The Nanny's Secret

ALSO BY E.V. SEYMOUR

STANDALONES
My Daughter's Secrets
The Widow's Boyfriend
My Lying Husband
The Nanny's Secret

KIM SLADE THRILLERS
The Patient
The Housekeeper's Daughter

THE NANNY'S SECRET

E.V. SEYMOUR

Joffe Books, London
www.joffebooks.com

First published in Great Britain in 2024

© E.V. Seymour 2024

This book is a work of fiction. Names, characters, businesses, organizations, places and events are either the product of the author's imagination or are used fictitiously. Any resemblance to actual persons, living or dead, events or locales is entirely coincidental.
The spelling used is British English except where fidelity to the author's rendering of accent or dialect supersedes this.
The right of E.V. Seymour to be identified as author of this work has been asserted in accordance with the Copyright, Designs and Patents Act 1988.

Cover art by Nick Castle

ISBN: 978-1-83526-749-3

For Ian

PROLOGUE

Thirty years before

In a moment of horror she snatches for the handrail and misses. Arms shooting wide, she plummets backwards, like a skydiver dropping from a plane.

The staircase is steep, brutal and, at three storeys, an instrument of torture. Spindles clatter her head. Threadbare carpet, burns her skin. A body that once was loved is beaten black and blue by each and every tread. Travelling at speed, limbs flailing, she has no breath to cry out despite the agony and terror. A newel post, sturdy and unforgiving, smashes her in the face. Then over and over she goes, in a grotesque impression of a cartwheel. And she keeps on going, faster and faster, until her neck twists and there is a sound like the crack of a whiplash.

After all the shouting and arguing, she didn't predict what was about to happen. She should have.

CHAPTER ONE

ALICE

The hard slap split her lip and loosened a tooth. The punch cracked a rib, the second knocked the air clean out of her. Pain assaulted Alice Trinick from three different directions.

'Look what you made me do?' he raged.

Doubled up, Alice gasped, 'Stop, Sean, please, *please*. I'm sorry. I didn't mean it.'

Strong labourer's hands grabbed her by the ears and yanked her upright. Even Sean's brown hair seemed to shoot up in indignant tufts. Tiny angry lines spiralled out from his eyes and across the edges of his dark stubbly cheeks as he gripped her upper arms. Alice cowered from a furious face that was right in hers, the combined smell of unwashed man and whisky-fuelled breath hot and overpowering. Would Sean, who claimed to love her, break her nose again?

'How many times have I told you to shut up with your bloody stories?'

'I don't know . . .'

'HOW. MANY. TIMES?'

'Too many.'

'When will you ever learn?'

'I'll stop. Promise. Please don't hit me,' Alice sobbed.

'It's the only way I can get it through your thick skull. I mean, what's *wrong* with you?'

'I don't know.' Tears sprang to Alice's eyes. The inside of her mouth tasted of rusty metal. 'Please don't hurt me, baby.'

'Think you're better than me, do you? Is this what it's all about?'

'No, no.' His grip tightened, now pinching the tender flesh on the inside of her arm. Spun out with fear, Alice's eyes searched the room. Where were his cigarettes, his matches, his lighter? Dread grabbed her by the throat.

'Think because you always have a nose in a book you're smarter? Is that it?'

'I'd never think that, Sean. You're the cleverest man I know.'

His chiselled chin tipped up. Pride swelled his bony features. 'Been reading too many of them rags-to-riches novels, that's your problem. Fills your head with all sorts of crazy ideas.'

'I know, Sean. I won't do it anymore,' she pleaded.

He looked deeply into her eyes, his grasp on her less intense. 'I guess you can't help yourself.'

Sensitive to the change in stance and tone, Alice dared to take a breath. First the physical and then the psychological; punishment was punishment, all the same.

'I'll try, Sean. I'll really try to be good. Honest.'

He searched her face as thoroughly as his hands invaded her body. Fear didn't make her shout, didn't make her run. Weighing a ton, it sat on top of her and pinned her down.

'What are you, Alice?'

She licked the blood from her bottom lip. 'Rubbish.'

'And who are you?' He elevated a thick ugly eyebrow.

'Nobody.'

'And who am I?'

'Somebody.'

'And why you need me.' With a greasy smile, he slid his arms around her, held her tight and whispered in her ear, 'No more stupid ideas. No more lies. Got it, babe?'

Alice froze and stared over Sean's shoulder at the wall. In a life of stories and false hopes, she vowed to escape. And when she found her dream, she'd make everyone, including Sean Stamp, pay.

CHAPTER TWO

ROSE

'What on earth have I done to deserve this?'

I stared down at the tray of fresh orange juice, warm croissants, luxury pot of jam and proper coffee — not the instant variety. I didn't think I could ever recall Raff bringing me breakfast in bed. Sleepily, I drifted through a mental list of anniversaries. My birthday was in October. We'd married in the month of June and it was now the end of July.

'Can't I treat my gorgeous wife once in a while?'

Raff plonked down next to me, thankfully without his boots on, though he was ready for work. Dressed in jeans and a T, my husband was a tree surgeon, also offering landscape and ground maintenance services. His build reflected his occupation — tall and broad across the chest, with biceps like rocks. He regularly worked on Sunday, especially during the busy summer months when his skills were in high demand.

'Well, I think it's a lovely idea and thank you.' I cuddled up next to him and deposited a soft kiss on his smoothly shaven cheek.

'You're welcome, Rose.' His brilliant smile gave his impossibly youthful face the appearance of a lead singer in a teen band; you'd never guess he was thirty-five. Short blonde spiky hair — styled by none other than yours truly, intriguingly grey-green deep-set eyes and wide nose, a little bit turned up at the tip. His soft full lips, perpetually tilted into a smile, reflected his sunny disposition. Despite his mischievous nature — all those who graduated from the Royal Agricultural College in Cirencester had naughty running through them — Raff possessed a genuinely tender side. A proper softie — and it was the thing I loved most about him. I'd done moody and magnificent and decided I didn't like it.

'What are your plans for the day, hun?'

'The usual.' I scooped raspberry jam onto my croissant and sank my teeth into it. Flakes of pastry flew all over the duvet. 'Pop to see Mum and Dad. I might see if Florence is around later now that she's flying solo.'

Florence Sadler was my oldest friend. We'd known each other since my mum and dad moved the family to Gloucester, from Wolverhampton. Florence's husband, Jamie, was Raff's best mate. 'Jamie's one lucky devil,' Raff said.

'Not sure Florence would agree.' An electrician, Jamie had recently flown to Dubai on a short-term contract. Financially, it made sense, but Florence worried about potential difficulties associated with maintaining a long-distance relationship. Personally, I thought a challenging climate and cultural differences would send Jamie back home sooner than later. Raff had no such concerns.

'No-brainer. Look at all the loot he's going to earn.' Raff conclusively crossed his arms and settled in, which I thought a little odd, but nice for me; Raff was normally out of the door by seven thirty, rain or shine.

I sipped my coffee. 'We're all right, aren't we? The business is flourishing. I'm backed up with clients at Crowning Glory.'

'You'd earn more if you owned your own salon.'

I swallowed a sigh. We'd been around this so many times.

'Dad has offered to lend you the capital,' Raff pointed out.

'I don't want a loan from your parents. They've already done more than enough for us.'

'I get your reluctance, but it's not as if they would be *giving* it to you.' Coming from money, Raff didn't seem to have a problem with handouts; it all seemed part of the same "money never an issue" gig. I came from a modest financial background. 'And it would be way simpler than running to the bank,' he insisted.

Agreed. One look at my pay cheque and any bank would be heading in the opposite direction. According to my dad, banks were great when you had money and crap when you didn't. 'Until *we* can afford to buy a home instead of renting, it's off the table, Raff.'

'Not if we go and live with my parents at Blackthorn.'

I turned sharply.

'Why are you looking at me like that?'

'I'm not.' I was. Had something heavy fallen on Raff's head?

'Rose, you couldn't look more surprised if I'd hacked into the Pentagon.'

Overstating it, although not far off. I really didn't want to move in with my in-laws even if they did live in Blackthorn House, a dirty great fourteen-acre estate in the Cotswolds with tennis courts, indoor pool and several cottages or "lodges" as the family called them. Thank goodness it didn't have a stable block because I'm terrified of horses. The only surprise: it didn't have a helicopter landing pad.

I rubbed an eye as if I'd got soap in it. 'Is this your thought for the day or have you been hatching it for some time?' *And cooking it up with his parents*, I thought anxiously. There's nothing Celeste and Benedict would love more than to have their entire brood around them. They'd reminisced about it often enough.

'Think about it,' Raff said, unable to conceal his enthusiasm.

I didn't need to. It was all laid out in black-and-white: Blackthorn House lay a few miles outside Cirencester where Raff had a unit on an industrial estate to house garden machinery. He routinely carried out work on his parents' land; it was one of our main sources of income. I could see the clear benefit to him, less so to me. After dating on and off — more off, if I'm honest, after Raff took it into his head to disappear to New Zealand — I was still getting the hang of marriage. I didn't fancy the added complication of living alongside my in-laws.

'Now that the parents have wound up the wedding venue business, there's bags of room. We don't have to do it forever,' Raff maintained in response to the alarm marching all over my face. 'It would only be until we've saved enough to put down a deposit for our own place.'

I couldn't fault his logic but, unprepared to bid farewell to independence and freedom, was determined to give a counter-argument my best shot.

'Living with your parents will mean I have to drive to work every day.' We rented in Charlton Kings, a suburb of Cheltenham. At the moment I could walk from home to Crowning Glory on the Bath Road; exercise without the sweat of going to a gym in my book.

'The Mini is a solid little motor,' Raff said, entirely missing my point.

'Yes, but—'

'And you love Blackthorn.' Raff had that expectant shiny look in his eye, the one he used when he wanted a free pass to go out with his mates.

True, I loved the grandeur of the place: the fancy-pants gated entrance with gold-tipped spikes set into Cotswold stone. I admired the long sweeping drive with grass running in a line down its middle, the avenue of trees and the row of poplars sitting on the hill behind the old house, the timelessness it embodied. The interior was a maze of cool lamp-lit corridors, lined with oil paintings; high ceilings and rooms containing glass cabinets crammed with memorabilia, or, depending on your point of view, old, if expensive, tat. I was genuinely privileged to have my wedding there. Benedict and Celeste were, and always had been, entirely warm and welcoming. They'd never suggested that my family were from the wrong side of the tracks, but the differences between us were obvious if unstated, certainly as far as my parents were concerned. My parents had never voiced it, yet I had the strong impression that they felt like poor relations. I was sensitive to my mum and dad's possible reaction to Raff's suggestion, quite aside from my own reluctance.

'Won't it feel overcrowded with Melissa and the kids?' I asked. Melissa was Raff's middle sister. She and her husband, Orlando, a high-flying lawyer who worked in London during the week, were living in the main house after their house sale had fallen through. Neither of them showed signs of relocating anytime soon.

'We wouldn't be living in the main house,' Raff said. 'We can have one of the lodges.'

'You've discussed it?'

Raff dry-swallowed. Yep, he had. *Great*, I thought, irritated, although I saw little point in getting shouty about it.

'It would be nice to spend more time with my niece and nephew,' Raff added, instantly putting me on high alert. If it were a choice between me running my own salon and having the large family Raff so desired, I knew which he would choose. Was this a sneaky way of getting me to warm to the idea of motherhood?

'What about Wren?' I asked.

Raff spread his hands. 'My kid sister's a free spirit. Who knows when she'll return?'

Which came as a relief. Beneath the "hey, man, everything is cool" beatific calm, Wren had the radiance of a brick. There was something a lot more manipulative trying to escape her folksy exterior. I liked Wren least of all Raff's family relations, of which there were tons. I was a reluctant only child so I sometimes found it overwhelming.

'Honestly, Raff, the prospect of four women under the same roof is daunting.' And never going to end well.

He took my hand, which I admit was unpleasantly sticky. 'Multi-generational living is a thing, Rose.'

A "thing" entirely alien to me. 'Look, I'd get it if your parents needed on the spot carers—' although God help me, I wasn't up for that '——but they're both fit and healthy with good years ahead of them. I'm surprised they haven't considered downsizing, travelling the world, spending the inheritance.' The last bit was a bit snarky, I admit.

Raff gave a little jolt. 'Blackthorn has been in the family for three generations. My dad grew up on the land. It's in our blood. *Of course*, my folks aren't going to give it up.'

'Exactly, which means we'll be expected to pay rent, which *means*,' I said emphatically, 'we will be in no better financial state there than we are here.' And I liked our cosy, two-bedroom house. It was the size of a shed, but it was our space, our place.

'Dad says we'll only have to pay a nominal fee to cover bills.'

'Seems like you've got all the bases covered.' I let go of his hand, pushed the tray away, flung back the duvet and climbed out of bed.

'Rose, please don't be cross.'

'I'm not,' I said. 'I'm going to the loo.' I needed a pee, but I also needed to cool and calm down. My pale cheeks burned hot at the thought of the family discussion that had taken place, one that affected my life, and yet from which I was excluded. This happened a lot in the mad and hasty build-up to our wedding. Fortunately, on the big issues, when I made my feelings clear, without exception I got my way.

Doing what I had to do, I flushed the loo and took my time filling the sink with cold water, scooping handfuls liberally over my face, patting it dry with a towel. Looking in the mirror I took in my shoulder-length hair, naturally dark although I often played around with colour. I like running it through with reddish highlights and have been known to tint it grey or blonde. Long ago were the days when I dyed it blue for a laugh. I have brown eyes, narrow at the edges. People have told me they resemble a cat's. Today their expression displayed hurt, rather than annoyance. My face is oval and my cheekbones "pop" when I smile. (I notice these things. The shape of a person's face is important for framing it with the best hairstyle.) My top lip is a little thin but I have great teeth, unaided by cosmetic dentistry. Despite my mood, I gave myself a toothy grin. *Better*, I thought, now grinning naturally. No point getting antsy over something that might never happen.

Bracing my shoulders, I returned to our bedroom where Raff was waiting for me. Slipping an arm around my waist, he drew me close and kissed my temple. He smelt of warm earth and sunshine.

'I'm so sorry, Rose. I should have consulted you from the off. I can see exactly how this must look.'

It looks as if I'm being stitched up, I thought.

'And,' he said solemnly, 'how you must feel.'

I drew away. All of it was true, but a hopeless part of me weakened under his mortified gaze. I really loved Rafferty Hugo Percival with all my heart. By all accounts his childhood had been idyllic. I could understand some deep part of him wanting to repeat it.

'We don't have to do this,' Raff said sincerely.

'Honest?'

'Cross my heart.'

I let out a sigh. Who was I to stamp on his dream without giving it proper consideration? 'Let me think about it, yeah?'

A wide grin broke across Raff's face.

'I'm not promising anything.' I wasn't that daft.

'Understood. I get it. Thank you.'

'I'd like to talk it over with Mum and Dad.'

'Of course.'

And Florence, I thought. Florence would understand and she'd offer solid advice.

Issue avoided, problem as yet unsolved, Raff released me. I followed him downstairs.

'What's the work schedule today?' I asked.

'Back-to-back mowing. Oh, and if that tapped bastard from the Grove phones and asks me to cut his hedges, tell him I'm not doing it while the birds are nesting.'

I smiled warmly. I loved the fact that Raff was so respectful of the land and cared about the environment.

'I might be a little later than usual,' he said.

'Oh?'

'Got to pick up fencing poles ready for a job at Blackthorn tomorrow.'

My smile faded. Whatever my parents said and Florence advised, I sensed how things were going to roll. Like it or not, I was going to be sucked into the Percival family vortex.

CHAPTER THREE

ROSE

I like dogs. Fergal, the Percivals' Irish wolfhound was almost as tall as me — an exaggeration — and wonderfully affectionate and gentle, rather like my husband. But Fuggles, the family's terrier, was a snappy, ankle-biting little bastard. It shed hair, had teeth like razors and made a beeline for me whenever I visited. All the way to Gloucester I sweated the small stuff because I couldn't contemplate the big stuff.

Mum was a florist, Dad a kitchen-fitter. They lived in a maisonette in Gloucester on an estate that bore no relationship to landed gentry. Houses sat on a grid of loops and cul-de-sacs, interconnected by pedestrian pathways. It probably looked cool back in the 1970s, not so much now, but it was still a place I loved because I'd spent my teens there. Their modest home was always scented with flowers, and Dad had recently installed a double Belfast sink with eggshell blue worktops and matching splash-backs. It looked lovely.

Mum ushered me through the door into the narrow corridor of a hall, and gave me a hug. Big-boned and blonde, with a talent for sensing when things weren't quite right, she gave me a knowing look.

'Raff all right?' My mum had a soft spot for my husband and it wasn't because he kept her and Dad supplied with free wood for their log burner. She thought he had "lovely manners" and "nice ways".

Glad to scotch any thoughts she might have to the contrary, I assured her he was fine.

'Just putting the kettle on,' she said. I often thought that this was Mum's sole occupation in life. Day or night, a pot of tea would be on the go. 'Do you want one, Bob?' she called to my dad who was in the lounge, fiddling with the remote.

I strolled in and gave him a peck on the cheek. 'Got a new telly,' he announced. Dark-haired, brown-eyed, goofy smile, I got my looks from my father, although I liked to think Mum's warmth of personality had rubbed off on me. I certainly displayed more of her patience, a trait unknown to Dad.

'It's huge,' I commented. It was and dominated the room to a ridiculous degree.

'It's so we can read the subtitles.'

'I didn't know you watched foreign films.'

'Your mum thinks it's good for us.' His tone suggested that he wasn't sold on the idea. 'You all right?' His eyes were glued to the screen, fingers stabbing at the handset. I'd offer to help but my dad was stubborn and didn't like to be defeated by "*bloody technology*".

'Uh-huh.'

Dad cut a glance that said *wassup* and returned to the challenge.

Before I had time to burble an answer, Mum popped her head around the door. 'Tea's in the kitchen.'

'Coming,' I said.

'Can't you put that thing down for a minute, Bob Sutton? Your daughter needs our advice,' Mum said.

Dad rolled his eyes and cast me a sheepish grin.

We sat at the kitchen table, a ceremonial pot of builder's best taking pride of place. Mum had got out her best china tea set, indicating my worry was taken seriously. In times of crisis, and we'd had a few, she'd been known to add a drop of brandy. Fortunately, we were not at the point where neat spirit was required.

When we were settled, Dad said, 'Spit it out then.' This drew a sharp look from Mum who rested a hand warmly over mine. Her limpid blue eyes were soft and sympathetic.

'What's the problem then, Rose?'

'Not a problem, as such,' I answered breezily. 'More of a decision I'm struggling to make.' I revealed Raff's suggestion.

My mother relaxed in relief. Dad visibly bristled.

'Why do you have to live there when you could live here? You could have your old room back.'

'Don't be soft, Bob.' Mum's laugh was jittery.

'I'm not,' he snapped. 'It's a perfectly—'

'Lovely idea,' I cut in, taking some of the heat out of Dad's reaction. When I say *some*, it wasn't quite enough.

'You only want her to move there so you can visit,' Dad said, unappeased, to Mum.

'And what's wrong with that?' Mum retorted, wide-eyed. 'It's a beautiful place.'

'With beautiful people.' The sarcasm in my father's voice was unmistakable. It all stemmed from the wedding. Mum had got tipsy and, despite being over a decade younger than Benedict, (my parents had me when they were in their teens) she had made her attraction to my father-in-law's creepy charisma a little too noticeable. It didn't help that Dad had felt marginalised financially. Too many times, Celeste and Benedict, in their generosity, had assured my parents that they were happy to foot the bill for the catering, the chocolate fountain, the booze, the string quartet in the morning and the live band and fireworks in the evening, among dozens of other items of expenditure. To my dad's mind, he'd been dissed. It hadn't helped when my nan, (same age as Benedict) had banged on about "funny stuff" regarding her counterpart, Raff's grandmother, Maud, a frail if doughty character, who was barely civil to Celeste, her only daughter, and, seemingly following family tradition, Celeste barely speaking to her eldest child and Raff's big sister, Violet. Violet had worn the most enormous hat, I remembered, and left straight after the church ceremony. Caught up in celebration, I'd barely given it a thought at the time. Now it loomed like the proverbial elephant in the room.

Rattled, I said as calmly as I could, 'If you're going to argue, I'm leaving.'

'Sorry,' Dad said and looked it. 'Sorry, Lindsey, love,' he added sheepishly to my mother.

Mum topped up his teacup, apology accepted.

'It wouldn't be very feasible for us to move in here, Dad,' I said, affectionately touching his hand. 'Most of Raff's work and business lie on the other side of the county.'

Dad conceded my point with a grunt.

'If things were different, we'd definitely consider your kind offer.' I was keen to ensure his feelings weren't too bruised.

'There you are,' Mum said, looking at Dad. 'It's not about taking sides.'

Outnumbered, Dad gave another grunt.

'The way I see it, Rose,' Mum continued, 'it's a wonderful opportunity for you both. Most young people of your age would leap at the chance, and think of the money you'll accumulate so you can be truly independent to buy your very own first home.'

I ran my finger in circles over the plastic-coated tablecloth.

'And you're thirty-one now,' she continued. 'I'd already got a twelve-year-old at that age.'

My eyes shot up. 'And your point?'

'Don't hang around too long to make her a grandmother,' Dad said with a loose grin. My heart went out to my mum. It would never replace the child she lost, my little sister; it couldn't. Having arrived pressured by one problem, I left pressured by two.

CHAPTER FOUR

MELISSA

Melissa Rhodes squealed with delight. 'You're coming home, Wren, but that's marvellous.' God alone knew she could use the emotional support. Two small children and a husband away did her head in. Dad was a darling and often played with the kids to give her a little personal time, but it wasn't the same. She felt lonely and Orlando was such a grump when he returned from London for weekends. She hated it when he left yet, perversely, by Thursday night, dreaded the prospect of his return.

'Don't tell Mummy and Daddy yet,' Wren warned. 'Won't be for a couple of months.' Melissa suppressed an instant streak of disappointment. 'How are the parents?' Wren continued.

'All good.'

'They're not missing the business?'

'Not at all. Mum spends most days out to lunch. She travels to London regularly for meetings with friends. A couple of weeks ago, she went to watch some West End musical.'

Melissa grinned at the sound of Wren feigning a retching noise. 'And the house thing?'

'Don't ask. It's fallen through — again. On the plus side, we'll still be here when you come back.'

'But that's great.'

'And, guess what, Rafferty and Rose are moving in.'

'You're shitting me.'

'It's not official, but that's the word on the wire.'

'God, it's going to be a crush.'

'It's not as if there isn't enough room.'

'I'd rather hoped to bag the Granary. Have summit talks taken place?'

'Nothing has been decided.'

Melissa could practically hear Wren's brain cranking up and, no doubt, scheming.

'Was this Raff's idea?' Wren asked.

'Think so.'

'And how is my big bro?'

'Same old: sunny, easy-going Raff.'

'It will be lovely to see him.'

'And us, I hope,' Melissa teased.

'Absolutely — got so much to tell you, Liss.'

'Can't wait to hear about your travels. Where are you now?'

'Berlin.'

'Why not catch a flight home?'

'What?'

'If you come back sooner, you could have first dibs on accommodation.' Melissa wasn't above a little manipulation of her own.

'Can't,' Wren said shortly. Returning to the subject of Raff and Rose, she said, 'Are they really planning to bunk up with us?'

'You're averse to the idea?'

'No-oh,' Wren replied, in a wheedling voice. 'I just can't for the life of me see Rose agreeing to it.'

'Why ever not?'

Wren snorted a retort. 'C'mon, Liss, she's not really one of us, is she? She doesn't really fit.'

'Of course, she fits. She's Raff's wife.'

'Yeah, but she's not from the same tribe.'

'Wouldn't that be incestuous?'

'You know very well what I mean.'

Melissa did. 'Don't be horrible.'

'I'm not. I mean Rose is nice enough and I can see why Rafferty fell for her feline looks and *come into my lair* eyes, but that voice, 'nuff said.'

'You're such a snob.'

'I'll take that as a compliment. You have to admit our sister-in-law is limited.'

Melissa briefly closed her eyes. Sometimes her sister could be so mindlessly pompous and cruel. At times, Wren reminded Melissa of Orlando. 'Well, *I* entirely disagree. *I* like her. *I* like her regional accent, which is pretty mild, actually, and *I* for one am going to make sure that she feels a valued part of the family.'

'Bully for you.'

Melissa was too irritated to speak.

'What?' Wren asked in the ensuing silence.

'Nothing.'

'I promise I'll play nice when I come home.'

'It suits you so much better.'

'Received and understood, big sister. Any other hot news?'

Melissa hesitated. She wasn't quite sure how to put it. 'Orlando wants me to go back to work.' *And earn your bloody keep* were his exact words.

'What on earth for? He earns oodles.'

'His job is highly pressurised.'

Wren gave a snort. 'Orlando's made for pressure, thrives on it.'

'He gets tired.' If ever Orlando found out she'd been discussing him, there would be hell.

'Stress is an absolute killer, Liss. Hot yoga and Echinacea should do the trick.'

Melissa blinked. She didn't like to picture the consequences of making such a ludicrous suggestion to her husband.

'More importantly,' Wren continued, 'how do *you* feel about a return to the rat race?'

'Torn.' And guilty. 'I'd like to wait until the children are older, at least until Edgar's out of nappies. He's only just had his first birthday, and Autumn is yet to start proper school.'

'Goodness, I've missed so much.'

'The kids are little, Wren, and it's only for such a short period of time.'

'Believe me, I get it. Those foundation years are vitally important. Every moment is precious. You don't want to miss a thing: first words, walking, first day at school, cuddles.'

Wren sounded almost dreamy, Melissa thought, not like her at all. Had travelling mellowed her sharp edges? Wren had never shown much interest in Melissa's children. Perhaps her biological clock was on the tick.

'Although I have to say I get where he's coming from,' Wren said, ruining it.

'Do you?' Melissa felt crushed.

'You were always smarter than Orlando.'

Melissa could have blown kisses down the phone. 'You really think so?' Her eyes gleamed with gratitude.

'I *know* so. How many female chartered surveyors do you know?'

'Not many, although more women are coming into the profession.' God, for all her irritations and, at times, her very un-Zen-like qualities, Melissa missed her little sister.

'Although that's not going to help with your current predicament.'

Her husband-sized predicament, to be precise. Maybe if Wren had been around and not travelling the globe, things wouldn't have got sticky with Orlando. He didn't mean to, but had a nasty habit of talking Melissa down at any and every opportunity. Wren was a firm believer in elevating a woman's self-esteem. *Belief in one's self and the vision and power to dream* was her sister's mantra. In Wren, Melissa saw her very own cheerleader.

'Playing devil's advocate, would the sky fall in if you did go back to work?'

Melissa frowned. Yes, it bloody would. She said as much.

'Just thinking aloud, Liss.'

Which wasn't helpful. The issue needed proper consideration not off the cuff philosophy.

'Surely, Mummy and Daddy could step in,' Wren suggested.

'Not for five full days a week.'

'Why not? Other grandparents do.'

'They're in their sixties, not forties.'

'Sixty *is* the new forty,' Wren said airily. 'Anyway, with Auntie Rose and Uncle Rafferty on hand, it should be a doddle.'

Melissa could have screamed with frustration. She'd learnt the hard way not to. 'They have jobs too,' she said with false calm. 'Rafferty is trying to build a business. Rose works long hours at the salon and she'll be doing more travelling by living at Blackthorn. Maybe you could help out. Autumn is always talking about her auntie Wren.'

'Me?' Wren practically choked. 'My feet won't touch the floor when I get back.'

'With what?'

'Stuff.'

'What stuff?'

'Wait and see.'

'Ooh, sounds exciting.'

'Thrilling, actually.'

'New man?'

'Don't be silly.'

Melissa's cheeks scorched. Another of Orlando's phrases and so similar to their mother, it sounded less belittling coming from Wren, yet still contained an unpleasant reminder.

'Do you really think Orlando will insist? You know what he's like. Are you sure he's not just messing with you?'

'I think he's serious.'

'Then you must talk to him and explain how you feel, although, to be fair your hubbie isn't big on emotions.'

An understatement, Melissa thought.

'Sent away to one of those awful public schools when he was four, it comes as little surprise,' Wren said. 'Perhaps he could try cranial massage. It's brilliant for releasing repressed emotions and trauma.'

Even if it worked, which Melissa very much doubted, it would take years to cure four decades of damage. Stupidly, she'd believed marriage and stability would provide salvation for her husband. Instead, Orlando had succeeded in bringing her down to his level. Better not to feel a thing than experience the reality of pain.

CHAPTER FIVE

ROSE

I dropped Florence a WhatsApp message from my car.
You in?
Yep, bored and lonely.
Drink?
Fantastic.
I'll bring a bottle.
That bad?

I didn't know how to answer so didn't reply. Mine was a first world problem and some wouldn't even consider it a problem at all. What's not to like about living in luxury?

Popping to a nearby supermarket, I chose a bottle of finest Pinot Grigio and drove to Cheltenham where I managed to squiggle the Mini into the only available free parking space a couple of streets away from Florence's one-bedroom apartment in Fairview.

Engrossed in *the decision*, I barely registered the weather other than to notice that the sun was out and it was warmish, which it should be for the time of year.

Stone steps led to a private entrance. Outside the front door, a bistro set, comprising two chairs and small circular table, was prepared in readiness; Florence had already parked a couple of wine glasses on the table.

'Am I glad to see you,' I said with a big smile. Florence was the human form of liquid sunshine. Naturally fair-haired, she had wonderful treacle-coloured lowlights that I suspected she had done in the most expensive salon in Cheltenham. Collar-length, her hair flicked up at the edges to perfectly frame her heart-shaped face. She gave me a proper *bestie* hug after which I unscrewed the bottle, poured the wine — a small glass for me as I was driving — and we sat down.

'Sundays are so lonely without Jamie. Honest, Rose, I thought I was going to lose my mind this morning. I cleaned the flat — it's so titchy it took me less than forty minutes — did a heart-attack inducing session at the gym, went for a swim afterwards, walked back to the flat, changed into a dress, loaded the washing machine, picked up a book, put down a book, called Mum — she was out — wandered out for a walk and . . . Oh God, I'm sorry, there's me rattling away like a machine gun and I haven't even asked how you are.'

I burst out laughing. It felt great.

'Good,' Florence quipped. 'Clearly, your world hasn't entirely collapsed.'

'Whatever gave you the impression it had collapsed?'

'Tone of voice — dead giveaway.'

'You know me too well.'

Florence grinned. 'Identifying nuances is part of the job description.'

'Nuances, huh?' I said, taking the piss.

'Subtle differences in tone and meaning,' Florence said in an affected plummy voice that sounded far too similar to my in-laws. 'When you're in the divorce game it pays to work out who is a problem for whom.'

'Duly noted.'

'Hey,' Florence said, taking a large glug of wine. 'Got my first proper live case to manage.'

'Well done you.'

'As a paralegal, it's all under supervision. The woman — she's my client — is ever so slightly edgy, which comes as no surprise because she's been to hell... Sorry,' she said. 'There's me banging on again. Normally I'd have Jamie to drown with conversation.'

'How's he getting on?'

'Seems okay. The prospect of seven and a half grand a month makes his absence more tolerable.'

I whistled between my teeth. Had Jamie's decision to go and earn a fortune influenced Raff's barking idea?

Florence fell silent, lifted her glass and viewed me over the rim: my cue to spill the proverbial beans.

'Raff wants me to move in to Blackthorn so we can save for a deposit for a house.'

I didn't get so much as an elevated eyebrow. Typically, Florence asked me how it would work financially, if it came with conditions, whether there were practical considerations, like division of labour with me expected to pitch in with cleaning or cooking in the main house.

Appalled at the thought, I couldn't answer a single question because I'd no idea. 'We've only discussed it in principle. Nothing has been agreed.'

'But Raff is keen?'

'Super-psyched about it. I mean I get it. His was an idyllic childhood and part of him hasn't quite let go.'

'You have to admit you'd be living in a pretty plush environment.'

I would. I hadn't forgotten the first time I'd set eyes on Blackthorn House. I'd stood slack-jawed, barely able to speak.

'Although I've always thought it slightly creepy.'

This took me by surprise. Florence had never mentioned it.

'It's very old, I guess, but I've never picked up on a haunted vibe.'

'Whatever that is,' Florence said with a grin. 'Ignore me. Raff does a lot of work there, doesn't he?'

'Yes.'

'So he's already committed.'

I nodded.

Florence looked thoughtful. 'When did all this come about?'

'This morning.'

I knew what she was thinking. I hadn't wasted time in seeking advice. In other words, I'd panicked.

Florence tapped a square polished nail on the table.

'Have you talked to your parents?' Florence was fond of Mum and Dad and recognised the perceived "imbalance of power" as far as my father was concerned.

I nodded.

'And?'

'As you might imagine, Mum's all for it, thinks it's a great opportunity.'

'And Bob?'

'Not so keen.'

Florence viewed me kindly. 'And what does Rose think?'

'Rose is at a loss.'

'Hmm.'

'You see my dilemma?' I so hoped Florence would.

'It might be fun.'

'That's not the first description that springs to mind.'

'Is your reluctance connected to money and status and feeling you don't quite belong?'

We'd had the same conversation before I'd married Raff. It had arisen after I'd overheard Wren bitching to Melissa about my appearance, the way I spoke, "cutting people's hair for a living" *blah-de-blah*. According to Wren, Raff could have chosen a Sasha, an Arabella, an India or a Zara. Instead, and to her huge irritation, he'd chosen a humble girl from the Midlands, named after a common garden flower. (Not quite how Wren had put the last bit). As Florence knew only too well, the conversation was burnt into my psyche. The saying about sticks and stones only hurting is utter crap. Words hurt way more.

Wren undermined me so much it made me wonder what on earth Raff saw in me. He lived in a world I didn't inhabit. Florence, as ever, had cut to the chase: *'Do you love him, Rose?'*

'I do. I really do.'

'And he clearly adores you.'

'He does.'

'Then where's the problem?'

'Rose . . .' Florence prompted me, dragging me back to the here and now. 'Is it to do with a sense of not belonging?'

'Not really,' I answered, less than truthfully. Whether I liked it or not, Raff and his family ticked to a different beat and it was tribal. 'I'm married to Raff so, as far as I'm concerned, I belong.'

'Is it loss of freedom that's bothering you?'

'Mostly.'

'Then establish ground rules before you agree.'

'Like what?'

'It's all about managing expectations,' Florence said, slipping into work mode. 'Are you expected to take meals at the house?'

Celeste was an excellent cook, but I didn't fancy being drawn in to regular family dinners. 'I have no idea.'

'Find out and, if so, how many times a week? Then there's the thorny subject of visitation rights.' She grinned in answer to my mystified expression. 'Whether it's okay for friends to visit.'

'Of course it will be okay.' The Percivals were nothing if not party-loving.

'Do you think they'll lock up the booze cupboard?' Florence asked, semi-serious.

'They don't have a cupboard. They have a cellar.'

'Gets better and better.'

I wasn't finding it quite so alluring. 'Goodness, this all sounds so over the top.'

'Trust me, it will pay to get things clear before you embark on playing Happy Families. The last thing you want is to be treated like the resident hairdresser.'

'Celeste wouldn't allow me within ten metres of her head with a pair of scissors.'

We both laughed, breaking some of the tension I felt. 'You get on okay with her, don't you?' Florence asked.

I had to agree that I mostly did, although we'd got off to a rather embarrassing start after Raff had told me his mother's maiden name was de Grey and I'd assumed she was French. My boss, Jerome, is Marseilles born and bred, so I asked him to coach me to speak colloquially to impress her. I'd got quite fluent and launched into things the second I was introduced. Imagine my embarrassment when Celeste confessed, in impeccably cut-glass English, to growing up in Warwickshire. Once we got that out of the way, I discovered a capable woman. Aside from running a wedding venue business while bringing up four children, she raised funds for the local church, was popular in the community and, in her spare time, ran a friendship club. She'd always treated me kindly and with respect and regularly asked after Mum and Dad; I didn't believe it was in a lame bid to curry favour with me.

Florence tilted her head to one side. 'And Benedict?'

He was more difficult to quantify. In his head my father-in-law was part landed gentry and part hippie. In the summer and in an effort to reclaim his youth, he was prone to wearing black sleeveless vests, (the skin on his upper arms was a little bit crinkly) teamed either with tight-fitting jeans or loose-fitting chino shorts. It puzzled me because he looked pretty good for an old guy. His steel grey hair and beard was neatly trimmed. The smile in his eyes suggested a mischievous nature, which he'd definitely passed on to Raff, although, unlike his son, Benedict's eyes were deep brown. He'd be so much more appealing if he dressed to reflect his age.

Florence asked about Wren and I explained she was still away, *thank God*, and then told her about Melissa's situation.

'Crikey, she's still living at Blackthorn with the kids and Orlando?'

'Orlando's away most of the week.'

'Good.'

'Why do you say that?'

'Why do you think? He's a shit.'

'Florence,' I spluttered.

'It's true. He's so damn smug. No idea what Melissa sees in the man. He was horrible to her at your wedding.'

Thankfully, it passed me by, although I was really surprised to hear it. 'I've never had a problem with Orlando. He's usually nothing short of charming.' *And deferential*, I thought, although I had to admit, a man of inexhaustible energy, having a tendency to look over my shoulder in the middle of a conversation.

'That's because you pose no threat to his ego.'

'Is that supposed to be a compliment?'

'Sort of,' she said with a grin. 'I always thought Melissa way superior to him.' An attractive woman, bone-thin and a little bit highly-strung, Raff's middle sister exuded fragility. 'Wasn't she a surveyor before she married Golden Boy?' Florence asked.

'Specialising in period properties. Pretty successful, too.'

'Explains why Orlando's jealous of her.'

'Do you really think so?' A slick city lawyer, I found it unlikely.

'He called her *neurotic* in front of a room full of people.' Florence's top lip curled with contempt.

I was astonished.

'It was so embarrassing. Honest, Rose, if Melissa ever contemplates divorce, I'm her woman.'

I loved Florence for her crusading spirit but I wasn't about to pass the message on.

We lazed silently in the sun and watched the world float by. Florence stretched her arms above her head and flexed her toes. 'I don't feel as if I've been much help.'

'No, you have.' I tossed back the remains of my drink and refilled her glass.

'Do you think you might buckle up and go for it then?'

'Makes sense.'

Florence eyed me in a way I found unsettling. 'What does your gut tell you, Rose?'

There are things you tell your best friend that you wouldn't dream of saying to your parents. But even this was too difficult for me to admit: *Run,* I thought. *Run for your life.*

CHAPTER SIX

ROSE

After tumbling temperatures of cloud and rain in a washout August, I took a few days' holiday and we moved to Blackthorn amid a heatwave in the first week of September.

I was reluctant to give up our little home and put furniture into storage, but was forced to admit that our new pad, situated to the west of the main house, was smart. The front door led into a teeny lobby with coat hooks above a window seat and with somewhere to park boots and shoes beneath. Straight ahead, a wet room, no bath, containing luxury toiletries, robes and lots of fluffy white towels. The open-plan living area comprised a dining room and lounge. It had polished wooden floorboards, a sofa, two leather tub chairs, a table big enough to seat four people at a push and, joy of joys, a wood burner with logs already piled up on the hearth. From the dining area two steps led up to a small kitchen that magically housed a dinky washing machine as well as an eye-level grill, hob, oven and fridge. We had too much food because Celeste had doubled up and filled the cupboards with goodies from the local farm shop. I didn't know what to do with a pot of quince jelly. *No more scrape the mould off and hope for the best*, I thought. Upstairs: a large bedroom with built-in wardrobes, a queen-sized double bed and far-reaching views across the grounds and beyond. A Velux window above ensured that at night we'd be able to see the moon and stars.

We had a courtyard garden with containers and patio furniture and a view of the woods beyond. Importantly, the lodge was some distance from the main house and I didn't mind the walk to the parking area, outside the Granary on the eastern side, to pick up my car each day. I'd even persuaded myself that the drive back and forth to Cheltenham would give me time to prepare mentally for the working day ahead and decompress on the journey back.

Crossing to the window I couldn't help but admire the vast proportions of Blackthorn, with its oak-framed porch, stone mullion and stained glass windows, turrets and towers, no matter what Florence thought about it being spooky. It was easy to picture the people inside: the cleaners, the occasional cook and elderly gardener. It wasn't on the scale of Downton Abbey but, with its vast rooms, high ceilings, swag curtains, panelling and antique furniture, it could definitely stand in as an understudy.

I was reading the instructions for the washing machine when Raff strode in. He'd been out dry-stone walling first thing. 'Hey,' he said. 'All unpacked?'

'Not much to it.'

His hair was tousled and there was a fine film of perspiration across his brow. Wearing a tight T, tanned to perfection, he looked hot and I didn't mean it in the literal sense. He caught my expression, slipped his arms around me and grinned.

'Do you think we should test the bed?'

I raised an eyebrow. 'Now?'

'Why not?'

I glanced in the direction of the house, which I had to admit was a long way away.

'Nobody is going to come in,' Raff said.

'I know but . . .'

Slipping his hand in mine, he led me to the front door. 'See this,' he said, 'it's a lock.' He turned the key. 'There. Works like magic.'

I gave him a wry smile then, laughing like a couple of naughty kids, we raced upstairs.

Horny as hell, Raff was already naked before I'd slipped out of my skirt.

'Shouldn't we close the curtains, or something?'

'Rose, nobody can see unless they've got a telescope.' He launched himself onto the bed. 'Anyway, who cares?'

I cared but lust got the better of me. Aching with desire, eager to feel his skin against mine, I stripped off. We were just getting down to it when there was a loud knock at the door.

'Fuck,' Raff let out.

Or rather not, I thought, frustrated. 'Want me to go?'

Raff elevated a sexy eyebrow. 'Perhaps if you answer stark naked whoever it is will go away.'

Unsurprisingly, I wasn't prepared to put his theory to the test. I grabbed a robe and padded downstairs to find Benedict on the doorstep. I couldn't think of a worse person to virtually catch us at it. Benedict is not an emotionally illiterate man and, in the space of seconds, I read several expressions on his face: shock, embarrassment followed by confusion about what to do next. He had two choices: make up a lame excuse and offer to come back later, or blunder on. He blundered.

'Rose . . . um . . . good to see you've settled in. Found everything, I hope. Anyway, thing is . . . um . . . we're having a BBQ this afternoon, a sort of welcome party. Hope you can join us. Oh, and no need to bring anything, just your good selves. Well . . . um . . . I'll leave you to it. I mean . . .' He cleared his throat. 'See you later.'

And wearing his trademark black vest with the name of a band I'd never heard of emblazoned on the back, he sloped away, flip-flops crunching on the gravelled drive.

'That was awkward,' I said, slipping off my robe and into bed beside Raff.

Letting out a deep belly laugh, Raff reached across and wrapped me in his arms. 'Did you actually speak?'

'I was too dumbstruck.'

'Not like you.'

'Raff, it was your dad, for goodness' sake, and it was obvious he knew what we were doing.'

Two lines appeared between Raff's eyebrows. He drew back a little. 'He didn't comment, did he?'

'Of course not.'

'Didn't look at you . . . I don't know . . .'

'What are you getting at?' I let out a frustrated sigh and looked into his eyes. The grim expression was so fleeting I thought I'd imagined it. Transformed by a smile that lit up the room, he said, 'Come here, you gorgeous woman.'

CHAPTER SEVEN

ROSE

My dad's barbeques were smoke-filled affairs with burnt sausages and underdone chicken — essentially, food poisoning on a plate. Professionally orchestrated by outside caterers, the average Percival party proved a very different experience.

Loved-up and strolling hand in hand with Raff onto a terrace positioned outside the drawing room — *lounge* where I come from — we were handed a glass of champagne by a young guy with a topknot who served bottles of beer and wine from barrels filled with ice. Three separate gas-fired barbeques catering for meat-eaters, pescatarians and vegetarians were already aflame. The kitchen area buzzed with activity as three young men in chefs' whites carried out plates of food and salads onto trestle tables.

The family were gathered underneath an awning on a raised lawn with late summer roses, exotic-looking shrubs and plants, which no doubt my mum could identify. I spotted purple-headed asters, cornflowers, clown-faced pansies and fuchsia.

Other than the family, there were loads of guests, some I recognised. Dress code went along the lines of tropical shirts and stone-coloured chinos for men; cool floaty numbers for women.

To the sound of chinking crystal, lively conversation and debate revolved around the heat and, perversely, best places to winter when the climate turned colder. There was a definite carnival atmosphere. Parked on a tartan rug, baby Edgar rolling around next to her, Melissa gazed out from underneath the shade of a large Japanese maple. (So Raff had informed me.) I waved to Melissa who waved back with a languid smile, as if she didn't quite have the energy to respond more demonstrably.

Belting up the steps, my husband scooped four-year-old Autumn into his arms and swung her around to squeals of little girl laughter. 'Put me down, Uncle Raff. Put me down.' Fergal and Fuggles could be heard barking chaotically from inside the house.

'Raff, for goodness' sake,' Celeste cried, 'you'll make the child sick.'

'She loves it.' Raff deposited Autumn on the lawn with a thump. From the delighted look on Autumn's face, she really did.

With an indulgent laugh, Celeste glided towards me. Effortlessly chic, grey-blonde hair styled to reveal a high forehead, suspiciously line-free, Celeste wore a simple blue cotton midi shift dress with a scoop neckline, and white pumps on her feet. Her pale blue eyes were hidden beneath a pair of designer sunglasses that matched her outfit.

Kissed on both cheeks, I was enveloped in a heady cloud of Chanel perfume, my mother-in-law's signature fragrance. 'Lovely to see you, darling,' she said. 'Have you got everything you need, Rose?'

'And more,' I replied, catching sight of Benedict man-hugging Raff from the corner of my eye. We're not that tactile in our family, my mum the exception. My dad's barely concealed expression of horror as Benedict clapped an arm around his shoulder on a first introduction still made me chuckle. Apparently, Granddad and Uncle Gary nearly passed out at the wedding after receiving similar treatment.

'Raff says you've sensibly taken time out to settle in,' Celeste said.

'Only a few days.' I hadn't really wanted to but Mum had persuaded me that it would be a good idea to "acclimatise", as she put it. Anyone would think I was going to live in Singapore where the humidity is sweltering.

Celeste rested a warm hand on my arm. 'Anytime you want your parents to come over, they're most welcome. Friends, too,' she said. I nodded enthusiastically and recalled Florence's advice, which, to my shame, I'd foolishly ignored. 'This is your home now,' Celeste said firmly.

I was probably overly sensitive. The finality with which my mother-in-law uttered those words was like a door slamming shut in my mind. Instinctively, I glanced over my shoulder and caught Melissa's faintly lost gaze.

I smiled and, seizing the opportunity to escape, headed off towards her. She looked nothing short of grateful to see me.

'Roasting, isn't it?' Melissa said as I sat down next to her. I'm not great with babies and was relieved to see that red-faced Edgar had conked out and was quietly snoring. I agreed. 'Love your dress.'

'Thank you.' It was one of Raff's favourites: short with shoestring straps in a gorgeous shade of buttercup yellow.

'Is it too soon to ask how you're finding life at Blackthorn?'

'I'm hating every second of it.'

Melissa crumpled in alarm then, catching my grin, burst out laughing. It sounded like the tinkle of wind chimes. 'You absolutely had me,' she confessed, pressing a hand to her chest.

'Worth it to see the look on your face,' I teased. 'Seriously, the lodge is lovely and your parents, as always, are extremely generous.' I gazed across the tightly manicured lawn to the barbeque. 'They're laying on quite a feast.'

'They've been staging events like this for a long time,' Melissa reminded me.

And they were very good at it. I'd never gone to one of the Percival bashes and been anything less than impressed.

'So how's it going?' I asked companionably.

'All good,' she said, shiny-eyed.

'No Orlando?' I trained my eyes on the house as if he'd suddenly materialise in front of a window, or pop out of a doorway.

'He had a work thing and is driving back this morning.'

'Doesn't he normally catch the train?'

'Apparently he took the car because he has a surprise.'

'For you?'

She nodded in feverish anticipation and fixed me with her liquid brown eyes. 'He called me late last night. No idea what it is.'

'Ooh, exciting,' I said.

Melissa checked her watch. 'Should be here any moment.'

A middle-aged woman with a bottle of fizz offered to freshen our drinks. Melissa instantly stuck her glass out. I put a hand over mine, politely declining. That was the other thing about Percival parties: it was too easy to get loaded.

Melissa asked about my job. Finding questions like this difficult to field, I came out with a stock reply: *busy*.

Resting a hand tenderly on Edgar's back, Melissa said, 'Orlando wants me to go back to work.'

She looked quite miserable at the prospect. 'It's a difficult decision, I guess.' And one I was delighted not to have. 'Can't you defer it?'

Melissa shrugged and gave a tight little smile. 'No doubt, we'll work it out.'

Changing the subject, I asked, 'Have you heard from Wren lately?'

'Spoke to her a week ago. She's still in Berlin, although she hopes to be back in the UK soon. It will be so good to have her home.'

I nodded, hoping my sunglasses masked the horrified expression in my eyes.

'Oh . . .' Melissa beamed then, as if she were seeing double, her eyes narrowed in confusion.

I followed her gaze to the terrace where Orlando stood, sharp-nosed, square-jawed, a vision of rugged confidence. Next to him, stood a pretty young woman barely out of her teens. Tall and slim, smiling shyly, she looked bewildered, as if she'd planned to travel to Aberdeen and wound up in Milan. Her tousled hair was red with distinctive dark roots, a very popular style at the moment, and fell in ringlets. I craned my head to see. Maybe she was a work colleague, or trainee paralegal.

At first, we were the only ones who seemed to notice the arrivals until conversations stuttered, petered out and, one by one, people turned to view the newcomer in the pale green crop top and wraparound ankle-length skirt. She wore sunglasses so it was impossible to read the expression in her eyes, yet the way she stood, stiffly, her hands bunched as if she were prepared to strike, struck me as someone feeling under pressure. My heart instinctively went out to her; I understood what that kind of intrusive scrutiny felt like.

Unusually flushed, Raff zeroed in on the arrivals. Celeste followed suit, suspicious, it seemed. Benedict stood mildly apprehensive and curious. Beside me, Melissa trembled. Tense lines ran from her mouth to her chin.

'Who is she?' I hissed.

Melissa shook her head and snatched at her drink.

Was this what Orlando had promised his wife? If so, some surprise this had turned out to be.

It took Autumn to break the spell the woman's unexpected arrival had cast.

Skipping innocently down the steps towards her father, Autumn gazed up at the mysterious stranger. 'Who are you?'

The woman squatted down to my niece's level. 'My name's Alice,' she answered. Her voice was low and husky and a curious amalgamation of West Country and Midlands.

'Are you Daddy's friend?'

The woman looked to Orlando as if she didn't know how to answer. Gallantly, Orlando stepped in, a wide smile on his narrow features, and in a booming "listen up" voice, said, 'Let's give a warm welcome to our children's nanny and newest member of the family, Alice Trinick.'

I watched as Celeste turned round and gave Melissa a long slow look that would make grown men tremble.

CHAPTER EIGHT

ROSE

It was as if someone's mobile phone had rung loudly at the start of the Christmas Carol Service, ruining the chorister's solo. Collective jaws on the floor, the Percivals stared at the culprit, in this case, Alice Trinick. I couldn't quite see why her arrival was such a big deal; a response shared by my brother-in-law who, unfazed, looked pointedly at the man with the topknot and demanded a drink.

Glass in hand, Orlando sprang up the steps, two at a time, joined his in-laws and pecked Celeste on the cheek.

'You know how much I hate surprises, Orlando.' Celeste's voice was haughty and strained.

'Where's the problem? It isn't as if this wasn't on the cards. Melissa is barely coping.'

I braced as Melissa muttered something under her breath, drained her glass and raised it aloft in a bid to signal to one of the servers that it was empty. I tried to catch Raff's eye but he was engaged in a low, urgent conversation with his dad.

'What do you have to do to get a drink around here?' Melissa complained loudly. Immediately, one of the servers dived for a bottle and sprinted towards us.

'Tell me to mind my own business,' I began in a low voice, 'But why did your mum . . .'

'It's fine,' Melissa said, snapping on a brittle smile.

Glass refilled — this time I gratefully accepted a top-up — Melissa practically necked her drink in one go.

'Are you okay?' I tried again, feeling awkward.

'I'm tired, that's all.' Melissa glanced at her sleeping son. Exhaustion was not the best advert for motherhood, although I didn't think fatigue the main reason for Melissa's nosedive in mood. We had Alice Trinick to thank for that.

I glanced towards Celeste, who stood ruler straight, locked in a silent exchange with Benedict. There were so many weird undercurrents I was in danger of getting caught up and sucked beneath. The second I got Raff alone I planned to drag it out of him.

Trying to appease and slow Melissa down, (wasn't there a law for being drunk in charge of small children?) I said, 'Maybe Orlando was trying to do something nice for you.'

Melissa turned the full force of her febrile gaze on me. 'Nice? He's a bastard.'

The next moments were the slowest of my life.

'*Rose*,' Orlando said, making me start. I scrambled to my feet and accepted a rather clumsy embrace. Seemingly oblivious to his wife's distress, Orlando plumped down next to Melissa and tucked an arm tightly around her shoulders. 'Hello, *you*,' he said.

'Go away,' Melissa snarled.

'What a welcome. And there's me thinking you'd be delighted to have a little extra help with the children,' Orlando continued jauntily though with a distinct lack of sincerity. He glanced up. 'This is how she repays me, Rose.'

Desperate to be left out of it, I stammered what I hoped was a non-contentious reply.

'Celeste says Alice can have the room next to ours,' Orlando informed his wife.

'Mummy agreed?' Obviously feeling stitched up, Melissa was wide-eyed in astonishment.

'She did, indeed.'

'I don't know how you pulled it off.'

Neither did I. Celeste was not a woman who caved easily.

'Charm and personality, darling.'

Melissa threw my brother-in-law such a poisonous look I swear to God if Orlando were ever found in lots of little pieces on the compost heap, it would be Melissa's fault.

Unperturbed, he reached into his pocket and pulled out a set of car keys, dangling them in front of me. 'Would you be a sweetheart, Rose, and show Alice to her room?'

'Well, I . . .'

'As this was your idea, why don't *you*?' Melissa's expression remained ugly with reproach.

'Because, my sweet, I've had a hell of a journey and I want to spend some time with my lovely wife who, it has to be said, looks a little teensy bit the worse for wear.'

'Screw you, Orlando.'

'Now then, Lissie, play nice.'

Melissa shook him off and sat up straight. 'You have no idea the damage you've done.'

'Sorry, darling, but now you've lost me.' He drummed his fingers on his chin. 'Oh *that*,' he burst out. 'I suppose, when you only have a baby to converse with, overthinking is an issue. Talking of which, let's see if my son is a little more hospitable.'

'He's asleep, Orlando. Leave him be,' Melissa warned.

Undeterred, Orlando picked Edgar up and jiggled him awake.

Before war broke out, and itching to know what *that* referred to, I headed for the terrace where Alice was trapped in conversation with Hector Finch, Benedict's accountant and the most boring individual on the planet. Annoyingly, Raff had wandered off to speak to a woman with a wide-brimmed hat about the redesign of her garden. I looked to Celeste. Intent on getting the party restarted, she was issuing instructions with semi-automatic delivery to the caterers.

Apologising to Hector for the interruption, I sidled up to Alice. 'I'm Rose Percival.' Alice looked none the wiser. 'Mrs Rhodes's brother, Raff, is my husband.'

'Of course,' Alice said haltingly. She swept her sunglasses from her face and parked them on the top of her head. Freckles dusted her high cheekbones. She had naturally shaped dark eyebrows and, beneath, her eyes were deep brown. Apart from the kink in the bridge of her nose, she was weirdly similar in appearance to Melissa.

'I've been asked to show you to your room,' I explained.

'My bags are still in Mr Rhodes's car.'

And why someone else had been given the job of lugging baggage in the heat rather than him, I suspected. 'No prob,' I said.

Unsurprisingly, Alice was ill at ease though I did my best to make her feel at home as we trooped onto the drive in search of Orlando's Alfa Romeo.

'Trinick is an unusual name,' I said.

'My dad's Cornish,' Alice replied.

'Oh, I love Cornwall. My parents used to take me there for holidays.'

'Whereabouts?'

'Falmouth, mostly, and Newquay.'

'My family live in Polruan, round the corner from Fowey.'

A place I'd definitely heard of. 'How lovely. You must miss it.'

'I do but it's very expensive, hardly any work, and awash with second home owners.'

'Don't they have children that need looking after?'

'They do, and they pay good money, but employment is only guaranteed for a few months of the year. My last job was in Birmingham,' Alice said.

Which accounted for the slight Midlands undertone. 'You're going to find country life very different from the big city.'

Alice's eyes brightened. 'That's the idea.'

I cupped a hand over my brow against the heat haze and spied Orlando's dark blue Alfa Romeo sandwiched between an Aston Martin DBX and a Porsche Carrera. I marched off, Alice's long-legged stride easily keeping up.

Popping open the hatch, I was surprised to see only two holdalls. 'Is that it?' I didn't go anywhere without a ton of luggage.

'I travel light.'

There's light and there's practically non-existent. Puzzled, I hefted one bag, Alice the other and we headed back to the house and through the vast front door and into a wide reception hall. The smell of fresh flowers and polish was strong enough to knock out the combined doggy pong from Fergal and Fuggles.

A couple of shabby sofas gathered around a large stone fireplace like elderly solicitors in a member's club. An abandoned game of Scrabble sat on a coffee table. Huge ancestral paintings hung on the walls. Books — loads of them — huddled together on bookshelves. I was accustomed to the stately home vibe. Not so Alice. With a look of awe I recognised so well, she followed me up a wide oak staircase to the first floor.

A proper boy's room, the room allotted to Alice still smelt comfortably of Raff. A miniature battlefield arranged on an occasional table was all that remained of his teenage obsession with Warhammer. Scary-looking figurines, with skulls for heads, stared out of towers at similarly ferocious figures brandishing fearsome weapons. Books on rugby, self-sufficiency, the environment and garden design sat helter-skelter on a shelf over the double bed. Matchbox cars were arranged along a window ledge; collector's items, I'd often suspected. Alice viewed her new surroundings with wonder, as if she were dreaming. It was quite sweet, really. She looked at me and swallowed.

'Rose,' she began, a cautious note in her voice.

'Yep?'

'When I arrived not everyone seemed that pleased to see me.'

'Oh that,' I said breezily. 'Take no notice.'

'It was embarrassing.'

'I came in for the same treatment when I met the family for the first time.'

'Really?' Relief flooded her face.
'Honest.'
'Thank goodness. I thought I'd done something wrong.'
'Not at all.'
'You live here too?'
'In one of the lodges. It's only temporary,' I said, feeling marginally disloyal. 'I guess we ought to be getting back.'
'Would it be okay if I stay here for a bit?'
'Aren't you hungry?' I was starving.
'Not really and I won't be long,' Alice said.
'Then I'll leave you to it.'

CHAPTER NINE

ALICE

Astoundingly, the stories Alice had heard about the Percival Estate were true. The house and grounds were more opulent than she'd dared to imagine. Swathed in Cotswold light, that bathed everything in a warm yellow glow, they exceeded her grandest expectations.

With her ear pressed against the door, she listened to Rose Percival's retreating footsteps. Having already designated it a relationship worth cultivation, Alice knew exactly who Rose was. It was reassuring to see that Rose was the type of person who could prove useful in smoothing Alice's way into the hierarchy of the family. Judging by the less than warm reception from the Percivals, with their hard expressions and braying voices, Alice would need all the help she could get. Despite assurances to the contrary, Alice very much got the impression that she, the new arrival, was not welcome. Quite simply, Mrs Rhodes didn't want her there.

A quick investigation of the place she would briefly call home revealed an en-suite bathroom containing a roll-top bath and shower. A large sash window overlooked a kitchen garden and tennis courts. Ghost hills, enshrouded in heat haze, could be glimpsed far away.

The room contained a fridge, in which there was a pint of milk and bottled water, still and sparkling. On an occasional table, a tea tray set out with kettle, sugar, two mugs and a tin of shortbread; at her bedside, a glass, magazines and sci-fi novel, with dog-eared pages. She'd stayed in hotels — cheap, admittedly — that were not so well equipped. *Posh living*, Alice thought, sinking dreamily onto the double bed and helping herself to a biscuit. She could get used to it — and she would until she'd got what she'd came for.

She was astonished that a crazy idea, conceived in a moment of desperation, had brought her this far. From the beginning she'd foreseen a number of potential obstacles. The plot would have been dead from the start if her godmother, a woman Alice had not previously seen for many years, had confirmed her mother's secret to be pure fantasy. Safe in the knowledge that what she'd been told was true, Alice had located the Percival family's whereabouts through an online article publicising the winding up of the Percival's wedding venue after many years in business. Melissa's society wedding to Orlando Rhodes and, next, Rafferty Percival's marriage to Rose Sutton, had helped Alice sketch in background details. Information gathered on the internet revealed a surprising amount about the "players", as she termed them. Alice knew what they did and where they worked. The next stage and most difficult had been to find a way in. This was where Orlando Rhodes' glossy P.A. and legal secretary, Belinda Hart, proved indispensable.

Alice had upped her game, procured a mani and a pedi, had her hair done professionally, and splashed out on an expensive new wardrobe, after which she'd pretty much stalked the woman until, one bright morning, Alice had employed "the spilt drink trick" in a café where Belinda routinely picked up a cortado and skinny latte. *Accidentally* splashing her glass of orange juice over Belinda's designer shirt and trousers, Alice had apologised profusely, offered to pay for the dry cleaning and insisted on buying Belinda breakfast the next day. One conversation led to another, followed by an exchange of phone numbers, nights out at clubs and bars and, before Belinda knew it, Alice had her in her web. When Belinda's quest for a nanny for her boss was mentioned, Alice put herself forward as the perfect solution. She'd even provided good character references (forged, naturally). In exchange for a number of drinks, a mother of an old mate from school had posed as one of Alice's former employers. Hiring domestic help wasn't really covered by Belinda's job description and she was easy enough to fool. Orlando Rhodes was a slick bastard with an acid tongue, a man of high intelligence equalled only by his opinion of himself, yet when he'd recruited Alice Trinick he had no clue that Alice had, in fact, recruited him.

Swiping the pillow next to her, a big smile across her face, Alice hugged it to her chest as tightly as her own little secret. Standing out there in the dry heat, with all those superior faces staring at her, Alice's focus was on one man only: *I'm coming for you, Benedict Horatio Percival. I'm coming for you.*

CHAPTER TEN

ROSE

I scoffed my own body weight in chicken wraps, couscous and bean salad, downed more wine than was good for me and talked to a lively man who bred horses — not my favourite subject — and glad-handed and spoke to a number of others whose names I couldn't remember but whose faces I'd never forget. Separately and earnestly, Celeste and Benedict asked me if I was having a lovely time, to which I answered in the affirmative. The same could not be said for poor Melissa, who looked achingly miserable. Alice, I noticed, remained conspicuously absent, which was probably a smart move. I couldn't blame her for not being able to face the onslaught of interest. By the time Raff and me could politely return to our living quarters, I was practically bursting a blood vessel with frustration. Scrap my legendary patience.

'What the hell was that all about?' I asked Raff.

'All what about?' Shoes off, sprawled on the sofa, his eyes were semi-closed. I suspected he was pretty fried and while I'd had a ton of booze, my brain was positively fizzing with theories and possibilities.

'C'mon, Raff, don't be dense. The newcomer. The nanny. The person your mum and dad were gawping at, including you, I might add.'

I sank down next to him and swung my legs up into his lap.

'Ouch! Watch where you're parking your feet.'

'Good, I have your attention.' I snapped a smile. 'For a nasty moment I thought Orlando had imported a mistress. Judging by the assembled reaction, I wasn't alone.'

'Orlando's a prat but even he wouldn't stoop to something as low as that.'

'It didn't stop Melissa having a right go at him.'

Uneasy with relationship talk — weren't most men? — Raff's eyes travelled to the direction of the kitchen. 'I need some water.'

'Not until you tell me what all the fuss is about. And don't say I'm overthinking, which is what Orlando told your sister.'

'Ancient history,' Raff said, with a yawn.

'Obviously not as far as Melissa is concerned.'

'That's Melissa for you.'

'Raff, that's not very nice.'

'Well, you know how temperamental she is.'

'You sound like your brother-in-law.'

This was met with a sharp look. 'Thanks very much.'

I gave his arm a playful punch. 'Sorry.' Raff was nothing like Orlando. *Thank God.*

'Accepted. Now can I get a drink?'

'Not yet. What do you think of Alice?'

'What sort of a question is that?'

'A simple one.'

'I barely exchanged more than a few words with her. No, I tell a lie,' Raff said, 'one word: *hello.*'

'Then why the big deal?'

'There is no deal.'

'Raff, she caused a stir.'

'You're imagining it.'

'Rubbish.'

I'm excellent at staring people out and I didn't hold back now. 'Why is it that I feel I'm being told to back off?'

Raff scrubbed a hand through his blonde locks, making it even more spiky than usual. 'Okay, okay.' Raff held his palms up. 'I give in. Jesus, Rose, you're like a bloodhound.'

I'd never been compared to a dog. A curious cat, for sure.

'We had a nanny when we were kids,' Raff said.

It wasn't the earth-shattering answer I'd expected. 'And?'

'That's it.'

Most definitely that was not it. 'Did she make you stand on the naughty step, tie you up, beat you, or something?'

'Don't be ridiculous.'

I let that pass. 'What was her name?'

'Shona, I think.'

'You *think*?'

'Rose, I don't remember. I was a little boy.'

'What about Violet? Would she remember?'

Raff pursed his lips in the way that all the family did whenever his eldest sister was mentioned. 'She would have been ten or eleven.'

'So this was . . .'

'*Yonks* ago.'

'Can you put that into modern English?'

Raff flashed a grin. 'I was six, Wren a toddler and Melissa was about eight.'

No wonder he didn't remember.

'Is Shona a Scottish name?' Raff asked, as if it had only just occurred to him.

'Think so. And you really don't remember a thing about her?'

'Nope.'

Then why would the presence of one nanny spark memories of another because I was pretty sure it had?

'How old was Shona?'

'Search me. You don't notice stuff like that when you're a kid. Oh, and after her, we had another nanny: Mrs Cole.'

'Is that what you actually called her?'

Raff did that hazy-eye thing again. 'Think her name was Beatrice. She was a right dragon.'

'She lived here?'

'No, she had a family of her own.'

'Older than Shona then?'

'Dunno.'

'How long did she stay?'

'Shona or Mrs Cole?'

'Both.'

'Mrs C probably five or six years, maybe, until I was thirteen.'

'And Shona?'

Raff shrugged his broad shoulders. 'You'd have to ask Melissa. Second thoughts, scratch that idea.'

'Did Shona leave for another job?'

'How should I know?'

I gave him a look, the one that says: *I'm only getting half the story. Where's the rest?*

Defeated, Raff cleared his throat. 'All right. It's a bit delicate.'

'How delicate?'

'Shona died.'

'*Jesus*, here, at Blackthorn?'

'Of course not,' he said tetchily.

'Sorry, but bloody hell, Raff.'

'It was really bad for my parents because Mum and Dad felt that if she'd stayed, she might have lived.'

'She wasn't murdered, was she?' Fine hairs stood up on the back of my neck.

'Christ, no.' Raff looked quite pissed off with my suggestion.

'Heart attack, disease, accident, what?'

'God, you're impossibly nosy.'

'Curious,' I corrected him. 'Did Orlando have any idea the effect his actions would have?'

'Who knows? My brother-in-law is a professional shit-stirrer.'

After what I'd witnessed that afternoon, I had to agree. Florence's slur about him sprang to mind.

'It would have been better if Orlando had consulted them,' Raff said.

I thought about that. Did Orlando know about the dead nanny and chose to ignore it anyway? 'It's not very fair on poor Alice.'

'It's not very fair on Mum and Dad,' Raff countered. 'It was a huge thing in their lives and why they rarely mention it.'

And seemingly far from forgotten. 'I'm sorry about that, but Alice isn't daft. She knew something was up the second she arrived.'

Raff elevated an eyebrow.

'Me and my listening face,' I reminded him. People tell me all sorts of stuff, particularly when they have their hair in my hands. 'You should have seen the stinking look your mum gave Melissa, as if she was in on it.'

'No way would Melissa have sanctioned a nanny.'

'Then she must remember what happened.' I gave Raff a meaningful look.

'You *cannot* ask her.'

'Why not?'

'Anything Melissa claims to know she got off Violet and Violet is a drug-taking liar.'

'Not at eleven years of age, I hope.'

He pinched the top of his nose with flat fingers. 'I worry about you, sometimes.'

'Raff, I've been here barely twenty-four hours and all hell's broken loose. I listened to all your arguments and because I love you, I agreed to bunk up with your parents. But I never imagined being plunged into some kind of family psychodrama. I'm really starting to question what we're doing here.'

He looked solemn and serious and grateful. Good. 'I appreciate everything you've done,' he said. 'I know it hasn't been easy. Honestly, I promise it will all blow over.'

I gave him a look that told him I was prepared to give him the benefit of the doubt. Mostly. 'Fair enough, but I expect to be included, not excluded.'

'Okay, okay,' Raff said, caving in. 'But you have to understand I only know this from Melissa and, to be frank, as much as I love my sister, she has a fertile imagination.' He took a breath. 'Shona's death was an accident.'

'What kind of accident? Car, horse riding, motor boat . . .'

'Hell, Rose. Give it a rest. I think she had a fall, or something.'

'Where? Down a cliff?'

'How the bloody hell should I know?'

No wonder Alice's arrival had raked up a shit storm of memories. When horrible things like that happen within a family they travel down the generations and assume almost mythical status.

'Had she been drinking?' I pressed Raff. If you drink and fall your body is so relaxed you wind up with bruises, instead of serious injuries. This was not based on scientific knowledge, but according to one of my more colourful clients who worked in medical negligence insurance.

Raff blew out through his full lips. 'If you keep asking me questions I can't answer, you're going to get me on repeat: I. Don't. Know.'

I wrinkled my nose in apology.

'Seriously, Rose, I don't have the foggiest recollection of the whys and wherefores — and neither does Melissa.' The warning note in my husband's voice was designed to scare me off. I was only marginally repelled. 'As far as Mum and Dad are concerned,' Raff continued, 'the world has moved on.'

'Until today.'

He let out a noise: part snort, part sigh.

'And maybe not for Violet.' This was a risky move.

'What are you talking about?' Raff's sharp expression could have cut stone. 'Violet was always going to go off the rails.'

According to family folklore, Violet had got into the Cheltenham drugs scene in a big way as a teenager and fried her brain. Had her nanny's death triggered a deep-seated emotional reaction? Was this why the family had virtually disowned her? Now a forty-something, she lived as a recluse in a shack in the Forest of Dean.

'Can I get some water now?' Raff said, in a "please, miss" voice.

I let him go. My mind was less accommodating.

'So let me get this straight,' I called to Raff. 'Shona worked for your parents and then she left and died.'

'Yep,' Raff said, drinking deeply.

I wondered what made her leave. I also wondered whether I had the courage to ignore my husband's advice and ask Melissa.

CHAPTER ELEVEN

MELISSA

Melissa had stayed for as long as she could bear, then parked Edgar with her father, scooted past Orlando, dashed back to the house, hurled upstairs, away from the hubbub and threw up in the nearest lavatory. It was the shock, not the booze. She didn't believe Orlando could be so cruel. And why did he choose a *looker* and not someone like Mrs Cole, Shona's replacement? He *knew* he was lighting a tinderbox. She'd warned him not to think about employing a nanny while they were living at the house. And now her mother believed she'd sanctioned it.

Running cold water from the tap, Melissa scooped a handful into her mouth and spat it out. What would happen now? Would those memories, the ones she'd blocked, resurface? The events that had taken such a toll on her older sister, Violet. The cradle of all her problems, Violet had never been the same since.

Melissa put the seat down on the loo and sat on it. She'd tried — and failed — on several strained occasions to explain to Orlando what it had been like back then. She'd struggled because her memories were hazy, open to interpretation, according to her husband, and it was too easy for him to dismiss them. *Shit happens* had been Orlando's contemptuous response. Worse, he'd called her neurotic (a view he shared with her mother so it was doubly hurtful). *Facts*, Orlando had demanded, of which there were few: Shona Reid, her beloved nanny for three years, had fallen out with her mother, was subsequently fired, and died soon after in a horrible accident.

This did not do justice to the emotional fallout for her and Violet. First, there had been the fear generated by grown-ups arguing, second, the terror of Shona, someone they loved, leaving. After she'd gone, confusing silences, shut doors, whispered and quickly abandoned conversations plagued their home.

And then two police officers came to Blackthorn, and Violet, it was always Violet, hung over the banister and eavesdropped.

They killed her, Violet shrieked hysterically.

That's horrible and you're horrible, Melissa had yelled back.

Not, not, not.

Frozen with sadness, Melissa withdrew into herself. Violet, the brightest of them all, took a different path. She rebelled, argued, cheated, stole and lied. As the weeks and months passed, Melissa strived to be good, to work hard at school and achieve because this is what her mother demanded of her, unlike her dad who loved all his children unconditionally and made no demands at all. Viewing Melissa's high grades and excellent behaviour as betrayal, Violet made colourful accusations and allegations that she could not prove. Finding no audience, she discovered drugs instead and hung out with deadbeats. At seventeen, she left home before she was kicked out, an outcast.

Melissa stood up and crept out onto the thickly carpeted landing. The party still in full swing, she drew a deep breath in and stared down into a muddy pool of dark imagining. Scum filmed the surface. God alone knew what really lay beneath.

CHAPTER TWELVE

ALICE

Lies and locked doors kept you safe, Alice thought darkly.

Sensitive to violent noise, she'd spent an uncomfortable night listening to her employers arguing. Hands clapped over her ears did not prevent parts of the alcohol-fuelled row from seeping through.

Much like musical compositions, heated exchanges had their own tempo, with plenty of staccato and crescendo. Horribly, it reminded her of Sean. That was the problem with abusive partners. Even when they were miles away, they remained as close to you as a clammy second skin.

At first, Alice thought she'd been rumbled. Why else had her presence stirred up anger and suspicion? It wasn't as if anyone knew who she really was. *Then* there might be a problem.

But as dawn broke, Alice had assembled enough of the shattered fragments of abuse hurled the night before to create a disturbing tale of guilt and death and, intriguingly, Benedict Percival was firmly at its centre.

She had a little think about that.

Alice's arrival had lit a spark and set light to a piece of family history that even her mum hadn't known about. And that meant her mother wasn't the first victim. Perversely, it served Alice's purposes.

The success of her scheme relied on her staying in post long enough to pull it off. The best she could do was prove that she was good at her job, indispensable even, and a valued *member of the team*, to quote Orlando Rhodes' fruity-voiced P.A., Belinda. The unknown factor, the wild card, the single element that could cock everything up, was Sean.

Vigilant, Alice stood at the window, scanning for sight or sound of him, or anyone lurking in the shadows and who didn't belong.

She'd learnt to tell the difference between a soft footfall that meant trouble and one that was harmless. She could divine a change in engine note — the hallmark of the kerb-crawler — and a fast car shooting past, designed to scare her shitless. Senses highly-tuned, she recognised when she was being watched. Honing her powers of observation over many months, she had meticulously checked her tracks since leaving Sean and her last position and the one before. Always on the move. Always on the run. Never ever going back. Because going back meant *him* and that ended up in a black eye and broken ribs and split lip, if she were lucky. If not . . .

Hearing Edgar's cry, Alice drew on a robe thoughtfully left for her on the back of a door and slipped out onto the corridor and into an adjoining room in which the children slept, shielded from their parents' heated altercation.

Edgar had wriggled out of his sleeping bag and, clutching the bars of his cot, pulled himself up.

'Clever boy,' Alice crooned. At the sound of her voice, Edgar gave her a gummy smile.

Alice reached over, inhaling his yeasty fragrance. 'Hello, little man,' she said. Some day she'd like children of her own but it would have to be with a man she could trust, someone special, someone who didn't beat the crap out of her.

Giving Edgar a cuddle, she carried him into the bathroom and changed his nappy. Autumn was already stirring by the time Alice returned to the bedroom.

'Can we have chocolate croissants for breakfast?' Autumn asked.

Alice was given no instructions other than to get the children up and dressed. 'I don't know. Are they allowed?'

'Ooh, yes.'

'Do you know where they are?'

'Granny has a special cupboard.' Autumn stuck her warm hand in Alice's. 'Come on, I'll show you.'

Back out into the corridor, Alice noticed the door to the Rhodes's room ajar.

'I'm going for a run around the lake,' she heard Orlando announce. Seconds later, he appeared in shorts, T-shirt and running shoes. He seemed perky for a man who'd spent half the night growling at his wife.

'Morning, Alice. Did you sleep well?'

'Fine,' she lied.

'Good to see you're acquainting yourself with the children. I'm afraid Melissa isn't well.'

'I'm sorry to hear that.'

Orlando's jaw clenched, suggesting he didn't feel quite the same level of sympathy. 'Could you amuse the children this morning?' he asked brusquely. 'I recognise it's an imposition and isn't quite what we agreed so, if you'd like to take some personal time tomorrow, please feel free to do so.'

'Thank you, Mr Rhodes.'

'Orlando, please.' He turned to go and then turned back. 'Oh and we'll be assembling for drinks in the drawing room around midday, prior to Sunday luncheon.'

Alice nodded. 'Is it okay if I give your daughter chocolate croissants for breakfast? I didn't like to presume.'

Autumn hopped up and down on one foot. '*Please*, Daddy, *please*.'

Orlando grinned, tousled his daughter's hair. 'You can have anything you like, my darling.' He looked at Alice. 'Well done. Seems you have everything under control.'

Alice smiled sweetly. That was the plan.

CHAPTER THIRTEEN

ROSE

Raff woke me at stupid o-clock with a kiss. 'Hey,' he said.

I had a mild hangover and kept my eyes tight shut. Next, I felt a hand on my thigh, morning breath in my face. 'What?' I mumbled, as if I didn't know.

'Come here,' he whispered. 'I want you.'

So me he had.

Afterwards, Raff took a shower while I dozed and blearily mapped out my day: a lovely walk through the woods, phone call to Mum, gossip with Florence, and then, when Raff got home, tapas, with all sorts of yummy goodies, shared over a bottle of wine. The second Raff bounded up the stairs from the wet room and burst in, phone held high like a grenade he was about to lob, I sensed my plans were to be blown to pieces.

'Just been on WhatsApp,' Raff announced. (The siblings had a WhatsApp group for hot news. As if we needed any more.) 'Wren's on her way home.'

Oh crap. 'Today?'

'Should arrive in time for lunch. Mum wants us to join them for a roast to celebrate.'

I suppressed a groan and dived under the covers. It was 23 degrees Celsius. The thought of a big hot Sunday lunch — and when I say *big* I wasn't joking — left me queasy.

'It's great news, isn't it?' Raff plunged his legs into a pair of stone-coloured shorts. 'Have you seen my navy shirt?'

I directed him to the wardrobe.

Hang on a moment. 'It's Sunday,' I said. 'Aren't you working?'

'Change of plan.'

'Right,' I said, mildly irritated that Wren had so much pull. 'You getting up soon?'

So unsubtle. Turning over, I tugged the sheet up to my nose; it made my feet stick out. 'There's no rush, is there?' I could have blithered on about Sunday morning lie-ins but Raff had that pumped-up look in his eye, like when he'd drunk too many cups of coffee.

'Said I'd give Dad a hand getting the Granary ready.'

'For Wren?'

'Yep.'

Lucky Wren, I thought. It was bigger than our place and there was only one of her. Worse, it would mean I'd have to walk past her door each workday to pick up my car.

'There can't be much to do,' I said.

'It's been used for storage so we need to shift stuff out before we can make it hospitable.'

I made a non-committal noise and stretched my arms above my head. Raff continued to hover. 'What?' I said.

'I thought it would be nice if you offered to give Mum a hand in the kitchen.'

Capable ran through Celeste's DNA. She would be fine without me and I had a nasty feeling I'd get in the way. More importantly, I didn't want to set a precedent. 'Sure,' I said. 'No problem.'

Raff leaned over and kissed me softly on the lips. 'Thank you.' He went to leave and then changed his mind. 'You, okay, Rose?'

'Uh-huh.'

'No more wild theories?'

'Cross my heart.'

He gave me a funny look as if I were plotting something the second his back was turned. He knew me too well. The moment he was out of the door, I counted to twenty and reached for my laptop.

A number of keywords banged into Google succeeded in listing death notices of much-loved grandparents aka nannies, yards of stuff on fatal accidental falls throughout the UK the previous year, and current information on nanny and babysitting services in Gloucestershire. Nothing involving a woman called Shona who'd checked out almost thirty years previously.

With great reluctance, I dragged myself out of bed, downed fresh juice and forced myself to eat a slice of toast, showered, dressed and cleaned my teeth. As a precaution, I drank a glass of milk to line my stomach before pre-lunch drinks — ruinous affairs. I couldn't rely on my tried and tested excuse for not drinking: *I'm driving*. At this rate I'd need to resort to: *I'm on antibiotics*. Except, living in the goldfish bowl of Blackthorn House, someone would demand to know the type of specific infection that required such heavy-duty medication.

Giving my hair a good brush, applying mascara and a slick of lipstick, I looked more human and was good to go. Still, I loitered.

I phoned Mum and got Dad who moaned about his beloved football team "cocking it up". Mum hovered, like she always does, until Dad said, 'Right, better pass you over.'

'Everything all right, Rose?'

'Yes,' I said.

'Settling in?'

'I think it might take a little time.'

'Bound to. Go on then, what's your new lodgings like?'

I told her.

'Sounds lovely and cosy for the two of you.'

Except it wasn't the two of us. It was the whole family.

Misreading my less than enthusiastic response, she asked, 'Everything all right with you and Raff?'

'When I get to see him, yes.'

'Don't you worry about a thing. It will all work out, you'll see.'

After that, I dropped a coded text to Florence that said I was missing her already, in the hope that she'd respond, but she was offline. I walked into the garden outside the kitchen and watered tubs of geraniums and cyclamen, wishing that I could stay there all day and watch squirrels abseiling down the tree-trunks. Basically, I wanted to be anywhere but at the big house. The whole dead nanny issue gnawed at me and, unlike Melissa and contrary to what Raff thought, I wasn't normally given to fanciful ideas. How can you explain when something in your gut tells you there's more to a story than is apparent on the surface?

I was so late putting in an appearance that Raff had finished sorting out Wren's new living quarters and was playing hide-and-seek with Autumn in the garden. Hilariously, Autumn's idea of hiding was to conceal herself behind Alice. Everyone could see my niece's mop of curly blonde hair peeping out. Alice entered into the spirit of it and laughed with my husband; it was nice to see Raff making an effort with the newcomer.

'Where's Edgar?' I asked Alice.

'Gone down for a sleep. We were up early this morning.' Strain tugged at her eyes. She looked really whacked.

'Everything okay?' I asked, sympathetic.

'Cool,' Alice replied, a little too brightly. About to go and do my daughter-in-law duty in the kitchen, she asked, 'I was wondering how far it is to the nearest town.'

'By car, it should take around fifteen minutes to Cirencester, nearer twenty-five to Cheltenham.'

'Is there a bus?'

'Not sure.'

'Could I get a cab?'

'You *could*. When were you planning on going?'

'Mr Rhodes said I could have the day off tomorrow.'

'I'm not going anywhere.'

'Oh, no, I couldn't possibly . . .'

'Don't be soft. It would be nice to have some company,' I said, ignoring Raff, whose eyeballs were boring a hole in the side of my head.

'You're sure?' Alice looked as if she couldn't believe her luck. 'Let me pay for petrol, at least.'

'You can buy me a coffee instead.'

That settled, I mooched from the garden into the house and into a storm of activity and an atmosphere thick with mother-daughter recrimination. The Percival kitchen is vast. Flagstone floors that look as if they were laid in the Dark Ages; a large, intimidating Aga; a Welsh dresser covering an entire wall. It was all terribly posh yet shabby. Mum, as incessantly curious as me, had taken a sneak peek once and, appalled, declared it unhygienic.

Vegetables, in various stages of preparation and assembly, littered the work surfaces. Melissa aimlessly whisked eggs and flour while nursing a cup of green tea at a refectory table that must have measured over two metres in length. Dark shadows ringed her eyes, as if she hadn't slept for a week. She looked up mournfully and I was sure I caught the faintest whiff of cigarettes. Orlando and Benedict, looming in the background, were engaged in a spirited discussion about which wine to serve as an aperitif. I noticed that Benedict was wearing an expensively tailored fitted shirt over a smart pair of chinos, the flip-flops swapped for loafers. Celeste, apron on, peeled potatoes and openly fretted whether the joint of beef would be big enough.

'Wren doesn't eat meat, Mum,' Melissa reminded her.

'I *know* that, dear,' Celeste snapped. 'I'm not talking about Wren. I'm talking about the extra person.'

I wanted to speak Alice's name but chickened out. 'Can I do anything to help?'

'You could lay the table,' Celeste replied briskly. 'For God's sake, darling,' she said to Melissa, 'can you hurry up? The batter needs to chill. Why on earth didn't you use the food mixer?'

'Because it makes far too much noise,' Melissa replied.

'Don't be wet. Oh, give it here.' Celeste snatched the whisk and bowl clean out of Melissa's hand. 'Make yourself useful and go and see to the dogs in the boot room. I'm not sure they've got enough water in the heat. And do buck up, Melissa.'

'I've been telling her that all morning,' Orlando chimed in.

Throwing him a thunderous look, Melissa slowly got to her feet and wandered towards the door, pausing on the threshold. 'I think Edgar's awake. He's crying.'

'Well go and get the nanny,' Celeste sniped. 'That's what she's paid for.'

'I'll go,' Benedict said cheerily.

'No need, sweetheart.' Celeste looked pointedly at Orlando.

'On it,' her son-in-law said, obedient.

'Christ, Edgar is *my* son,' Melissa exploded. With a hand already reaching into the pocket of her dress, fumbling for cigarettes, she tore outside.

God, I thought, *could the return of the prodigal get any worse?* Worried about my sister-in-law, I shot after her. Melissa moved at incredible speed in the direction of the woods. I had visions of her disappearing into the undergrowth and never finding her.

'Melissa,' I called. 'Wait. Slow down.'

Either she didn't hear, or pretended not to. Undeterred, I kept running. By the time I caught up with her, she was resting her back against an oak tree, smoking a cigarette, and I was practically vomiting up my lungs from the exertion.

'I'm all right,' she said, sad-eyed.

'No, you're not.'

Melissa took a deep drag that seemed to calm her. 'This is so screwed up,' she said softly.

'What is?'

'Everything. Me, Orlando, the bloody nanny — I'm quite capable of looking after my own children, thank you very much. As for my mother, I do a better job than she ever did.'

'Right,' I said. What else could I say?

'I'm so disappointed.' Tears flooded her eyes. 'I'd so hoped that Orlando would give me something nice, something to treasure, that said we're still all right. As you might have gathered,' Melissa said, with a weary sigh, 'my husband and I are not seeing eye to eye at the moment.'

'I gather children can put an enormous strain on a marriage,' I said tentatively. Not that I had the first clue.

Melissa peered through the trees as if somewhere, amid the dappled light, she'd find the answers she craved. 'I thought having kids would fix things.'

'Oh,' I said.

Melissa inclined her head and smiled. She really was very pretty. 'I can see you're surprised.'

'I am.' I'd no idea that their problems started before Autumn and Edgar were born.

'I'm biased, naturally, because Raff is my brother,' Melissa said, 'but you're lucky to be married to such a gentle and uncomplicated soul.'

I smiled warmly. I was.

'The trouble with Alpha males, like my husband,' Melissa continued, 'is they're difficult to manage and contain. They have such high expectations of themselves and of their partners.'

'I'm sure you more than fit the bill.' I genuinely wanted Melissa to feel better.

'Kind of you to say, but as disappointed as I am in Orlando, he's equally dissatisfied with me. I'm aware that, one day, he'll leave me.'

Shocked by Melissa's candour, I said, 'Do you honestly think so?'

'He'll probably wait until the children are grown and flown.' Melissa exhaled a languorous plume of smoke and narrowed her eyes as if envisaging life without him.

'Melissa, you can't think that.' It was such a horrible way to live.

'Why not? It's the truth.'

'Can't you talk to him, tell him how you really feel?'

'What's the point?'

'Surely, he'd listen if he knew how unhappy you are?'

Melissa's smile was thin. 'Orlando only listens to dissect, spin and dish it back. You know the worst thing? It's the contempt he displays towards me — so humiliating.'

I didn't like the sound of that. 'He doesn't hit you or anything, does he?'

'I don't think he can be bothered.'

'I'm sure he doesn't mean—'

'Look, can we not discuss it anymore? It's all so depressing.'

My sister-in-law's honesty made me bold. I waited a beat. 'Is this connected to the arrival of the nanny?'

Her eyes flared. 'What?'

'Raff told me about the nanny you had when you were children.'

'We had several.'

'I meant Shona.'

Melissa's expression darkened. 'Did he now?'

'Not in detail,' I added quickly. 'He was too young to remember.'

'He was.' Melissa flicked an *I think we're done here* smile. 'Wren will be here any minute. I really think we should be getting back, don't you?'

The shutters had come down with a thump on the conversation. My bad.

CHAPTER FOURTEEN

ROSE

'Where the hell have you two been?' Raff was pink-cheeked and unusually snippy. 'Mum's been doing her pieces.'

'We didn't realise the time,' I said mildly.

'*Lunchtime*,' he snapped.

'No need to be snarky,' Melissa said. 'Doesn't suit you, little brother.'

I held my breath, waiting for a backlash that never came. I guess Melissa could pull big sister rank.

'Has Wren arrived?' I asked.

'She's been delayed and said to start without her.'

'What a shame.' Now who was being snarky?

Under Celeste's reprimanding gaze, Melissa and I slunk in and were handed glasses of pink fizz. Not bad as a consolation prize. I very much got the impression that Benedict, sitting one leg across the other, ankle turned in, was poised to hold court. And I was right.

'Living together in a community is about mutual respect and cooperation,' he announced, as if giving a presentation. 'We all value individuality and freedom.'

This, I could sign up for. I took a happy sip and let the bubbles travel up my nose.

'So,' Benedict said, in a voice like oiled walnut mixed with mahogany, 'to maintain open channels of communication, I believe we need a few house rules. Nothing proscriptive,' he added, glancing at me. The champagne on my tongue tasted instantly sour. 'I suggest regular Friday night suppers and Sunday lunches will give us all the opportunity to come together as a family and air any potential grievances.'

I glanced at Raff who hiked an eyebrow, hugely enjoying my obvious consternation. *You'll pay for that later*, I thought.

After Benedict's welcome speech, I didn't recall much else. I was put at one end of the table between Raff and Alice. Melissa was next to her, with Edgar in his high chair; on the opposite side Autumn was next to Orlando who sat next to Celeste. Benedict, as master of the house, took pole position at the head of the table, carving great slices of beef onto plates already embellished with Yorkshire pudding. In a flurry of culinary activity, tureens of vegetables were handed around, gravy dispensed, horseradish and mustard offered. Orlando did what he always did: made sure our glasses were topped up with wine. Chatter turned to the weather, Wren's arrival and England's chances at rugby, a sport in which I had little interest. Deluged by noise from the children and clatter of cutlery, and Percival business, mostly concerning the management of the land, I tuned out — though I did cotton on to a couple of snippets of conversation from Raff and Alice about her family.

'My dad, he's called Jago . . .'

'Jago?' Raff burst out.

'It's Cornish,' Alice enlightened him. 'He's an ops manager at a brewery.' This immediately sparked a conversation between Raff and Orlando about the merits and flavours of various craft beers. We'd finished our main course when Benedict ceremoniously tapped the side of his glass with a spoon. My heart sank.

'I'd like to make a toast,' he announced. 'Raise your glasses, everyone. Here's to us living together in perfect harmony.'

Oh, God, this is so cheesy, I thought, noticing the sly glance Orlando gave Melissa. After the conversation in the woods, I feared a scene, something our family didn't really go in for. Bickering was one thing, flat-out rowing unheard of. Perhaps that's why I found conflict hard to handle.

Smoothly oblivious, Benedict continued, 'I'd also like to give a special welcome to my son, Rafferty, and my lovely daughter-in-law, Rose. I hope you'll be very happy here at Blackthorn.'

Celeste enveloped me in a warm smile that told me I was forgiven for my late appearance. I received it, mildly embarrassed.

'Let's not forget Alice,' Orlando boomed.

In the space of seconds the emotional temperature in the room dipped from jolly to seriously awkward. Pale-faced, Celeste cast a helpless glance at Benedict who looked as nervous as a groom before his wedding. *Thank God for Raff*, I thought, as eyes alive with good humour, he leapt to his feet, raised a glass and said, 'And here's to Ma and Pa for their kindness and generosity and especially to Ma for the splendid lunch.'

'Hear, hear,' I said. Call me a creep but I was desperate to change the mood. Catching on, Edgar bashed his bowl with a spoon, resulting in a show of spontaneous if slightly nervous laughter. I never thought I'd be more grateful to a one-year-old. Normal service resumed and puddings served, I was about to tuck into plum crumble when the sound of a baby crying stopped everyone in their tracks. Merrily plastering his high chair with custard, it wasn't Edgar. The sound appeared to emanate from the hall.

'What the . . .' Benedict began.

'I'll go.' Celeste threw down her napkin and stood up. She'd barely made it more than a few steps when, with a dramatic flourish, the door to the dining room swung open and Wren stepped inside. Shorter than Melissa, she had a petite build, a mane of curly white-blonde hair and green eyes that could pierce armour plating. In her arms, swaddled in a blanket, a bawling infant. 'His name's Kai,' Wren announced, in a voice that didn't take prisoners. 'And he's mine.'

CHAPTER FIFTEEN

ROSE

Apart from becoming entangled in the generally astonished reaction, I had the single advantage of being an outlier and not emotionally involved. After the universal *Oh my God*, Benedict was like a man bewitched, Celeste, a woman abandoned on a desert island. Orlando's superior expression was laced with boredom. I couldn't tell what Melissa thought because she was assiduously attending to Autumn's runny nose. Alice, on the other hand, looked appalled. She appealed to me with a glance that signalled S.O.S. It didn't take brain surgery to deduce that her workload had exponentially increased.

Raff was the first to hug his sister and study his new nephew. He slipped his hands beneath the tiny bundle. 'Can I?'

'Help yourself,' Wren said. 'My arms are killing.'

'Wow,' Raff said in wonder. 'You kept this pretty quiet, little sister.'

Celeste hurried over and regarded her new grandson with apprehension. Benedict, who'd sidled over to join the familial huddle, took it in his stride. He beamed widely at the sight of the latest addition to his tribe.

'Why on earth didn't you tell us, Wren?' Celeste asked.

'I wanted it to be a lovely surprise. A new playmate for Edgar and Autumn.' She chucked a glance at Melissa who was giving absolutely nothing away. I wondered if she felt hurt that her sister had failed to confide such a profound piece of news.

'Kai is a foundational name,' Wren announced to anyone daft enough to listen. 'It means keeper of the keys and earth.'

I think we all tuned out when she blithered on about the importance of combatting negative energy.

'He's very handsome,' Benedict said, breaking Wren's flow. 'All that lovely dark hair.'

'And the father?' Celeste asked, rather pointedly, I thought.

'We're not together.'

'But, Wren, darling, Kai is so little.'

'And in fine hands,' Benedict said briskly. 'Where's all your stuff, sweetheart?' he asked Wren.

'What stuff?'

'Baby equipment,' Melissa said, crowding round.

'You don't need much at this age,' Wren said, drawing a puzzled frown from Melissa.

'How old is he?' Celeste asked.

'Four months,' Wren replied.

'So you had him in Germany?' Melissa piped up.

'Berlin, yes.'

'In hospital?'

Wren pulled a face. 'No. I had a home birth in a yurt.'

'In a *yurt*?'

'What's wrong with that?'

'Risky, I'd have thought,' Melissa said.

Wren shrugged. 'Wasn't too awful. I had an excellent doula.' She leaned in and threaded her arm through her sister's. 'And absolutely no pain relief.'

'It's not a competition.' Melissa laughed lightly.

'Just sayin'.'

Sometimes I was really glad not to have a sister, although I mourned for Poppy, even after all these years. I glanced at

Alice and realised Poppy would have been around the same age, had she survived. Aware I was the only person in the room not paying homage, I ventured over.

'Hi, Wren.'

Looking me up and down, as if appraising a prize heifer to be sold at market, she said, 'Hello, Rose.'

I glanced over her shoulder at Raff and the baby. My heart ached because I could see how much he wanted one of his own.

'Right,' Wren said crisply, 'must pop to the loo and freshen up. Got anything to eat, mother?' she addressed Celeste. 'I'm absolutely famished.'

My cue to escape, I whispered in Raff's ear about *leaving the family to it*. Casting an apologetic glance in Alice's direction, I headed outside.

The heat of the day had not subsided. It was suffocating and airless, much like the atmosphere in the house. I crossed the lawn, skirted an ornamental pond and headed towards a long avenue of trees where the air felt fresher. At the end there was a folly where I sat on a cool stone ledge and thought about what I'd let myself in for.

After my little sister died when I was twelve, my parents poured all their love into me. Poppy had a rare form of liver cancer that meant she was sick for most of her short life. You need to experience happiness before you can view sad and tragic events with any degree of perspective. And I had all of that and more. But I still missed her terribly. While I was sure that Celeste and Benedict loved their children, I wasn't certain they loved them as individuals. Out of all of them — and obviously I couldn't include Violet — I think Raff came out best. Perhaps it was that old landed gentry thing of the favoured son. Even though the sisterly bond was strong, Melissa and Wren were madly competitive and each sought approval from Celeste. I had no problem with my mother-in-law, but I did feel at times she wasn't very kind to Melissa. Perhaps it explained Melissa's fragility and why her powers of perception remained exceptionally intact. No expert in sisterly relations, I had the clear impression that she didn't buy wholly into Wren's account of her son's birth. I thought it was pretty suss too and couldn't help but be curious about the identity of Kai's father.

The sound of snapping twigs caught my attention. Glancing up, I saw Raff striding towards me, clutching two glasses in one hand, the neck of a bottle of red wine in the other.

'Hey,' he said. 'Budge up.'

I sometimes thought those often repeated words would be inscribed on my husband's gravestone. I grinned and shifted along the ledge.

'Couldn't take any more excitement?' He poured a glass and handed it to me.

'You have to admit Wren showing up with a child in tow is unusual.'

Raff gave a snort. 'Typical Wren.' He took a deep drink. 'It's pretty amped inside. Mum's dazed and Dad is gaga about his new grandson. He's already giving instructions to Alice.'

'Why? Kai is Wren's responsibility.' I sounded preachy and I didn't care.

'Well, yeah, but as Alice is here already, it's a pity not to make use of her.'

'Raff, that sounds so exploitative — and it's not what she signed up for.'

'Why do you care?'

'Because I'm looking at it from her point of view.' *And I'm an outsider, like her*, I thought.

Raff's expression softened. 'You sound like Florence.'

Good, I thought. Florence was particularly impressive when defending underdogs. It was one of the things I admired about her. 'While your dad means well,' I said, 'he isn't Alice's employer. What were Orlando and Melissa doing while he was *issuing instructions?*'

'Glowering at each other. You could cut the atmosphere between them with a rusty blade.'

'Not exactly good for Autumn and Edgar.'

'Agreed.' Raff swallowed some wine. 'Do you think Liss and Orlando will divorce?'

I drew back. 'How long have you known the marriage is in trouble?'

'Longer than you, by all accounts.' Sometimes, Raff astounded me with his emotional intelligence. 'Melissa hasn't said anything then?'

I recognise when my husband is fishing. 'No breaking news.'

'But you'd tell me if there were?'

'Yes.' It was only a tiny white lie.

'And you didn't ask about the other thing?'

'Never got the chance.' Which was sort of true.

He let out a relieved sigh. 'And *we're* tight, aren't we?'

'*We* are fine.' The rest of his family were the problem.

Appeased, Raff stretched out his long legs and we sipped and sat companionably, staring into the shade.

'I wonder who Kai's dad is,' I said, at last.

'Rose Percival,' Raff teased, slipping an arm around my shoulder. 'You wonder far too much.'

I guess I did, and I wasn't going to apologise for it.

CHAPTER SIXTEEN

ALICE

Benedict stood meekly before her. 'I apologise, unreservedly.'

After tapping on Alice's door, he'd seemed reluctant then hesitant, but in he'd finally come and that pleased Alice ridiculously. It meant she had set the bar; she had power.

Alice took a seat in the tub chair by the window and didn't let him off the hook. In minute detail she listed everything she'd done since the arrival of the youngest daughter, including clearing up Duplo, putting away sticker books, changing two dirty nappies, sterilising bottles, feeding Kai who was ravenous, giving Edgar and Autumn their teas, bathing and settling three children, each with their comforters, and reading Autumn a bedtime story. It was hours later and she was exhausted. No way was she heading downstairs to listen to that bloody awful woman's travelogue and sign up to her mutual admiration club, however attractive Benedict made it seem.

'It's not what I signed up for,' Alice said, stony-eyed.

'And I'm immensely grateful,' Benedict said. 'I really shouldn't have spoken to you the way I did. It was rude and wasn't my place and the last thing I want is for you to feel like the hired help.'

This was going better than expected, Alice thought. Very deliberately, she tucked a lock of hair behind her ear to reveal the curve of her high cheekbones. 'Appreciated,' she said in a husky voice. 'You had me worried.'

'Which is entirely unforgivable of me.'

He couldn't take his eyes off her, sick bastard. It confirmed what she'd already been told and reinforced her desire to take him for everything he had, *everything that should have been her mother's and now hers.*

'Right,' Benedict said, flashing a dazzling smile. 'So we're all good? No hard feelings?'

'None taken, Benedict.' She was deliberately familiar. He didn't complain.

Alice stood up, walked slowly towards him, drawing close enough for him to catch the fragrance of the perfume her mother told her she used to wear. 'I don't think I've ever met a Benedict before.' She found his eyes, let hers settle on his and held his gaze. She swore he was trembling.

'Anything you need, feel free to ask.' His voice sounded hoarse.

'I will.'

'Perhaps I could show you the house if you're free later tomorrow, a sort of guided tour. Show you the ropes,' he burbled. 'There's lots to see.'

'That would be useful, thank you.'

Wrapping him in her warmest smile, she opened the door and saw him out.

What a weak-willed, pathetic man you are.

CHAPTER SEVENTEEN

MELISSA

'*Jesus Christ*, get a shift on, Melissa. I'll miss my train.'

'I'm driving as fast as I can, Orlando.'

'You're driving like a snail because you're worried you'll be pulled over and breathalysed.'

'Don't be ridiculous.' Unfortunately, Orlando was right. Blindsided by first her sister-in-law's intrusive line of questioning about things that didn't concern her and then Wren's arrival with babe in arms, she had reached for the Chablis.

Determined to needle her, Orlando said, 'You're hungover as hell.'

'And whose fault is that?'

'Just listen to yourself. It's always someone else's fault.'

'That's not true.'

'You blame the kids for your fatigue.'

'It's not supposed to be taken literally.'

'Shona bloody Reid for . . .'

'I've already warned you,' Melissa bit back. 'Don't you ever say her name.'

'Why not? That's what she was called. Why, for heaven's sake, you keep a shrine to a dead woman in what passes for your brain eludes me. So typical of you to play the victim.'

Melissa chewed her lip, a fragment of a long-forgotten conversation fluttered through her mind. The words had come from her mother and addressed to her sister, Violet.

'And let's not forget your dad's role in all this.'

Melissa slammed on the brakes so hard she thought the airbags would go off.

Orlando jolted forward. 'Shit . . . fuck . . . ow . . .'

High colour in her cheeks, Melissa turned the full force of her fury on him. 'Slander is a serious offence. As a lawyer you should know that.' The sharp note in her voice held a warning. *You really want to push it?*

Unaccustomed to his wife answering back and visibly shaken, Orlando placed his palms up. 'All right, all right.'

'Do I make myself clear?' Goodness, where did that voice come from?

'Truce?'

'I'm not the one who's fighting,' Melissa said.

The rest of the short journey along country roads passed in cold, stony silence. Melissa found herself literally counting the seconds before her husband climbed out of the car.

Taking the turn for the Grade II listed train station, Melissa followed the wide leafy drive to the entrance and pulled up outside with ten minutes to spare.

Get out, she thought. To her annoyance, Orlando stayed right where he was.

'What are you up to today?'

She met his imperious grey-eyed gaze, recalling how once, early in their relationship, she thought he'd have great genes and make good father material, the importance of which her mother had impressed upon her. 'Why do you want to know?'

Orlando's perfectly straightened teeth glittered with a smile. 'Showing an interest. Isn't that what you want from me? Thought you'd be pleased.'

It would take a lot more than that to please her. 'I'm meeting Ava.'

'Ava Cartland?'

The note in his voice suggested disapproval. *Tough*, Melissa thought. She and Ava, who worked in property management, had been friends for years. 'We're off to the Cotswold Water Park with the children.'

'Not spending it with Wren seeing as she's just got back?'

'I didn't know she was coming and I arranged to see Ava weeks ago.'

He gave her a curious look, as if he didn't quite believe her, then leaned towards her and deposited a dry kiss on her cheek. 'Be good,' he said, stepping out with a briefcase tucked under his arm.

The second the passenger door shut, Melissa hit the central lock. A tiny act of defiance, which felt good.

In a calmer mood and without Orlando's constant barracking, she considered the events of the past twenty-four hours. Melissa had believed she and Wren were close. They'd communicated lots while her sister was away, yet Wren had never uttered a single word about meeting anyone, let alone getting pregnant and giving birth. Trawling back through previous conversations, there had been no clues and if there had been, Melissa had missed the lot.

You can be so dense, Mummy used to say when she was little. Her mother had been full of admonitions when Melissa was growing up. *Don't do that. You don't want to turn out like Violet, do you?*

Strange how at times of severe stress, her mother's casual cruelty would emerge from the depths of the past, a past that Melissa's curious sister-in-law was taking too much interest in. Melissa liked Rose enormously and she was certain that Rose meant well, but it was critical she was headed off as fast as possible. If you dislodge a dirty deeply-buried stone, something cold, slippery and repellent was likely to wriggle out from underneath. It was why, subconsciously, or consciously, every single one of the Percivals, Violet included, had finally signed an unwritten pact never to speak, conjecture, speculate or lay claim to know what really happened to the children's nanny. Best it stayed that way.

CHAPTER EIGHTEEN

ROSE

After a lie-in, I showered, washed my hair, dressed, crunched across the gravel towards the Granary and actively prayed that Wren wouldn't hear, or spot me. If she had, she'd made herself scarce; suited the pair of us, I suspected. Picking up my car, I drove up to the house to collect Alice, parked outside and ran straight into Melissa in the hall.

'Hiya,' she said brightly.

Happy and energetic, the difference in my sister-in-law was astonishing. It was as if the crushing anxiety that had sat heavily on her back yesterday had fallen away.

I stared as packed lunches were assembled, bags loaded with baby paraphernalia and children strapped into car seats.

'Where's Celeste and Benedict?' I asked.

'Mum had to run into Cheltenham to collect essential baby supplies. Dad, bless him, is looking after Kai.'

'Where's Wren?'

'Saluting the sun in the garden and no doubt giving herself a pat on the back for getting us all running around after her.'

'A tricky yoga pose,' I said with a dry smile that made my sister-in-law laugh. It was nice to see Melissa back to her old self, even if it only lasted until Orlando's return. 'Is Alice about?'

'Think she's in her room.'

I turned to go.

'Rose,' Melissa said.

'Yes?'

'Thank you.'

'For what?'

'Listening.'

'You don't need to thank me.'

'Well it was appreciated.'

Warmth flooded over me. Perhaps I was making too big a deal of living at close quarters.

'And I'm sorry I was snippy with you yesterday. Shona meant a lot to us.'

'I'm sorry I dredged it up.'

'You didn't do anything wrong.' She seemed about to expand then, glancing at her watch, changed her mind. 'Well, must fly.'

Thoughtful, I found Alice on the landing talking animatedly to Benedict who threw back his head and laughed at some shared joke.

'Hello, Rose,' he said, beaming broadly.

I greeted him and asked Alice if she was all set to leave. She wore a thin vest top, the label sticking up, shorts, sandals on her feet, revealing painted toenails in a funny shade of yellow, a canvas bag slung over one bare shoulder.

'Nearly,' Alice replied, then addressing Benedict, 'You'll be all right with Kai?'

'I will now you've got him off to sleep.'

'I promise I won't tell Wren.' Alice's smile burst with intrigue. 'Bye, Benedict,' she said cheerily.

'Have a lovely time, girls,' he called after us.

'You should have seen him this morning,' Alice prattled when we were in the car. 'Striding around with baby Kai strapped to his chest in a sling.'

'Benedict tends to be a hands-on grandpa.'

'I think it's nice. He's dead clever with giving Kai his bottle, too.'

I glanced at Alice sideways. 'Isn't Wren feeding the baby?'

'She says she couldn't.'

For someone who espoused healthy eating and natural living, Wren would take an inability to feed her child hard. It made me feel bad for not always thinking the best of her.

We fell into conversation about favourite bands and I discovered that she liked listening to Miley Cyrus and Taylor Swift and we shared a mutual admiration for Billie Eilish and Raye.

'Oooh, I love her. Raff's old-school in musical taste,' I told Alice. 'He likes Lou Reid, J.J. Cale, Neil Young. When I first met him he listened incessantly to Slipknot.'

'He'd get on well with my brothers,' Alice said.

'How many have you got?'

'Three — they're older than me.'

I found a free parking space in Watermoor Road. From there, we criss-crossed through side streets of historic and more established properties to the centre of Cirencester.

'I'd kill for a coffee,' I said, suggesting a café at the end of Black Jack Street. About to cross the road near the Bear Inn, a pub on the corner of Dyer Steet, Alice, I noticed, appeared to hang back. She glanced over her shoulder and seemed nervous.

'You, okay?' I said.

'Um . . .' It was as if Alice's brain was telling her to move but her feet wouldn't budge.

'What is it?'

Forehead suddenly beaded with perspiration, Alice was breathing hard, her complexion pale and wan. 'I'll be okay. Give me a minute.'

Spotting a bench close to the town hall, I linked my arm through hers and practically dragged her over the road towards it. Forward motion appeared to snap her out of whatever had spooked her.

'Thought I saw someone,' Alice explained, breathy. In answer to my questioning look, she broke into a smile. 'It's nothing. I have a few trust issues.'

I never know what to say when people make big personal revelations, especially in public places. I was keen to pry, but not keen to be *seen* to pry, so I kept my mouth shut.

Spotting my uncertainty, Alice squeezed my arm. 'Me being silly. Come on, let's go.'

Hitting the square, we got caught up in a craft market. People were already milling about among the stalls. Alice appeared to relax. Safety in numbers, it seemed.

The café was busy with tourists, predominantly American and Chinese. I found a table near the front, recently vacated and facing the street. While I shifted debris to another table, Alice ordered and paid. She seemed composed as she sat down with her back to the window.

'This is nice,' she said, sunnily. 'Can I ask you a question?'

Alice was smiling so I didn't think it was going to be the kind of tricky question Orlando might aim at me, at least I hoped it wasn't. 'Knock yourself out,' I said gamely.

'Did you always want to be a hairdresser?'

'Honestly, I didn't know what I wanted to do. Keen to earn my own money, I started off as a Saturday girl, sweeping up and making drinks for clients, progressed to washing hair, and it sort of went from there. I actually have a Level 3 in hairdressing and a Masters in colour.'

'I didn't know you could get proper qualifications.'

'Oh yeah and I've done competitions and got awards. Never go anywhere without my scissors.'

'Really?' Alice was wide-eyed. 'You mean you've got them with you now?'

I nodded. 'Here, check these out.' I pulled a leather pouch from my bag and, slipping out the blades from their chamois cover, let them nestle in the palm of my hand.

'Wow!' Alice exclaimed. 'They look sharp.'

'Very. They're Japanese and made from cobalt and alloy.'

'Expensive?'

'Over five hundred pounds. They were a thirtieth birthday present from Mum and Dad,' I explained, putting them away.

'Why on earth do you carry them with you? Not for protection, I hope.'

'God, no,' although I guessed, technically, they could be viewed as an offensive weapon. 'Habit,' I said. 'I used to work at a salon where the owner was notoriously late opening up. Clients would be clamouring outside the door so, to hit the ground running, I always had my scissors at the ready. Saved all the faffing about trying to find the right pair.'

'Smart,' Alice said. 'Although I wouldn't want to meet you down a dark alley at night.' She grinned.

'Can I ask you a question?' *Fair's fair*, I thought.

'Sure, fire away?'

'How did you stumble across Orlando?'

Alice let out a laugh. 'I didn't. It was all down to a chance meeting with Belinda, his secretary.'

'You're friends with her?'

'You could say. We met in a café when I worked in London and hit it off.' Before I could pursue it, Alice asked, 'So where are you from originally? This isn't your natural stamping ground, is it?'

I shook my head and gave a potted history, including our move from the Midlands to Gloucestershire. I didn't tell Alice the reason why. I didn't say that, in the wake of my little sister's death, it was my parents' attempt at a new start and made with the hope it would heal broken hearts.

'You met Raff at school?'

'At work. He bowled in, sat down and said he wanted a mullet hairstyle.'

'*Seriously?*'

'He did it for a dare. I was only twenty, new to the salon. I thought it a terrible idea.'

'What did you do?'

'Kept a straight face and suggested it would look more cool if I shaved his entire head.'

'Gotcha,' Alice burst out exuberantly. 'So you've been together all that time?'

'Not exactly.' Mum kept spouting that the road to true love never ran smoothly, or some such. I took a more realistic view. 'We were a bit on and off, to be honest. Then when we were getting it together, finally, Raff took it into his head to visit an uncle in New Zealand who wouldn't be able to make it to our wedding. It was supposed to be for a few weeks but, captivated by the place, turned into a couple of months.'

'That must have been hard on you.'

'Annoying but I sort of got it. New Zealand is a great country to study the cultivation of trees, which is Raff's thing. He's a tree surgeon,' I explained. 'The good thing about the experience was that it affirmed our total commitment to each other. It taught us to value what we both wanted. The rest, as the saying goes, is history.'

'I think that's lovely,' Alice said, sipping her drink.

'What about you? Anyone special?'

'No,' Alice replied with an easy smile. 'I'm not ready to settle down.'

Our drinks arrived: two double-shot lattes. I faffed about with sugar and, eyes down to stir in a spoonful, noticed some strange marks on one of Alice's arms.

Quick to follow my gaze, Alice said, 'Chicken pox scars from when I was a kid.'

'Ooh, nasty.'

'You should see my brothers. They came off much worse.'

'What do they do?'

'Lee's a delivery driver, Jace works for a building society and Stu . . . well, he does a bit of this and a bit of that,' she said with a grin. 'One's married, the other two have partners.'

'No nieces or nephews?'

'Nah, my mum — she's a medical receptionist — reckons she's too young to be a grandmother.'

'I wish she'd talk to *my* mum,' I said wryly.

'Desperate for a grandchild?'

I nodded. 'I'm an only child.' The small pebble of grief that unexpectedly rose to the back of my throat confirmed the lie. I didn't know Alice at all and Poppy was too precious to discuss with a stranger. 'The three of us are pretty tight.'

'Not like the Percivals.' Alice raised a dark eyebrow and lifted the mug to her lips.

It felt as if she were fishing. Unhappy with the change of tone, I played it cool and didn't respond.

Alice took a sip of coffee. 'Don't get me wrong, the kids are fine, but . . .'

'You didn't plan on having three. I'm sure you could renegotiate your terms.'

'It's not that.'

Her brown eyes locked onto mine in a way I found intrusive. 'What is it then?' I asked.

Alice bunched forward and placed a warm, overly familiar hand over mine. 'You and Raff are okay, but the rest, well . . . the atmosphere . . . it's . . . um . . . toxic.'

I smothered my surprise by swallowing some coffee.

'I'm not used to working in environments like that,' Alice continued, 'and it's not good for the children. My very first night, the Rhodes had a hell of a row.'

'All married couples argue.' Actually, Raff and me didn't, or didn't much. 'I'm sure it will easily resolve.' *Curses*, I thought, unhappy with confirming Melissa and Orlando's marital difficulties with the new nanny. The inquisitive side of me wondered what had been said. The more inquisitive side wondered why Alice was making a big deal of it. And it was exceptionally early to start making pronouncements about atmospheres, good or otherwise. I thought it symptomatic of her age. Naive, she had a lot of growing up to do.

Alice put down her mug and casually asked, 'Do you know Violet?'

I instantly flared inside. 'Celeste and Benedict's eldest daughter. What of her?'

'I only caught snatches of conversation,' Alice was keen to impress, 'but Mrs Rhodes got angry with Mr Rhodes and accused him of having an opinion of her based on lies.'

I lifted my drink to my lips to mask my interest.

'Mrs Rhodes mentioned someone called Shona Reid.'

Alice's eyes never shifted from mine. It took everything I had not to go, *Oh my God*. 'Never heard of her.'

'From what I could make out she was a nanny who looked after the children when they were small.'

I shook my head, feigning ignorance.

Alice glanced down and ran a slender finger around a knot of wood in the table. She seemed to be struggling with how much to say and how to say it. I was absolutely desperate to ask; silence was a better option.

'She got fired,' Alice said, eyes darkening.

I did my best not to jolt. 'For what?'

'Not sure. Something pretty serious.' Alice fixed me again with a look that refused to let me go. 'Two months after she left Blackthorn, she was dead.'

Either Melissa was extremely foolish for blabbing at high volume, or Alice was insanely nosy and a terrible gossip. It put me on edge, made my skin itch. Quickly changing the subject to holidays and, finding little traction, I blithered on about work. Alice nodded and smiled and asked questions in all the right places while the dull expression in her eyes told me she wasn't listening. I sensed her weak effort to engage was no more than an act designed to either be polite, or fool me. Perhaps she was plain bored, or I was more of a Percival than I originally thought.

We drank up and I showed her around town: shops and eateries first, then past the museum and up Cecily Hill towards the Bathurst Estate. Alice, again, seemed weirdly ill at ease out in the open. It was as if she expected an assailant to jump out from behind a tree at any second.

'Could we go back?' Alice begged at last.

''Course,' I said.

We returned to the main part of town and walked past the estate agents and solicitors in Castle Street and eventually found ourselves outside the Church of St John the Baptist in the main square.

'We could go inside, if you want. It will be cooler.'

Alice pressed a hand to the side of her head. 'Bit of a headache coming on.'

She looked quite pale and clammy. 'I'll take you home.'

'Sorry to be a spoilsport.'

'You're not.' I'd wanted to drive up to the industrial estate to see if Raff was about, but scrapped the idea.

'I'll feel better in the car,' Alice assured me. 'It's the heat, I think.'

She had a point. The temperature was well over 80 by the time we reached my Mini and it wasn't yet noon. I banged on the air con as soon as I started the engine.

Alice fell quiet, hunkered down and stared out the window. Frankly, and despite the fact she'd slotted in a tiny piece of a bigger puzzle, I was glad to drop her back.

Shona Reid, I thought. *What exactly did you do?*

CHAPTER NINETEEN

ALICE

Get in. Get out. Before Sean finds me.

Alice had Sean to thank for her panic attack. She hadn't made it up. It was as real and debilitating as ever. If there was a bright side, it had made her seem vulnerable to caring, not so sharing, Rose.

Alice clasped her hands behind her head on the pillow and ran back through the conversation in the café. Adept at making shit up, Alice had played a blinder with her family history. Telling people what they wanted to hear was easy as long as you listened first. There was Rose believing Alice came from a nice stable background, like hers, when Alice's childhood experience had been one of cold silence, never a cross word spoken until her mother vamoosed when Alice was ten and her real brother, Craig, was only seven. The names of her fictional brothers were picked from men she'd hooked up with before she met Sean, though she'd used a little embroidery when describing their occupations. Lee was a thief and Jace a drug dealer, Stu was Stu and she never expected to see any of them again.

On sticky ground with her scars, she'd compounded it by voicing negative observations about the Rhodes too soon, although Alice believed she'd redeemed herself by dropping Shona Reid into the conversation. Wrong-footed and quick to deny, Rose had failed to convince that she'd never heard of the woman. She knew, all right, *and* Rose knew that Shona had died. Whether she knew the detail was doubtful. She also appeared ignorant of the reason for Shona Reid's dismissal. Alice wondered if it would change Rose's opinion of her father-in-law if she knew.

Alice had no doubt that Benedict found her attractive. She'd seen the way his eyes gleamed when engaged in conversation, his laugh so vibrant and easy. Men like him didn't change even when they wanted to. He was a man turned on by vulnerability, perceived or otherwise, and Alice had a plan to appeal and exploit the sensitive side of his nature.

As if by magic, a tap at the door signalled his arrival.

Alice pushed herself off the bed and, barefooted, greeted him.

'Hi, ready for the tour?'

He had the bearing of a man about to go on a date, she thought. Hair freshly washed, clean chinos, nice shirt. She slipped on some sandals.

'I'm all yours,' she said, meaning it, and followed him downstairs.

Trailing from room to room, admiring the architecture, she let him drivel on about Blackthorn's ancient past, how it had been a hideout for Royalists during a period of history when Parliamentarians had held the town. Every painting and "objet d'art", as he termed it, came with a history lesson. She'd never been interested at school and wasn't interested now, but she tilted her head, gazed deeply into his eyes, their shape and colour so similar to hers, making it clear that she was hanging on his every word. When the huge cost of maintenance of Blackthorn was mentioned, she made suitably sympathetic noises.

'It must be quite a burden,' she said.

'One I'm happy to bear. I feel it's my duty to secure it for the next generation.'

Pompous arse, Alice thought, beaming appreciatively. 'I'd love to see the grounds.'

Impossible to cover it all, Benedict suggested they visited the Orangery, a posh greenhouse in which large-leaved plants bore down on her, full of threat and warning.

'Goodness, it's hot in here,' she said, fanning her face with a hand and surreptitiously undoing another button of her sleeveless shirt. In passing, she asked what the rest of the family were up to.

'Celeste is out for the day on community business and Melissa is with the children at Cotswold Water Park,' Benedict replied.

Out of the way then, Alice thought, thrilling inside. Stepping back into the sunshine, they travelled down a flagstone path. Benedict was droning on about the various plants in the garden. *Screw that*, she thought, accidentally on purpose missing her footing. Pitching towards Benedict, his arm shot out and caught her.

'Steady,' he said.

She clamped a hand on his wrist and gazed up into his eyes. 'Thank you.' She swore she felt him tremble.

'The flags are a little uneven.' Apologetic creases either side of his dark eyebrows, he asked, 'You okay?'

'I am now.' Her smile was designed to eat him alive. Did she imagine him hanging on to her longer than was strictly necessary?

Back in the vast, draughty hall, Benedict assumed the air of a man about to unveil a statue of a much-loved historical figure.

'Stand in front of the fireplace,' he told her, with a ready smile.

She did. Wide enough for two big men to sit on either side of the grate, the marble mantle was flanked with ornate wooden panelling with pictures of birds inlaid into the marquetry.

'What do you see?' he asked.

'A fire,' Alice replied, with a laugh.

Benedict came up behind her. A pulse hammered in her chest. Alice held her breath. He really was a sleazy bastard. She didn't flinch when Benedict rested his broad hands on her shoulders. She wanted him to believe that it was the most natural thing in the world.

'Now look again at the crow on the right of the farthest panel.'

Alice craned forward, narrowing her eyes. 'I still don't get it.'

'Look at its tail.'

She drew back. 'It's a lever.'

'And for good reason.'

Benedict approached and, with the palm of his hand, pushed it against the bird, resulting in the entire panel springing ajar. Another push revealed a secret chamber.

'Very Harry Potter,' Alice exclaimed.

'You can go inside,' Benedict said.

Not likely, she thought. 'Only if you go first.'

'Fair enough,' he remarked.

She followed. Stale musty air tinged with wood smoke and earth enveloped her. A low level bench ran along one wall to accommodate a family of four, possibly more, sitting side by side.

'It feels quite cramped.' Her eyes strained to make out Benedict in the swallowing darkness.

'Better to be claustrophobic than dead.' His voice echoing from deeper in the compartment contained a mysterious ring.

'Why do I think you have another trick up your sleeve?'

At once the place flooded with natural light. Benedict laughed at her from the other side of a door that led out into the garden.

'An escape route,' he said.

'Perfect,' Alice said. It really was.

CHAPTER TWENTY

ROSE

I'd returned to find our bed made and the breakfast dishes in the sink washed up and put away. Perversely, it irritated the hell out of me. I didn't like the idea of Celeste snooping around our home. Deciding to tackle it head on I sent a message that didn't convey nearly how cross I was.

Hi, Celeste. Very nice of you to tidy up but there's really no need.

I went to the loo and heard my phone ping with a message.

Can't take the credit, I'm afraid. I sent our cleaner, Flavia. She will be coming every Monday and Friday morning. And she'll be collecting your laundry too. Enjoy!

I didn't want our washing collected. I could do it myself. Feeling thoroughly snookered, I let out a groan. *What's not to like?* Mum would say, quickly followed by *It's nice to be nice, Rose.* I still didn't want mine and Raff's undies picked up by a stranger and fired off a message to that effect.

If I were honest, my trip out with Alice had made me out of sorts and edgy. Too hot to sit around indoors, I took a bottle of cold water from the fridge, grabbed a pair of walking boots and, retracing my steps from the day before, turned left out of our temporary home and into the throat of the woods.

An established path led through all ten acres, though I'd never walked the full extent. Raff first brought me here many years before, shortly after we met. I think he was trying to impress me and, shallow as I was then, I *was* impressed. It's where he'd played as a child, building dens, playing hide-and-seek and pretending to be a soldier on lookout from the tree house Benedict had built for his only son. Fancifully, I wondered if I could hear the echo of children's voices drifting through the trees, mingling with birdsong. Cutting through a kissing gate, my heart gave a lift. It was here Raff got down on one knee, and very romantically asked me to be his wife. The place held good memories; it was magical to me.

And yet . . .

Rain had been torrential during the month of August but, here in the woods, in its own microclimate, the earth had begun to dry out and the path felt crumbly beneath the soles of my boots. Twigs snapped. Autumn leaves crunched. I picked up a stick for no other reason than it was there. Pale sunlight trickled through a canopy of beech and oak, creating a strobe effect that dazzled my eyes. My ears tuned to the distant noise of geese heading off for their winter holidays. The smell of earth and bark was strong, with an undercurrent of moss and ivy. It reminded me of Alice, the scent she'd worn, its fragrance as cheap as the clothes on her back and sandals on her feet. I was brought up never to judge a book by its cover and I appreciated that Alice was dressing down deliberately because nobody in their right mind wore their best clothes when caring for small children, but Alice was on a day off. I had to ask would a woman as sophisticated as Belinda Hart, with her Tote bag and Gucci purse, befriend someone less than glossy and expensively groomed?

I'd met Belinda once when Orlando had pulled a ligament and she'd driven him back to their old house when I'd been visiting. A class act, Belinda had legs up to her ears and dressed like a model. If you could bottle "posh" and flog it, she'd be used in every TV ad campaign. By comparison, the clothes Alice wore looked as if they'd been bought straight out of a supermarket clothing concession. The canvas bag slung over her shoulder that morning matched the bargain basement holdalls in which she'd carted her belongings. I was no snob and couldn't have cared less but the image Alice projected was not who she was. Animal instinct, of which I had in spades, told me so.

Those marks on her arm were not old wounds. They were recent and, worryingly, the shape and size of a lit cigarette. Had I imagined Alice changing the subject from her to me too quickly? Why had she previously mentioned working in Birmingham but not London? A slip, a lapse in memory, or false trail? Was it anger I'd seen briefly flare in her eyes when she told me that Shona had been fired, or was I mistaken? And what, if anything, did that mean?

I passed what could be euphemistically called a lake; in reality, a stretch of green murky slime with edges so indistinct, I kept well away. Fungi grew near the water's edge and clung to the stumps of old trees. At least someone had the presence of mind to nail a lifebuoy to a post in case of an accidental fall into the water. A shiver tiptoed up my spine. What sort of accidental fall had claimed Shona Reid's life? Why had she been fired and were the two events connected?

Where the undergrowth became more unruly, the path suddenly narrowed and faded to a maze of jagged and tangled edges. I had to watch my step to avoid stones and tree roots that protruded eager to trip me up. Midges or small biting things flew into my face.

Out in the woods, time ticked differently. The air throbbed with heat and the deeper I ventured, the darker the light, as if the earth had been scooped up and flung through the trees. No wonder I couldn't get a signal on my phone.

About to turn back, I noticed a thin track of flattened ground as if someone had walked that way recently. Intrigued,

I followed it through waist-high brambles and nettles, my arms outstretched above my head until the path magically opened out into a copse. From here I spied a metal roof illuminated in the distance where a shaft of light pierced the canopy of trees. Inexorably drawn, I strode on and the track opened out into a clearing. There, a timber-framed shack stared belligerently back at me, as if I were disturbing its peace. Thick plastic sheeting had been nailed across makeshift windows, making it impossible to see inside. Its corrugated tin roof looked sturdy and weatherproof. I drew near to its red-painted door and, glancing over my shoulder, which was silly of me because I was completely alone, I pushed it open and went inside.

The floor was bare earth, the interior simply furnished. There were a couple of battered old armchairs, a stripy canvas beanbag and a day bed that might well have been rescued from a junk shop. An old-fashioned oil lamp sat on a scratched and worn drop-leaf table. With no evident electrical supply to the building, the lamp would serve as lighting. The portable gas fire in the room would form the heating. A bit dangerous, I thought. A cupboard on the wall revealed glasses and mugs. A wooden box, pushed up against one wall, contained a number of old toy cars and trucks, a very old Barbie and some dried-up colouring pens. Guessing it was a superannuated hidey-hole for the children down the generations, the place didn't look as if it had been used recently, but then how would I know? Feeling vaguely guilty and uneasy, I headed for the door and, about to let myself out, noticed a gold drop earring on the ground. I crouched down, picked it up and placed it in the palm of one hand. Art deco in style, the shape distinctive, it resembled a tiny fan. I could have left it right where it was. I could have placed it on the table for someone to find. Instead, I pocketed it and, in a thoughtful mood, made my way back to what passed for civilisation.

CHAPTER TWENTY-ONE

ALICE

'One more won't make a difference,' Celeste insisted. 'It will only be for the morning while we sort out a car for Wren.'

'I know but—'

'And Kai's *so* little.' To emphasise the point, Celeste lifted the baby aloft as if he weighed no more than a bag of sugar.

'It isn't what was agreed,' Alice protested.

'Agreed with whom exactly?'

'Mr Rhodes.'

'But Mr Rhodes isn't here and in his absence—'

'*And* Mr Percival.'

Celeste's cheeks flushed pink, in contrast to her suddenly pale lips. *Good*, Alice thought, the dart she'd launched had hit home.

Alice was in the kitchen clearing up after breakfast. Autumn was busy colouring in a picture at the kitchen table and Edgar scooting around in his baby walker when Celeste, Kai clutched to her chest, had hijacked her.

Collecting herself, adopting a disarming smile, Celeste changed to a more *right-on, sister* approach. 'When it comes to little ones, men don't really understand. It's down to us women to sort things out, don't you think, Alice? Surely you could make an exception?'

'But I've already cleared the morning's activities for the children with Mrs Rhodes,' Alice persisted. It wasn't their day to attend the local nursery in the village so Edgar and Autumn were scheduled — because *schedule* was Mr Rhodes' signature word according to his wife — to play outside in the shade, hats and sunblock on, before it got too hot to move and Edgar needed his nap. Having another small person, a baby no less, would scupper her plans.

'Kai will sleep,' Celeste insisted.

'Not all morning.'

'Then he'll play in his crib.'

'Where he will cry.'

'Then let him.'

Alice stared at Celeste in astonishment. 'I don't hold with that.'

'I'm not asking you to.'

'I still—'

'I *have* had some experience, Alice. Four of my own and they've all turned out just fine. The old ways are often the best. If it's extra payment you're after . . .' Letting the words drift away, Celeste wrinkled her small nose as if the mention of cash created an unfortunate stink.

'I'm not looking for more money.' *Not from you, at least.*

Celeste's white teeth glittered and for a moment Alice could see the family likeness between mother and her youngest daughter, Wren. 'Perfect,' Celeste said handing her grandson over. 'Don't forget he needs his feed. We'll see you after lunch.'

Autumn piped up, 'Where are you going, Gran?'

'Out with Auntie Wren and Mummy, sweetie.'

'Can I come?'

'Not today, but Gran will bring you something lovely back from the shops.'

Autumn's eyes widened with glee.

'Goodbye, my cherub,' Celeste said, kissing her granddaughter on the top of her head then, hips swinging, breezed out.

Alice stared after her. 'Cow,' she muttered under her breath.

After counting to ten, Alice set about settling little Kai. She warmed his bottle, changed his nappy, fed and winded him. Bored and wanting attention, Edgar yowled to be taken out of his walker and Kai, drawing his small knees up to his chest, screamed in pain. Hands clamped over her ears, Autumn yelled, 'Why is he crying?'

'Colic.' Agitated, Alice was unsure which child to go to first. Red-faced, tears streaming down his cheeks, Edgar flailed and, in his frustration, crashed the walker against the Aga, almost tipping it over on the uneven surface and bashing his head. Edgar shrieked in pain and fear.

'No, no, no.' Desperate for somewhere she could put Kai down safely so she could pick up the other child, Alice popped him on the table and hoped to God he wouldn't roll off.

'Everything all right?'

Alice glanced up to see Benedict. Concern shone in his dark eyes. Yes, she was panicked. Yes, she could use some help. But, yes, this was too good an opportunity to miss and one she hadn't even engineered so, without hesitation, Alice promptly burst into tears.

CHAPTER TWENTY-TWO

ROSE

Raff was often late home during the summer months. While domestic customers didn't want their lawns mowed in the evening, contract work for churches and surgeries posed no problem and could be carried out for as long as the light held. The evening before was no exception.

After my foray in the woods, I came back, ate a chicken salad and was already in bed with a book by the time Raff walked through the door. I've been with Raff long enough to realise that deluging my husband with questions or information is not a smart play after a hard day's physical labour. In answer to his *How was your day?* I smiled, made a non-committal reply and was already asleep by the time he'd rifled through the fridge, wound down and came to bed. Up early, he was out of the house before I'd come to.

Rattled the day before, I thought a good night's sleep would make any reservations I harboured about Alice and the whole mystery surrounding Shona Reid's death fade away. Instead, my fears had ballooned overnight.

Florence was the only person in the world I'd message before eight in the morning. I dropped her a WhatsApp, suggesting that

I pop round to hers that evening. Waiting for her reply, I clambered out of bed and stole downstairs to make a cuppa. I found a note from Raff propped against the kettle.

Sorry, Rose, finished off the milk with cereal. Mum and Dad will have tons.

Great. The last thing I wanted was to beg a favour from my in-laws. It also made me look hopelessly inadequate. Milk, for God's sake, a staple; wasn't as if we'd run out of luxury chocolates. Call me pathetic, but I cannot function without an infusion of tea first thing. Scrabbling around for jogging pants and sweatshirt, I pulled them on, slipped into trainers and set off for the *big house*. I'd gone all of twenty paces when Wren homed into view, wet hair around her shoulders and wearing a teeny bikini that clung to her yoga-toned physique like a second skin. I didn't think I'd ever had abs like that. Too late to turn back, I plastered on a friendly smile.

'Hiya,' I said brightly.

'Morning,' Wren said.

'No Kai?'

'Mum has him.'

'That's handy.' I didn't mean it to come out wrong. From the pinched expression on Wren's face, it obviously did. 'I went for a swim,' she said pointedly. 'One of the many benefits of coming from a large family, one can share the load.'

One can, I thought. 'It wasn't a criticism, Wren.' I winced at how needy I sounded.

'And wasn't interpreted as such. Anyway, nice to see you, but must dash. I'm shopping for a car with Ma. She hates it if I'm late.'

Suitably chastened, I walked up the rest of the drive and, on reaching the house, tapped on the door. When nobody answered I walked straight in to the hall to the sound of raised voices echoing from the kitchen. Dogs were nowhere to be seen, probably in hiding.

'For Chrissakes,' I heard Benedict bellow.

'I saw you. You had your arm around her.'

'Celeste, I was merely behaving like a decent human being. Dumping another child on the poor girl is far too much to expect of a youngster.'

'Your shirt was wet with her tears.'

'Alice was upset.'

'You gave that woman the same look you gave that . . .'

'Don't you dare go there,' Benedict exploded. 'When will you get it through your head, there was nothing going on?'

'You really expect me to believe that after all we've been through?'

'Yes, I do,' Benedict barked. 'And, for God's sake, have some respect for the dead.'

Sudden silence made me hold my breath. I didn't like to picture the expressions on their faces. It was Celeste who broke the impasse.

'I do respect the dead. Of course, I do, Benedict. You know that better than anyone.'

'Well then,' Benedict said, sounding only slightly more dialled down. 'Alice has been here less than a couple of days. Do you seriously think so little of me?'

'Honestly, I don't know what to think.'

At the sound of the kitchen door slamming, I shrank into the shadows and watched as Celeste flew up the stairs, tears streaming down her face. As quietly as I could, I slipped back outside. Taking a circuitous route back to the lodge, via the Granary, I fled.

Stumbling back inside my temporary home, I slammed the door shut and turned the key. A nasty picture was formulating in my mind. Had Benedict had an affair with Shona — was she '*that woman*'? Was this the reason for Shona's dismissal? And what did they really mean about 'respecting the dead'?

It was a relief when my phone pinged with a message from Florence.

In bed with heavy cold. If you don't mind my germs, come whenever you like.

I did like and headed off for a shower. I could pick up milk on the way.

CHAPTER TWENTY-THREE

MELISSA

They'd gone to Cotswold Mini in Cheltenham, a flagship showroom, and then, after Wren declared she really wanted an SUV, to the Toyota dealership where Wren had set her eyes on a cherry-red Rav 4, 2.2 TD, Automatic, with leather seats. The model name was *Invincible*. *How apt*, Melissa thought sardonically. In a peculiar mood all morning, Mummy had sprung for it and, in celebration, declared that they should lunch at Petit Coco, a French restaurant on Bath Street that served classic French food in a dimly lit cellar.

Sitting in the back of her mother's Range Rover, Melissa tuned out as Wren banged on about the health benefits of toxic detoxes and hot yoga. Had Melissa known that Kai was to be dumped on Alice, she would have offered to stay. Wren behaved as if her life could carry on as it always had and that the baby would, like it or lump it, fit in — when every parent recognised that it was the other way around. Despite Wren's claims to the contrary, have baby will travel, didn't work. Not that Mummy would agree. She'd got quite arch when Melissa expressed surprise at Kai's absence. Sacrifice was not a word with which either her mother or sister were familiar.

But then there was the other thing.

Indulging in a rare leisurely early morning swim with her sister that very morning, Wren, madly competitive, ploughed up and down until she'd swum forty lengths. For a woman with a baby she had terrific energy. More suspiciously, Wren's worryingly slim build was free of stretch marks. Over a year on, Melissa still hadn't shifted her baby weight. It made her wonder whether Wren had an eating disorder. Was she purging herself in order to keep her weight down? Melissa guessed lunch would provide the acid test.

Parking in Bath Parade car park, it was a short stride to the eatery. At Celeste's instigation, Melissa found herself sitting opposite her mother and sister as if she were being interviewed for a position in senior management. Without fuss, Celeste ordered G&Ts, ice and lime, not lemon, and enquired about the fish of the day, which was halibut.

'Lovely,' she said. 'Melissa?'

'I'll have the same.'

Wren settled for French onion soup followed by baked Camembert. Interesting choice and packed with fat, Melissa observed. The wine arrived, was poured and glasses chinked.

Celeste was first to take a sip. 'How nice it is to have my girls around me.'

'Lovely to be back home,' Wren said.

Melissa smiled to herself. With any luck it wouldn't be for much longer. After spending the day with Ava she'd hatched an escape plan and, to her delight and surprise, Orlando had agreed in a phone conversation that very morning. The call had gone better than she'd dreamed possible. Either Orlando was astounded by her bullish idea or too busy with work to respond negatively. *Or*, Melissa thought, feeling a sugar rush of pleasure, *he liked the new, improved and decisive version of his wife.*

'We should do this more often,' Wren continued. 'There's a different dynamic without the men around.'

Melissa smiled at feeling more confident, more like her old self, in control and clear-sighted.

Wren's small eyes burned into Melissa's. 'Is everything okay with Orlando?' The question came out of nowhere, jolting Melissa out of her good mood. Was the dismal state of their marriage that obvious? She'd never have Rose down for a tittle-tattle. 'What made you say that?'

'He seems more Orlando-like than usual.'

'I haven't a clue what you're on about.'

Celeste laughed lightly. 'Neither do I. Orlando is Orlando. You've obviously been away too long, Wren.'

But Wren stood her ground. 'He's definitely more edgy, brittle, more don't give a flying fu—'

'That's enough of that,' Celeste interjected sharply. 'Your brother-in-law does a marvellous job in difficult circumstances.'

'What difficult circumstances?' Melissa hadn't quite eradicated the conversation shared between her husband and her mother about *Melissa barely coping*.

'No need to get het up,' Celeste said with a tepid smile. 'Working in a hard, brutal corporate environment, he is the man with the sword.'

'Goodness, Mummy,' Wren said, exchanging a ribald look with Melissa, 'you make him sound like a gladiator.'

'Don't mock. Protecting his clients from anyone who is dangerous to their interests is an extremely challenging business. And a young family always poses a strain on a man. Poor boy is still getting used to living with his in-laws.' Celeste laughed lightly. Supposed to sweeten thinly veiled criticism, she seemed entirely unaware that she'd scored the equivalent of an own goal, as far as Melissa was concerned. Sensing a "Put up or shut up" moment, Melissa thought it time to drop her delicious piece of news.

'Not for much longer,' she announced.

A line appeared on Celeste's smooth brow. 'I don't understand.'

'We're moving out, Mummy.'

'Is your house purchase back on?'

Melissa shook her head and took out her phone. A few clicks, and the property available to see online, she pushed her mobile in front of her mother and sister who huddled around it as if it were a small fire. 'Ava has found us a lovely place to rent at Sapperton.'

Celeste glanced up. 'Ava Cartland?'

Melissa nodded.

'But that's ludicrous,' Wren burst out.

'I have to agree,' Celeste said sniffily. 'A place like that will cost the earth.'

'Mates' rates makes it affordable *and* it's closer to the train station, meaning we avoid the mad dash on Monday mornings. *Plus* we can take Alice with us so she'll be out of your hair.'

Celeste opened her mouth and then closed it again. Wren looked as if someone had hit her in the face with a shovel.

'But what about Kai?' Wren wailed when she'd recovered from the mortal blow.

'What about him?' Melissa took a silky sip of wine.

'He needs routine. Alice can't go. I need her help.'

'I'm sorry, Wren, but she works for us, not for you.'

'You've discussed it with Orlando?' Celeste interjected.

'This morning on the phone.'

'I don't believe it,' Wren said sharply.

Melissa could well imagine her sister lobbying Orlando. Wren could be exceptionally persuasive. It was a horrifying thought. Hoping for a rare show of support, Melissa cast an appealing look at her mother. In reply, Celeste steepled her fingers together and touched her chin, her expression unreadable. Seconds ticked along like minutes. Melissa's stomach curdled inside; it still mattered to her what Mummy thought.

'It may well be for the best,' Celeste conceded, at last.

'But, Mummy,' Wren began in a voice thick with self-pity.

'Not now, Wren,' Celeste snapped. Addressing Melissa, she asked when they were planning to move.

'A couple of weeks.' Melissa beamed. 'No chain *and* it's empty.'

CHAPTER TWENTY-FOUR

ROSE

'*Shu-ut up*, you serious?'

Propped up on pillows, tissues to hand, Florence gaped. In a litany of revelations the one that got her fired up most was the overheard argument between Benedict and Celeste. Up until that point, she'd sniffled her way through my more ripe speculation. It had to be said my best mate looked absolutely hideous: shadows under her glassy eyes, red nose, raw skin.

'Benedict is an attractive man,' I said. 'But is he honestly sketchy?'

'Never tried it on with you?'

'God, Florence, of course he hasn't.'

'Don't look so shocked. In my line of work you see all kinds of human behaviour. So you think he's more of an appreciator than a player?'

'If you must put it like that, yes. Honestly, Florence, I genuinely can't imagine him playing away and definitely not with the children's nanny. Celeste would kill him and it-it's all so . . .' I struggled to find the right word.

'Banal?'

'*EastEnders*,' I said, although the Percivals were as far away from the goings-on at the Queen Vic as I was from royalty.

'I've always thought him a bit tactile, for my liking, but hey.'

'That's just the way he is.' I felt quite protective of my father-in-law.

'If you'd nominated your brother-in-law,' Florence said, 'I wouldn't have been in the least surprised.'

After spending time with Melissa and seeing them together, I couldn't quite cast Orlando as a philanderer, although I had to agree with Florence he wasn't particularly nice to his other half. Scratch that: they weren't very nice to each other.

'*If* it were true about Benedict,' Florence continued, 'it would explain why everyone is spooked.'

I shook my head. 'Everyone's spooked because Shona Reid is dead. Ghosts leave long shadows.'

Florence's eyes watered. Her nose twitched. I took cover as she let out a hurricane of a sneeze. 'Sorry,' she said miserably. 'Only if they're disturbed.'

'Is this your way of telling me to stop speculating?'

'What I think and what you'll do are two separate things.' Florence blew her nose vigorously. 'I'm assuming you're not going to tell Raff what you overheard?'

'God, no.'

'Good. It would only stir up a shitload of trouble.' Florence reached for the glass on her bedside table and downed two flu capsules with water.

'Poor you,' I said sympathetically.

'I'll live. What's the new nanny like?'

Good question. I'd been surprised that Alice had got out of her depth so quickly. Weeping all over Benedict, according to Celeste, Alice wouldn't last long. 'She's hopelessly inexperienced.'

'Not exactly a character defect.'

'It is if you have three small people to look after.'

'Typical of Wren to take advantage,' Florence said. 'Other than that, what's Alice like as a person?'

'Seems okay.'

Florence gave me a hawkish look. '*Seems* and *okay* — understatement of the year.'

'She's nice to the children.'

'I should hope so.'

I shrugged. 'I don't know. There's something about her that doesn't stack. And she naively made assumptions about me.'

Florence frowned. 'You?'

'She was a little too matey.'

'Maybe she was looking for an ally.'

'If I'd overheard an argument on my first night, I wouldn't confide it to another member of the family then fish for the low-down.'

'Jeez, Rose, I'd hate to be you. Not everyone and everything is dodgy.'

My answering grin was slack. 'You're probably right.'

'When are you back to work?'

'Tomorrow.' Couldn't come soon enough.

'Things will get better,' Florence said. 'You'll see.'

'And so will you.'

Leaving her to sleep, I left and drifted around the shops for a bit. Spa towns such as Cheltenham are great when it's wet, less so when the sun is belting down. Heat bounced off every building, sapping the life out of anything that moved. Thoroughly overheated, I drove back to Blackthorn. In the closed cool confines of my car, I thought Florence was right. Every family had its secrets and inconsistencies and I was seeing problems where none existed. Who was I to pry?

Resolute, I parked my car and walked the short distance to the lodge. I planned to catch some late afternoon rays in the garden. No sooner than I'd sat myself down, the noise of crunching gravel announced I had company. Over the low picket fence, Melissa stood, bright-eyed and animated in a way that suggested she'd had a liquid lunch.

'Hiya,' she said. 'Hope I'm not disturbing you.'

'Not at all. Come in.'

'No, it's fine. I won't be long. I wanted to tell you myself.'

'Tell me what?'

'We're moving out.'

'Nothing to do with us moving in?' I gave a wet laugh.

'God, no. You're the most sane person here.'

Embarrassed, I said, 'Raff will be disappointed. Me, too.' And I was.

'It's for the best.' Melissa lowered her voice. 'It's all got a little crowded with Wren's return and, rather than outstay our welcome, I thought it would be good for me and Orlando to have our own space again.'

'I get it.' I felt envious. 'Is it far?'

'A few miles the other side of Cirencester. You and Raff will come and visit, I hope.'

I assured her we would. 'When are you leaving?'

'A couple weeks.'

'How exciting,' I said. 'You're taking Alice with you?'

Melissa's face clouded. 'She's not very happy about it.'

I expressed surprise. 'It should be the answer to her prayers. She definitely didn't want to take on Kai as well as Edgar, no offence.'

'None taken,' Melissa said. 'She's being positively perverse. Would you mind talking to her?'

'Me?'

'She seems to like you and you've spent more time with her than any of us, other than the children, that is,' Melissa said with a smile.

'I'm not sure she'll listen. I hardly know her.'

'Would you try? I've got Wren lobbying from the opposite camp.'

In that case I'd give it my best shot and told Melissa so.

'I'd be so grateful, but, ah well,' Melissa said brightly. 'If Alice leaves she leaves.'

'Surely, it won't come to that?'

Melissa gave a breezy shrug and turned to go and then turned back, suddenly serious. 'Rose?'

'Yes?'

Now she'd got my attention, indecision engulfed her features. I got the impression something was bothering her, had been for some time and she didn't quite know how to go about resolving it.

'It would be better if you leave the past in the past.'

She didn't spell it out but I knew what she was on about: Shona Reid. The dead. I swallowed and felt my chest hitch. 'Okay.'

'Don't believe all that you hear.'

'It sounds like a threat.'

'I'm looking out for you, you understand?'

'I think so.'

She looked solemn and sad and vaguely apologetic. 'No good can come of it, do you see?'

'Can I ask one thing?'

Melissa shifted her slender weight from one foot to the other. 'One, and then we will never speak of it again.'

I hesitated. My mind suddenly tumbled with questions, some sure to cause offence. I decided to go to the beating heart of it all.

'Was it really an accident?'

Melissa blinked. 'I believe Shona slipped on some stairs and broke her neck.'

CHAPTER TWENTY-FIVE

ALICE

Two weeks to snare him. That's all she had. Shocked, Alice had thought of nothing else; she was consumed by it. *This was Celeste's work*, she thought, darkly examining events since the morning.

Weeping all over Benedict was a genius move. Alarmed, he'd put his arms around her, smoothed her hair, spoken to her softly, his mouth warm against the top of her ear. So close, she could smell his distinctive aftershave. The trap had been sprung and she had snared him. Then Celeste, hatchet-faced, appeared out of nowhere and Benedict sprang back, as if Alice were a burning, flaming torch. Alice believed she'd be sacked on the spot. Celeste had done it before and would do it again. Instead the old witch snatched Kai up and ordered Alice to take Autumn and Edgar outside. Summarily dismissed, Alice fled across the terrace, over the lawn, without sunhats or sunscreen for the children, and parked them in a gazebo.

'Why is Granny cross?' Autumn asked.

'No idea,' Alice lied. 'Sometimes grown-ups get a bit scratchy.'

An anxious wait followed until, later, Benedict, with Kai attached to his chest in a sling, found her. He didn't look embarrassed or sorry or as if he'd been carpeted. He was bullish, in command, like a man pushed once too often and wasn't putting up with it anymore. She could have cheered. Head held high, he apologised for any misunderstanding and suggested that she return inside to the recently converted playroom while the Good, the Bad and the Ugly, as Alice thought of them, cleared off on a shopping trip. He hadn't flinched when she'd touched his arm and assured him she didn't want any trouble. And he'd *smiled*. Everything would be fine, he'd said. Too right, it would. She thought she had it in the bag.

But then Celeste plotted to get rid of her. Alice was sure she was behind Melissa's decision to move her family out.

Wren was Alice's only hope. Alice didn't like the Percival's youngest daughter, a selfish stuck-up moo, but if Wren's necessity for help extended Alice's stay, she'd be more than happy to work for the woman. Caring for a baby would be a doddle and, without the distraction of the other kids, it would give her more time to concentrate her efforts on Benedict. From what she'd observed, Wren had more clout with Celeste than Melissa so it could smoothe her way back in.

Feeling a good deal more upbeat, Alice pulled on a robe and gazed out of the window. There were so many places she could meet Benedict in secret. She'd have to tread carefully; couldn't afford to be anything other than discreet. Only when the old bat was properly out of the way could Alice pounce. It was of paramount importance that she chart Celeste's movements, and find out when she was safely at a distance.

Alice headed for the shower. *Fourteen days, and then I'll be out of here.*

CHAPTER TWENTY-SIX

ROSE

Insomnia in your own home is a pain; insomnia in someone else's is intolerable. I hadn't planned to return to work bog-eyed, but sleep evaded me. How absolutely grim to slip downstairs and, rather than breaking an arm or leg, or bashing your head, you snap your neck. I couldn't help but shudder at the thought.

Raff, as still as a dead man, would be up in a couple of hours so I crept downstairs in bare feet and silently poured myself a glass of milk from the fridge.

My best friend had suggested I stop digging. My husband had advised me to back off. *No good can come of it*, Melissa said. And my sister-in-law wasn't the threatening type, yet her warning went beyond urging restraint. To my ears, that meant something very bad had taken place. After what I'd overheard in my in-law's kitchen, I couldn't help but think that jealousy and passion sat at the heart of it.

'What are you doing up?'

My gaze swivelled to Raff, bleary-eyed. Engrossed in my own dark thoughts I hadn't heard him.

I stretched my arms above my head. 'Couldn't sleep.'
'Something bothering you?'
'Not especially,' I said, evasive.
He slipped his arms around me, nuzzled my neck. 'Rose Percival, I always know when something's up.'
Which was true, yet I feared telling him about the private grief I'd stumbled across that morning. Raff wouldn't be cross — wasn't his style — but he would be hurt. Easier to sell it to myself that I was protecting him by saying nothing when, in reality, I was protecting me.
'I'm out of my normal routine. I'll be better once I'm back at work.'
'Talking of which,' Raff said, glancing at his watch, 'I might as well crack on.'
'Mug of tea, first?'
'If you're making, I'm drinking.'
I put on the kettle and chucked teabags into two mugs. While the water boiled I asked Raff what time he'd got in.
'After eleven. Went for a drink with Tom at the Black Horse.'
Tom the Tree, as we knew him, carved elaborate sculptures out of dead wood. 'How is he?'
'Same: skint but happy.'
Raff scratched the back of his head. 'Then I ran into Wren who gave my ears a good bashing.'
I let out a groan. Wren was a meddling idiot. If Wren would only keep her sticky beak out of things, we'd all be better off.
'She told you all about it?' I said.
'*It* as in Melissa and Orlando moving out?'
I nodded.
'Mum and Dad will be disappointed,' Raff said. He could tell from my face that I thought it an overreaction. 'Personally, I think it's a good thing.'
'You do?' I was surprised.
'Sure.'
'Bet you didn't share that opinion with Wren.'

Raff gave a sloppy smile. 'As if.'

We spent a lovely hour together. It reminded me of our honeymoon in the Maldives. The two of us in our own little private world. No distractions. Nobody to defer, or answer to. Did I feel more sorted after our early morning conversation? Not really. Not at all, if I were honest.

Eventually it was time for us both to leave. 'Promise I'll be home earlier tonight,' he said, kissing me on the doorstep.

'Takeaway Indian or Chinese?'

'Chinese. Have we got any beer?'

'I'll pick some up.'

He headed off to Cirencester as I hit the road for Cheltenham. Parking was a nightmare, like I knew it would be. Crashing through the door with seconds to spare, I hurled greetings at Jade and Mandy, the receptionists, nodded *bonjour* to Jerome, before scooting through to the staff area to dump my stuff and then hit the ground running. Back-to-back appointments of cuts and colours, toners and highlights with established and new clients, lasted beyond the morning. My coffee went cold and I barely had time to have a pee. I was mixing up a tint for my next lady, a woman with amazingly curly hair that challenged me to tame it, when Jerome asked if he could have a word.

'As long as it's speedy,' I said, following him into his lair, a darkly lit room that would not look out of place in a bordello in Bordeaux.

If you were asked to draw a picture of your idea of what a typical Frenchman looks like, Jerome would be that person. He was one walking Gallic shrug. A shock of thick black hair, beautifully cut, crested a wide forehead. His dark eyebrows framed deep-set, hooded eyes the colour of old tobacco. His nose was wide and large, his top lip generous and out of proportion to the bottom. Parking his rear on the desk, he crossed his arms and viewed me over the top of his glasses (not the trendy ones with big frames, but colourless, without discernible edges.) I felt like a mouse being sized up by a bird of prey.

'I've heard from Manchester,' he said.

'About my application?'

Jerome nodded.

I caught my breath. With everything else going on I'd pushed it to the back of my mind. What seemed like a lifetime ago, I'd applied to a new degree course unique to hairdressing. It was pretty hardcore, involving chemistry and psychology. Competition was stiff. There were only 110 places nationwide. It involved a lot of homeworking with online lectures, but Jerome had promised that if I were successful, he'd award me time off each week to study. It wasn't all a one-way ticket. He figured that, with an extra qualification, he could charge more for my services.

'And?' I said, hardly daring to dream.

A big smile splashed across his fleshy features. 'Congratulations. You got through.'

'Crikey,' I said. My knees actually went wobbly.

'You'll need to choose a couple of subjects for your dissertations.'

'Already thought about them.' I'd briefly flirted with unusual genetic conditions like spun glass syndrome, a complaint that normally starts in childhood and leaves hair completely uncombable. I'd discounted it due to its rarity and, instead, contemplated the risk of potential strokes following backwashes, and the causes and effect of female-pattern hair loss. I'd refused to make a firm decision because I didn't want to jinx it.

'Bon,' Jerome said, making a shooing gesture with the tips of his long fingers.

Dismissed, it was around three thirty before I could grab a sandwich. Bolting it down, I picked up my phone and saw two missed calls from Alice. Damn, I really didn't want to go on a charm offensive on Melissa's behalf, but if I say I'll do something, I do it. Perhaps I'd collar Alice later. Better still, maybe she'd had a rethink and decided to view the move with the Rhodes more positively. In the light of Melissa's warning,

I was convinced the sooner Alice exited Blackthorn House, the better for everyone.

My next client was a woman who wanted her hair dyed the colour of red cabbage. After her: one of my regulars. Mrs Mariner, or Jude as she preferred to be called, used to live in South Cerney, a pretty thriving village outside Cirencester, and had recently moved to Cheltenham because she preferred the golf club there. We fell into the usual conversation. *Been anywhere nice lately? How are the family? Got any plans for your wedding anniversary?* She chatted away while I popped her into the massage chair, washed her locks, applied conditioner, gave her a head massage that made her positively purr and, after a rinse, settled her back down with a flat white while I shaped and styled.

Most clients want to talk. A few prefer silence. I'm demon at identifying which is which. My nicer clients ask as many questions as I ask them because they are genuinely interested. Mrs Mariner was no exception.

'How's that lovely husband of yours?'

'All good,' I said. 'Sorry, Jude, could you uncross your legs?'

'I always forget,' she tutted, parking the soles of her shoes flat on the bar in front of her.

'You don't want a lopsided cut,' I said with a laugh.

'That would never do,' she agreed.

'Obviously, Raff is pretty busy this time of year,' I continued, picking up the thread of the conversation.

'Got to cash in while you can. Feast or famine when you're self-employed.'

'Indeed.'

I snipped and Mrs Mariner sipped. I excused myself to check on another client's colour and returned.

'Does hubbie still work at his parents' estate?' she asked.

'He does.'

'Did I ever tell you our daughter's wedding was held at Blackthorn?'

I stepped back in surprise. 'No way.'

'Almost twenty years ago,' Mrs Mariner said, 'when it was in its heyday. Nearly bankrupted us.' Her sparse eyebrows shot up and she gave a rueful grin.

'But it was a success?'

'A beautiful occasion. Sadly, the memory lasted longer than the marriage.'

'I'm sorry to hear.'

Mrs Mariner peered forward to look in the mirror. 'Could you trim a little more from the sides, dear?'

Flexing several locks of hair through the fingers on my right hand, I snipped away with my left.

'Did you know the Percivals well? I mean before you used Blackthorn as a wedding venue?' Shamelessly fishing, I hoped I didn't sound too nosy.

'I didn't really know Bacchus and Marnie very well.'

'Benedict's parents?'

'That's right.' Mrs Mariner lowered her voice in the way people do when they have unpleasant news to impart. 'Bacchus died quite young — heart attack.

'Maud, that's Celeste's mother, I'd known for many years. We were in the same bridge club. Quite a character, she moved to be closer to her family and lived at Blackthorn for a number of years after her husband Theodore passed away.'

'I'd no idea.'

'Well before your time, you understand. One would see the family at various functions.' Mrs Mariner nodded and briefly drifted off into yesteryear. 'I gather she's recently gone into rather a nice nursing home in Leamington Spa. Maud always had an eye to the nicer things in life.' Mrs Mariner spoke with obvious approval. 'I'd always rather admired Celeste who definitely took after her mother. She was the brains behind the business.'

I recognised Celeste was a powerhouse of a woman, yet I'd always thought Benedict, the extrovert with his verve and open way of thinking, had been the driving force. He'd grown up at Blackthorn and had a better handle on how it could develop, I'd mistakenly thought.

'Oh yes,' Mrs Mariner continued, in full throttle. 'Benedict's father, Bacchus, virtually ran the place into the ground. Saddled his eldest son with a terrific pile of debts. Benedict did the right thing in marrying Celeste de Grey. She literally saved him from penury. I'm not one to gossip but there are a lot of people who don't really care for her, particularly women of my age who've done nothing with their lives. I put it down to envy. When a man is ruthless in his pursuit of an ambition he is lauded. It doesn't work the same way for us women. Even now.'

Noise from the dryer drowned out further conversation. I swept as much loose hair from Mrs Mariner's neck as possible, trimmed a few rogue hairs and, grabbing a mirror, displayed the cut from the rear-view.

'Lovely,' Mrs Mariner concluded.

Accompanying my client to the desk, I reached for her jacket while she paid and made an appointment for six weeks' time.

I eventually escaped the salon around five thirty, flew into the supermarket and picked up dinner. I was looking forward to normality and an evening with Raff.

It wasn't quite so warm and the sky was milky white, threaded with streaks of blue, as I drove back to my new temporary home. Near the entrance, a small white van, like a vehicle used by tradesmen, was parked up on the verge. It wasn't exactly in my way, but it made navigating past tricky. I slowed down as a man in shorts and a T clambered out of the driver's side and came towards me. Tattoos on his limbs, he was of medium height and well built. Below a scrub of badly cut dark hair, and in a strongly featured face, he had drinker's eyes: small and bloodshot. His hands were coarse and calloused. Not the kind of guy you'd want to bump into in an alley late at night.

I poked my head out of the window. 'Everything okay?'

'I'm trying to find Cotswold House.'

A name like that was akin to looking for a grain of salt in a salt cellar in this part of the world. 'Do you have a name?'

'Carvel-Day.'

I shook my head. 'Sorry, never heard of them.'

He looked at his phone, stuck his tongue out in concentration. 'It's a washing machine,' he said absently. 'Duntisbourne, it says here.'

'Which one? There are three.'

'Really?' He looked aghast.

'Duntisbourne Abbots, Duntisbourne Leer and Duntisbourne Rouse.'

'Typical of the depot,' he muttered, stabbing at his phone. 'At this rate I won't get home until midnight. Don't suppose the people at the big house would be able to help?' He jutted his chin in the direction of Blackthorn.

'The Percivals? Not sure. You could try, I guess.'

Eyes back on the screen, he broke into a relieved smile. 'Hang about, Leer it is.'

'There you go. Mystery solved.'

'Sorry to have troubled you. And sorry for being in the way,' he called over his shoulder.

'No problem.' Bemused, I thought that the puffin logo was a sweet choice for a washing machine repairs company.

CHAPTER TWENTY-SEVEN

ROSE

Raff was already parked next to a red SUV that I guessed belonged to Wren. I slid the Mini into the space next to Raff's pick-up, crossed the drive and, toeing open the door, my arms laden with groceries, discovered an empty home. I stowed the beer and takeaway and, slipping out my phone, called him. He answered straightaway. In the background I could hear the clamour of a party in full swing. My spirits sank. He must have popped in for a drink on the way home and got waylaid.

'I'm at the house,' Raff announced. 'Come on up. Mum and Dad have put on a spread. We're all here.'

My spirits stayed right where they were: in the depths. 'But, Raff, what about dinner?' *What about our quiet cosy night together?*

'It will keep, won't it? Dad's cracked open the Dom.'

Originally mystified by the description, I was now fluent in champagne. Dom Pérignon was what Raff meant. 'Are they celebrating?'

'Don't think so.'

'Okay,' I said lamely. I'd wanted to tell him about the degree course. I'd needed to talk to him about things that bothered me and I couldn't nail.

Mortally pissed off, I freshened up and trundled up the drive.

Spontaneous parties fill me with dread. I hate it when the Percival siblings get together. Each reverts to what they were like as children, as if none of them ever grew up, had lives or significant others. *In Wren's case, nothing had changed*, I thought sourly. She'd obviously had a few because she sidled up to me and asked how her favourite sister-in-law was, as if there were a crowd of us. Raff, entirely in his element without Orlando, had taken it upon himself to make sure everyone had a topped-up glass in hand.

At my arrival he broke away from his mother, slipped a meaty arm around my waist and drew me close. 'Thanks for coming,' he whispered in my ear. I tensed and smiled. 'You're okay with it, aren't you?' he said, suddenly anxious.

'It's fine.'

He spun away and I caught Melissa's eye. She raised her eyebrows in acknowledgement before turning to her father for advice about a financial product designed to benefit her children. *Maybe she was talking to the wrong person*, I thought, recalling Mrs Mariner's remarks. Celeste had been and probably still was the financial brains of the enterprise and marriage.

There was no sign of Alice. On child duty, I suspected, feeling marginally guilty that I hadn't returned her calls. Celeste wandered over and slipped an arm through mine.

'Journey to work all right? I know it's an utter bore for you.'

'I'll get used to it.' The prospect of driving during the winter months remained daunting. It was not uncommon to have several inches of snow. A couple of years ago, the road between Cheltenham and Cirencester had been shut for days. I'd freak out if I were holed up at Blackthorn.

A great shriek of laughter split the air in two, Raff and Wren sharing a private joke that earned him a punch on the arm.

'You little mare,' Raff said, tickling his sister, making her screech. With a sly look in my direction, she cupped a hand over her mouth and muttered something that elicited tittering laughter from the others.

'High spirits,' Celeste said, wincing. 'If I were you, Rose, I'd go and help yourself to supper before the pack animals descend.'

Starving hungry, I headed towards the dining room and a table groaning with food. Piling up a plate with cold cuts, salad and crusty bread, I found a quiet corner in the adjoining garden room. Here the decibel level was more acceptable. I was halfway through a chicken leg when Benedict sloped in.

'Mind if I join you?'

My mouth full, I shook my head.

Astoundingly, he'd dyed his hair and beard. I hated to say it but it kind of suited him and I wondered when and where the hell he'd had it done. (I can always tell the difference between a salon colour and a home kit).

He sat down, parked one leg over the other and sank his teeth into a sausage roll, chewing happily. Removing a flake of pastry with the edge of a serviette, he said, 'I love my children but I prefer them individually. They're a nightmare when they're all together.' He pulled a silly face. 'How are you, Rose?'

'Good, thanks.' Finishing a mouthful, I continued, 'No Alice?' A horribly risky move I'd hoped for an illuminating response.

'Sulking in her room, I believe. My youngest daughter's bid to keep Alice here was thwarted by my other daughter. War will ensue,' Benedict said gloomily.

'Oh dear.' I'd heard other friends' parents talk about their children's enmities.

Benedict sighed wearily. 'I do so hate people to be unhappy, especially when they're under my roof.'

And that was Benedict all over, I realised. He was rubbish at people around him being sad. It really upset him.

'She'll come round,' I assured him.

He shook his head. 'Alice is strangely adamant that she's staying here. It's *what she signed up for*, she claims.'

'She's not exactly indispensable,' I scoffed. 'Nannies come and they go.'

Whether it was a trick of the light, I thought I saw an expression of pain flash behind my father-in-law's eyes. It put me on notice. Appetite gone, I sat up a little straighter. Benedict's gaze sneaked away to some faraway place.

'Perhaps I should take her something to eat?'

'What?' Benedict said, momentarily confused.

'Alice.'

'Oh yes,' he said, giving my knee a pat. 'That would be a kindness. What would we do without you, Rose?'

Celeste was right. The pack *had* descended. I rescued the last piece of quiche, picked through a jumble of remains and found a clean glass that I filled with water. I took the lot upstairs and tapped on Alice's door.

Alice's answering reply was borderline pathetic. I bowled in, armed with nothing more than a warm smile. She was sitting at the window, gazing out, before turning her attention to me.

She didn't say: *Oh, it's you.* Didn't need to. The light in her eyes was dull with disappointment.

'Thought you might be hungry.' I parked the plate of food on the table in front of her.

'Thanks.'

'Sorry I didn't return your calls. It was manic at work.'

'That's okay.'

Feeling a sudden swell of concern, I sat down on her bed and put my arm around her slender shoulders. 'Alice, don't you think this is all a little silly?'

She stared at me with her big brown eyes. Talking to Alice was like diving through an ocean. The deeper you reached the colder it got.

'Melissa is kind and, quite honestly, moving out should make life simpler.'

'I guess.'

'And you've got a couple of weeks to get used to the idea.'

She didn't look persuaded.

'Maybe Melissa could run you and the children out to Sapperton to check out the new place, show you your room.'

Alice hiked a shoulder. Hard lines tugged at her mouth. She didn't seem as pretty as she did when she first arrived.

'It's literally a few miles away and I'm sure Melissa will visit Blackthorn often enough,' I persisted.

The sad expression remained.

I was tired. I was fed up. Frankly, I was mystified. I'd had enough of playing nursemaid to the nursemaid. Time for a little tough love, as my dad would say. 'You know what, Alice,' I said, a weeny bit of snap in my voice, 'in this life, you have to make the most of it and grab happiness where you can. There's a hell of a lot of people worse off.'

She cut me a surprised glance that told me it had struck home. I didn't want to hurt or upset her, obviously, but I needed to get through. The rest of the family would not be so kind. Job done, I slapped my hands on my thighs and stood up. 'I'll leave you to it then. Night night.'

Downstairs, in my absence, numbers had increased exponentially. Some of Benedict's drinking buddies, mostly old boys with club ties, (one with a bow tie) whose wives had left them, had mysteriously appeared. There was a lot of chortling and sentences punctuated with *Humph* and *Splendid*. Wren had come up with the bright idea of playing the animal name game with a bevy of girlfriends. Celeste was talking to a long thin woman with a severe haircut about a forthcoming literary festival in the West Country. Talking to Raff, I spied Tom the Tree with his girlfriend, Amber. Queen of recycling, she was eternally on the lookout for turning crap into art and flogging it for more than I earned in a month. I wasn't jealous. I liked her style, her tattoos and her piercings. I liked *her*.

Amber was in full flight. An expressive person, she waved her arms a lot, jangling her bangles. 'If a piece is in bad shape, a repaint will bring it back to life. If it's of quality, a repaint is an absolute crime. Oh, hi, Rose,' she said, breaking off.

'Hiya.' I was glad to have someone I could relate to.

'How's it going?'

'Good.'

'Hope we're not crashing in. Raff said it would be okay.' Amber acknowledged him with a flick of her chin.

'And Benedict and Celeste are such a laugh,' Tom said.

That wasn't quite how I'd have described them. Was I reading too much into my in-laws, casting them as out-laws? I was starting to feel a right party pooper.

'Raff's doing us a huge favour,' Amber said.

'Yeah?'

'I've scavenged some oil drums, cheap as hell, from a restaurant. Raff's offered to store them for us at the lock-up.'

'Great but what do you need them for?'

'She's converting them into pizza ovens,' Tom said. Shaking out a cigarette from a pack, he announced he was heading outside for a smoke.

'Be with you in a sec,' Amber told him. Then turning to me, 'Once you get your own place I'll let you have one of my premium designs.'

'Could be a long wait,' Raff chipped in.

I gave him a look that failed to land as hard as I'd wanted it to. I'm pretty good at hovering and waiting my turn to slide into a conversation. With so many on the go, it should have been easy. Truth was, I felt invisible. It set me thinking about my mum and dad, about my nan, who'd moved in with us for a while when my parents had to spend long periods of time at the hospital with Poppy. It made me remember cups of tea and tinned salmon sandwiches with crisps and pickled gherkins, companionably eaten in front of the TV. Warm, dignified, comfortable affairs.

I wandered into the snug to catch some quiet. Comfortably furnished, a little bit on the shabby and lived-in side, this was where Celeste and Benedict hung out when flying solo. I imagined them with trays of food on their laps in front of the TV on winter evenings. Photographs of their children and now grandchildren decorated the walls. Wren, a flaxen-haired child, with big green eyes and gappy smile, seemed a lot more biddable then than she was now. Raff, a typical lad, with dirty knees to match his dirty face, had been caught on camera clambering up trees, a younger Benedict, powerful and vital, with jet black hair — which seemed funny because, up until tonight, I'd only ever known him with grey — already several branches above Raff's head. And then there was Melissa, shy and awkward in her school uniform. I stared at her pale little face; saw the hopelessly lost expression in her eyes. If I hadn't known better I'd have thought her a sickly kid. *What happened to you?* I asked, *and why was Violet notable by her absence?* Had she been disappeared deliberately from the family hall of fame? And was this connected to the mysterious and long dead Shona Reid?

Another photograph caught my eye. It was of a young Celeste and Benedict at someone's party. They typified the golden couple, happy and relaxed and absolutely smashing it personally, socially and professionally. I wondered when it was taken. I wondered if, beneath the surface, resentments simmered.

Unaccountably homesick and keen to escape, I found Raff and explained I was walking back to the lodge. I gave his arm an apologetic squeeze. Before he could persuade me to stay, I slipped outside and padded down the steps to the gravelled drive. It had turned dark and felt cooler. In my flimsy dress, I felt a shiver trickle down my spine. Close to the lodge, almost home, I heard a noise: a rustle through the trees, the sound of twigs snapping. Badgers, foxes and squirrels, I thought, listening to an owl hoot in the distance. I would have paid it no attention at all if I hadn't noticed a thin beam of light, glimmering through the trees.

CHAPTER TWENTY-EIGHT

ALICE

Plates littered with leftovers, abandoned glasses of wine, empty bottles, dirty marks on the tiled floor — was that vomit in a plant pot? — Alice picked her way through debris the following morning and thought it disgusting to leave such a mess for the cleaner.

Clearing a space, she set up camp for breakfast and wandered into the boot room to warm bottles in the microwave for Kai and Edgar. Waiting for the milk to heat, her throat closed over in fear. There, on the side, near the back door, a pack of cigarettes. She'd recognise Sean's brand of smokes anywhere. *Quitting will improve your health. Smoking risks blindness and infertility.* She didn't want his health improved. She didn't want him fertile and able to raise another human being in his own image. She wanted him gone.

Rushing to the back door, she checked that it was locked. It was. Next, she stared out of the window, feverishly scanning the grounds. How had he got past the electronic gates and entry system? *Don't be a fool*, Alice thought. Sean had reached her before and he would reach her again. Dared she confide in Rose? But then, if she did, they'd arrange for her to leave as soon as possible.

The microwave beeped, signalling Kai's milk was ready. With shaking hands, she took out the bottle and pressed the teat to the back of her hand. Too hot, like a lit cigarette against her skin.

Dazed with fear, she tried to get a grip. There were bound to be smokers at the party. It was sheer happenstance that a pack had been left on the side.

But it's Sean's particular brand, Alice's internal alarm system shrieked back.

Her legs almost giving way, Alice turned, her desperate gaze tumbling onto a calendar hanging next to a chalkboard for shopping lists. A mine of information, Alice studied it as if it were the contents of a will to which she was the sole beneficiary. Written with italicised flair, Benedict's appointments revolved around fun: drinks and lunches, tennis and squash. Celeste's were of a more official and practical nature: parish council and committee meetings, appointments with solicitors and accountants, the date for picking up a prescription — Alice wondered what that was for — and then, joy unconfined, she stumbled across one little word that said so much: AWAY. Heart tripping, Alice peered closer at Celeste's spindly handwriting. A literary event in the West Country in a week's time and Celeste would be away for three whole days. *But it was cutting it fine*, Alice thought with a frown. A day after Celeste's return, she was destined to leave Blackthorn forever.

'Morning.'

Alice gave a start and whirled round.

'Sorry, didn't mean to give you a fright,' Benedict said.

He looked rough, she thought. Not so sparky around the eyes and his skin looked moist and blotchy. He wore a dressing gown over pyjama bottoms and his feet were bare, which wasn't exactly a novelty.

'I came down for orange juice.' He scratched his head absently.

'Let me get it for you,' Alice said, bright and keen to oblige. 'Why don't you sit down in the kitchen — if you can find somewhere,' she said, laughing lightly.

Benedict nodded with a peaky smile. 'Bit of a party last night.'

'Feeling worse for wear?'

'Regrettably, yes.'

'You'll soon feel better,' Alice said, practically dancing towards the fridge. *Look at me. I am young and vibrant and beautiful. I am youth personified. I am the antidote to lost years and the promise of good things to come.* She felt sure that his gaze was glued to her every move and gesture. Finding a clean glass — not easily done — she parked it in front of him with a sexy smile. Holy crap, up close and personal, he smelt like a distillery.

'You're a treasure,' Benedict said, drinking deep.

This was more her line, Alice thought, resting a warm hand on his bare arm. 'Top-up, Benedict?'

His eyes found hers. She was certain she read desire in his expression, the filthy pervert. Leaning gently towards him, she thought, any second now and their lips might touch.

'Daddy,' Melissa burst out.

Alice straightened up so fast she cricked her neck.

White-faced, Benedict said, 'I had something in my eye.'

Alice suppressed an inner smile. Benedict was covering for her, for *them*.

Melissa's stony gaze crushed. 'Kai is awake,' she said, indicating the door with a nod of her head.

'No problem.' *Except it was*, Alice realised, swallowing hard.

CHAPTER TWENTY-NINE

MELISSA

Horrified, Melissa stared at Alice in retreat and rounded on her father.

'What was that all about?'

'Absurd, but the girl has a crush on me.'

'You don't say.'

'Lissie, don't be like that.'

'Like what?'

'As if I'm engendering it.'

'I know what I saw.'

'What you think you saw. My God, why is it that everyone in this household believes I'm some kind of ancient Lothario. You're as bad as your mother.'

'Can you blame her?' It felt odd to defend Mummy but, on this occasion, she deserved backup.

'That was uncalled for.' Her father gave a pained sigh. Melissa chewed her lip. Governed by silence, she reached for the right words and, awkwardly fluffing it, grabbed hold of the wrong ones.

'Really, Daddy, wafting around the house in your dressing gown, what did you expect?' So much easier to reprimand him for what she knew than what she thought she knew.

'I'm not clairvoyant. I'd no idea Alice was going to be up and about.'

Melissa raked his face for lies. A post-party assignation in the kitchen seemed as unlikely as it was risky. But Melissa's eyes were not deceiving her. There was definitely something going on. She loved her father and hated to think the worst of him, but Alice was very pretty and she was a nanny. Cold slid down between Melissa's shoulder blades. Could she honestly believe that the attraction was all one-sided? Fleeting memories, imposters, pulled her in for an unwanted cuddle. Shaking them off, Melissa ducked and darted away.

'Well, next time be more careful. If you know she's attracted to you, steer clear.'

'But it's my house,' Benedict said, affronted. 'I refuse to sneak about in my own home.'

'Nobody is asking you to. It's about pragmatism.' Christ, was he so naive? From the time she was old enough to understand, she'd been aware that her father was like a magnet to women. It wasn't simply his good looks; it was his charismatic and endearing personality. Up until this morning, she'd so wanted to believe he'd never, ever strayed, no matter what anyone thought or said. Not even Violet.

'Is it a crime to be nice?' Benedict asked, obviously hurt.

The word "crime", coming from her father's mouth, set Melissa's teeth on edge. She gave him a hard stare. 'It pays to be more discriminating.'

'Life lessons from my daughter.' Benedict shook his head sadly.

'Daddy, I'm looking out for you, that's all.'

'I know. Probably best we don't mention a word of this to your mother.'

Melissa froze inside. How many times had she received admonitions to keep her mouth shut? To survive in this family it paid to be deaf, dumb and blind.

'I don't . . .'

'You know how she gets,' Benedict said, beseeching.

Just say it, Melissa thought, *just blurt it out*. It was only the two of them in the kitchen. Nobody else was up, apart from bloody Alice. Did Melissa have the courage to confront the past? Did she have the guts to drag out the elephant in the room and parade her, definitely female, in front of her dad? Did Melissa have the stones to finally ask him once and for all?

A drumming sensation inside her chest beat a tattoo.

Were you really in love with Shona, Daddy?

Was it really an accident?

And if it wasn't, did you . . .

Melissa cleared her throat. 'The sooner we leave and take Alice with us, the better.'

'I will miss you so much, sweetheart, and little Autumn and Edgar, of course.'

'Then we shall visit often.' *Without Alice*, Melissa thought firmly.

CHAPTER THIRTY

ROSE

I told Raff about my degree course the second we had a minute to ourselves.

'Unreal,' he said, 'what a clever wife I have. Does it mean you get paid more?'

'It should do.' After Jerome had taken his cut.

The weekend came and went. Orlando returned home and left. I kept my head down all week and spent the following Saturday morning at my mum and dad's.

'How are you settling in then?' Mum asked.

'Fine,' I lied, not feeling good about fibbing to my mother.

'Told you so.' Mum saw the good in everything and everyone. Mind, if something seemed off, you were toast and there was no point of return.

'Not long until your holiday,' I said for something to say.

'You're right,' Mum said, bright-eyed. 'Pity you and Raff can't get away for a bit.'

'Wrong time of year for us.' And winter holidays were so expensive. There had been mutterings about us joining Raff's folks for a skiing trip. As I'd never skied and didn't fancy it, I'd rejected it out of hand.

'You're looking tired, Rose,' Mum said, in that knowing way of hers.

'Too much partying.' Not so far from the truth.

Walking in the woods later, I wondered about the strange light I'd seen on the night of the party. With the benefit of hindsight, I reckoned it was someone carrying a torch. The big question: who and why?

Feeling wary, I didn't go as far as the shack and took a different route that followed a path flanked by bright red rosehips and rogue blackberry bushes. Rays of sunshine nosed in through the trees. It was quiet and peaceful. I should have felt "centred", as Wren would say. Instead I felt untethered and strangely ill at ease.

Raff returned home knackered after a day of chainsawing logs and, for once, we had an idyllically quiet night in. We ate homemade lasagne (my mum's) with garlic bread (supermarket's) followed by Eton Mess (dropped off by Celeste). My only contribution was the wine to which I could lay no claim. Cuddled up on the sofa, the pair of us nice and mellow, I topped up our glasses.

'What did you get up to today?' Raff asked.

I told him. He looked aghast.

'Promise you won't go into the woods again alone?'

'Why not?'

'What would happen if you tripped and fell in the lake?'

'I'd swim and climb out.'

'You're a rubbish swimmer.' Which was true. 'But even if you swam like Wren, I'd be worried. The sides are damn slippery. It's very cold and nobody would hear you.'

'Okay, I get it. I'll avoid the lake.'

'It's not only that. You might fall and bash your head or skewer yourself on a fallen branch.'

'God, Raff, when did you become so risk-averse? It's ridiculous considering you handle the most dangerous implement known to man on a daily basis.'

He slipped out his phone. '*This* keeps me safe. You can't get a signal in the woods. I'm serious, Rose. Take it from a tree surgeon.'

I half-laughed. 'Are you forbidding me?'

His mouth assumed one straight, tight line. 'I'm cautioning you. If you want to ignore it, not much I can do. But don't say you weren't warned.'

He snatched up his glass and drank. I followed suit. Silence wrapped around us like a lethal piece of barbed wire.

Keen to break it, I said, 'Can anyone walk the woods?'

'You mean members of the public?'

'I wondered if it's accessible from the road.'

'They'd be trespassing if they did. Why do you ask?'

'No reason.'

His face creased with a smile. 'You are a funny girl.'

I inclined my head on his shoulder. 'Am I forgiven?'

'Nothing to forgive.' He dropped a kiss on the top of my head. We sat like that companionably, drifting through a game show followed by a documentary on wildlife. Giving every impression of concentrating on what we were watching, my mind was elsewhere until I was practically bursting. There was never going to be a good time to say what I needed to say.

'Raff,' I said, at last.

'Yep.' Eyes on the screen.

'You know when you drank all the milk and told me to go to your folks to pick up some more?'

'Ye-es.'

'I overheard them quarrelling.'

'Okay.'

'It sounded pretty serious.'

'All rows sound pretty serious.'

'I know, but . . .'

'Was it loud and noisy, or cold and snarky?'

'There are grades of argument?'

He cracked a lopsided grin. 'Rose Percival, you know there are.'

I supposed it fell into the cold and snarky. 'Your mum was really upset.'

Raff muted the TV and turned towards me with a long look. 'What was it about?'

'The past.' I didn't dare drop Alice in it.

Raff tensed. I knew then that sharing a confidence was not my best idea. I should have bailed. I should have made up a feeble lie. I should have resorted to describing a silly argument that blew up out of nothing. Then I thought of Shona Reid, her death, and accident. I thought of Florence's advice and the warning from Melissa. Everyone wanted me to forget about it. Florence to protect me; Melissa to protect herself.

'Your mum thinks that your dad had a fling with Shona Reid.'

Raff's eyes shot wide. 'Did she actually accuse him?'

'Not in so many words.'

'How many bloody words? Jesus, Rose, how much of the argument did you actually hear?'

'Enough.' I hated to see the pain in his eyes.

He was sitting bolt upright now. 'Are you sure you didn't get the wrong end of the stick?'

'I don't think so.'

'Even if it's true, what am I supposed to do with it?'

'Well, I . . .'

Realisation of what I was hinting at flooded his face. 'Bloody hell, Rose, are you suggesting that this alleged affair had something to do with Shona's death?'

Raff never got really angry. Pale-lipped, he looked absolutely blindsided.

'I'm not saying that, no.' Self-preservation prevented me from blurting out that I'd spoken to Melissa. 'Look, I'm sorry, but I didn't feel it fair to keep it from you. We've always been straight with each other, haven't we?'

His hard expression softened. 'We have, yes. We don't have secrets.' He took my hand and kissed it to prove that, whatever else was going on around us, we were solid.

'Selfish of me but I didn't want to carry the conversation and not tell you.'

'Okay,' Raff said. 'I respect that.' Everything about the way he sat, more relaxed and open, suggested he was recalibrating. 'What was actually said?'

I closed my eyes, reached for what I'd overheard in my mind. It was important I got it right. It was also important I edited the row to protect Alice. 'Your dad sounded cross and asked when she, referring to your mum, would get it through her head that there was nothing in it.'

'And what was Mum's reply?'

'*You really expect me to believe that?* Those were her very words.'

'And you're sure they were talking about Shona?'

'Well, yeah,' I said, suddenly unsure.

'Mum said her name.'

'No, she said *that woman*.'

'Aha.' Raff broke into a grin, spotting a hole in my argument. 'You heard a row and took it out of context.'

Annoyingly, he had a point. 'Maybe,' I conceded. 'Not that it makes it better.'

'Rose, we had a number of nannies. Not that I'm suggesting anything scandalous went on with any of them,' he added quickly.

'Of course not,' I said, eager to squash the thought.

'Or anyone else for that matter. Dad isn't that type of guy. He's devoted to Mum.'

From my perspective, it had always looked that way. I'd no reason to question it and, according to my client, Mrs Mariner, Benedict owed his wife everything. I made some inane comment in agreement and sipped my wine.

Raff settled back in his seat like an old man looking back on his life and deeply content with what he'd achieved. He let out a happy sigh. 'Thank God we cleared that up. I love Melissa,' Raff said, 'and I adore the kids but, after these last few days, I won't be sorry to see them move out. Then things can get back to normal.'

Whatever that meant, I thought.

CHAPTER THIRTY-ONE

ROSE

Sunday lunch was a subdued affair. Even Benedict was quiet, desperate to neither be seen nor heard, it seemed. Wren nursed a hangover that rendered her speechless — *thank you, Lord*. Chipping into conversation with Orlando about their new lodgings, Melissa's eyes occasionally darted between her father and Alice, who was too involved with the children to notice. If it weren't for Celeste and Raff rattling away, the meal would have been excruciating. I focused on my plate and the food in my mouth. I wasn't feeling great in a way I couldn't quite identify. A bit tired. A bit headachy. A bit sniffly — just slightly off, like milk on the turn.

After the meal was cleared away, Melissa strong-armed Wren to help her wash up. Raff took the kids outside to the designated play area. Alice disappeared to her room and Benedict and Orlando decamped to the drawing room with a bottle of brandy. Lost, I found Celeste sitting on the terrace with a small glass of whisky. She was smoking a cigarette like an aging 60s pop singer, bored and tired of life. She very rarely smoked and, though I didn't comment, she read the surprise in my expression.

'In extremis.' She puffed out a perfect smoke ring, looking effortlessly cool. If it weren't bad for your health, I could be persuaded to take it up. Not knowing how to respond, I gave the mere suggestion of a sympathetic nod.

'Children,' Celeste stated, as if it were the answer to a politically loaded question. 'When they're small they break your arms. When they're grown-up they break your hearts.'

Bearing in mind all her children were fully-formed adults, I wasn't certain to which "child" she was referring let alone what said child had done. 'Has Raff upset you?' I couldn't think how.

'Raff? Goodness, no. Boys are so much more straightforward, as you'll discover when you have one of your own.'

Reluctant to discuss my absence of maternal instinct with my mother-in-law, the sympathetic, listening expression on my face took a hike.

'The girls in our family have always been the problem,' Celeste continued, taking an expansive drag from her cigarette. 'They're so much more complicated emotionally and that never changes.'

'Am I included?' I asked, in an attempt to lighten the conversation.

Celeste viewed me through glassy eyes. Pretty drunk, I thought. 'Nothing temperamental about you. If you were a vehicle you'd be a Land Rover Defender, I swear.'

My heart sank. Dull and solid was what she meant.

She touched my arm. 'Raff chose well when he chose you.' Celeste issued a tight laugh. 'I daresay Benedict's mother thought the same of me.'

Because you had the brains and the connections, I thought, recalling Mrs Mariner. Because you could bring the money.

'Not that my mother would agree,' Celeste continued.

'You didn't get on?'

'Different animals,' Celeste said, with a wet laugh. 'We had a falling out, not uncommon.'

'What happened?'

'Happened?' Celeste's eyes scanned the distance as if the reason for the disagreement were to be found in the tree line. 'Do you know,' she said, turning sharply towards me, 'it seems utterly ridiculous, one of those family things that sparked the most dreadful kerfuffle, yet I'm blowed if I remember what it was about. It was all so long ago.'

Lies cower within a voice and Celeste's grovelled and sneaked away.

'You don't know Granny Maud, do you?' Celeste reached for her glass and sipped her drink.

'We met briefly at our wedding.'

'Nobody loves a grudge more than my mother. I'm certain she takes it out each night and gives it a polish. I don't think even she remembers anymore, but there you go, families for you. Enough of my rambling,' Celeste said abruptly, as if she suddenly realised who she was talking to. 'How are you finding life at the lodge?'

'Good,' I said, 'and I like the fact it's close to the woods — all that birdsong and wildlife.'

'I never go there.'

'*Never?*'

'Beating my way through the wilderness is not my idea of fun and I have better things to do with my time. Besides . . .' She skidded to a halt and glanced away.

'Yes?'

'If I'm honest, Rose, I wouldn't go there alone.'

'Oh, the lake? Raff told me to be careful.'

'No,' she said slowly. 'I wouldn't want anything to happen to you.'

Alarm flared inside me. 'That sounds like a threat.'

'No, no,' Celeste said with a bright smile. 'I didn't mean you specifically, darling. Ooh, I don't know. It's so remote, hostile even.'

'How can you say that when your children played there when they were little?'

'A very long time ago.'

That again. Every time I posed a question, the evasive reply was steeped in history in a narrative I could never contest. I wondered again, who the hell had been walking through the trees on the night of the party. I didn't ask Celeste for an opinion because I knew I wouldn't get a straight answer.

* * *

On Monday, my day off, I wanted to get on with coursework for my degree. I'd already written a mandatory thousand-word introduction, stating my aims and aspirations, including the possibility of using my qualification to enable me to get into education and teach (always a good sell). Life had different ideas. I knew I was coming down with something for sure the moment I woke up and could barely prise myself from bed. Alternately hot and cold and shivery, my legs ached and pain lanced straight through one ear and out the other. Whatever Florence had caught, I now had, and I wasn't happy about it. Dosed up and dragging myself into work on Tuesday, I lasted until lunchtime.

'I do not want you here,' Jerome said, wagging a finger in his typically forthright fashion. 'Go home and don't come back until you are better.'

I drove to Blackthorn, parked and, gathering all my strength, limped to the lodge. Feeling absolutely awful, I hauled my aching limbs upstairs and, exhausted, crawled, fully clothed, beneath the duvet. Utterly pathetic, I phoned Raff and explained that I was no better than I had been early that morning and actually felt worse.

'God, Rose, I told you not go to in. You sound terrible. I'll come home.'

'No, I . . .'

'I'll see you in half an hour.'

Almost to the minute, Raff walked in brandishing painkillers and cold and flu preparations. Weak as a newborn, I let him peel me out of my clothes and put me to bed properly.

'Sorry,' I said, teeth chattering.

'Don't be daft. Now take this.' He pushed a glass of water and two cold and flu tablets into my hand. I swallowed them down and lay back on the pillows. The room swam in front of me. All I wanted to do was sleep.

'Will you be okay?' His face was a picture of concern.

I gave a pathetic smile. 'I will now.'

'I can stay, if you like.'

'No, you go.'

'Shall I ask Mum to look in on you?'

'Emphatically no.' If I wanted anyone it was *my* mum, not someone else's and definitely not Celeste. I had images of her throwing open windows and encouraging me to pull myself together.

'All right, if you're sure?' He stood, anxious, blonde eyebrows drawing together.

'Raff, stop hovering.'

A sudden smile lit up his face. 'Good to see you haven't entirely lost your spark. I'll leave you to it then.'

He'd gone no more than a few paces. 'Raff,' I called after him.

'Yep?'

'Thank you.'

'Love you,' he said.

'Love you more.' And then, feeling mildly better, I fell asleep.

CHAPTER THIRTY-TWO

MELISSA

'This will be your room,' Melissa said, with a flourish. 'See, you have the top floor all to yourself.'

Alice responded with a flat stare. She couldn't have looked more disinterested if she'd tried.

The grand tour of their gorgeous seventeenth century stone cottage, with double aspect vaulted ceiling and inglenook, had taken a good half hour. The entire time Melissa's brain had been shrieking: *Keep your mitts off my dad.* The more Alice wandered around like a wet weekend in a Paris summer, the more convinced Melissa was that Alice really was mooning over Melissa's father.

It. Was. Ridiculous.

And scary.

Orlando knew enough to understand that the arrival of a nanny at Blackthorn would trigger bad memories and dig up a past, best left buried. If he'd seen what she saw that morning, if he'd caught the way Alice looked at her dad, God alone knew what he'd do with it.

Determined to press on against a wall of indifference, Melissa pointed out the view from the garden from where she

149

could see Autumn belting around the lawn with Ava's son, Niall. Clutching Ava's hands, Edgar was currently tottering along a path flanked by late lavender.

'Come and see,' Melissa said encouragingly.

Alice wandered over as if she were being herded into the back of a lorry run by people traffickers.

'Do you think you could show a little more enthusiasm?'

Alice regarded Melissa with reproach. Her chin wobbled. Her doe eyes glistened. 'Sorry.'

Not for nothing was it called the hardest word, Melissa thought, strongly resisting the urge to give her nanny the mental equivalent of a shake. It was too bad, particularly as Wren was barely speaking to her. To say her sister felt murderous about Alice leaving was an understatement.

'Right then,' Melissa said briskly. 'Let's scoop up the children and get them back to Blackthorn. With my mother away, it will be just you and me.' And a to-do list as long as her arm. Her mother never went anywhere without leaving detailed instructions.

'And Mr Percival?' Alice asked.

'He's out to supper with old friends,' Melissa replied crisply.

A spontaneous "oh" seeped from Alice's lips. Crestfallen didn't really cover it, Melissa thought. Not a vindictive woman, she couldn't help but savour the moment.

CHAPTER THIRTY-THREE

ROSE

I didn't know what time it was when I came to. Something had definitely woken me up. Disorientated and trying to get my bearings, I reached for my phone.

'Hello, Rose.'

I blinked, dazed. Next Melissa's head popped around the door.

'Oh, it's you,' I said.

'I've just picked up a message from Raff. Goodness, Rose, you look awful.'

'So I've been told. Did you come simply to admire the view, or what?' I pushed a feeble smile.

'Had I known sooner I'd have abandoned my visit to the new house.'

'How did that go?'

Melissa tilted her hand. 'So-so.'

'Don't tell me, you took Alice with you?'

Melissa elevated an eyebrow and seemed about to expand but swerved a more considered reply and, instead, announced she'd brought lemons and super-strength Manuka honey. 'Would you like me to make you a hot drink?'

'I'll try anything.' Although I felt better for a sleep I'd acquired a new symptom: my tonsils felt as if they'd been seared with a blowtorch.

'Be with you in a tick.'

Melissa scurried off and I listened as my sister-in-law rifled through cupboards and drawers. The kettle hissed, protesting at the interruption in its otherwise peaceful afternoon. Seconds later, I was clutching a mug. Melissa sat on my bed.

'Don't get too close,' I croaked. 'I'd hate you to catch this.'

'Trust me, when you have small children your immune system gets a thorough workout. I'll be fine. Anything else you need? Tissues, medicine?'

In that moment she sounded remarkably like her mother, not that I told Melissa this. I randomly wondered if Celeste was like her mother, Maud, and what Maud was really like.

I shook my head. 'Raff has already sorted it.'

'You've lucked out there. I'd have to be dying before Orlando took any notice.'

Melissa's phone rang. She glanced at me with a grin. 'Speaking of which.' I watched as she took the call.

'Hey.' Whether or not it was for my benefit, Melissa sounded positively perky. 'That's incredibly short notice,' she said, with a slight frown, 'Right . . . what a bore . . . *crikey* . . . yes, I see . . .' From the depths of my bed I heard Orlando's rumbling upper-class voice, although I'd no idea what he was saying. Melissa's tone and facial expressions suggested surprise, comprehension and, briefly, shock, although not of the *this is going to hurt* kind. 'I will . . . of course . . . until next weekend then, bye,' Melissa finished.

I hitched the sheets up to my chin. 'Problem?'

'Middle Eastern property buyers with suitcases full of cash.'

'That's a *problem*?'

'It is for Orlando. He's got to work the weekend.'

'So he's staying in London?'

'That's about the size of it. With you out of action and Mummy away, it's going to be a quiet weekend.'

I sank back into the pillows. I could cope with that.

CHAPTER THIRTY-FOUR

ALICE

Written in Benedict's stylish hand, the note was found under Alice's door. She read it again and thrilled.

Committing the message to memory, she tore the paper into tiny pieces, as instructed, and flushed it down the toilet. *Not so smug now, Mrs Rhodes*, she thought. And take that, Mrs Percival.

The afternoon had been a humiliating trail around a house she had no intention of living in with an employer who sensed her father's animal attraction to Alice. What was it with these stiff-lipped women? Benedict's romantic track record was his problem, not hers. It had been her mother's too.

Alice sat down. He had wronged her mum. End of. And did the Percival women make Benedict's life a misery? Did they hell! Infuriatingly, whenever Alice got close to him, either his wife or daughter would pop up to ruin it and then blame her. High time the gods, or whatever, cut Alice slack. She was running out of time and the longer she stayed, the greater the chance of Sean hunting her down and tearing her away. The prospect was terrifying. Each time he dragged her back, the worse his temper.

But then, *yay*, Benedict had come to the rescue.

She *knew* he wanted her.
She'd *read* it in his eyes.
She'd *felt* it in his touch.
Screw the supper with his frigging old fogey friends.

At midnight, romantic old fool, she was to travel through the priest hole rather than struggling with the locks on either the front or back doors. Who knew Benedict Percival had a taste for drama? Alice pictured herself slipping downstairs while the rest of the household slept. She wasn't sure what Benedict had in mind but she was absolutely certain about how far she would let him go. Definitely not as far as he'd like, but far enough to embarrass and shame him. When she had him at the point of no return then she would strike.

Alice practically punched the air in triumph. Benedict Percival had a choice: pay up and she'd go away quietly and he'd never hear from her again, or she'd scream the bloody house down, accuse him of sexual assault and then tell *everyone* his big secret.

Whether it was true or not.

How about that?

CHAPTER THIRTY-FIVE

ROSE

Feverish, I tossed and turned and dreamed of the lake. I'd slipped and plunged in headlong. Through the trees, whispering voices mocked: *should have stayed away; should have run; we warned you.*

My limbs wouldn't work and I was getting nowhere. Unable to climb out, slime clung to my clothes, dragging me down as effectively as a concrete overcoat. The more I struggled the deeper I sank. Stagnant water up to my chest rose to my chin, then mouth. If it reached my nose, it would be over. In the distance a bright white light offered rescue that would never come.

'Rose, Rose.' Raff's cool hand lay on my forehead.

'What? Oh, thank God.'

He slid his arms around me, pulled me up to his chest, as if he'd reached into my nightmare and rescued me from the sludge and terror of impending death.

'Hush, it's only a dream.'

'It was so real,' I gasped, scared.

'This is real, you and me, here. Go back to sleep, babe.'

And I did, and when I woke again stars sprayed across the night sky and all was impossibly quiet.

CHAPTER THIRTY-SIX

ALICE

The staircase whined and noisily complained. Alice feared it would give her away and sound the alarm. What she'd do if Melissa found her she hadn't considered.

And there were the dogs, particularly that vile little terrier with its incessant yapping. So far, the mutts hadn't reacted. Perhaps they considered her friend and part of the family, not foe. Perhaps Benedict had shut them in the barn as he had on the night of the party.

One step and then another . . . easy does it.

She'd chosen her prettiest dress. It had a plunging halter neck and, because the temperature had dropped, she had draped a soft pink shawl around her slim shoulders, the last present her mum had gifted her and, therefore, right and proper. Not that Alice would need it; Benedict couldn't wait to keep her warm. On her feet, white pumps, similar to those worn by Celeste. Alice twitched a smile. While the cat's away . . .

Within sight of the vast fireplace and the entrance to the priest hole, Alice was almost dizzy with expectation. How much was Benedict good for? How much could she squeeze out of the old bastard? Was he already waiting, salivating over the thought of another conquest?

In your dreams, mate.

Silently crossing the floor, Alice thought she'd never felt so alive.

The catch gave easily. She stepped inside, closed the door softly behind her. The smell of damp and wood smoke was strong and cloying. It felt colder than the first time and she experienced an involuntary shiver.

She expected a sign, light, a murmured greeting, an endearment, perhaps an expression of surprise. There was nothing. No sound. No flood of illumination. Was he waiting for her to stumble through the void and out into the night? Was he loitering for her on the other side of the door in the garden? Was he a tease? Did he think the silent dark would make it fun?

She strained to see. Her night vision stubbornly refused to oblige. Many frightened people had huddled together, hidden here before her, she thought with a bump. Had their terror left its own imprint on the walls, in the contained space, in the darkness?

Sudden fear tapped her on the shoulder. Her palms sweated, her pulse rate increased. Unnerved, she wanted to call out, let Benedict know to *please, please* appear and release her.

In the pitch black the walls shape-shifted, closing in. Raw fear robbed her of speech. What if nobody came? What if she were sealed in, entombed? What if she could not be heard even if she screamed?

What if Benedict, tumbling to the truth, had set a trap? What if he'd lured *her*?

A horrific thought, she realised that the warning signs were there from the outset. The accidental death of one nanny should have been sufficient to trigger an alarm and alert her to the danger.

Focused, clever, driven, she had not listened. She had not seen. She had not read the room.

Her heart pounded. Loud. Noisy. Deafening. Yet the silence surrounding her was acute and sharp and it hurt. Dread coiled around her.

Then she heard a sound, imperceptible at first. He *was* there. She could hear him breathing.

'Benedict,' she whispered, arms outstretched, fingers sifting through the darkness. 'It's me, Alice.'

And suddenly a figure appeared: warm, solid and dependable and . . .

Oh my Christ.

Instantly recoiling, palms up, she backed away. Her heel banged against a wall. The shape advanced, slowly, with precision. *Knowledgeable*. In an instant she saw it all, read what was going to happen next and realising there was nothing she could do to prevent it.

With nowhere to run, nowhere to hide, she reached an arm behind her, scrabbling to find the catch, fingertips grazing, nails breaking, sobbing in frustration.

'No, no,' she gasped. 'Don't hurt me. Not this.'

She didn't think of the pretty things she wanted to buy with the money she'd hoped to extort. She didn't think of the life she could have had or the fresh start she could have given to her little brother, Craig who, of all the people she knew, deserved a shot of good luck. She thought only of the terrible, *terrible* mistake she'd made.

Pressure on her throat was crushing, pressure behind her eyes worse. They felt as if they would explode out of the sockets. Opening her mouth to yell, no scream came out.

No words.

No breath.

Nothing.

CHAPTER THIRTY-SEVEN

MELISSA

Melissa woke to the shattering sound of Edgar's cry. Glancing at her phone, it was well after his normal waking time. *Where was Alice?*, Melissa thought in irritation. Was she on a go-slow in protest at the trip to the house yesterday?

Grabbing a robe, Melissa was met by Autumn in her PJs.

'Mummy, Mummy, Edgar is sad.'

Melissa took her daughter's hand. 'Then we'll cheer him up and go and hunt Alice,' she said brightly.

'Hunt Alice. Is it a game, Mummy?'

'Absolutely,' Melissa replied. 'You run ahead, but don't go into Alice's room, not until I'm with you. Okay?'

'kay.'

Soothing Edgar was simple; he was such an easy little boy to please. Picking him up and holding him close, Melissa gave him a cuddle that made him gurgle with pleasure. What the hell did she need a nanny for? How else was she to have gorgeous *never to be forgotten* moments like this?

Changing Edgar's nappy, Melissa trailed out onto the landing. 'Have you found her?' she called to her daughter.

In the spirit of hide-and-seek, Autumn was examining the space underneath the big desk on the landing. 'I can't see her, Mummy.'

'Have you tried the laundry room?' Melissa asked, more to keep the game going than in any hope of finding Alice inside.

Off Autumn sped. As predicted, Alice was nowhere to be found.

After the first rush of annoyance, it occurred to Melissa that perhaps Alice was ill. Perhaps she'd caught Rose's appalling bug. Guilt stole over Melissa for giving the girl such a hard time.

'Dear me, Autumn. Let's try Alice's room.'

Dancing ahead, Autumn reached it first.

'Wait,' Melissa said, 'let Mummy knock.'

'Why?'

'It's only polite.' Then, tapping on the door, she called, 'Alice, it's Melissa. Are you okay?'

Nothing.

'Can we go in, Mummy?' Melissa met her daughter's excited gaze and felt an unaccountable hitch of misgiving.

'Tell you what, why don't you go down to the kitchen and find Gramps?'

'Aw . . .'

'He'll make you breakfast and you know he loves to see you first thing.'

'I don't want breakfast. I want to find Alice, like you said.'

'I know, but she might be poorly.'

Tiny hands on tiny hips, Autumn channelled her inner diva. 'So?'

'So when people are poorly, sweetie, they don't like an audience. They want to be left alone.'

'But you don't *know* she's poorly. You made that up.'

Sometimes her daughter's ability to see through her was startling. Melissa squatted down to Autumn's eye-level. 'Could you please do as I ask?'

'Edgar gets to see Alice and I don't.' To make the point, Autumn stamped her bare foot. 'It's not fair.'

'*Life* isn't fair.' The snap in Melissa's voice, although not pleasant, did the trick.

Sullen-faced, Autumn thumped down the staircase, one step at a time.

Straightening up, Edgar dead weight in her arms, Melissa knocked once again and rested one hand on the door handle. Its touch awakened a fleeting recollection. Her grip tightened, yet she couldn't move. Stock-still, the memory, once thin and lost, swelled and took shape, pushing away the years. She was with Violet. Beset with panic, and the horrible anxiety of losing the person who loves you most in the world, they were searching desperately for Shona.

Melissa cried out, her voice a screech, 'I'm coming in.'

She swept inside to a room that had the stripped and empty appearance of a recently exhumed grave.

Melissa clasped Edgar tighter.

Examination of the bed revealed that, stone cold, it had not been slept in or, if it had, not recently. No clothes, such as they were, hung in the wardrobe; no belongings huddled together in the single set of drawers. The bedside table harboured a tin of biscuits. *Hard to estimate if any had been eaten*, Melissa thought, peering inside. There were two full bottles of water and a pint of milk in the mini-fridge. The bathroom presented a similar picture. No toiletries although the sink contained evidence that a tap had been recently run. Beginning to fuss, Edgar wriggled in her arms, indicating that he'd had enough of being clutched and demanded freedom. Melissa placed him belly down on the carpet and, at a loss, slumped into the only chair. What would Orlando say?

Her perplexed gaze measured the empty room. So this was Alice's reply to the move. She'd never any intention of falling in with Melissa's grand plan. Why Alice couldn't have been honest and simply said so, Melissa couldn't understand. It wasn't as if she were unapproachable. And why choose the night to sneak out?

Had she left because of him?

Had Daddy told the truth?

Melissa screwed her eyes up tight. She didn't want to remember Violet's furious face. She didn't want to recall what was whispered in corners, what was shouted in closed rooms when she and Violet were supposed to be asleep.

Collecting Edgar, Melissa padded downstairs and found her father in the kitchen with Autumn. Over toast and juice, they were playing a game of Snap. He glanced up.

'Have you found her?'

'She's gone.'

'Gone gone, or gone for a walk?'

'She's cleared out.'

'I see.'

'Is that all you have to say?'

'What else is there to say?' Benedict glanced at Autumn. 'In the circumstances, it's for the best.'

'What I don't understand is all the cloak and dagger.'

'SNAP!' Benedict shouted.

'That's not a snap, Gramps. Look.' Autumn spread his cards. 'That's cheating.'

Christ, Melissa thought, *I need to get out of here.* And then a thought, unbidden, leapt out and smacked her on the head.

'Have you been outside this morning, Daddy?'

'No, why do you ask?'

'Here,' she said, pushing Edgar into his grandfather's arms. Speeding outside across the hall, Melissa checked the front door. It was locked, so how had Alice made her escape?

Unless, and as irrational as it sounded, Wren had snaffled Alice and was hiding her at the Granary. Melissa wouldn't put it past her sister.

Still in her nightwear, Melissa let herself out and crossed the gravelled path to Wren's at roughly the same time as Wren, Kai in her arms and mobile crooked into her neck, was making her way to the house.

Dressed in what Melissa would describe as her yoga gear, Wren gave a hearty wave. Melissa waved back and waited.

'Wisdom comes from love in action,' Wren said to whoever was at the other end. 'Yeah, I get it, Serge . . . but . . . okay . . .' Ending the call and ruefully observing Kai, she had the look of a new dog owner that regrets buying a puppy for Christmas. 'God, will I be glad to off-load this one. Had me up all night. Honestly, Liss, I don't know how you do it with two. What?' she said, verbally skidding to a halt.

'You haven't seen Alice?' Melissa asked.

'If I had, do you think I'd be standing here now? Isn't she with you?'

'She's left.'

'*Left*? She can't. I've got a class to prepare for.'

'Her room is entirely bare.'

'Oh, that's great.' Wren stamped a foot in a very similar way to her small niece. 'This is all your fault,' she cried, rounding on Melissa.

'Don't be wet.'

Wren's eyes widened to the size of pizza bases. '*Me*, wet? You're the one limping around, looking bloody miserable all the time. If I'd known you'd become so pathetic, I wouldn't have bothered coming back.'

Once, Melissa would have crumbled under such an attack. Once, she would have agreed that it was her fault. To hell with that.

'Not to worry, you won't have to put up with me a moment longer. Nanny or no nanny, I'm out of here.'

'What, you can't . . .'

'Mum's left a list of instructions in the kitchen. Oh, and I suggest you change your son's nappy before you make a start.'

Heading for freedom, Melissa turned on her heel and left Wren standing.

CHAPTER THIRTY-EIGHT

ROSE

I woke to find my fever broken and Raff, dead to the world next to me, snoring with all the gusto of a petrol-powered lawn mower. I gave him a hearty shove. He grunted and rolled over.

It's strange when you've been out of it for hours. I found myself checking all my limbs to make sure they were still attached to my body and in the right place. Satisfied that I really was feeling better, I sat up and, light-headed, swung my legs out of bed. Feet firmly on the floor, I headed for the bathroom on wobbly pins, peeled off my pyjamas and took a shower. *Bliss.*

I was dressed when Raff finally stirred and cocked open an eye.

'You're looking better,' he mumbled.

'I am.'

'What time is it?'

I told him.

'Oh, God,' he groaned, pitching out of bed. 'I'm going to be so damned late.'

'Late for what? You're your own boss.'

'Doesn't matter.' He staggered about and reached for underwear and trousers. 'Christ, that was a hell of a night. What on earth were you dreaming about?' He ran a hand under his stubbly chin.

'Don't remember,' I lied.

'I never thought I'd say this but we have to have a spare bedroom when we eventually buy our own home. Then you can shout as loud as you like.' He pulled on a T over his head.

'I was shouting?'

'At one stage, yes.' He frowned. 'Are you sure you don't remember?'

I shook my head very slowly. 'Want me to make you a cuppa?'

'Won't have time.' His feet pounded downstairs and he was out of the door before I'd said cheerio.

At least having our place was still on Raff's agenda, I thought happily. There had been times during the last couple of days when I thought we would be trapped at Blackthorn forever.

I made myself tea and toast and considered what to do for the rest of the day. I could have gone to work. I *should* have gone to work. Technically speaking, I could have signed into an online lecture and started my first module. Instead, I trawled social media for signs of the Alice Trinick I knew. She wasn't on Facebook. She didn't exist on X. She was absent from Insta and she didn't appear to subscribe to TikTok. None of it was conclusive — maybe Alice shunned social media. I simply needed to find some indisputable evidence of her official existence, something that would confirm she spoke the truth because, when it came to Alice, I sensed truth was a stranger.

Alice had described Fowey as her home. I found ten breweries close enough to employ her father as Ops Manager. Most breweries listed senior members of staff. Some didn't. Those that didn't, I phoned. Nobody had employed a man going by the name of Jago Trinick.

Bemused, needing fresh air, and despite my mother-in-law's warning, the woods beckoned. Reaching for a pair of shoes, imagine my surprise at seeing Wren loitering outside my front door, a muslin over her shoulder with what looked suspiciously like baby vomit on it. The big smile plastered on her face didn't fool me.

'Heard you weren't well.' A good opening gambit, it made me more suspicious. No way was I letting her over the threshold.

'I'm better now, thanks,' I replied cagily.

'Not going to work?' The strangely hopeful ring in her voice suggested she wanted to come inside for a proper girly chat. I couldn't think of anything worse.

'Not yet.'

'Great, could you have Kai?'

'No way.' I'm not usually this direct, but the situation absolutely demanded a very definite negative. No ifs, no buts.

'It would only be for a couple of hours.' Her shiny white teeth rested on her bottom lip, a sad face accompanying the wheedling tone.

'I'm probably still contagious.'

'Surely—'

'Wait a minute,' I interrupted, 'where's Alice?'

And then it all came out. *Alice gone. Melissa going. Mummy absent.* Essentially, and to quote Wren: *I'm in the shit and need your help.*

Contagious or not, I stepped outside and pushed past Wren.

'Where are you going,' Wren cried.

'Where do you think?' I called back.

I headed up the drive to the house and walked in to find Melissa tearing into Benedict. God alone knew where the children were. Hopefully, playing and out of earshot.

'What on earth were you thinking, Daddy?'

'I didn't realise it was such a big deal.'

'Christ Almighty,' Melissa burst out. 'Have you any idea how this looks? Have you no sense of self-preservation?'

I've seen my sister-in-law upset. I've seen her angry. This was different. Fear generated her anger; I reckon you could power the grid with that level of raw emotion.

Feeling like a bouncer splitting up a fight, I waded in. 'What on earth's going on?'

Melissa tossed her head. 'You tell her,' she spat at her father.

'Alice has left and my daughter is under the impression that it's my fault for conducting myself in an inappropriate manner.'

After the initial silent *bloody hell*, I slipped out my phone and called Alice. The line didn't connect. Didn't even go straight to voicemail. No, she'd definitely had enough and didn't want to be found. I reached for something calming to say. "A misunderstanding," seemed like a good option in the circumstances, but it missed by a couple of miles. Scandal is like an earthquake; it sends tremors into unknown and unexpected places. I'd heard of history repeating itself but everyone knew the history books could be altered.

Melissa wasn't done. 'Why else show the bloody girl the priest hole?'

'What priest hole?' I chipped in. I only had four GCSEs. One was in history. Occasionally, random crap came in handy for a pub quiz. I remembered that during the Elizabethan era, they were created for Catholics to escape persecution and torture. I never realised there was one at Blackthorn.

'The one in the dining hall,' Benedict said. 'And there was nothing funny going on.' His normally smooth features contracted into numerous tight pointy lines.

'When did Alice leave?' I asked.

'Some time during the night,' Melissa replied.

'And the dogs didn't stir?'

Benedict and Melissa exchanged anxious glances. 'No,' they said in unison.

'So she left through the front or back door?'

'Neither,' Melissa said, eyes widening with realisation. 'Both locked from the inside. She must have left through the priest hole.'

And, right now, I couldn't blame her. 'Has anyone checked?' I pressed.

Benedict led the way. I trooped behind him with Melissa.

I watched as Benedict fiddled with something on the panelling. At once, a door, previously concealed, sprung open. It was incredibly dark and I had a memory of a film that terrified me: big fish, jaws open, and a man called dinner.

'I'm not going in there.' Melissa recoiled, white-faced.

'I will if someone fetches a torch,' I said.

Benedict patted his trousers and pulled out a box of matches. They were the long type used for lighting open fires and wood burners.

I struck a match and, holding it aloft, stepped inside. A few paces into darkness you could strangle by, I held my breath.

Christ.

CHAPTER THIRTY-NINE

ROSE

A fist of fear clenched inside me.

I didn't know what I expected to find. It wasn't this.

I'm not superstitious, religious or spiritual, but the foetid air felt messed up, disturbed and replaced with something rotten and decayed, something inherently evil. It put me in mind of the whispered warnings, the helpless drowning terror in my dream.

'Can you see anything?' Melissa called. Her voice bounced through the chamber, boomeranging off the walls and smashing me in the face.

'No,' I shouted back.

I pictured priests huddled together, noble families that sympathised with Mary, Queen of Scots, Elizabeth I's great rival. To be discovered would mean painful death at the stake — *Jesus* — or on the scaffold. Whatever had gone down inside Blackthorn felt more recent, yet there was nothing to suggest that Alice had passed this way. But just because I'd found no evidence didn't mean she hadn't been there. For a young woman keen to cover her tracks, it made sense.

And that bothered me enormously.

My only real experience of the macabre was when my nan, (Dad's mother) passed away. After the undertaker did what undertakers do she was brought back to her house and put in the dining room on the dining room table in an open casket. I'd been taken in to say my goodbyes for the final time. (Not Dad's best idea.) Dead was dead. Nan didn't smell, or anything gross like that, yet the little room reeked of her. Viewing her waxy bloodless face, devoid of expression, I thought she'd already gone someplace else. She was there, but not there and all that remained was the shadow of her existence. I got the same creepy feeling here.

Thin flame spat into the darkness. I pressed on, pain tightening my hunched shoulders, fighting my way through imaginary cobwebs and demons. Breathless, I came to a door, which I put my shoulder against and pushed open. Buttery sunshine tumbled in. I was never gladder to get outside and see the light and breathe fresh air.

Spun out, I walked back around to the front of the house and let myself in. Melissa and Benedict seemed to be engaged in an uneasy truce in the drawing room. No drawing going on, naturally. I'd always thought it a place for words. A powwow room where high-level discussions about the estate and family took place over drinks, against wood panelling and wood fires in the winter, crunchy leaves blowing through the trees in the autumn, chintz and dusty sunshine in the summer. A room for all seasons, the drawing room was the beating heart of Blackthorn. If we were in the middle of a murder mystery, this is where we would assemble and be told who dunnit. Autumn sat cross-legged on the floor, studying a picture book. Edgar rolled around on the carpet, picking up dog hair and all sorts of crap and putting it in his mouth. Disgusting.

'No sign she was ever there,' I announced, sinking into the nearest chair, a battered leather beast with thick padded arms. Alice *had* been there. She just wasn't there anymore.

'See,' Benedict said, palms up.

In answer, Melissa slapped her thighs, stood up and announced she was going upstairs to pack.

'Do you want a hand?' I hoped to corner her.

'Sweet of you, but no.'

I watched as she disappeared with Edgar, Autumn trailing along behind. Benedict followed the little girl with his eyes. He looked like a man who had won the lottery a decade ago, spent the entire fortune, and wound up penniless. Melissa's insinuation that her father was a letch loomed large.

Deeply uncomfortable, I'd have scooted if it hadn't been for Wren bursting in.

'Does anyone know where Mummy is, because sure as hell she isn't at any literary festival?'

'Don't be silly, Wren,' Benedict barked. 'I spoke to her only last night. She and Amelia are having a wonderful time.'

'Daddy, I've literally got off the phone to Amelia who is, indeed, having a wonderful time, but Mummy isn't with her.'

Benedict paled. 'I don't understand.'

'Mummy cried off, said she wasn't feeling well.'

'Well, where the hell is she?'

'There has to be a logical explanation,' I said, struggling to squash flat the thought that Celeste's timing left a lot to be desired. Surely, there was no connection to Alice's disappearance? It had to be coincidence, hadn't it? With a queasy feeling, I wondered what Celeste was up to. In my head I was thinking *alibi*.

'I've even rung around hospitals in the West Country,' Wren said, sounding put out to have actually had to do something.

It staggered me how someone so innately lazy and eager to delegate any task, small or large, to others, was capable of this level of activity. Did I detect a note of panic?

My gaze swivelled from Benedict to Wren and back again. Wren was not the only family member unnerved. Benedict's skin had turned grey. In the space of seconds he'd aged ten years. Was this how he'd looked at the news of Shona Reid's death?

Benedict stood up, distracted.

'Where are you going?' Wren asked in alarm.

'Out,' he said.

'I'll come with you.'

'No,' Benedict said, uncharacteristically brusque.

'But, Daddy . . .'

He stalked off. We both stood, bewildered. Keys rattling, door slamming, gravel crunching, car starting, we caught sight of Benedict's Lexus speeding down the drive, dirt spitting and tail lights flaring.

I had a terrible sense of déjà vu followed by *now what?* I fully expected Wren to renew her plea and dump her baby on me, but the chaos of the last couple of hours had a more profound effect. Muttering under her breath, Wren announced that she was going out and taking her baby with her. Untroubled by her mother's disappearing act, Melissa followed soon afterwards, claiming that she'd come back for the rest of her things later.

Left entirely alone, I set to work.

CHAPTER FORTY

ROSE

If a house could talk, I wanted it to sing a popular soundtrack from my era at the top of its voice. Only then would I be persuaded that everything was fine and dandy.

Instead, complete and utter silence fuelled my strong desire to find evidence that would exonerate Benedict from the charge of infidelity, past and present, account for Alice's sudden disappearance and Celeste's equally mystifying vanishing act. Fired up, I sped upstairs and went straight to Benedict and Celeste's bedroom.

I viewed drapes that cost more than my monthly salary, large sash windows with breathtaking views over Blackthorn land and those of neighbouring estates; a vast bed with a million cushions, a couple of plush easy chairs *and* a sofa; a desk (I vaguely remembered that Raff had informed me it was called a Davenport), gorgeous wallpaper and dove-grey panelling. Bedside lamps were antique. A chandelier, a revelation of glamour and style, hung from the ornate ceiling.

Celeste's taste in reading was highbrow and literary with Booker prize-winners among her stash; Benedict's was thriller and spy fiction. I headed for his side of the bed and noticed the latest novel from Mick Herron on the bedside table.

I discovered Benedict's man drawer in a mahogany chest. It revealed old currency, pocket-sized tissues, painkillers (not wise with little kids about, I thought), three boxes of gold cufflinks, a small torch, a mini screwdriver, a set of brown shoelaces, unopened, and a couple of USB connection leads. No wallet. Old receipts indicated long lunches and a recent visit to Gardiner Haskins in Cirencester where he'd purchased several tins of paint and a hammer. The last item made me swallow. *Don't be so ridiculous.*

Unlike Benedict's higgledy-piggledy approach, Celeste's items were arranged as if each inhabited their own select space and didn't care for disruption. Undeterred, and with only a smidgeon of guilt, I pored through perfumes (Chanel and Jo Malone), another set of pocket-sized tissues, printed minutes of a parish council meeting (yawn), a jewellery box — risky — and a password code book — very risky. I flicked through the latter and discovered nothing particularly eye-catching. More out of curiosity than believing it might prove a game-changer, I opened the jewellery box and was surprised to find a rose gold bracelet with the clasp broken, a cheap necklace that had seen better days and an assortment of trinkets and mismatched earrings. Obviously, the good stuff was held elsewhere, probably in a safe, except I didn't know where this was. Even if I did, I was no safecracker. Sifting through the bling with my fingers, I sat back on my haunches with a start. Nestled in my hand, Art deco in style and in the shape of a tiny fan, was the twin-sister to the earring I'd found at the shack in the woods, the place Celeste claimed never to visit.

She could have lost it years ago, I told myself. Yes, that made sense, which came as a relief in a series of incidents that stubbornly evaded explanation. I hastily put it back.

With seconds ticking by, I didn't know how much longer I had before someone turned up. I could blag it with Benedict — *maybe* — but Celeste was a different proposition. What if she was out of contact because she was driving and on her way home? Coming face to face with me in her bedroom, she wouldn't accept my lame excuse that I was trying to trace her whereabouts.

Stomach jittering with nerves, I had one last piece of furniture in my sights: the walnut writing bureau. Four drawers ran down the side with highly polished knobs like buttons on a military dress coat. To my disappointment, each section proved empty. I moved on to the leather-inlaid desk with a sloped lid like a piano top. Lifting it open revealed a treasure trove of compartments, again, every one of them empty. No, I lie — I found a fifty-pence piece. The less I found, the guiltier I felt. These were my in-laws; people who, for the most part, accepted me as one of theirs and here was I snooping and prying. And yet I couldn't stop myself. It was as if, let loose in places I wasn't supposed to be — like Alice in the priest hole — I was on a roll.

And then inspiration struck.

Raff was a terror for cramming his pockets with all sorts of nonsense. I've unearthed packets of chewing gum, mints, bits of tree, a written reminder to buy a birthday present for me — seriously damping down the surprise element — paper clips, receipts and, once, a half-eaten rock bun. Some of these wound up in the washing machine. *Pockets next*, I thought.

Heart hammering, I stole into the dressing room adjoining the en-suite bathroom. Beautifully fitted wardrobes flanked three walls. Celeste's clothing dominated. Whether dress, shirt or skirt, she obviously had a thing for pale coral and soft pink, splashed with the odd shade of blue. Her shoe collection displayed similar taste. Benedict chose a more limited palette: olive greens, greys, navy and the occasional pink. He favoured brogues for winter wear and loafers for summer. His trademark flip-flops were nowhere to be seen. (I couldn't remember if he was wearing them.) Coats and jackets hung in separate compartments. Glancing over the entire wardrobe, this definitely divided into His and Hers.

I started with Benedict's and ran my fingers through the pockets of a very nice bankers-style trench coat in dark blue. Next: gilets and fleeces, followed by a battered short leather number, circa 1980. Right at the end, a waterproof jacket, favoured by the hunting, shooting and fishing fraternity. It had two deep pockets at the front with two fleece-lined hand warmers at the side. A bulge in the left pocket revealed a hip flask. I unscrewed the top. The strong whiff of brandy completely neutralised the equally strong scent of Celeste's perfume. Nerves properly jangling, I resisted the temptation to take a swig. A fan of homespun philosophy, my mum always tells me that if you want something badly enough you have to make things happen. So I did and then seriously wished I hadn't.

CHAPTER FORTY-ONE

ROSE

The photograph was zipped inside a security pocket in Benedict's all-weather jacket. I didn't know how long it had been there. Perhaps it was moved around in the same way a fleeing dictator with a bounty on his head sleeps in a different location every night. Is this what Melissa had suspected all along? I dreaded to think what would happen to Benedict if Celeste unearthed it. Crinkled and in colour, it measured roughly six by six centimetres and displayed a young woman with a glorious mane of red hair that fell around her shoulders. Her complexion was milk-white. Her eyes were bright blue and she laughed at something, or someone. If you could bottle joy, she was it. A tight-fitting sweater suggested a full figure, a check-print mini-skirt displayed long legs. It's difficult to estimate height from a photograph, but I thought she was taller than average. On her feet, shoes with thick heels and a bar across that I'd only ever seen in my mum's wardrobe. These were the visual details of the stranger with the big heart. And yes, silly as it is, this is what I read and I like to think I'm pretty good at reading people. I also recognised where the photograph was taken. Iconic, with shops on both sides and swirling white water below, the bridge on which the woman stood was Pulteney Bridge in Bath, roughly an hour's drive away. To remove any element of doubt about the woman's identity, her name was written on the back of the snap in faint pencil: *Shona*.

Why would Benedict carry around a photograph of Shona Reid if she hadn't meant something special to him?

I am a champion eavesdropper — I put it down to my lonely child upbringing. Not that it was Poppy's fault, she was poorly and demanded so much of my parent's time and energy. For the most part I was happy in my own world, the one where children didn't get sick and die. The problem with overheard conversations is that you only receive snippets taken out of context. You might be able to catch a tone. Rarely can you observe the body language of the speakers. You can't divine their facial expressions. You can't read the atmosphere. In other words, you can be wrong. Suddenly, Celeste's accusation didn't seem a case of naked jealousy. No wonder the poor woman feared history was about to repeat itself with Alice's arrival. I'd thought Melissa was too hard on Benedict. In the light of my discovery, she could have been right to accuse her father of *inappropriate behaviour*.

Whatever the truth, it made me sad to think that Shona Reid, someone this lovely, with everything to live for, had met such a shocking and untimely end. God, Shona was probably my age when she died.

And that set me thinking about the nature of her death. An accident, everyone said. What if it wasn't? What if my gut reaction all along spoke of something steeped in darkness.

Fear burst into the back of my throat and lobbed a stun grenade.

I'd read about serial killers who carried trophies to remind them of their victims. No, don't go there. If only I could get hold of Alice and prove that her disappearance had an innocent explanation.

Slipping out my phone, I took a snap of the Shona picture and, with trembling hands, slipped the photograph back inside the jacket, zipped it up and prayed nobody would notice.

Creeping out onto the landing, I nearly passed out at the definite noise of someone tramping around below. It wouldn't be Melissa. I doubted it would be Wren. That left Benedict or Celeste who, no doubt, would have some explaining to do. Not that I could blame the woman for going walkabout after my recent discovery.

Stealing downstairs, my destination the front door, I had to cross the big hall, a Grand Canyon of a room, with obstacles that to my mind, were designed to trip me up, or give me away. The sound of footsteps got louder and it occurred to me that whoever was on the prowl was not about to cut in from either the drawing room or snug, but from behind me. Crap, I was about to be rumbled.

Deciding to front it out, I whipped round and came face to face with a cross looking woman with *don't screw with me* eyebrows. To hell with that, I'd had enough shocks and surprises to last me a lifetime.

'Who are you?' I demanded to know.

Towering above me and solidly built (think shield-maiden), the stranger let the full might of her imperious gaze crash down and crush me into the flagstone floor.

'My name is Carmen Albescu,' she announced in a thick foreign accent I couldn't place. 'I have come for my baby boy and I will not leave until *you*,' she said, poking me hard in the chest, 'give him back.'

CHAPTER FORTY-TWO

ROSE

Things thudded into place, which was saying something when it came to the Percivals. The mystery over Kai's dad, the fact that Kai looked nothing like Wren, Wren's inability to breastfeed and her surprising lack of maternal affection (which I'd never considered to be a case of postnatal depression) made perfect sense. As I understood it — and I had no experience to support the view other than trashy real-life magazines — women who snatched other women's babies, were often unstable due to an inability to have children of their own or had sadly lost an infant. Usually, the abductor became obsessively besotted with the baby they claimed to be their own. They loved them. They cared for them. This. Was. Not. Wren.

In the seconds it took me to put that lot together, Carmen was advancing on me with clenched fists. Despite the language barrier, it was easy enough to deduce that the woman with the beautiful face and murderous eyes wanted to rip my head off. And she was tall. Very.

'No, no,' I said, palms up. 'It wasn't me. It was my sister-in-law, Wren.' Yes, I really said that. What a snitch.

Once I'd vociferously stated that I was no kidnapper, which took some doing, I did what my mum taught me to do in a crisis. I invited a marginally calmer Carmen into the kitchen, made her a cup of tea and listened to her tale of woe. In stuttering English she explained that her baby, whose real name was Marius, was trafficked for four thousand pounds.

'Oh my God, your baby was snatched?'

'By my dirt bag of a father.'

I stared goggle-eyed. What a greedy, heartless tosser. The big question: how was Wren involved in such a despicable act?

Fat tears cut a silent path down Carmen's cheeks. 'He is my baby. It is not right what has been done.'

It wasn't. I rested my hand on her knee, gave it a pat and handed her a clean tissue from my pocket.

'Thank you,' she said, drying her eyes. If I cry, my nose goes red and my mascara runs, sending tramlines down my cheeks. In distress, Carmen was even more stunning. Big, dark, liquid brown eyes in a perfectly oval face, she could have been a model and certainly had the height and figure. She was the kind of woman that would even have looked good dressed in an old coat covered in cement dust and rescued from a skip.

'Is my baby well?' Carmen asked, sudden desperation in her eyes. 'He is not sick? He is cared for?'

'Yes, yes,' I said. 'Until today, he had a nanny looking after him.'

Her jaw dropped. Her eyebrows formed the shape of arrowheads. '*Another* woman?'

I sensed that Carmen's emotional temperature was generally set to high. It wouldn't take long to dial it up to max.

'She was lovely,' I said, thinking *was she?* 'Very caring. There are a number of children here. Well, there were,' I finished awkwardly. Keen to diffuse Carmen's sudden spurt of anger, I asked, 'How did you find us?'

'I talk to people. I get information.' The dark expression on her face was accompanied with a dramatic toss of her head. 'The thieving bitch who took my baby hired a fishing vessel.'

The thought of Wren stowing away with a ton of haddock almost made me laugh. I was smart enough to keep my face straight.

'I know one of the men,' Carmen explained. 'Your sister-in-law is not so good at keeping her mouth shut. She is . . . how do you say . . . *poser?* She showed pictures on her phone, her lovely house, her grounds, her life, her . . .'

I tuned out and, glancing at the kitchen clock, wondered who'd return first. I hadn't yet processed Celeste's vanishing act, the issue of the earring and, the bigger problem, the photograph.

The weight of Carmen's expectation sat heavy on my shoulders. In her eyes I was the link, the person who could facilitate the release of her son. I was a fixer. In desperation, I called Raff. I had a shedload to tell him.

'Hiya,' he said, all fresh and bright.

My husband's ability to bounce back after a bad night's sleep never ceased to amaze me. If I didn't get a good eight hours, I was like an extra from *The Walking Dead.* I didn't mess about. 'We have a problem.' Several, actually.

'Uh-huh.' Still with the game voice and fluffy attitude. He'd be thinking the fridge was broken or my car wouldn't start.

'Kai isn't Wren's baby.' I let that sink in and then, making eye contact with Carmen, I continued, 'and his mother is sitting right in front of me in your parents' kitchen.'

'Bloody hell.' No doubt it took the shine off his morning. Wait until he heard what else I had to report but, in the immediate crisis, Alice and Celeste's disappearances would have to keep. I wasn't going to fess up to rummaging through his parents' wardrobes either. I'd have to think of some other way to explain what I'd unearthed. *Maybe.*

'Raff, I wouldn't normally ask but . . .'

'I'm up the road at Stoyle Manor. Be with you in fifteen.'

Thank God the cavalry were about to arrive.

'Your husband?' Carmen said.

'Yes.'

'He will not like what he hears.'

'No.'

'The woman who took my child,' Carmen said suspiciously. (I was imagining blades and meat-cleavers.) 'Where is she?'

'Out, but I'm certain she'll be back soon.' I bloody hoped so.

'Who else lives here?'

I told her.

'This place,' Carmen said, with an elegant hand gesture that encompassed the general area in which we were sitting, 'it is very grand, very big.'

'Yes.'

'You live here too?'

'Passing through.' And quickly, *please*.

CHAPTER FORTY-THREE

ROSE

Raff was as good as his word. Whatever he really thought, he didn't let on. Switching up to full-on practical and business-like mode, he warmly shook Carmen's hand on introduction. I guess the short drive had allowed the shock to subside. I, for one, was still reeling.

'You have toilet?' Carmen asked.

I showed her the cloakroom. Raff practically pounced when I joined him in the kitchen. 'Jesus Christ,' he hissed. 'Do you think she's who she says she is?'

I was taken aback. Raff's smooth and considerate mask hadn't slipped. It had fallen and smashed into a zillion pieces on the floor. I pictured myself picking my way through.

'I don't think she's lying.'

'It's a scam.'

The thought hadn't occurred to me.

'Bet this was all cooked up in Bucharest.' Raff's lips twisted in disgust.

'You can't deny Kai bears a striking similarity to Carmen.'

Raff gave a snort. 'He's a *baby*. At that age they don't look like anyone.'

'He has similar colouring and his eyes are brown.'
'Down the paternal line.'
'His mysterious dad. Right,' I said cynically.
'You're suggesting Wren is lying?'
I was suggesting a lot more than that. 'Well, there's a very simple way to find out. A DNA test should do the trick.'
That was as far as we got before Carmen strode back in.
'I am hungry,' she announced.
Raff gave me a "told you so" look and said he was going outside to make some calls.

Thankfully, Carmen had simple tastes. A quick raid of the pantry, more a grocery store, unearthed cold ham, cheeses, pickles and artisan crackers (according to the blurb) with packaging that cost more than the ingredients.

I made more tea (for my benefit) and watched Carmen eat like a wolf. Maybe Raff was right. Maybe Carmen Albescu wasn't her real name. Florence always says that to make a lie stick, you flavour it with truth. I could easily picture a chance conversation in a bar in which Wren had boasted and shown photographs of her folks' place back home. As I recalled, Wren claimed to have given birth to Kai in Berlin, not Romania.

'Good,' Carmen said, pushing the plate away and patting her tummy. 'Now we wait.'

And so we did. Running out of small talk and in danger of losing my mind, I was pleased to see Raff saunter back in a better mood than the one with which he'd left.

'Ma's on her way back,' he announced.
'From where?' I asked casually.
'The Lit Fest.'
'According to Wren, who spoke to Amelia, your mother cried off. She was quite adamant.' Not strictly true, but it got the message across.

'Wren's such a drama queen,' Raff said, tutting. 'Ma had a tummy bug and, not wishing to pass it on, stayed in her room for twenty-four hours.'

'That's what she told you?'

Raff cracked a smile. 'Rose, you've got to stop being so suspicious. Not everyone lies.'

'Much people do,' Carmen chipped in, glowering.

Grateful for the show of support from an unlikely direction, admittedly, I recognised that when the two people you care most about in the world point out the same character defect, they usually have a point. What was it Florence said? *Jeez, Rose, I'd hate to be you. Not everyone and everything is dodgy.*

'Has your mum spoken to Benedict and Wren? They were really worried, Raff.'

'Misunderstanding all smoothed over,' Raff insisted.

At the sound of tyres on gravel, he glanced out of the window. 'Dad's back with Wren and . . .' Raff shot me a look, '. . . the baby.'

Carmen leapt to her feet as if someone had thrown boiling oil over them.

'I think it's important we all stay calm.' I was anxious to avoid a scene while realising one was inevitable. Equally keen to avoid a punch-up, Raff offered to act as the advance party and "have a word".

I shook my head. 'Let's see Wren's reaction. If the baby is hers, she'll stand her ground. If not, she'll crumble.'

With three pairs of eyes focused on the door, I thought Solomon had got nothing on me. But then Solomon hadn't had Wren Percival to deal with.

CHAPTER FORTY-FOUR

ROSE

I once saw a catfight kick off outside a pub in the middle of Gloucester. It wasn't pretty. Thank God, Benedict had been carrying the baby.

For a tall big-boned woman, Carmen moved at astounding speed. I had time to catch the look of blind astonishment on Wren's face before Carmen lumped Wren one and followed up with a flurry of sharp slaps to her face.

Hands clamped to her head, Wren let out a heart-attack inducing scream that sent Raff running to her side. Undeterred by someone bigger and heavier, Carmen continued to throw punches and it took all of Raff's strength to restrain her and not before she'd gouged a hole in his face. Alarmed, Benedict handed me Kai, aka Marius, and went to assist.

'I bought him fair and square,' Wren yelled.

'*Bought*?' Anger surged through me. 'You can't buy a baby. It's illegal.'

'Rose, please,' Benedict said, clasping Wren tightly.

'You see, I tell you, this woman is a witch,' Carmen thundered. To make the point, she gave Raff a sharp jab with her elbow in an attempt to shake him off.

'Are you going to be good?' Raff's voice was uncompromising.

'I want my child.' Carmen's dark eyes found mine. 'Please,' she said, appealing to me.

With Wren throwing me death stares, I handed Carmen the baby. Carmen gazed at him in wonder, stroked his cheek with her finger then, quite unconsciously, unbuttoned her blouse and put the baby to her breast.

'Bitch,' Wren cursed.

'Shut up and sit down,' Raff told her.

Good on you, I thought.

Benedict turned to Wren with a pained expression. 'Darling, Rose has a point, I'm afraid.'

'But, Daddy, this is so unfair,' Wren whined. 'Kai's grandfather only wanted his grandchild to have a better life in the UK. I was doing him a good turn.'

Yeah, four thousand pounds worth of good turn, I thought.

Carmen glanced up. 'This is bullshit,' she said. I couldn't have agreed more. Not that this deterred Wren.

'He told me his daughter had got pregnant by a married man.'

The poisonous edge to Wren's revelation would have felled most. I glanced at Carmen. Unconcerned, she didn't deny it.

'She's dirt poor,' Wren said, eager to lob another accusation. 'She could never afford to give Kai—'

'His name is Marius,' Carmen said, her gaze entirely focused on her baby.

'... the kind of life he could have here,' Wren continued. 'Think of all the advantages: a lovely home, proper schooling, a career, a *future*.'

'Without his birth mother,' I said. 'In a country that isn't his own.'

Wren's green eyes shrivelled to two nasty little dots. 'You're not going to go all nationalistic on us, are you, Rose?'

'I'm going all truthful on you, Wren, a quality you're unfamiliar with.'

'You little—'

'Raff, why don't you and Rose go back to yours and take Wren with you?'

Oh, great, I thought, glaring at my sister-in-law. I could see what Benedict was doing. He wanted us to go away, calm down and kiss and make up. Fat chance.

'I'm not going anywhere,' Wren said. 'Kai is mine.'

'And this is my house and you will do as you're told,' Benedict growled. 'Your mother will be home soon.'

This seemed to have a loosening effect on Wren's resolve. She didn't look happy about it, but she took a step towards Raff.

'Rose?' Benedict said. I tried and failed to banish the photograph I'd found of Shona Reid from my mind.

'No,' I said, 'I'm staying.' I wasn't going to leave Carmen on her own with Benedict.

Raff threw me a puzzled look but didn't argue. 'Okay, if you're sure.'

'I hope you've got booze in the house,' Wren muttered, following Raff out.

CHAPTER FORTY-FIVE

MELISSA

Melissa could breathe again.

After picking up groceries and essentials for the rental in Sapperton, she'd spent the last few hours stocking the fridge in their new surroundings, making up beds and settling the children. Edgar was easy enough to please. Autumn, an inquisitive little girl, was less biddable. She'd asked straightaway, 'Where's Alice?'

'She's gone home to see her mummy and daddy, darling,' Melissa replied.

Anxious that her child would miss her grandparents and ask more awkward questions, Melissa had read stories, played games and allowed Autumn to watch a cartoon on her phone. Melissa swore that the tranquil, uncomplicated environment was as good for her children as it was for her.

Yet how soon before the ghosts of her childhood seeped to the surface to haunt her? Not long.

Melissa fiercely loved her father to the point of blindness.

She'd heard the rumours — how could she not? And Violet had her theories and had paid a terrible price for voicing them. But rumours and theories didn't amount to the truth. There's a huge difference between being told something and believing what you're told. Even if Dad *had* strayed thirty years ago, it didn't mean that Shona's death was anything other than an accident. It definitely didn't indicate that Alice Trinick's disappearance was some kind of action replay. She'd been with the family for less than a month, for goodness' sake.

Yet Rose's deathly white gaze after creeping inside the priest hole was all too evident, as if she'd seen something that defied reality, as if the house was finally giving up its secrets to a stranger. Melissa shut her eyes, bunched her fists, mentally shutting out and shutting down. She should have found it easier now that Alice was gone. *Should have.*

Had Dad lied about his attraction to Alice? Stumbling across them in the kitchen the morning after the party, Melissa was certain she'd seen them behaving intimately. What was her father thinking by showing Alice the priest hole? Did he plan some kind of assignation with her in the garden? Melissa had practically been forced to wrench a comment out of him. And he'd looked so shifty.

Her temple throbbed with thinking. Melissa placed her hand to her head to try to ease it. Hunting for Alice that morning had reawakened old memories of her and Violet's frantic search for Shona, a woman who had loved them and cared for them more than their own mother. With two distracted parents nurturing a fledgling business on a tight budget, it was Shona they went to when they were sad, Shona they wanted to please and Shona who made them happy. She was the one constant in a chaotic home life and they had loved her. When she left, their world changed forever. Afterwards, Violet didn't veer off the rails. She hurtled. Raff and Wren were too young to appreciate the seismic consequences of Shona's dismissal. Rightly or wrongly, Violet blamed their mother and, ever since, Melissa had taken her father's side on everything. In the light of what she'd witnessed more recently, and probably unfairly, her mother, with her bossy ways and officious manner, was such an easy woman to cast as a villain. One thing was certain: her mum would be delighted to see the back of Alice Trinick. She'd never wanted her there in the first place.

CHAPTER FORTY-SIX

ROSE

Thrilled to be home, Celeste breezed in with a big smile.

'Darling,' she gushed, throwing her arms around Benedict, hugging him tight. My father-in-law's stiff body language suggested he wasn't as easily persuaded by his wife's explanation as his son.

I had to admire Celeste's front. She was lively in her dismissal of such a "silly misunderstanding". Wren's panic had seemed genuine enough as had Benedict's grumpy reaction, as had Raff's calm reassurance. Truth was, I no longer recognised what or who to believe.

'Hello, Rose,' Celeste said chirpily. 'Where is everyone?'

I looked to Benedict. *Your mess. You explain.* As soon as Celeste's car headed up the drive, he'd suggested that Carmen take Kai into the snug, while he broke the news of her existence to his wife. Feeling protective, I decided to adopt a low profile and join her. Hiding in plain sight was a trick I'd perfected since I'd been involved with the Percivals. You learnt more, although clearly not enough, I thought, nipping next door.

Celeste's response to "the Carmen situation" could probably be heard all over the county. Certainly, Carmen's poor grasp of English proved no barrier. We exchanged nervous glances and Carmen grasped her baby a little tighter. 'I go,' she said, suddenly standing up.

'Where?'

'Home.'

Judging by the determined set of her jaw, I think she really meant to walk straight out of the house, down the drive and hitch a lift, rucksack on her back and Marius in her arms. I didn't know whether Carmen had a ticket, money, or a plan. The similarity with Alice's predicament startled me. Both trapped women. Both dead keen to escape. While I was summoning up the courage to offer Carmen a lift to the train station, Benedict bowled in, followed by Celeste. Meek was not a word I'd use to describe my mother-in-law and God alone knew how Benedict had managed it, and yet she stood dutifully beside him, like a politician's wife playing a fake role for the camera.

'Carmen,' Benedict said, wearing a greasy smile that showed his teeth. 'Please, we want you to stay as our guest.'

I didn't know whether Carmen looked to me for a translation or advice. I minutely shook my head. *Go. Leave. While you can.*

'She can have Alice's old room,' Celeste blustered.

'What about the baby?' I stuttered.

'I think we can make an accommodation,' Celeste replied, meeting my eye. 'Until we've reached a reasonable solution.'

The edge in her voice cut into my bones. She would back Wren and, despite Wren's absence of maternal instinct, I couldn't see my sister-in-law giving up Kai easily. Carmen, on the other hand, would fight like a tigress for her son. It could never end well.

'I'll shoot across to the Granary to fetch the baby's crib and blankets,' Benedict announced, clearly keen to be doing rather than listening. With an unsettling sense of déjà vu, I showed Carmen to Alice's room. I felt queasy walking inside. It was cool and empty and there was no suggestion of recent habitation. Eager to leave, I felt Carmen's warm hand on my arm.

'Thank you,' she said.

'You're welcome. I . . .'

'Yes?'

I cleared my throat. 'Phone,' I said, 'Do you have one?'

Carmen nodded. 'I'll put in my number,' I said, gesturing what I wanted to do. 'Anything you want, I'm in the lodge at the bottom of the drive.' I entered my contact details.

Carmen nodded again and I thought how blissfully happy she appeared now that she was reunited with her child.

At the lodge, Wren was banging on to her long-suffering brother about how she'd spent the last ten years "figuring out her life" and, "Oh my God, how personal growth hurts so much" and now that she had got life sorted/figured, it had all "gone to ratshit". Raff glanced across with a "Help — get me out of here" expression as I parked myself on his lap. Before Wren continued to dribble on I gave the low-down on what had been agreed at the house.

'What?' Wren exploded.

'It's Carmen's child,' I countered.

'Yes, but . . .'

'There is no *but*. You're lucky Carmen isn't going to prosecute you.'

'I beg your pardon?'

'She's right, Wren,' Raff said. 'You've done some dim things in your life but this has to be the stupidest.'

'Well, thanks very much for the brotherly support.' Surging with anger, Wren drained her drink and slammed down her glass. Before anyone could remonstrate, she jumped up and headed for the door. I made to move but Raff stopped me.

'Leave her,' he said. 'Any more of her bloody whining and I'll report her to the police myself.'

I slipped my arms around his neck and gave him a hug. 'I'm so sorry about all this.' I was but I was also glad we were on the same side.

'Not your fault. What a shitshow.'
'Did Wren tell you about Alice?' I asked.
'She did. Blimey, it's all happening today.'
'I suppose.'
Raff inclined his head. 'What's up?'
'I thought Alice might have said something to me rather than upping and leaving.'
'You weren't that matey with her. She's only been here five minutes. And Alice was never happy about moving with Melissa and Orlando.'
'I know but...'
He drew away. 'But what?'
'Oh, it's nothing.'
He squeezed my ribs. 'Fibber.'
'It's so strange. Both doors were locked. The dogs didn't make a sound. The security alarm never triggered.'
Raff frowned. 'That *is* strange.'
'Melissa and Benedict think she might have escaped through the priest hole.'
His eyes screwed up in surprise. 'Seriously? Did Alice even know about the priest hole?'
'Apparently, she did.' Colour rose in my cheeks. 'Where do you think she went?'
'Home, I guess.'
Wherever that was.
'You have to admit, Alice was a little strange,' Raff said.
Stranger than any of us realised, I thought.

CHAPTER FORTY-SEVEN

MELISSA

'I knew it,' Melissa barked, triumphant. 'No way in hell had Wren given birth to the baby, but trafficking? She's really surpassed herself this time.'

This was the conversation she imagined she'd have with her mother who'd phoned to break the news. Instead, Melissa said: 'Oh dear. What an appalling state of affairs.'

'Quite,' her mother said crisply.

'What are you going to do?'

'Act quickly.'

Melissa felt a pinch of alarm. 'How?'

'Pay the woman off and let her go quietly.'

'With the baby, of course.'

'Unfortunately, I see no other option.'

'Surely, it's for the best, Mummy.' *Surely, even you can see that.*

'I suppose. I was rather enjoying having another baby in the house, especially now you've moved out.'

Melissa refused to take the bait and embraced silence.

'Poor Wren is beside herself,' her mother continued.

'I'm sorry to hear that.' If Wren was beside herself it was with frustration and petulance. Glad to be miles away from the metaphorical crime scene, Melissa glanced affectionately at her children. Autumn was playing quietly at the kitchen table with Play-Doh. Edgar was rolling around on his play mat.

'How was the literary fest?'

'What? Oh that, yes. Apart from my twenty-four hour tummy bug — so annoying. Poor Daddy thought I'd gone walkabout.'

'Why would he think that?'

'With my head down a lavatory I wasn't taking calls.'

'But you're all better now?'

'Fighting fit. And how are you getting on without help with the children?'

'I'm enjoying it.'

'Good.'

The trite response suggested to Melissa that this was not the answer her mother wanted to hear.

'And have you spoken to Orlando?'

'Not recently, why?'

'Shouldn't he be informed about the Alice situation?'

'There is no situation,' Melissa said.

'He's bound to be annoyed.'

He wasn't entitled to be annoyed, Melissa thought, though her mother was probably right. She had a knack of reading her son-in-law's moods and foibles. 'Anyway, Mummy, I'd better let you get on,' she said, cutting the call mercifully short.

CHAPTER FORTY-EIGHT

ROSE

I couldn't wait to escape to work on Saturday morning. As far as I could glean, high-level negotiations were taking place in a febrile atmosphere — was there any other? — at Blackthorn Central. I suspected that some underhand deal was in the offing and said as much to Raff over a hurried breakfast.

'Like what, Rose?'

Chewing a piece of toast, I shrugged and swallowed. 'Marius is Carmen's baby. What is there to discuss other than a refund and a ticket home for the pair of them?'

'What about Wren?'

'What about her?'

'She's obviously formed an attachment—'

'You think? She doesn't seem that bothered to me.'

'That's harsh.'

'It's true. She has as much maternal inclination as . . .' I was going to say *me* but thought better of it, '. . . a crocodile.'

'Actually, they're quite affectionate with their young,' Raff said seriously.

'Get you, David Attenborough.'

He cracked a smile. 'But Wren has a point about the kind of life Kai could have here other than the one he'd have in Romania.'

'That's not her decision to make. And aren't you a teeny bit prejudiced?'

'What?'

'A lousy student trip to Bucharest is no way to judge a country.'

'You got me,' he said with a grin. Drawing me close, toast and all, he said, 'We're lucky, aren't we? Everyone around us in crisis and there's us completely out of it.'

Hmm, I thought, planting a big buttery kiss on his cheek. Disentangling myself, I went to clean my teeth before following Raff out of the lodge to our vehicles. Raff went one way in his pick-up, me the other in the Mini.

If I have time, I study my client list for the day. Most are regulars, as much in need of a reassuring natter as a haircut. I could count on the fingers of one hand, clients who nodded and smiled and expressed thanks to your face then, the moment they got home, reached for a phone to complain about the style or colour. Worse if they post a stinky review online. When I noticed that Judith Mariner was scheduled in, weeks early, I collared Mandy, our receptionist, and asked if there was any particular reason for Mrs M's appointment.

'Special occasion,' Mandy said. 'We were only able to fit her in because you had a cancellation.'

The special occasion turned out to be an award ceremony for Mr Mariner in which he was to receive a Lifetime Achievement award for services to commerce.

'It's at the Savoy. Going to be quite a do,' Mrs Mariner informed me, as I snuck a towel around her neck. 'I have to look my best.'

'When is it?' I asked, washing her hair.

'Tomorrow night. We're catching the train later.'

A kind woman, Mrs M asked about my family and Raff's. Flushing with the lie, I gave the standard "they're fine" replies.

'I feel quite guilty for not visiting Maud as often as I should. We're all so busy these days; a standard excuse, I'm afraid, but it's the truth.'

'I'm sure she'd understand.' The germ of an idea seeded at the back of my brain. 'Which home did you say she was in?'

'Did I? Oh, it's one of the better ones. Doesn't smell of cabbage and urine and the staff are friendly. Believe me, it's not always the case,' Mrs Mariner said, with a meaningful expression. 'Wintercourt Residential Home is very much the upper end of the care home spectrum and quite civilised. Mind, it costs a fortune, not that this poses a problem for Maud de Grey. Guests — that's what they call them — even have a sherry in the evenings before dinner.'

I smiled. 'That's nice. Have I taken enough off, Jude?'

'Perfect,' Mrs Mariner said.

Later, when I finished work, I dropped Carmen a message:
Are you okay?
Yes.
Is Marius okay?
She posted a big smiley emoji back.

Conscience salved, I drove home. Raff arrived earlier than usual for a Saturday in September and cooked a mean spaghetti Bolognese. He didn't suggest we saw Wren, or dropped in to the parents. It was just he and I and a bottle of wine shared over a nice dinner and a movie. Making love felt natural and fun and I wasn't hung up about someone watching, or bursting in with breaking news. Next morning, Raff asked if I was seeing my folks as usual.

I reminded him that they were on holiday in Lanzarote. 'Thought I'd pop over to Florence's. Weekends are so miserable for her without Jamie.'

'I'm hoping to be done by lunchtime. Thought we could slope off somewhere.'

'What? No Sunday lunch with the parents?' I joked.

'Thought we could all do with a little space. How does the Golden Cross sound?'

'You'll never get in.' Sunday lunches were legendary. I reckoned there was a black-market trade in bookings.

'Table is already set for 2.00 p.m.'

'My hero.' I gave Raff a hug and promised to meet him back at the lodge in plenty of time. 'I'll drive so you can enjoy a pint,' I told him.

I found Florence at home rearranging the clothes in her drawers Marie Kondo style. 'Christ, I'm bored. Not quite *let's clean the oven* bored, but you get the picture.'

'Sounds great to me,' I said.

'Cuppa?' Florence said with a penetrating look.

I watched as she chucked tea bags into two mugs and boiled a kettle. 'How's the new client?' I asked.

Florence's face fell. 'The new client went back to her husband.'

'Well, I guess that's good.'

'Until next time,' Florence said. 'Anyway, you didn't come here to ask me about work.'

'No.' Raff had been so thoughtful I felt guilty for giving voice to my worries. Confiding in Florence would spare Raff from me whining on about his parents. At least, that's how I sold it to myself.

'Am I to gather that life with the in-laws isn't panning out?'

'I don't know where to begin.'

'At the beginning?'

'This has a beginning, a middle and end.'

'I love a good story.'

So off I went.

'Alice upped and left?' Florence broke in.

I swallowed hard in an effort to forget the creepy, claustrophobic sensation I'd experienced in the priest hole.

'Cleared out.'

'Should make life easier.'

I didn't say yes, didn't say no, and continued until I'd finished.

'Bloody hell, Rose. You actually went through Benedict and Celeste's wardrobe?' Florence was aghast.

'Means and ends,' I said stoutly. 'Here, take a look.' I brandished my phone with the picture of Shona Reid on it.

Florence gaped. 'What a glorious-looking woman, so full of life.'

'That's what I thought.'

Florence looked up sharply and pushed the phone back into my hands.

'You go poking around in other people's business you're going to get burned. I'd hate to think what someone would find in my dirty linen drawer.'

Florence had never so much as had a parking ticket, let alone something worse. In answer to my questioning look, she elevated an eyebrow.

'You didn't tell Raff that you'd been on a detective hunt through his parents' belongings, did you?'

'No.'

'Promise me, you'll never say a word.'

'But what if . . .'

'Rose, Rose,' Florence said, exasperated. 'Seriously. *Everyone* has skeletons in their cupboards.'

'That's what I'm afraid of.'

'Look,' Florence said, running a hand through her hair, 'it's sad what happened, but Shona Reid's death was a tragic *accident*. Whatever went on beforehand is nobody's business.'

'Then why is everyone behaving so weirdly about it years later?'

'Because they *cared*.' Florence leaned towards me. 'You have to stop this, Rose. Your ridiculous compulsion to unearth imaginary secrets will eat you up and—' she raised an index finger '——it will affect your relationship with Raff.'

Ouch. I quietly sipped my tea.

'I'm telling you as a friend,' Florence said gently, clearly scared she'd hurt my feelings.

'I know.' I sounded sheepish. I felt guilty; no way was I going to miss the opportunity to pay Maud de Grey a visit.

'We're good?'

'Yes.'

Glad to have my agreement, Florence sat back with a wide grin. 'Now dish the dirt on Wren and the Romanian lady.'

CHAPTER FORTY-NINE

MELISSA

Melissa was taken aback. 'You think it funny?'

Orlando could be so perverse. She'd phoned him to tell him about Wren and Carmen, and Alice's sudden departure. Bearing in mind the seriousness of what Wren had done and the trouble her husband had personally gone to in order to hire Alice Trinick, she'd expected him to be plain furious on both counts.

'The thought of Wren's face when cops turn up with an arrest warrant is priceless.'

'God, you think it a genuine possibility?'

'Depends on whether this Carmen woman wants to press charges. What's your take?'

Melissa didn't have a take. She'd sneaked back to collect some belongings and ordered the rest of their stuff to be brought out of storage and delivered. She'd been introduced to Carmen and that was that. 'I don't know,' she said tersely. Whatever Orlando thought, it was no laughing matter. 'I expected you to be more upset about Alice.'

'Oh Malice Alice,' Orlando joked. 'Don't you see, after all the fuss, it provides the perfect solution. She leaves. Celeste is happy. You're happy. Win-win.'

Melissa blinked. Orlando sounded quite strange. Perhaps it was the pressure of work. She asked him how it was going.

'Abundantly under control,' he replied.

'It was worth staying in London then?'

'Most definitely. Should make a tidy pile from it too. How's the new place?'

Again, this was not like her husband. He never took an interest in domestic matters. 'I think it's going to work very well.'

'A pity it's not on the market. Perhaps it's something we should explore.'

'You're serious?'

'Why not? The school's good there, isn't it?'

'Outstanding.'

'Have a word with Ava. Get the lay of the land.'

This was going better than she could imagine, and she needed his support after the unsettling conversation with her mother. 'That's a great idea.'

'Looking forward to seeing it.'

'You're home next week as usual?'

'Wouldn't miss it for the world.'

He sounded warm, upbeat and genuine, more like the old Orlando who'd won her heart. Perhaps standing up to him and taking decisive action had proved she wasn't the weak and incompetent person he'd come to despise. Maybe they really did have a future together. She blossomed when Orlando was nice to her. It was so reassuring to hear him take an interest in the things that mattered.

But . . .

It also troubled her, too, reminding her too much of how her mother used kindness and caring as a weapon.

In the wake of Violet's abrupt demotion from sensible eldest child to banished outsider, Melissa was elevated from second child status to daughter number one. '*You're so clever, Melissa. Nothing like Violet, thank goodness. Such lovely manners, I can take you anywhere. I'm always on tenterhooks with Violet in case she causes a scene.*' At first, Melissa had revelled in her mother's approval until Melissa realised how miserable it made her big sister and how unkind her mother was.

Once Violet upped and left, her mother's expectations of Melissa became a burden too hard to bear. Yes, she excelled at exams. Yes, she obtained a degree with honours. When Melissa developed an eating disorder her mother's response was to worry about her losing her looks, not her life.

But did it make Mummy a wicked person? Melissa sighed and went into the garden to check on her children. No good ever came from trawling through past hurts.

CHAPTER FIFTY

ROSE

Bruised by my conversation with Florence, I threw myself into making Raff's Sunday as happy as possible. We enjoyed a lovely long lunch, bumped into Amber and Tom the Tree on the way back to the car park and, taking a detour, spent a happy couple of hours at the Fleece, before pushing off back home.

Where all hell broke out.

I don't know how long Wren had been sitting at her window, waiting for our return. I'd hardly parked the car when she flew out, pinch-faced and tear-stained, and threw her arms around Raff.

'Hey, hey,' he said. 'What's wrong?'

'It's Kai,' she sobbed. 'He's gone.'

Cold trickled down my spine. I viewed Raff over Wren's head. 'Let's go inside.' Between us, we manhandled Wren to ours. She threw herself down on the sofa and held her face in her hands.

Mumbling through her fingers, she said, 'That bloody woman has taken him.'

'What?' I said, confused. 'You mean he's not missing but with Carmen?' Typically, Wren had allowed the pair of us to believe that something truly awful had happened. I flared with anger at her for giving us such a fright.

'Daddy and Mummy did a deal.'

I looked at Raff who looked at me and shrugged. More forgiving than me, he crouched down next to his sister. Gently prising her fingers apart, he asked Wren to explain.

'*They* said it was for the best. *They* didn't even tell me until after she'd gone and taken my baby.'

Enough of the dramatics. 'When did Carmen leave exactly?' I said.

'This morning.'

'When this morning?'

Wren viewed me with reproachful eyes. 'How should I know? I was asleep.'

I imagined Carmen trudging off down the long drive, thumbing a lift, the baby in her arms.

'What do you mean about a deal?' Raff asked.

'Obvs,' Wren said with a flat stare. '*You* saw her. She had no money, only the clothes on her back. How else would she leave without assistance, fucking gold-digger?'

'Let me get this straight. You don't know whether the parents gave her a penny?' Raff asked, frowning.

'What do you think they've been discussing, *moron*?'

'Don't speak to your brother like that,' I flashed.

'It's okay,' Raff said, patting the air. 'She's upset.'

And so was I. One woman going walkabout was one thing; another, too much of a coincidence. I sparked with fear. Had Carmen gone of her own free will, or had something happened to her? But then there was the baby. Nobody would hurt him, would they? My stomach gave a nauseous lurch. I reached for my phone.

'What are you doing?' Raff asked.

'Sending Carmen a text.'

Wren eyed me unkindly. 'You're cosy.'

I took no notice.

I hear you left. Safe travels. Message if you can.

Wren was still whinging. 'Money was all the parents talked about. How they wanted to support her. They obviously don't think I'm good enough to be a mother, which is so *so* shit of them. Nobody gives a damn about me in this family.'

'You selfish cow,' I exploded. 'For God's sake, will you shut up and listen to yourself?' I didn't know who was more startled: me, or Wren, or Raff. Too many weeks of weird goings-on, as my dad would say, had taken its toll and I'd just about had enough. They gaped at me as if I'd declared I was going to participate in the bobsleigh event at the Winter Olympics. Now I'd started I was going for broke. 'All you've ever done is *take*, Wren. You're the same age as me and look at you. You've never done a decent day's work in your life because Mummy and Daddy fund your lifestyle. You want a roof over your head. You're given a roof over your head. You want a car. You're given a car. For once in your entitled existence get over the fact that you can't have exactly what you want. Well, boo-bloody-hoo.'

'Wow!' Wren's face was hard and challenging and I didn't give a damn.

'The baby, who is called Marius incidentally,' I continued, 'was never yours to have and you're bloody lucky nobody is doing you for trafficking. Good on Carmen for having the balls to get the hell out of here.'

And with that out of my system, I turned on my heel and sped upstairs to bed.

CHAPTER FIFTY-ONE

ROSE

I felt as if I'd downed three Espresso Martinis. Too wired to sleep, I listened to the bark of sharp voices and the front door opening and slamming shut. I don't know what time Raff came to bed. I hate angry silences and pretended to be asleep.

Raff was wide awake and staring at the ceiling when I woke early.

'Hey,' I said.

'Hey, you,' he said, snuggling in.

'I shouldn't have . . .'

He pressed a finger to my lips. 'You have nothing to apologise for. Wren is a spoiled brat and she had it coming to her.'

'I could have chosen my words better.'

'A thick skin like Wren's requires sharp penetration. And you certainly did that.' He grinned and gave my shoulder a squeeze.

'Will she forgive me?'

'Probably not and not your problem.'

Warm relief trickled over me. I'd genuinely believed Raff would close ranks. Blood thicker than water and all that.

'Where did you go last night?' I asked amiably.

'Up to the house to talk to the folks.'

'And?'

'Wren was telling the truth. The parents organised and paid for Carmen's train fare and flight from Heathrow and refunded her money with another three grand as a goodwill gesture.'

'Did a cab collect her?' I wondered why we hadn't heard it crunching up the drive. The one benefit of staying at the lodge we saw all the comings and goings but then, I remembered, we were out for most of the day.

'Dad drove them.'

I buried my face in Raff's chest so he wouldn't see the *Oh* on my lips and the concern glinting in my eyes. *Don't think about it*, I told myself, remembering Florence's advice. Don't look for trouble.

Eventually, it was time for Raff to make a move. Sliding out of bed, he asked me what I had planned for the day.

'Might see Melissa's new gaff, although I ought to get on with some coursework.'

'How's that going?'

'Erm . . . it's going.'

'Slacker.'

I stuck out my tongue. 'It's been an age since I did proper research and writing.'

'You'll soon get into the swing,' he said, cheerfully heading downstairs to the shower room.

I reached for my phone, checked my messages. Nothing from Carmen. Didn't mean anything sinister. She couldn't be blamed for putting the Percivals behind her. As far as she was concerned, I was one of theirs. Next, I dropped a message to Melissa.

Are you in today? Thought I'd pop over.

Out this morning at nursery then visiting local primary school for Autumn. This afternoon would work.

Around three?

Perfect.

Raff padded upstairs, damp and with a towel around his waist. 'Who were you messaging?'

'Melissa.'

'Cuppa?' he asked, getting dressed.

'Please.'

Off he went and returned with a mug of tea for me and a huge bowl of cereal for him. He munched companionably, sitting on the bed. We'd done all the talking we were going to do and, finally, he left for work with a kiss and a promise to see me later.

Getting up, I wondered how long it would take me to drive to Leamington Spa.

* * *

Mrs Mariner was right about the home.

Set at the end of a long drive that not only rivalled but outdid Blackthorn, Wintercourt was a grand old place with Rapunzel-style turrets and towers, east wings and west wings and low windows from which it was possible to see its aged residents peeping out to admire the view. Wide stone steps led up to what might be described as a portcullis in castle circles; bold and forbidding, the doors defied entry. In front of these: an ornamental pond with, at its centre, the statue of a large fish, water gushing out of its mouth.

I parked in the designated visitors' area behind a huge hornbeam hedge, crossed a drive plastered in creamy-coloured stone, scaled the steps and pressed an entry buzzer and waited. The weather was definitely on the change: sun threatened by rain and its heavy henchman, wind.

It took an age for anyone to answer. The prospect of being caught in a bureaucratic nightmare regarding my visitor status seemed all too real. What was I thinking? That I could simply blag my way in? Stressing that my trip was a mad waste of time, a cultured woman's voice finally answered.

Assuming a confident and purposeful tone, the one I used for job interviews, I said, 'My name's Rose Percival. Would it be possible to visit Mrs Maud de Grey?'

'Is she aware you're coming?'

'It's a surprise.'

'And you are?'

'Her grandson's wife, Rose.'

It went horribly quiet. The woman with the voice would be checking with Maud and Maud would be wondering why a loosely connected relative had randomly pitched up to see her. Perhaps her old mind was reaching back to the wedding and the spat she'd had with her daughter, Celeste. I had images of a couple of burly security men showing up and escorting me off the premises. Wincing inside, this had to rate as one of my more rubbish ideas.

'Hello,' the voice said again. 'Mrs de Grey is happy to see you. You can come in now.'

And with a click and buzz, the gates swung open and I stepped into a small entrance hall and then into a large fragrant smelling room with light grey painted panelling and stupendously comfy chairs. In the middle of the marble floor, a vast Persian rug and a table with an arrangement of fresh sweet peas and roses. A couple of elderly ladies glanced up from reading newspapers and smiled. An elderly gent wheeled towards me and beamed a gummy hello. They all looked well and lucid and cared for, not a cardigan button out of place. Tranquillity and its cousin, serenity, oozed out of every furnishing, painting and floor covering. They were surpassed only by their residents and, as I discovered, staff.

A lady in a navy suit approached, her ash blonde hair swept into a ponytail and coiled to create a chignon that framed her aquiline features. She had blue intelligent eyes that complimented the warm smile on her face. I pegged her to be in her fifties. I knew she was staff because she wore a lanyard and her nametag told me her name: Frances.

'You must be Rose,' Frances said, extending her hand, which I took and shook in what I hoped was a firm and convincing handshake. 'Maud doesn't receive many visitors,' Frances continued, 'so this is rather a treat. Have you come far?'

I told her.

Frances gave a wise nod, which I think she did often. I surmised she was one of those rare souls who had wisdom running through her DNA. 'Follow me,' she said and I gladly did.

Up a couple of stairs, along a thickly carpeted wide corridor, I spotted signs for a library, conservatory and activities room. I imagined a lot of elderly folk engaged in tai chi or singing along to Michael Bublé — my mum's favourite. Everywhere I looked, old folk were smiling and conversing, as if posing for an advertisement promoting senior, dignified living. One old boy, with a terrifically seamed face, wobbled past me on a walking frame.

'Morning, Frances,' he said.

'Morning, Frederick,' she replied.

I didn't believe the inmates were drugged up on happy pills and, if they were, I wanted some. It was all rather surreal and reminded me of my only encounter with an incredibly expensive hotel with a Michelin-starred restaurant (Raff had taken me there to celebrate our first wedding anniversary).

At the end of the corridor, bi-folds led out onto a wide terrace with views of a ha-ha and rolling fields dotted with sheep and cows.

'Here we are.' Frances tapped lightly on an adjacent door and pressed her ear to the wood, listening for a reply.

In response to a scratchy, 'Yes, come in,' we walked inside.

An open door in a small lobby area gave a glimpse of a walk-in shower with seating and grab handles. A couple of yards further on, the space opened out and it was huge.

Chintz floral drapes hung from floor to ceiling windows. A single chandelier to rival any in Blackthorn, a two-seater sofa, a writing desk, a built-in TV (which wasn't on), a coffee table and easy chairs inhabited a room filled with photographs and fine china. At the far end, a Super-King-sized bed cast its imperious gaze, as if wondering what I was doing there. In the middle of old-school luxury, sat Maud who, blinking like a baby chick, regarded me with an expression of pure delight, as if I were a long-lost friend.

'I'll leave you to it then,' Frances said. Digesting how exactly I was going to tease out information from decades ago without causing a stir, I had a sudden urge to exit with her, but Maud had other ideas. Beckoned by a bony finger that, I suspected, brooked no nonsense, I joined her in front of the window.

'Take the weight off your feet then,' Maud said, eyeing me.

I did as asked and sank down into a firm chair the colour of oxblood. Up close, I could see Celeste in Maud and Maud in Celeste, the only massive difference being Maud's advancing years. At ninety-three, her hair was white and thin and wispy, unlike her iron-grey eyebrows. Her eyes were blue, washed out to the colour of lilac. Her make-up, especially her foundation, had settled in the numerous lines on her face, giving her the appearance of a piece of antique porcelain. Pale pink lipstick on her lips matched the pale pink varnish on her nails. The jewelled rings on her bony, arthritic fingers resembled knuckledusters. A tiny woman, she wore a heather-coloured cardigan over a dark blue blouse with pearl buttons over tweed trousers. Her thighs were the diameter of my arms. But what she lacked in physicality, she made up for in robust personality. Without her uttering more than a few words, I sensed a long-lived life in which she didn't give a toss about anyone or anything. A "character", I thought.

'My goodness,' Maud said, 'aren't you a bonny girl?'

I wasn't certain whether she meant I'd put on weight since the wedding — I had — or the comment was nothing more than a bland throwaway remark, to be accepted as a compliment.

'And your mother, how is she?'

The question took me by surprise. As far as I was aware, Mum had never exchanged more than a polite sentence with Maud at the wedding. 'Um . . . she's very well,' I replied.

'Excellent, such a capable woman, I'd always thought. And my grandson, how is he?'

On safer ground, I replied, 'Raff's very well.'

'A pity he couldn't come.' She sniffed, eyes sharp.

'He would have loved to, Granny Maud,' I said, blushing with guilt. What would Raff say if he knew what I was up to? 'But he's extremely busy.'

'And you, dear?'

'Day off from the salon.'

'Ah, yes, Rose the hairdresser,' Maud proclaimed. I felt like one of those characters in the picture books I'd read as a child: *Bob the Builder, Mr Tick the Teacher, Mrs Vole the Vet*.

'And the rest of the family?' Maud asked. 'Benedict and so on, are they well?'

I guessed "so on" referred to her daughter. 'Oh yes,' I said, a little too brightly. 'Benedict is . . .' I faltered.

'As hopeless as ever?' Maud cut in with a twinkly smile.

'Well . . .'

'Don't get me wrong: I like Benedict and he's got his work cut out with that daughter of mine, but . . .' Maud stared off into the distance. I held my breath, not daring to put thoughts into her head or words into her mouth. 'He's hopeless with money,' she finished, after a little start that made me wonder if that was what she was really going to say. 'And my grandchildren?' Maud asked.

'Melissa has two little ones now.'

'Edward, isn't it?'

'Edgar.'

Maud repeated the name, rolling it around her thin lips, as if trying it out for size before committing it to memory. 'No, I haven't met him. And the other one,' she said, 'Wren?'

'No children,' I said in a thick voice.

'I should think not,' Maud said firmly.

If you only knew, I thought.

'And poor sad Violet, how is she?'

'Violet?' I started in surprise. 'I haven't seen her since the wedding.'

Maud's face darkened. 'It was never right. Plain wrong, in fact.'

'What was?' Did she mean Raff and me getting married?

'The girl never got a fair shake. Odds stacked against her from the start. I blame the parents.' The lines around Maud's eyes contracted and she had that faraway expression again as if she knew precisely what she was on about and expected me to know too. It seemed like a familial trait.

'Granny Maud,' I said softly. 'What exactly do you mean?'

'Violet,' she said sharply, as if I were deaf. 'When they adopted her they should have left it at that.'

It took a moment for me to realise exactly what she'd revealed.

'Violet's adopted?' This was definitely news to me. I'd heard a lot about Violet over the years but never that she wasn't a Percival by blood. Did Raff and his siblings know?

'That's what I just said,' Maud said in a loud "do keep up" voice.

'As soon as Celeste got pregnant, little Violet was toast.' She clapped her thin hands together to make the point. *Children are not puppies*, I said. You can't take them back if they become tiresome or wet the bed.

'And Melissa was such a sweet-looking child, not a bit like Violet who was quite coarse-featured, as I recall. Parents again,' Maud said, rolling her eyes theatrically.

I was speechless. Firstly, because Violet's adoption was such a protected secret and, secondly, Violet's problems had begun well before Shona Reid came on the scene; it put a different slant on Violet's grievance with her parents.

'And what a child needs most in situations like that is stability and certainty,' Maud declared. 'Not distracted parents attempting to make a living from the building equivalent of a corpse. That's why Bonny Cole was so important.'

'Mrs Cole?'

'No, no, not that old bat,' Maud said. 'The other one, the one the children liked, the one they got rid of.'

I blinked in confusion. Aside from blanching at the phrase *got rid of*, Maud appeared to be mixing up Mrs Cole with her predecessor. I was looking for points of contact. Instead, they were entirely failing to connect. I had to wonder whether Maud's account was reliable, or the product of a slightly scrambled brain.

'The girl who left under a cloud,' Maud insisted, willing for me to recall an event that I had no knowledge of.

'Theodore would remember,' Maud said, tersely tapping the arm of her chair in agitation. 'I'll have a word when he comes home.'

Theodore, Maud's husband and Raff's grandfather, was an orthopaedic surgeon. He'd died shortly before Wren was born. I swallowed the sinking feeling that was working its way up from my stomach.

'Busy man, you know,' Maud prattled on. 'Probably setting someone's leg or whatnot.' She leaned forward with a conspiratorial gleam in her eye and patted my knee. 'Now that's settled, what say we have a glass of sherry? You'll stay for luncheon, won't you?'

CHAPTER FIFTY-TWO

ROSE

I didn't stay for sherry or lunch.

Apart from the weird comment about my mother, Maud had seemed quite lucid until . . . well . . . she didn't. It was like overhearing snippets of fascinating conversations while waiting in a queue to see your favourite band at a gig. In the general noise and commotion of people at last allowed through, key words got obliterated. What part of Maud's conversation contained truth? What was unadulterated garbage? Memories undoubtedly faded over time. Some got chewed up. Others remained entirely intact. I couldn't navigate which was which.

All this travelled through my brain as I drove the hour and a quarter journey back to Cirencester. After slotting into a space in Watermoor Road, I sped into town on foot, bought chocolate for Autumn and Edgar, flowers for Melissa and treated myself to a sandwich and coffee in a little café in a mews off Black Jack Street, or Flapjack Street as Autumn referred to it, which I thought hilarious. Dragged kicking and screaming against its will, my mind landed in an unruly heap on Maud's take on Benedict. She liked him well enough yet there was a definite "but" about his shortcomings with finance, which confirmed Mrs Mariner's opinion. However nobody had alluded to him having a wandering eye. After the discovery of the photograph, I wasn't too sure how I felt about my father-in-law at close quarters. Like Florence, I'd always believed him to be attractive but on the level. Keeping a picture of a woman he'd known briefly from thirty years ago signalled a stronger connection, perhaps love, or obsession, or both. Not the kind of question I could easily discuss with Melissa. And still no word from Carmen, and nothing but deadly silence regarding Alice's whereabouts.

It took me fifteen minutes to reach Sapperton. It was a sweet Cotswold village of high laurel hedges, renowned for its canal tunnel and Arts and Crafts influence — I'd looked it up on Wikipedia one day. It also had a highly-acclaimed pub favoured by the London set.

I found Melissa's new home and immediately appreciated its attraction. Not simply its visual impact; the fact it was a good five miles from Blackthorn made it infinitely appealing.

The front door popped open and Autumn, in an apron plastered with flour, skipped out to greet me. 'We're making cupcakes,' she announced, cake mixture in her hair.

'My favourite,' I replied, bowling in.

'And we've made tiffin and brownies. Daddy *loves* brownies,' Autumn said, wide-eyed.

I fought my way through a hallway crammed with storage boxes and general paraphernalia, in various stages of deconstruction.

The Shaker-style kitchen was a picture of homely chaos. Edgar had devised his own game by seeing how many cupboards he could open to reach into and upend the contents. Saucepans and various pieces of culinary equipment clattered out with a tremendous din; the more noise, the greater his delight. Melissa gave him an indulgent smile and, pink-faced, greeted me with a hug. I handed her the flowers.

'Can't remember the last time someone brought me roses.' She scooped Edgar out of the way to find a vase before he smashed it. 'Sorry about the chaos.'

She wasn't wrong about that. 'Do you want a hand?'

'Would you? Once we've got this lot squared away we can sit and you can tell me the latest.'

Not all of it, I thought, reaching for a pair of rubber gloves.

Once plates and bowls were rinsed, the dishwasher stacked, work surfaces washed down and the floor swept, Melissa parked the children in another room with their toys, and put on the kettle for tea.

Finally, settled at the kitchen table, Melissa eyed me over the rim of a fine china teacup. 'How's the baby snatcher?'

'You haven't spoken to Wren? I thought you were close.'

'She's not answering my calls and, frankly, after what my sister's done, it's probably best she doesn't.'

'She's not speaking to me either.' I lowered my voice. 'We had a falling out.'

'I'm not surprised. And the child's mother?'

'She left.'

'With the baby?'

I nodded and told Melissa what Raff had told me.

Melissa thought for a moment or two. 'I suppose that's good. Orlando joked about the police issuing a warrant for Wren's arrest.' Shame on me: I couldn't help but thrill at that possibility. 'I guess the fact that Carmen was paid off and safely escorted off the premises, so to speak, means criminal action is less likely.' Melissa took a delicate sip and put down her cup. 'Terribly grubby and embarrassing though.'

I grunted agreement.

'What?' Melissa said, picking up on my unease.

'You don't think it strange there are two disappearing women?'

'Disappearing?' Melissa repeated in a frozen voice.

'Both gone, never to be heard of again.'

'A little dramatic, if I might say.'

I gave her a straight look and shrugged.

Flickers of alarm radiated across Melissa's features. She glanced at the door and back, as if afraid someone was listening in. 'You really think there's more to it?'

'Warming to the possibility.'

'But that's awful, Rose. Carmen and Alice each had perfectly logical reasons to leave. And there's the baby,' Melissa said, flinching in alarm.

'I know,' I said softly. 'Maybe I'm wrong about Carmen but I'm less certain about Alice. How was she able to leave without triggering the security lights at Blackthorn?' And when those came on the whole estate lit up. 'Even if she escaped through the priest hole, she'd have to exit through the gated entrance.'

'Perhaps she did but nobody noticed. I'm so tired these days it would take a nuclear explosion to wake me up.'

And I was ill and out of it, I remembered. 'Unless,' I said, hitting on an idea, 'she headed out through the woods.'

'Risky, and would Alice know how to negotiate her way to the road in the dark?'

'There's a CCTV camera embedded over the front door at the house, isn't there?'

'There is.'

'So Alice's escape should be picked up.'

Melissa nibbled at a nail on her little finger. 'You've checked?'

I cracked a smile. 'Not my place to, but your mum and dad could take a look.'

'Yes, I see.'

'And there's the dogs. Fuggles yaps at the wind, never mind another human being.'

'Cupcake?' Melissa asked, not so skilfully changing the subject.

'Lovely,' I said, helping myself. 'Aren't you having one?'

'Not hungry.'

I made appreciative noises in between eating cake. Melissa's gaze drifted. Obviously uncomfortable, she said she needed to check on the children. She took her time and I suspected it was to recalibrate her emotions. When she returned she sat down, more relaxed, and stretched out with a sigh. 'I do love it here and the school are happy to take Autumn.'

'That's handy.'

Melissa gave an awkward nod and glanced at the clock. She wanted me gone. It was now or never. 'I visited Granny Maud this morning,' I blurted out.

'Did you?' Melissa sounded casual. Her expression was anything but.

'When I get doddery that's the kind of place I want to wind up in.'

'I hear it's rather grand.'

'Just a bit.'

Melissa pushed the tip of her finger around the rim of the saucer. 'Did you have a specific reason to visit?' *So unsubtle*, I thought.

'Curiosity,' I answered with a level look.

'How is Granny?'

'A little muddled, not in an alarming way,' I added. 'Pretty well, actually. Definitely up for a sherry.'

'That's Gran for you.' Melissa broke into a relieved "on safer ground" smile.

'She said some surprising things.'

'Oh?'

'She made out that Violet is adopted.'

Her face filled with genuine astonishment. 'That's rubbish.'

'It's not true?'

'Of course it's not true. Granny is obviously mistaken.'

'She was very convincing.'

'Granny always favoured Violet,' Melissa said with a tight laugh. 'I think she blamed our parents for Violet going off the rails and wasn't particularly silent about it. It was Gran who ensured that Violet had a roof over her head. To this day, she still pays the rent on her home.'

'Not your parents?'

'They contribute in other ways, or at least Daddy does,' Melissa said vaguely. 'Either way, the whole *Violet was adopted* story is simply that: a tall tale.'

And you've heard plenty of those, I suspected. 'Maud must have got the wrong end of somebody's else's stick,' I said affably.

Melissa chewed her lip and tipped her chin. 'What else did Gran say?'

'She asked about the family.'

'Did she mention Mummy?'

I shook my head.

'Still handbags at dawn then,' Melissa said, in a lame attempt to make light of it.

'What was the argument about at the wedding?'

'General mother-daughter crap, I expect.' Either Melissa didn't know or she was being evasive. 'So what else did you talk about?' she asked.

'You.'

'Me?'

'And the children.'

'I should take them to see her but two small people on the rampage might disturb the peace.'

'It would shake things up nicely,' I agreed with a grin.

'God, you didn't tell Gran about Wren and the baby?'

'Give me some credit.'

'The shock would probably kill her.'

'I think it would take more than that.'

'Yes,' Melissa said with an indulgent laugh. 'So that was it. Nothing of significance?'

What are you angling at? I wondered. 'She did say something a little odd, actually.'

'Apart from the fact my sister is adopted?' Melissa's smile was thin.

'She mentioned a woman called Bonny Cole.'

'Bonny?'

225

'I initially presumed it was a reference to Mrs Cole, the dragon nanny.'

'Kind of. Bonny was Beatrice Cole's daughter.'

'I'd forgotten Raff told me Mrs Cole had a family. What about Mr Cole?'

'According to Mummy, he left the family to live with a woman in Germany. Bonny occasionally babysat us, not that we needed a lot of supervision by then. In the evenings mostly, you know, if Mummy and Daddy had to attend an event.'

'How old was she?'

Melissa frowned. 'Sixteen, something like that. Goodness, haven't thought about Bonny in years.' She broke into a smile. 'Raff had a crush on her.'

'He's never said.'

'Why would he? Have you mentioned all your schoolgirl infatuations?'

Melissa had a point. Around the age of twelve, I had an insane thing about a lad called Geoff who kept chickens. It was too embarrassing to share with anyone, especially my husband.

'How long did the Coles work for the family?'

'Five or six years. It was only the last couple of years that Bonny was more on the scene. They left when Mrs Cole decided to take up a post in Cornwall.'

My stomach tightened. Cornwall was where Alice Trinick claimed to originate. 'It was Mrs Cole's decision?'

'Yes. Why do you ask?'

'No particular reason. Simply getting my bearings.'

'Not easy to do with us lot,' Melissa said, her smile dry.

CHAPTER FIFTY-THREE

MELISSA

Melissa was consumed by doubt.

Had Alice disappeared?

Or had Alice gone walkabout, without a word?

And if she had, where was she now?

Why did Gran say that Violet was adopted?

And why, in God's name, was Rose poking her nose in and shining a light in dark, forgotten places? Was it only insatiable curiosity, or was there more to it? Did she *know* something?

Unable to settle, unable to think, Melissa slipped out her phone and called a number she hadn't used in a very long time. Whether or not it would be answered was open to question.

It rang and it rang and then, finally, the call picked up.

'Yes?'

'Violet, it's Melissa.'

Melissa was accustomed to waiting several beats. Whatever drugs Violet had taken during the rocky years had done irreparable damage to her brain. Everything Violet said and did happened in slow motion.

'Who?'

'Your sister.'

'Oh . . . oh . . . yes. Hello,' Violet said timidly.

'I'm sorry it's been so long.'

'Are you?' There was no challenge, more regret for Melissa feeling the need to apologise.

'How are you keeping, Violet?'

'Well, I think . . . and you?'

Melissa clung to the nearest piece of furniture. 'I'm good. Quite well, actually.' She blithered on about the new home she'd rented. Told Violet that the children and Orlando were fine. She'd no idea if any of it resonated with Violet and knew better than to make direct references to their parents, even though Melissa knew their dad gave his eldest daughter an allowance.

'How's Puddles?' Violet's cat was always a safe topic of conversation.

'Exceptionally pleased with himself . . . He caught a rat yesterday . . . Did I tell you that . . .' Violet drifted into silence.

'Tell me what, Vi?'

'I'm writing . . . a book.'

Last time, Violet had been writing a symphony though she didn't play and didn't read music. 'How wonderful. No, you didn't say.'

'Yes . . . it's for children . . .'

Children, Melissa baulked.

'Based on . . . Puddles.'

Thank God, Melissa thought. 'Autumn would love to read it, I'm sure.'

'Autumn?'

'My little girl, your niece.'

'Oh . . . yes . . . I see.'

'Talking of children,' Melissa began tentatively.

'Ye-es?'

'I heard a silly rumour today.'

'Gossip, you mean.' Violet's voice hardened.

Melissa frowned, regretting that her clumsy approach had put Violet on guard. She decided to dump her original question about Violet's parentage in favour of another. 'Do you remember when we were small?' Melissa swore she heard Violet's breath hitch.

'I think I do, yes.'

'When you were really little and I was born?' Melissa knew that children had sparse or no recall before the age of three.

'It's a very funny question, an interesting question but ...' Violet briefly puttered out as if needing more time to consider. 'I might remember when you came home from hospital. Daddy bought me a rabbit.'

Melissa smiled at her father's typically thoughtful nature. But then she remembered that Violet was wrong. She and Raff had not been born in hospital. Their mother had given birth at home, on the bathroom floor, in Melissa's case. Maybe Violet meant Wren. She said as much.

Violet didn't respond.

'Vi, it doesn't matter,' Melissa said earnestly. 'Silly, really.'

'We played in the woods a lot,' Violet said, sudden warmth in her voice.

'We did. You became an expert den-builder.'

'Yes, yes, that's right,' Violet said, animated. 'And we'd steal food from the pantry for our picnics. You used to like those funny biscuits ...'

'Wagon Wheels.'

'Yes, with marshmallow in the middle.'

'And Raff would charge about like a mad thing, climbing trees and pretending to be on the lookout for enemies.'

'He fell out of the tree house.'

'God, yes,' Melissa exclaimed. They'd been scared shitless. Too terrified to get the parents, Violet had run with all her might to fetch help. 'Shona came to the rescue,' she said.

Melissa heard a long intake of breath. Had she pushed it too far, too quickly?

'Vi?'

'Yes?'

Melissa shut her eyes tight.

'I loved her,' Violet said, a catch in her voice.

'I know,' Melissa said softly. 'We both did.'

'She should never . . .' Again, that weird sense of drift. Talking to Violet was like communication with a submarine thousands of metres below the ocean's surface, the time delay massive from the command centre in Violet's brain to relaying the message through her lips.

Melissa waited patiently in the silence.

'She should never have gone,' Violet finished.

How different the paths their lives would have taken, Melissa thought sadly. Lost in a romanticised version of what might have been, she almost missed what Violet said next.

'Her brother died, remember?'

Melissa frowned and reached into the past with delicate fingers. How could she have forgotten?

'Yes, yes, you're right. Hamish, was that his name?'

'It was.'

A falling tree had hit the car in which he was riding, Melissa remembered. His girlfriend had been driving and she'd also been killed. How strange that Violet should retrieve this one single irrefutable fact from the debris of her mind. 'Do you remember the police coming to the house, Vi?'

No answer.

'Violet?'

Still no answer. Melissa winced, scared she was losing her sister.

'Which time?' Violet asked.

Melissa blinked at Violet's incredibly strong grip on the past, as if it were the only thing worth clinging to. There had been two visits in quick succession, Melissa now recalled. To her mind they'd become conflated into one event.

'After Shona died,' Melissa answered.

Another intake of breath and Melissa wasn't sure whether or not Violet was crying. She waited and waited and listened as Violet blew her nose. When she finally replied it was with surprising conviction.

'The question,' Violet said, weighing out each word, 'is why did Shona go to Bath and not return to Scotland?'

Melissa felt a deep fluttering of alarm in her chest. 'Violet, do you think . . .'

With a single click, the line went dead and silence coiled around her.

CHAPTER FIFTY-FOUR

ROSE

I had a bad taste in my mouth and it had nothing to do with the cupcake I'd eaten. I liked Melissa a lot. Aside from Raff, she was the most normal of the Percivals. I didn't claim to know her well, yet I knew her well enough to spot unease. All that lip chewing and swallowing and not-so-subtle diversions were dead giveaways. And then there was the Cornwall connection. Was it pure coincidence that Alice Trinick hailed from the same part of the world that Mrs Cole and her daughter had departed to, or was it another of Alice's deceptions?

Keen to let him know about my visit to his grandmother before Melissa inadvertently mentioned it, I called Raff on the way home.

'Hey,' he said.

Not great at going around the houses, I came straight out with it.

'Why on earth did you do that?'

I closed my eyes tight. 'For something to do.'

'Rose, it's a three hour round trip to Leamington Spa.'

'I like driving.'

'Since when?'

'Please don't give me a hard time.'

'I'm not. I'm surprised, that's all. And I thought you were supposed to be studying.'

'I have to be in the mood and,' I gabbled, 'I wanted to do something nice for your Gran. She doesn't get many visitors,' I said, cribbing a line from Frances.

'You are a funny woman,' Raff teased.

'And why you married me.'

'Among other reasons,' he said good-naturedly. 'Did you manage to fit in a visit to Melissa too?'

'I did.'

'She okay?'

'More than.' And loving living anywhere but here. 'What time will you be home?'

'Around six.'

'Fancy a pizza?'

'Perfect.'

I ended the call and wondered what to do for the next couple of hours. Raff was right about me studying. Technically, I should be looking at percentages and statistics: how many women had stroked out as a result of backwashes in the last five years. Instead, I changed my shoes and ventured into the woods. Not because I was going rogue. Not because I thought I'd discover answers to questions I couldn't get my head around. But because I fancied a walk to clear my mind and it had to be somewhere I wouldn't bump into Wren, Celeste or Benedict.

I took a similar route to start with and then branched off, taking care to circumvent the lake. The weather was definitely on the change. Under a dark, dark sky, I pictured sudden rain and flash floods. Raff's personal battle to tame the trees, to control the woods, to chop down and replant, burn off and fence in was stamped everywhere. I had the sneaking feeling that, despite his best efforts, nature would always win, would never be tamed, always get her own back. As if to make the point, I noticed that the forest had swallowed up the remains of a children's bicycle. It was red, with a chrome bell mottled by rust. I imagined all four Percival children when they were little, their voices loud and piping, playing tag or hide-and-seek. Violet, the eldest, leading the pack; Melissa, eager to please and fragile, joining in; Wren throwing a tantrum, and Raff, gentled by his sisters' influence, playing peacemaker. I wondered whether each would remember a game, a chase, a den, in exactly the same way, if the same event would be experienced through four separate and contradictory narratives. This was what I was up against, I realised, as I stepped more deeply into the Percival's pasts. Time distorts; what was is not always what is.

Melissa had confirmed Granny Maud's belief that Violet was treated badly. If Violet was adopted, perhaps she was regarded as separate and different to her blood siblings long before her hooligan tendencies kicked in. Or was she ridiculed for saying things that nobody wanted to hear because they were true? Had a woman died because of the Percivals, and, deep down, did Melissa know but, rocked by it, lacked the courage to admit it? My sister-in-law could be maddeningly inconsistent. I was never sure if she was going to be warm and lovely or, as if armed with a Taser, aim a remark with a barb attached to it — not on the same level as Wren — but enough to occasionally embed itself deep into my skin.

Pillows of cloud blotted out any suggestion of sun. The light was different this time. It sneaked between intensely green leaves. This was no Center Parcs with clear trails and elegant log cabins. This was wolves and witches and bad omens and rogue trees. This was treachery and betrayal.

A wood pigeon shot out, creating a racket. Spooked, I stood still, caught my breath and panicked that I'd never be able to find my way back.

I was rooted, breathing fast. The same haunting sensation I'd first experienced when I entered the priest hole travelled up the base of my spine to the back of my neck. Blackthorn is creepy, Florence had said.

Was I so stressed out by living in this godforsaken place that my mind was playing silly tricks?

Shaken to my core, blood thundering through my veins, I spun away on my heels. Knotted roots seemed intent on tripping me up. I slipped and slid. In unknown territory, I stumbled back the way I'd come until I reached a fork. Uncertain which route to take, I veered left and, hacking my way through undergrowth, found myself, to my surprise, at the rear of the shack. My relief in finding an identifiable landmark swiftly vanished when I noticed a dim light shining through the cracks in the wooden structure. Someone was moving around inside.

Jesus. Was it Alice? I madly wondered. Or could it be Carmen?

Fluttering with alarm, I stood transfixed.

Desperate to calm down and grab a mental foothold, my mind instantly tracked back to the night of the party and the gleam of torchlight through the trees. I hadn't known who it was then and didn't know who it was now. On impulse, I picked up a sturdy branch from a fallen oak, hurled it at the corrugated iron roof and darted behind a beech tree. The resulting clatter and noise deafened in the silence. The door flew open and I caught my breath as Orlando shot out, naked to his waist. Hair unkempt, feet bare, he wore only his boxers. Sharp-eyed, jaw jutting, he slowly surveyed the wooded landscape. I shrank back, my heart thundering so loudly in my chest, I swore he'd hear.

'What the hell was that?' a woman's voice demanded to know.

'Must have been a branch falling from a tree.'

'Thank God. Now come back and fuck me.'

I'd know that voice anywhere. It belonged to my mother-in-law, Celeste.

CHAPTER FIFTY-FIVE

ROSE

Knowledge isn't power. It's a burden as deadweight as a concrete overcoat. I wondered for how long my mother-in-law had been having an affair with my brother-in-law.

Dazed, I retraced my steps, stumbled back through the woods, branches snapping, brambles and nettles catching my skirt and grazing and stinging my legs. Thoughts tumbled and collided, smashing off and contradicting each other. *Benedict is good. He's bad, but not that bad. Celeste was a victim. Celeste is an adulterous bitch. Liars, liars — all of them. And what of Alice and Carmen and her baby?*

I returned to the lodge with a sharp, hot pain in my chest. Plunging through the door, I locked it shut and sank, grey and exhausted, onto the sofa. I had no interest in food, preparing it or eating it. I couldn't stop shaking. *Poor Melissa*, I thought. Poor Wren and poor Raff. I wasn't certain where Benedict sat on the misery spectrum. Maybe his wife's affair was a case of he had it coming to him.

But guilt threatened to knock me sideways. Insatiably curious, I'd picked apart my in-law's lives. I'd delved into their pasts. I'd uncovered things that should have remained hidden and, throughout, I'd kept the lot of it from Raff. He deserved better. I had two choices: stay silent and quit digging or come clean and ruin every belief he held about his parents.

I was still sitting, wondering whether or not and how to broach it when Raff bowled in. The smile on his face quickly faded.

'Christ, Rose, what's wrong?'

Everything.

I looked up with a wary gaze. In that split second I knew what had to be done. Lies weren't an option. There had already been too many of those. About to detonate a bomb that would shatter the family, I didn't know how to break it to him. It didn't matter if I were gentle or brutal. Acts were acts.

Anxiously, he sat down beside me, took my hand, eyes locking onto mine. 'It's not your mum and dad, is it?'

Nervous laughter rippled out between my lips. 'God, no.'

'Then what?'

'It's . . .'

'Yes?'

'I went for a walk in the woods. I know you told me not to. I found the little hut you used to play in as a kid and—'

'Babe,' he said, mystified. 'I'm not your keeper. You've done nothing wrong. I'd prefer it if—'

'You don't understand, Raff,' I insisted. 'I saw Orlando there.'

Raff drew back and frowned, perplexed. 'But Orlando is in London.'

'He isn't. There's no easy way to put this: he was with your mother.'

Still Raff didn't get it.

'They were together.'

He silently mouthed the words. God, he wasn't making this easy.

'They're having an affair.' It came out angry, which wasn't my intention. 'Sorry,' I blurted out and sped through the details, including me finding one of his mother's earrings in the cabin. (No way did I tell him I'd found its sister).

There's a lapse in time between hearing and understanding difficult news. I watched Raff's expression change from ardent denial to numb disbelief to frozen horror. His face drained of colour and the sparkle left his eyes.

'Are you absolutely certain, Rose?' he gasped. 'You've been acting a little strange lately.'

'Because of living here,' I snapped. 'It's doing my head in.'

I could tell from his face that he was deeply worried about me. Screw it, *I* was deeply worried about me. 'Raff, I am *not* seeing things. Orlando was having sex with your mother in the woods.'

His blue eyes found mine. His grasp on my hand tightened.

'Slow down and start again, Rose.'

So I did. 'I did not imagine what I saw at the hut. I'm so sorry,' I finished, chewing my bottom lip.

Raff jumped to his feet, stalked up and down, not that he could stalk very much in the contained space. White-faced, one hand punching the palm of his other, eyebrows drawn hard together, he appeared lost in some feverish internal monologue. I thought that if Orlando walked through the door right now, Raff would beat the living crap out of him. Quite how he felt about his mother, I didn't dare to imagine.

Raff stopped suddenly, his gaze raking my face. 'Does Melissa know?'

'You're the first person I've told.'

'Good,' he said, shaky. 'That's good.'

'What are we going to do?'

'I don't know. I need to think.'

'God, Raff, it's such a mess. And what about your dad?'

At the mention of his father, Raff's jaw slackened and his skin went the colour of curd cheese. I glimpsed something in his expression, regret perhaps, yet felt unable to nail it. His glance fell on the window, towards the house, and then on me. 'He mustn't know. Neither must Melissa.'

'But Raff, how can they *not* know?' How could I pretend otherwise? 'Melissa, of all people, deserves to know the truth.'

Raff didn't seem to hear. 'What time did you go to the woods?'

I told him.

'How long were you there?'

I told him this, too.

He nodded and seemed to come to a decision. I realised he'd gone from *we* to *him*.

'I'll give it an hour, let them have dinner and then I'll go up to the house.' His breath came in short bursts. He was so very pale.

'You can't. Look at the state of you.' I actually thought he might pass out. He wasn't listening.

'Dad likes to watch TV in the evening. I should be able to speak to my mother alone.'

'Is that a good idea?'

'Do you have any others?'

None that wouldn't smash everything to pieces. 'What if your father overhears?'

'He won't.' The set of Raff's jaw suggested he'd make very sure of that.

I spread my hands. 'What are you going to say?'

'I'm going to tell her to end it.'

'But how will you say you found out?' The thought of my husband telling his mother that I'd rumbled them scared the shit out of me.

'No sweat, I'll say it was me in the woods.'

I hissed with relief and gratitude. 'Thank you.'

Raff slumped back down next to me, scrubbed his fingers through his hair.

'I'm so sorry, Raff.'

'Not your fault.'

'Can I make a suggestion?'

He turned to me with a glassy stare.

'We leave. We go somewhere, anywhere, I don't care. We just clear out.'

'Agreed. I'm so sorry I brought you here,' he said, softly touching my hand.

'You weren't to know.'

Sombre, he viewed me with sad eyes and I had one single thought: although I'd now got what I wanted, I should have kept my mouth shut.

CHAPTER FIFTY-SIX

MELISSA

Melissa's sense of family loyalty was in jeopardy. She was scared and scared people do crazy things.

Violet had always been different from the rest of them, not for what she had done, but for what had been done to her. Defined as difficult from an early age, her eldest sister had never fitted in. Suddenly, the claim that Violet was adopted contained a ring of truth. It explained how Violet was much less adept at maintaining the party family line. It also meant that, bewilderingly, Violet had always known and yet had never breathed a word. How had she been silenced and what else hadn't she breathed a word about?

Melissa trawled through the fragments of their conversation. Reminded by Violet, Melissa recalled Shona's sadness at her brother's sudden, untimely death and Shona's fury at Celeste, her mother. Melissa did not remember which came first. In common with Alice, Shona had never announced her departure. She was there one minute and gone the next. She hadn't stayed to say goodbye. From an adult point of view Melissa understood the pain it would have caused, the questions that would be asked by two small children for which an emotional grown-up had no answers. But, my God, it had hurt them.

On shaky ground, Melissa cast her mind back, peeling away the years: giving birth to Edgar and Autumn, getting married, dating Orlando, university, job interview, first promotion, studying and studying, riding ponies, trying to please, please, please. She could remember the name of her first puppy, the registration of her first car, a Corsa, the phone number at Granny Maud's house. She could not nail the circumstances surrounding Shona Reid's departure and death. Crushing her eyes tight, she willed herself back to Blackthorn, to when she glanced out of an upstairs window at the noise of tyres on gravel and watched a police car travel up the drive. She recalled the deep sonorous ring of the doorbell, footsteps across the hall, her father's, she thought, hushed voices and then three pairs of feet disappearing into the drawing room. She remembered Violet's scared gaze clinging to hers, the secret wisdom children have of impending disaster, like a couple of embryonic fortune-tellers. They'd tiptoed down the staircase and each pressed their ears to the thick wooden door.

Melissa ground her jaw, squeezed her eyes tighter, catching snatches of conversation, not dissimilar to the stilted exchange she'd just shared with her sister. Brunswick Place was mentioned.

'I gather you're the owner, Mr Percival,' a man's voice, one of the police officers, said.

Melissa hadn't understood its significance at the time. Is that what Violet meant about Shona going to Bath and not back home? Was she suggesting that Melissa's dad had installed Shona somewhere else as his mistress? No wonder her mother had displayed more anger than compassion in the years since Shona's accidental death. It would be a terrifying and terrible way to find out about her husband's infidelity. Later, a foolish remark from one of the gardeners, employed to manage the grounds, revealed that Shona had died in a fall in which her neck was broken. That had sealed it for Violet.

'You fucking killed her,' Violet raged.

'I will not have you swearing in our home,' Celeste thundered.
'You did. You did. You did. She was too nice and you were jealous.'
'Benedict, for God's sake, take Violet out of my sight.'
'Get your hands off me, Daddy. It's all her fault.'
'Nobody is to blame,' Benedict said. 'It was a terrible accident.'

But what if it wasn't? What if one parent was instrumental in Shona's death? The question was: which one?

Alice Trinick's sudden departure suddenly assumed a sinister hue. What if history was repeating itself? What if Daddy was up to his old tricks? What if . . .

Melissa's head ached. Surprised at stumbling across her father with Alice the morning after the party, Melissa now wondered if it were connected to the cloak and dagger of Alice's departure. There was only one way to find out and that was to confront him.

Hatching a plan, she gave the children their tea, washed and dressed them for bed and phoned Rose.

243

CHAPTER FIFTY-SEVEN

ROSE

'Melissa,' I almost choked, eliciting an alarmed look from Raff. He shook his head vigorously and ran a finger under his throat.

'I've been thinking about what you said,' Melissa said.

'O-kay.'

'I need to talk to the parents.'

'About what specifically?' Conscious that Raff was watching my every word, I aimed to sound casual.

'Alice, among other things.'

I had a rough idea what *other things* meant and thought it a terrible idea at this very moment. 'Do you think that's wise?'

'It won't be easy but my mind's made up. I know it's a hell of an ask but could you come and look after the children for me?'

'What, now?'

Raff mouthed to me: *You know nothing*.

'Or I could drop them off at yours.'

I'm not great at thinking on my feet but fear galvanised me. 'I'd love to but I've got a roaring headache so it's bath and bed for me, I'm afraid.'

Raff cut me a puzzled glance.

'Tomorrow then.'

'I'm at work.'

'How about tomorrow night? What time do you get . . . oh . . .'

I heard a man's deep voice in the background.

'Didn't expect you back until the weekend,' I heard Melissa say and then to me, 'It's okay, Rose, Orlando's unexpectedly home.' *Bastard*, I thought, eyeing Raff who was listening as though his life depended on it. 'I won't trouble you further, Rose. Hope you feel better soon.'

Relieved Melissa ended the call, I wasn't sure how much time it would buy us.

'Phew, that was a close one,' he said. 'Imagine what might have happened if Melissa walked in when I was with Mum. God, do you think she'll leave the kids with Orlando?'

'You mean *shithead*? I don't think so.'

'He's got a bloody cheek turning up.'

'Guilty conscience.'

Raff glowered. 'I wonder what was so urgent.'

'With Melissa?'

'Yes.'

'She didn't say.' Technically true.

Raff's eyes widened. 'You don't think she's found out about the affair, do you?'

'She didn't sound like a woman about to eviscerate a man.'

'Good point. Obviously she doesn't know.'

'For now.'

'Rose,' Raff said, holding my gaze. 'I know it's going to drive you crazy but you have to keep your mouth shut for Melissa and the children's sake.'

It seemed keeping quiet was a family tradition. Despite what Raff said, I didn't rate my chances highly. In my book, Melissa had a right to know.

Raff glanced at his watch. 'I'd better make a move.'

For the second time that evening I questioned the wisdom of anyone blundering into Percival affairs and said so.

'If I'd really seen what you saw do you think I'd stand idly by?' Raff said.

No, Raff would have marched up to Orlando and decked him. He wouldn't have fled like me. 'I guess not.'

'There you go.'

I watched him leave and stride up the drive. Tired to my bones, I flopped back down.

I'd always thought Raff close to his mother and knew how much it would cost him to speak the words that no son should ever have to say. I'd no idea how Celeste would respond. Would she deny it? Would she defend and try to justify it? Don't be silly, I thought. Having an affair was one thing, having it with your son-in-law on a completely different level. Melissa deserved much better. And if Raff had the stones to confront his mother, I wondered if I had the stones to confront Orlando. Someone should.

Restless, I switched on the TV and switched it back off. My go-to would be Mum but, happily, she and Dad were out of the picture, drinking margaritas and pigging out on seafood. I thought about calling Florence. Bad idea. She would twig that something was up and any revelation about Orlando would fuel Florence's fire. Not that I blamed her.

While half my mind was chewing over the adulterous lovers, the other part was thinking about the night Alice went missing.

My heart gave a dull thud. I was poorly, Raff tucked up in bed beside me, attempting to sleep with a delirious woman. Melissa was in her bedroom, next to Alice's room, Benedict on the floor above. Wren was also at the scene of the crime, so to speak, in the Granary. They each had opportunity although what had been done and how it had been carried out without waking up the entire household eluded me, as did motive.

Crushed by the very idea of it, I dumped the thought but not before considering Celeste and Orlando, both away on the night in question, possibly with each other.

Or were they? A ball of fear lodged deep in my throat.

How could I forget the vile and murderous look my mother-in-law had thrown Melissa? How could I blot out the overheard conversation that revealed Celeste's jealousy — rich after what I'd seen and heard that afternoon?

But, I reminded myself, however much Celeste hated Benedict looking at another woman, she already knew that Alice was leaving to live in Sapperton so why bother running the risk of bumping her off? People were generally conservative in their actions. They only escalated to bad behaviour if they saw no other option. (God, I couldn't actually believe I was thinking like this.)

The more my confused mind tried to work it out, the more ridiculous my theories sounded. Nobody here had a reason to kill Alice, a young woman who had only recently set foot in Blackthorn. Even if they had a strong motive, they wouldn't be stupid enough to carry out a crime in situ, not after the stink created years before. One dead nanny was one thing, another plain unimaginable.

I glanced at my phone again, wondering if Carmen had been in touch. She hadn't.

Glum, I went to the fridge, helped myself to a glass of milk and rolled my mind back to the morning I'd spent with Alice in Cirencester. She'd been jumpy, I recalled. Actually, rather more than that, she'd been *scared*. Was she on the run from someone? Was this the reason she left, leaving no trace? Now that *did* make sense.

The sound of gravel crunching alerted me to Raff's return. He slipped inside, heat in his cheeks, and I didn't think it was from the brisk walk back. In two paces, he had his arms around me, buried his face in my neck and held me tight. I hated that he was so upset. I basked in the fact that I was needed.

'How was it?' I asked tentatively.

'Awful.'

'Did she deny it?'

'No,' he said wearily, drawing away.

'And?'

'There were tears. Lots of them.'

Manipulative cow, I thought. 'I bet,' I said mildly.

'It was a silly one-off moment of lust, according to Mum.'

'Do you believe her?'

'No.'

Neither did I.

'She was very contrite,' Raff continued. 'Terribly embarrassed and promised it will never happen again.'

'I should think not.'

'And she begged me not to tell you, or Melissa.'

Great, so I had to pretend to be Mrs Know-Nothing, despite being the only single living witness. I grimaced. Where the hell did that phrase come from?

'What about Orlando?'

'What about him?'

'Fair's fair, don't you think you should have a word with him, too?'

'I don't think that would be helpful.'

Raff could tell from the flinty expression on my face, I strongly disagreed. This was not a case of *least said soonest mended*, one of Mum's favourite expressions.

'Rose, you can't say anything.'

Too right, it would blow my cover. The thought of Orlando getting away without so much as a stern word in his ear frustrated me enormously. Maybe I'd work on Melissa and flag up the merits of divorce.

'So we carry on as if nothing has happened?'

'Pretty much.'

'Hmm,' I said. 'First thing tomorrow morning I'm looking for somewhere else to live. You cool with that?'

'I am,' Raff said fervently. 'Not sure I can stand any more drama.'

On this, we were in complete agreement.

CHAPTER FIFTY-EIGHT

MELISSA

Orlando couldn't have been sweeter. After surprising her with flowers, champagne and, thoughtfully, a dinner for two from Cook, he'd kissed her deeply and then bathed and put the children to bed while Melissa prepared vegetables, laid the table and poured the fizz. Her heart swelled with hope. Now that Orlando was home, (a kinder, more rested Orlando, no less) all the horrid stuff about her father and her mad desire to confront him about Alice's disappearance receded into the distance. She knew what Orlando would say if she confided her doubts. *Oh, no, Melissa, not that again.* And perhaps he was right. Melissa dared to believe that, with the pressure off at work for her husband, it signified a new phase in their relationship.

'The house looks as if it's coming together,' Orlando observed appreciatively. They were in the sitting room, glasses apiece, him in his favourite easy chair, legs spread apart, in Lord of the manor pose.

'Apart from packing boxes stacked to the ceiling in the guest bedroom,' Melissa said ruefully.

'Just as well Alice decided to make alternative plans. She's no great loss, don't you think?'

Ignoring the unpleasant ring in his tone, Melissa quietly sipped her drink.

'I'm not afraid to admit it, Lissie, but employing that silly little girl was a big mistake.'

'That's harsh.'

'It's true.'

'Whatever,' Melissa said evenly, 'I can manage well enough without her, although I'd feel happier if I knew where she was.'

'Why?' Orlando said, peeved.

'From a welfare point of view.'

'You care too much, darling.' He took a huge glug of champagne. 'When are we eating?'

'Are you hungry?'

'Famished.'

Telling Orlando that she'd push things along in the kitchen, his mobile rang. He viewed the number, cut the call and slipped the phone into his trouser pocket. 'Work,' he explained.

'Don't they know what time it is? You're entitled to a home life.'

Orlando's smile was wide. 'I love it when you feel the need to defend me. Honestly, I can loo—' His phone rang again.

'This is so tedious,' Melissa said. 'Who is it?'

'Belinda.'

'*Belinda*? I thought she'd have more sense.'

Orlando rolled his eyes, stood up and headed for the door. 'The law calls. I'd better take it.'

'No need to go outside,' Melissa trilled after him, but he was already gone. A good five minutes later, during which she'd put confit duck in the oven, turned roast potatoes and topped up the steamer for the green beans, he reappeared, strain on his face.

'Everything okay?' Melissa said. Clearly, it wasn't.

'Perfect.' His voice said one thing, his expression another.

'You're sure?'

'Absolutely.' He scooped up his glass, downed the contents and poured another. 'Say, why don't we take off tomorrow for a few days?'

'But you've only just got here.'

'You could use the break, couldn't you?'

'Well...'

'We could go to that little place you like so much on the coast.'

'Little Haven?' She was astounded. The plotter, the planner, this was not like her husband at all. If ever she wanted to book a holiday, he always needed six months' notice.

'That's the one.'

'But...'

'C'mon, Lissie, let yourself go.' He grabbed hold of her waist and twizzled her around, as if they were contestants on *Strictly*. 'The children would love it.'

'Yes, I realise that...'

'And we really should take advantage of the fact we're not constricted by school holidays.'

She was incredulous. 'Can you drop everything at work?'

'No problem,' Orlando said, bullish. 'After all the time I've put in, I'm owed.'

'Well, it's a lovely idea...'

'Then say, yes.'

'It's so sudden.'

Too sudden and after that phone call, Melissa thought, instantly on her guard.

He let her go and slipped out the phone, an instrument of suspicion, as far as Melissa was concerned. Dared she attempt to check the number when Orlando wasn't looking?

'I'll call Bill now.' The property owner, Melissa recalled. 'See if he can book us in.' Orlando inclined his head, a rascally look on his face. 'What do you say, Lissie? Let's go and have some fun.'

His eyes shone with ardour. His mouth, so often a sneer, was wide and laughing.

Oh what the hell. 'Yes,' Melissa agreed, with a big smile.

CHAPTER FIFTY-NINE

ROSE

I trawled through letting sites first thing. My heart sank when I saw how much the cost of rentals had gone up since the last time I'd negotiated somewhere for us to live. With a couple of possibilities in mind, neither in our preferred streets, I messaged Raff the details, and hoofed off to the salon.

Jerome was in full flow with one of his ladies, as he called them. Short, fruity-voiced and authoritative, she was complaining about a particular shampoo we stocked.

'It's ridiculously expensive, lasts seconds and doesn't lather.' The woman stood like a fullback on a rugby pitch.

'That is because you are not using it correctly,' Jerome countered. Not a man to be challenged, I spotted a particularly dangerous gleam in his eye.

'Here,' Jerome said, swiping a product from the shelf. 'Give me your hand.' Startled, the woman obliged. 'You pour a tiny little bit out, like so.' He pressed a smidge onto her palm. 'See, now you use *this* amount to get your hair clean. Without a clean scalp, the shampoo cannot lather. Next,' he said, as if he were hosting a cookery programme, 'you apply another little dab and, hey presto, lots of foam, lots of lather and with very little product.'

Not wishing to witness the outcome, I snuck out the back and poured myself a cup of coffee from the machine, warm, wet and caffeinated its only merits. Suitably fuelled, I powered through the morning, intermittently checking my phone to see if Raff had got back to me. When he finally did it was mid-afternoon and I was gobbling down a cheese and tomato sandwich in the staff area.

Sorry — out of signal and only just picked up. Can we discuss later?

Disappointed, I dropped him a thumb's up emoji. I thought that would be the end of it, but another ping on my phone alerted me to a second message and it wasn't pretty.

Mum wants to have a family dinner tonight.
What? Is she cracked?
Her way of making amends.
Again, is she cracked? I am not going to dinner.
It will look odd if we don't.
I don't care.
Please, Rose.
If you go it will look as if it was no big deal and she's forgiven.
I'm thinking more about Dad. He'd view it as a snub.
Tough.
Please, it's not his fault.
I won't be able to look Melissa in the eye.
She won't be there. She and Orlando have gone away for a few days.
Bloody coward.
Agreed. So what do you say?
NO.

Mandy popped her head around the door. 'Your next client is waiting, Rose.'

'Give her a magazine and a coffee. I'll be there in a second.'

Sod this, I thought, and phoned Raff. Before he could get in a word, I said, 'Your mother will know I know because she knows we tell each other everything.'

'I swore blind I hadn't told you. All you have to do is pretend.'

'*All?*' I screwed my eyes up so tight I saw spots. 'How do *you* feel about going?'

'I'd rather lie down on a bed of nails.'

'Well then.'

'But, like I said, I'm conscious of how Dad might react if we bail. We need to protect him if we can.'

'We can't,' I said stubbornly.

'For one night only, Rose, and then we'll go home-hunting tomorrow.'

'I'm working tomorrow.' I knew I was being awkward. I *felt* awkward.

'I'll finish early, drive into Cheltenham and meet you. We can view together and then go out to supper.'

Hmm. I recognise when I'm being manoeuvred, although Raff made a fair point about carrying on as if I hadn't a clue. Perhaps if I kept thinking of the escape route I could stagger through the evening. 'What time?'

'Drinks in the drawing room at six.'

'I'll be late.' No way was I tearing back to dance to Celeste Percival's manipulative tune.

'Get there soon as you can and we get to leave earlier.'

'Deal.' I ended the call with a heavy heart, slid a comb from out of my pouch bag around my waist, plastered on a smile and headed off for my next cut and finish.

CHAPTER SIXTY

MELISSA

With loo and *stretch your legs* breaks, the journey had taken them over five hours. It hadn't helped that Autumn had thrown up all over the Range Rover's leather upholstery. Normally, this would draw cold irrational hostility from Orlando but, after the initial *Oh my God*, he dealt with it as he might a legal battle: with ruthless efficiency. Melissa felt as if someone had abducted her husband and put an imposter in his place. She wasn't saying that she wanted the old one back, but at least she knew how to deal with Orlando's mercurial ways. The person sitting next to her, driving as if he had the Grim Reaper about to scythe off his head, remained a mystery.

And there were already too many conundrums in her life.

As they descended the steep hill to the bay, the sun glinted across the water, creating shades of mercury. Her spirits lifted.

'Look,' Autumn said to Edgar, pointing. 'Seaside.'

Following the road around, passing pubs and restaurants, older folk with dogs and young families, they drove up the hill past a complex of holiday homes on the left and a steeply wooded area on the right, eventually arriving at their rental, a large converted barn. Nothing barn-like about the interior: uber-modern furnishings and fittings, and a large kitchen with up to the second equipment that led out onto a terrace overlooking fields and with sea glimpses. They'd first stayed for a wedding anniversary treat and had been coming back for the past several years. Solidly booked up for months in advance, Melissa dreaded to think of the inducements Orlando must have offered to persuade Bill to let them have the barn at short notice. It smacked of desperation, almost as worrying as the phone call that triggered the "get me out of here" response in her husband. Orlando was clever. He was sly. She didn't think he had criminal tendencies, but you never knew in the murky legal world he inhabited. Had he done something underhand and potentially against the law?

'Right,' Orlando said, manhandling their baggage into the hall and into their bedrooms. 'Let's go and find somewhere nice to book in for dinner.'

'Ooh, am I coming too?' Autumn was oblivious to the fact that, an hour before, she had vomited up her lunch.

'Give me a moment,' Melissa said, 'I'd like to at least get the children's nightclothes unpacked.'

'Spoilsport,' Orlando mocked good-naturedly.

'Spoilsport, spoilsport,' Autumn joined in.

'Cheeky,' Melissa said, smiling at her daughter, then turning to her husband, 'Tell you what, how about you go on ahead with the kids? I won't be long.'

Autumn looked up expectantly at her father.

'If you're sure,' Orlando said, already scooping Edgar up, ready to prise him into his pushchair.

'Positive. We could rendezvous at the Castle.'

Orlando's smile, in a face unaccustomed to it, was like a rictus grin, Melissa thought. Without warning, he leaned across, over the top of Edgar's head, and kissed her full on the mouth. Startled by the open display of affection, Melissa's primary emotion was one of embarrassment. As if to confirm it, Autumn burst out with, 'Yuk.'

'Come on, you,' Orlando said, tousling the hair on his small daughter's head. The gesture was so reminiscent of Raff, Melissa couldn't help but wonder if Orlando had been coached.

Watching them trundle out, Melissa waited several beats, inhaling the silence and, feeling mildly giddy, let her pulse rate settle. It was too much to expect that Orlando had left his mobile behind, enabling her to take a deep dive, but she had another idea. Staring out of the large picture window, across the rural view, she mentally sketched out a game plan. It involved Belinda, Orlando's P.A.. Loyal to her boss, not to his wife, Belinda would lie for Orlando. It would take guile to force a wedge and break that trust in order to discover the truth.

Taking several deep breaths, Melissa put a call through to the firm and was then patched through to Belinda.

'Good afternoon, Mrs Rhodes,' Belinda said, in her smooth as syrup voice.

'Hello, Belinda. How are you?'

'Very well, thank you. And you?'

'Fighting fit.'

'Good to hear.'

'I wonder if you could help me.' Always a good idea to appeal for assistance; even horrible people liked to feel needed.

'I'll certainly do my best.'

'To be honest, Belinda, I'm a little worried about Orlando.'

'Oh?'

'You hadn't noticed anything amiss.'

'Can't say I have.'

'Only his work schedule has been quite punishing lately, what with weekends in the office.' Melissa let that hang and swore she heard Belinda clear her throat and reach for a glass of water. 'I very much fear he's become quite run down,' Melissa continued, voicing deep if fake concern. 'He's not sleeping properly and he's a little irritable. You know how it is.'

'Yes, I . . .'

'He never really talks to me in detail about his cases — likes to leave work at work, if you understand my drift, which is very considerate of him.'

'Yes, absolutely,' Belinda rallied.

'I wondered if I should be more in the know. I'm not asking you to betray a confidence, or anything like that.'

'Understood,' Belinda said, laughing a little too heartily.

'But after the difficult news you delivered yesterday evening, I really would like to be in a better position to support him.'

Belinda was too well-brought-up to splutter. The silence spluttered for her. Gotcha, Melissa thought. However devoted his P.A. she didn't want to be forced to provide an alibi to his wife.

'Mrs Rhodes, would it be possible for me to get back to you? One of the partners has entered the office to sign some papers. I'll be back to you in a jiffy.'

'Appreciated,' Melissa said. She counted thirty seconds and then phoned Orlando's number. As predicted, it was engaged. Melissa hoped Belinda gave him hell.

CHAPTER SIXTY-ONE

ROSE

I arrived fifteen minutes late, having changed my mind a dozen times about the good sense of turning up at all. And what did you wear to attend a *Sorry, I slept with your brother-in-law* type occasion anyway? How Celeste thought a nice family meal would redeem her was beyond me. I tried to think how it would play if a similar scenario had occurred in my family. A furious row, probably involving the threat of violence, followed by actual violence, and guilty parties thrown out on their ears and gossiped about for evermore. Did people in the upper end of society behave and act differently? The answer was a resounding *yes* and it bewildered me.

In the end I settled for navy culottes with an expandable waistband, (it was bound to be an extravagant dinner with large helpings of humble pie) an ice-white shirt and pumps. Everyone had gathered in the drawing room — where else? When I say everyone, I was surprised to see that Wren was absent.

'Hello, Rose, darling,' Celeste said, with what could only be described as an assessing gaze. She pecked me on both cheeks and it took everything I had not to confess that it was me who'd stumbled across her dirty assignation in the woods with Orlando. The frozen look on Raff's face as he leapt towards me with a glass of Kir told me I'd barely convinced anyone of my ignorance.

'You look lovely,' he whispered in a warm show of solidarity. 'Good day?' Raff asked loudly for the benefit of others.

'Fabulous,' I answered with a straight face.

Benedict bowled in with a tray of canapés: olives and smoked salmon blinis. 'Help yourself, everyone.'

He looked exceptionally louche. With the onset of cooler weather, spanner trousers, loafers and no socks had replaced shorts, T and flip-flops. Addressing me, he said, 'Don't suppose you saw Wren on your way here?'

I shook my head and took a sip. Alcoholic blackcurrant, cassis beat the hell out of Ribena.

'Where on earth is she?' Celeste burst out, annoyed, and then, as if realising it wasn't a good look, gushed, 'Look at us, so lovely for us to be together.'

'And on a school night too.' Benedict winked at Raff and me.

'Pity Melissa and Orlando can't join us.' Drawing a sharp look from Raff, it was worth it to see the fleeting expression of anxiety in Celeste's blue-grey eyes.

'They're at Little Haven, lucky beasts,' Benedict said.

Celeste glanced at her watch and then at Benedict. 'Do you think I should give Wren a ring?'

'It's certainly not like her to be late.'

It wasn't. Wren would sell her own child for a drink and knees-up. Resentful at being forced to play a game I despised, I felt belligerent. Perhaps it would be better if I feigned a migraine, slid out and left them to it. Considering how I could frame an excuse, footsteps and voices from the hall caught everyone's attention.

You can always tell when Wren is about to arrive. The atmosphere receives a turbocharge. Doors are flung open. Wren enters centre stage as if she's playing the opening night of *The Lion King*, which in Wren's head, she is.

To everyone's collective surprise, she was followed by a wiry and muscular youth. Freckles dusted his sunken cheekbones. He had cracked lips, pasty features and cold watchful eyes. From a grubby grey hoodie, the brim of a baseball cap protruded. Above black and well-worn trainers, his jogging bottoms finished at the ankle revealing white socks. His dark searching gaze alighted on everyone in the room, as if casing them for how much jewellery was on offer. I didn't think he was Wren's mate. He certainly didn't look like boyfriend material. He was around seventeen, possibly eighteen, difficult to tell because he had the drawn lean look that spoke of a hard upbringing, yet there was definitely something strikingly familiar about his features and then, with a gasp, I tumbled to it.

'Meet my parents,' Wren said, turning to the young guy. 'This is . . .'

'Alice's brother.'

The young guy rivalled Wren's scowl at me for ruining her punchline. He looked sullen and extremely put out.

Then I remembered. Alice had three *older* brothers: Lee and Jace and thingummy. So who was this?

'This is Craig and he's from Plymouth,' Wren said, elbows out and keen to prove that she had the inside track. 'I found him wandering outside the gates looking for Alice and invited him in.'

'I can speak for myself,' Craig glowered, instantly drawing colour to Wren's pale cheeks. 'Yes, I'm Alice's brother.' His accent was strong, West Country but harder, not like Alice's softer delivery.

'And your mum's a medical receptionist?' I said, recalling the story Alice had cooked up.

Craig's face cracked into a wolfish grin.

Catching on, Raff said, 'Don't suppose your dad works as Ops Manager at a brewery in Cornwall either?'

Craig barked a laugh at the absurdity.

Benedict angled his gaze. Intensity scribbled all over his face, he was as keen to unearth the real Alice Trinick as me.

Craig surveyed him with a hard smile then turned to Raff. 'Alice had you over good and proper, didn't she?'

'But why?' Benedict asked, spreading his palms.

'Why do you think?'

I didn't think Craig was a youth accustomed to wielding power but, my God, he was wielding it now and enjoying every second of it. 'Remember Bonny Cole?' Craig asked.

'The dragon nanny's daughter,' Raff muttered under his breath to me.

Benedict double-blinked. Next to him, every muscle in Celeste's face tightened. 'I do, but fail to see the significance,' Benedict protested, a little pompously, I thought.

Craig waited a beat, hugely enjoying the moment. 'Bonny is our mother.'

Raff jolted forward.

Craig fixed him with a grin. 'Clever bloke like you can work out the arithmetic.'

I stared dumbfounded. It wasn't the fact that Alice had lied and lied and, as Craig rightly pointed out, pulled one over; it was the implication of what he was saying.

Benedict looked as if he'd been shot; Celeste the woman who had pulled the trigger.

'Would someone please tell me what's so awful?' Wren said, confused.

Staring straight at Benedict, Craig said, 'My mother is the kid your dad promised the world to. And Alice is . . .'

'That's an utterly ludicrous and filthy lie,' Benedict spluttered.

Craig wasn't buying it. 'What I want to know, *Benedict*,' Craig said, 'is what you've done with my mum and my sister?'

CHAPTER SIXTY-TWO

ROSE

Benedict's face contorted into a mask of rage. Letting out a deep-throated growl, my father-in-law flew from one side of the room to the other and piled into Craig. Time stalled. I watched, aghast, as punches were thrown and blows landed. A flurry of fists and feet and no holds barred. Craig, younger, tougher and streetwise, was giving as good as he got. If this were a game of darts, he'd scored several bull's eyes and would have continued to do so if it hadn't been for Raff, temporarily stunned, wading in to his father's rescue.

Paralysed and not knowing what to do, struggling with Craig's ugly allegation, I found myself having the equivalent of an out of body experience. I couldn't help but watch in morbid fascination.

A table tumbled over, the antique lamp sitting on it crashing to the floor. Glasses and china followed. Wren let out a squeal and ran to Celeste, cowering in the corner of the large fireplace. As the tussle became more violent, Raff had Craig in a headlock and was walloping the hell out of him. A sharp jab from Craig's elbow and Raff howled and let go. Benedict slipped and fell down on one knee.

'Call the police,' Celeste screamed at me.

'No way,' Wren pleaded, hysterical.

I had enough functioning brainpower to figure out that cops draw heat and Wren was scared the story of Carmen and the stolen baby would leak out. Wouldn't look good if *that* hit the headlines.

They were all at it again and I wanted it to stop. This wasn't anything like the scuffle between Wren and Carmen where Raff had acted defensively. This was full-on *men at war*. Bizarrely, I wondered how much ice we'd need to soothe cuts and bruises. Nothing could be done about bruised egos. The dogs, reacting to the commotion, furiously scratched and whined at the door, yowling and barking. Thank goodness, Wren hadn't let them in.

'STOP, FOR CHRISSAKES.' My voice shrieked and nobody was more surprised than me.

Amazingly, Raff and Benedict, severely out of breath, broke away. Craig, blood running from his nose, fists up and pumped up, roared, 'Want some more, you posh fucking tossers?'

'You little shit,' Raff snarled. He would have gone back for an encore if I hadn't stepped in front of him. We were eyeball to eyeball. Panting heavily, zoned out, Raff looked straight through me. There was a mad glazed look in his eye and, in that heart-stopping moment, I wasn't entirely certain he wouldn't mow me down to get at Alice Trinick's little brother.

'That's enough,' Benedict panted, patting the air.

I threw him a grateful glance.

Everything went quiet, apart from the sound of crunching glass and china beneath the soles of our shoes. Wren righted the table. Nothing could be done about the lamp. Celeste reached out to Benedict who told her roughly not to fuss. I could see that he deeply regretted his loss of control, Raff not so much. He was studying a stain on the carpet, hand clasped around the back of his neck, the knuckles skinned, his breath coming in short, furious bursts.

'Let's go,' I whispered, resting my hand on his arm.

He looked up with a gaze that was hard and unforgiving, his face a mess of cuts and bruises. Already the skin above one eye was swelling. 'This I have to hear,' he said darkly. I didn't know whether he meant more about Craig's allegation or his father's defence.

With the threat of imminent attack over, Craig's stance relaxed. He didn't apologise. He didn't complain. It didn't seem to me as if he were going anywhere without answers. I couldn't get his accusation out of my head and, added to everything else I'd either witnessed or overheard, a deeply unpleasant picture paraded in front of me. It appeared that Shona Reid had been the start of Benedict's infidelity and it hadn't stopped there. It clearly connected in Celeste's mind. Her complexion was the same colour as an egg-white only omelette.

Everyone moved around Craig as if he had an incurable and contagious disease. Celeste switched off whatever was cooking and fretted about *everything* being ruined. *Understatement of the year*, I thought. Nobody listened and nobody had an appetite anyway. Wren disappeared to fetch a towel for Alice's brother to wipe the blood from his face. She took it upon herself to bridge the generation gap because, as Wren explained to her parents on the quiet in the kitchen, though not out of my earshot, *she understood where young people were coming from*. Benedict fobbed off questions from Celeste and his children and briefly exited to change his bloodstained shirt. Raff downed a glass of water and accepted painkillers from the emergency supply in my bag. And this *was* an emergency. In true Percival style, Benedict returned all cleaned up, as far as was possible, composed and back in control.

'Right, young man,' Benedict addressed Craig. 'I suggest we all sit down, have a cup of tea and talk in a civilised fashion so we can get our facts straight and work this thing out.'

CHAPTER SIXTY-THREE

MELISSA

The Castle was rammed with early evening diners. The weather still mild and warm, Orlando had grabbed a table outside with the children and was three-quarters of the way down a pint of lager when Melissa arrived. She'd expected him to look exquisitely uncomfortable. Instead, he seemed exceptionally pleased with himself.

'Got you a glass of Pinot,' he declared.

Typical of Orlando to front it out, Melissa thanked him stiffly.

'What took you so long?'

What took Melissa so long was the time taken to calm down and give herself enough distance to consider all the angles, one so sharp it practically cut off her nose. There was no other possible explanation for Orlando's deception: he was having an affair. The big question: with whom?

'This and that,' she said stonily.

Orlando twitched a smile, fastened his gaze and placed a firm hand over hers. 'You don't seem very happy, darling.'

Melissa stared him out.

His gaze intensified. 'Belinda called.'

'I know.'

'Said you were worried about me, which is entirely sweet of you.'

Melissa tipped forward and spoke in a low, controlled voice to protect the children. It was no less threatening. 'Orlando, can we cut the crap? Who is she?'

In a perfectly choreographed move, Orlando's body gave a little jolt of surprise. It did not temper the wily expression in his eyes or the smirk flirting across his lips. He knew she knew he'd been rumbled, Melissa thought, and yet he determined to play it like a lawyer in a courtroom: *my client is not guilty even though I know, sure as hell, he is.*

'Ah,' he said, a knowing light in his eyes. 'The phone call last night.'

'Who was she?' Melissa hissed.

'He, actually.'

Melissa pictured a furious husband hurling a fierce ultimatum.

Come on then. Out with it, she thought. Maddeningly, Orlando appeared in no hurry to expand. This could be the shortest away trip they'd ever taken.

'And?' she said, elevating an eyebrow, prodding him to continue.

Unfathomably confident, Orlando yawned. She felt a flicker of unease.

'I'd so wanted to protect you, sweetheart, but as you've clearly got infidelity on your mind and grasped the wrong end of the proverbial, I suppose I'll have to come clean.'

Misgiving assailed her. Was there honestly a logical explanation? Had she got it all wrong? Had she missed something? Anxiety grabbed her by the throat. If she'd made a terrible mistake, she'd never hear the last of it. Suddenly, her more recent emotional strides forward felt hollow.

Orlando patted her hand and sat back. He didn't say *pin your ears back and listen up.* He was too polite. But this was what she intuited from his demeanour. She recalled the embarrassing time she'd unaccountably discovered a red sock left in a white wash, turning two of Orlando's brand new Brook Taverner shirts pink. He'd been furious and patronising at the same time.

'We had a very nice chap working as an intern for us,' Orlando began. 'You know how it is, a favour for an old school chum wanting to give his son an instant-in to a prestigious law firm. Well,' Orlando riffed, still with the smug *I'm ahead of the game* bearing, 'to tell the truth, and I'll spare you the gory details, the young man, nice enough, mind, wasn't up to the mark. As *yours truly* was appointed his mentor, it fell to me to break the news that he didn't quite have what it takes for the rigours of property litigation.' Orlando paused, regarding Melissa with a *with me, so far*, expression, the kind a doctor bestows on a patient when explaining a complicated medical procedure that might go horribly wrong. Melissa swallowed and nodded. Yes, she was with him, goddammit. 'As you might expect,' Orlando continued smoothly, 'His ego was a little dented — fair enough — but he became quite abusive. Rather proving my point,' Orlando said with fruity satisfaction, 'and jolly threatening.'

Melissa's shoulders slumped. She felt foolish and stupid and judgemental, rolled into one. 'That's outrageous,' she stammered.

'Indeed,' Orlando agreed earnestly. 'I thought it would all die down — these things usually do — but then his father got involved and, to put it in common parlance, *cut up rough*. Came to the office, would you believe, demanding my head.'

Oh God, Melissa thought. 'Oh dear,' she said, hand against her temple in an effort to tame the thoughts spinning out of control inside her head.

'Since then, the daddy has been running a campaign of harassment against me.'

'What kind of harassment?'

'Making unpleasant phone calls, following me to the train station on one occasion. The situation has got quite ridiculous.'

Melissa jolted in alarm. 'It's not ridiculous. It's intolerable. You're a lawyer, for God's sake, surely you can take action?'

'In my vast experience, it's best to let these things die a natural death.'

'But, like you said, this is harassment. There are laws against it.'

Orlando pouted his lips, steepled his fingers, and assumed a lawyerly air. 'A very high threshold is required for harassment, darling. A long history of proven incidents is paramount and, as frustrating as it is in this instance, the high bar to push forward a convincing case has not been met.'

Melissa shifted uneasily in her seat and narrowed her gaze. 'Who is this man?'

'Nobody you know.'

'Was the phone call last night from him?'

'It was. He threatened to come to the house.'

'Jesus Christ, Orlando,' Melissa exploded, forgetting that small ears had excellent hearing.

'Mummy,' Autumn burst out.

Ignoring her daughter, Melissa said, 'Surely, this is an escalation and warrants a conversation with the police.'

'Charles would not be happy to draw that kind of attention to the firm.'

'Bugger, Charles,' Melissa said, even if he were a senior partner, reaching for her drink.

'Darling girl,' Orlando said expansively. 'The man doesn't know where we live.'

'But he could find out and,' Melissa lowered her voice, 'I'm on my own most of the week with the children.'

'And why it's being taken care of.'

Part of Melissa was relieved, the other brimming with trepidation. Did Orlando mean an alarm system was being put in, or her husband had employed rough men to do bad things? (She'd been reading Orwell). If she had to take a punt, she knew which it would be. She didn't dare ask and Orlando was content for her to drop the subject. 'So you see, Lissie, my sweet, I only have eyes for you. Now what do you fancy eating?'

CHAPTER SIXTY-FOUR

ROSE

Half the family looked as if they were waiting in A&E, the rest, for the jury to return after a particularly distressing trial. Self-appointed peace negotiator, Wren, took up residence next to Craig. Celeste and Benedict sat on the sofa opposite them. Raff and me sat in easy chairs. Beverages arrived though I didn't notice who made them. I was glad to drink a good old-fashioned cuppa and not booze, a sound move in the circumstances. Craig cradled a mug with three sugars, and helped himself to a plate of Digestive biscuits as if he hadn't eaten for days. Very noticeably, Benedict didn't respond to Craig's dodgy question *what have you done with my mum and my sister?* With jaw-grinding vehemence, he stated, 'I strongly refute your allegation.'

'Refute?' Craig questioned, mouth full.

'Deny,' Wren translated.

'I would add,' Benedict continued, pink-faced, 'that your mother was little more than a child when she visited Blackthorn, making your allegation all the more offensive.' His voice rose. Not quite the civilised chat we'd expected, I thought.

Craig's mouth was a thin straight line.

'For the avoidance of doubt,' Benedict began again.' I did not sleep with your mother and Alice is not my daughter.' He sounded overbearing and he looked thunderous.

'Your mother must have fallen pregnant shortly after she left Blackthorn,' Celeste sneaked in to Benedict's visible satisfaction. Craig's answer was to glower and grab another biscuit, plunging it into his drink.

Now Benedict had established the facts, as he saw them, he sketched out how Alice had come to live at Blackthorn. Craig looked interminably bored, as if he knew very well how Alice had inveigled herself into the family.

'Children's nanny?' Craig scoffed.

'She came with very good references.,' Celeste pointed out.

Craig displayed his cynicism by belching.

'She was great with the kids,' Wren said for nobody's benefit.

'I wouldn't go that far,' Celeste corrected her.

Benedict checked his wife with a look that would fell a charging rhino. 'We did everything to make your sister's stay here as hospitable and happy as possible. We treated her like one of the family.'

Not my father-in-law's best choice of words, I thought, seeing as Craig had got it in his head that Alice was Benedict's daughter.

'Did you promise her the world, like you did my mother?' Craig snarled.

Beside me, I felt Raff stiffen, though not as much as Celeste.

Benedict sighed and crossed his arms. 'I have no idea what you're talking about.'

'I do,' Celeste said, snap in her voice. 'The letter.'

Benedict's eyes briefly widened until a glance from Celeste reassured him and his expression changed to one of relief and gratitude. In that unique moment I saw them closing ranks. I saw how they'd each got each other's backs. I had to admit it was impressive. But in the age of email and text, who the hell wrote a letter these days?

'What letter?' Craig asked, as if reading my mind. It was the first time since he'd arrived that he came across as less sure of his argument.

'The one your mother sent several years ago, requesting financial assistance,' Celeste answered.

'Bloody hell,' Wren burst out. 'You never said.'

'A cheap attempt to take us for a ride, why would we?'

Celeste spoke with panache and *take that* delivery. Seemed to me that lying ran in the Trinick family. Wasn't this, after all, a sophisticated form of shakedown?

Craig raised his voice. 'Because she was owed, your husband . . .'

Celeste threw back her head and laughed, cutting him off. 'Your mother was a fantasist. Ask your grandmother.'

'She's dead,' Craig cut in. 'Keep your hair on,' he said in response to Wren slapping a hand over her mouth. 'She died of old age.'

'I'm sorry for your loss,' Celeste said mechanically. 'We liked Beatrice enormously. The same cannot be said for your mother, I'm afraid. Sixteen years of age, she swanned around Blackthorn as if she owned the place. Thought she'd got her feet under the table here for life. When your grandmother decided to leave us to live in the West Country, Bonny did nothing but whinge and whine, rather like your sister when it was mooted she moved to my daughter's home.'

I was having trouble keeping up with all the familial connections. We should have been talking exclusively about Alice. Instead, we were discussing Mrs Cole, *the dragon nanny*, and her daughter, Bonny.

On the attack, Celeste sat up straighter, her voice stronger. 'No doubt your mother passed her grievances and delusions on to your sister. Alice, I'm afraid to say, is a chip off the old block, and any suggestion that she is my husband's daughter is another naked attempt to extort money from us. I will not tolerate it,' she finished.

Benedict didn't say 'Well done, darling'. His expression said it all.

Craig opened his mouth to speak and closed it again. Before anyone filled the vacuum, I asked him the obvious question.

'Where is your mum now?'

'Cleared off when we were kids.'

'But that's terrible,' Wren said.

'I'm sorry,' I said because I was, although it exposed the hole in Craig's beliefs. 'How old were you when she left?'

'Seven.'

'And Alice?'

'Ten.'

Poor kids, I thought, but it begged a horribly obvious question.

'Does your dad say that Alice has a different father?'

'No, but . . .'

'You see,' Benedict pitched forward. 'It's all a pack of lies.'

I kept my gaze doggedly on Craig. 'Did your mum stay in touch after she left?'

Craig eyed me suspiciously, suspecting a trap. 'Flitted back a couple of times. Always talked about coming to get us, but the time was never right,' he said resentfully. 'She'd send birthday cards, sometimes shit presents. Don't look at me like that,' Craig said responding to Celeste's irritated expression. 'Last thing Mum bought us was a pair of trainers, two sizes too small and a shawl for Alice that would look good on an old lady. No offence,' he said, staring at Celeste. I heard a sharp crack. I think it was my mother-in-law's teeth grinding together. 'Bright pink, it was,' Craig said. 'Always from different postmarks and places. Lived the life of a gypsy, my mother.'

'When was the last time you heard from her?'

'Dunno. Five years ago maybe.'

'And you haven't heard from her since, no phone calls, no messages?' I needed to be absolutely certain.

Craig shook his head, disappointment etched into the hard lines on his face. I felt for him. His confidence had come from a mistaken, deeply held belief and, in seconds, it had been smashed to pieces. But I couldn't say I was sorry because it meant Benedict was in the clear.

Scenting victory, Benedict asked, 'When was the last time you heard from Alice?'

'A month ago. She messaged me. Said everything was going well. Never said what she was up to, mind, though I had a pretty good idea.' Craig wiped his nose on the side of his hand.

'I'll bet you did,' Benedict sniped.

'Point is,' Craig said, surly. 'She always stays in touch. Always. She would never go away and not tell me. Since Dad lost the plot, I'm all she's got. I know something isn't right.' He looked at each of us, eyes ablaze with conviction.

Keen to damp down his anger, I asked, 'When was the last time you actually saw her?'

'A year ago, maybe less. She always came home when she was in trouble.'

'What sort of trouble?' Raff asked.

'Bloke and black-eye trouble.'

My eyes widened. I remembered the cigarette burns on Alice's arms. I remembered how afraid she'd been. What if her old boyfriend had found her? Suddenly a new and ugly picture was forming in my mind. Drops of fear trickled down my spine.

'What's his name?'

'Sean Stamp, by name and nature.'

Raff exchanged glances with me. He was thinking what I was thinking. 'Where can we find him?'

'Anybody's guess,' Craig said with a shrug.

Not helpful. 'What does he look like?' I asked.

Craig frowned. 'Only met him once.'

'Try.'

'Built,' he said.

'Dark hair, blonde hair? Blue eyes, brown eyes?'

'Short hair like thatch. Brown eyes, size of piss-holes.'

My heart gave an involuntary lurch. 'I know him.'

Five pairs of eyes zeroed in on me. 'The man in the van,' I stuttered. 'He was delivering washing machines.'

'Nah,' Craig shook his head. 'Sean's never done a day's work in his life, unless you count dealing drugs.'

'But don't you see, it has to be him?' I urgently explained how I'd come across Stamp. Craig slowly seemed to catch on. The more I talked, the more uncertain and worried he became.

'Is Sean the kind of man who would stalk your sister and abduct her?' Raff asked.

Slack-jawed and a lot less macho, Craig confirmed Sean Stamp was exactly that kind of man. Craig's whole bearing shifted from bolshie and belligerent to sheepish and anxious, the answer to his sister's disappearance staring him in the face and, blinded by family folklore, he'd completely missed it. I felt sorry for him. Benedict was less forgiving.

'Why the hell didn't you consider this before? You do realise the whole time you've been living in some fantasy about what I've supposedly done to the women in your family, this man could be responsible for your sister's disappearance? God only knows what's happened to Alice.'

Raff turned to me. 'Do you remember anything about the vehicle, Rose. What about registration?'

I shook my head. Blindly, I tried to remember. 'It had a picture of a puffin on the van.' Then turning to Craig: 'When you saw Alice last, where was she living?'

'Stourport-on-Severn, but that was nearly a year ago. She won't be there now.'

Raff stood up. 'You're coming,' he said to me. 'It's the only lead we have.'

CHAPTER SIXTY-FIVE

MELISSA

It had been the most depressing evening. Melissa had barely touched her fish and chips. The more Orlando rattled on, the greater her despondency. She felt like the person who believes they smash it in an interview only to receive a *thank you but no thank you* text. All her judgements were off and it hurt. She had thought, of late, her old confidence was coming back. There was greater equality in her marriage after she'd started sticking up for herself and it felt good. Since the move from Blackthorn, she wasn't the little woman at home with the children, a lazy woman at that, according to Orlando. And now she'd given voice to a stunning lack of trust in her husband and handed him a weapon to be used against her at some later, opportune moment.

But — there was always a *but* with Orlando — did she honestly believe him? The story about a young disgruntled intern was believable. Less credible, the ex-employee's rampaging father. However protective a parent, it wasn't sensible to kick up such a fuss. And who was "sorting it out" and how? The obvious move would be to slap a restraining order on the guilty party. Melissa couldn't see Charles, senior partner at Duckworth and Prior standing for anything less.

They were back at their rental. Orlando had taken charge of the children and, cringingly, had run her a bath into which he'd poured her favourite oil, a calming blend of lavender and rose that was not doing what it said on the bottle. About to sink below the surface, her mobile rang. Nobody called her after nine o'clock unless it was an emergency. With a heavy sigh, she sat up, stretched a wet hand to a towel on the chair beside her, gave it a cursory dry and picked up her phone.

No *hello, how are you, how is Little Haven?* Wren plunged straight in. 'You'll never guess what?'

Melissa had had enough of speculation and said so.

'Gosh, you sound awfully cranky, Lissie. Thought you'd be living it up. Everything all right?'

'You can't live it up with small people,' Melissa pointed out dryly.

'Yes, well,' Wren said stiffly, and then proceeded to tell Melissa about the unexpected guest.

Melissa sat up so hard, water sloshed over the side of the bath. 'Alice's brother?'

'And there was an awful row and fight and . . .'

'Slow down,' Melissa barked. 'Over what?'

'Craig — that's Alice's bro — had got it into his head that Daddy had had a relationship with Bonny, you know Mrs Cole's daughter, *and* . . .' Wren paused for dramatic effect, 'that Alice was Daddy's daughter.'

Melissa's tired mind reeled back to the scene in the kitchen. It fast-forwarded to the blasted priest hole. *Oh. My. God.* She felt a terrible hammering in her chest.

'Hello, you still there,' Wren said, not without irritation.

Melissa staggered a response.

'Well, it's not true, *silly*,' Wren said.

'No?' Melissa asked weakly.

Wren bored on about a begging letter, *shakedowns*, as she put it, meaning requests for money, and described a family who, as she also put it, were several prawns short of a seafood salad. 'Delusional,' Wren said conclusively. 'Mummy said that Bonny used to waft about as if she owned the place. Obviously thought she'd got her feet under the table and then had the nerve to pass on the same spiel to her daughter, Alice.'

Crikey, Melissa thought, struggling to keep up. So crazy Alice had set out with the sole intention of robbing the man she believed had taken advantage of her mother. Did Alice honestly believe Benedict was her father? If she did, behaving in the way she had made Melissa queasy.

Still gossiping, Wren reported how Bonny had abandoned her children and taken off and disappeared.

Melissa felt a raw sensation in the back of her throat. What was it Rose had said? *You don't think it strange there are two disappearing women? Both gone, never to be heard of again.*

'Where is Alice's brother now?'

'At mine, snoring his head off in the guest room. Obviously I made sure he had a close acquaintance with soap and water first. The parents wanted him gone but I took pity on him. I'll boot him out tomorrow.'

'Where were Raff and Rose during all this?'

'Weren't you listening? They were *there*. I've never seen Daddy so worked up. Raff had to leap to his defence and would have punched the shit out of Craig if it hadn't been for Rose stepping in.'

'Good grief.'

'She's turned into a right jumped-up little detective,' Wren said scathingly, 'showing off and asking all sorts of peculiar questions.'

Melissa was getting an arm-ache and a headache.

'Raff was quite impressive, actually,' Wren continued, with the unstoppable delivery of a runaway train. 'But that's not all,' she said, warming to the big punchline, one that threatened to knock Melissa out cold. 'Alice had an abusive boyfriend.'

Melissa's heart rate picked up despite the warm embrace of bathwater. In no particular order she heard *puffin*, *washing machine*, and *Stourport-on-Severn*.

'So what do you think of all that?' Wren said, finishing breathlessly.

Melissa thought there was something sinister and strange going on.

CHAPTER SIXTY-SIX

ROSE

Raff was tight-jawed and tense. Pumped up, he looked like he wanted to hurt someone, anyone, to obliterate those ugly allegations and make the situation with Alice go away. My head hurt from contradicting emotions. I no longer felt like an outsider but an insider and I didn't like it at all.

Back at the lodge, I scrolled online and located Puffin Washing Machine Repairs, a unit next to a car park off Stourport's High Street. It took me a while to persuade Raff that searching for Sean Stamp at that time of night was not a good plan. 'No washing machine shop will be open now. We'd be better off going first thing tomorrow morning,' I said.

'What if he's beating the crap out of her? You heard what the brother said.'

'She's dead, Raff.' I couldn't shake the sensation. It was too strong, too rooted. Maybe it was because of what happened to Poppy, my little sister, but I've always felt a close affinity with death, not in a dark and dismal way, just that there is no point in denial.

His fair eyebrows pinched together. His eyes narrowed. Raff is not a man to patronise or pity; still less to have spiritual inclinations.

'Think about it,' Raff said. 'If the police had concerns, found a body even, they would have visited Blackthorn.'

Like with Shona Reid, I thought with a shudder.

'But what if she hasn't been found yet?' I countered. 'What if she's . . . God, I don't know . . .'

'Okay,' Raff said, eager to humour me. 'Suppose you're right. What do we do? Call the police?' He slipped out his phone, held it up, like it was a security pass to MI5. *I have your back and I will make this call if you want me to*, his expression said.

And tell them what exactly? Was there enough for the police to go on? Would they take a grave allegation, based on speculation and rumour, seriously? I said as much.

Raff sighed, slipped his phone back into his pocket, and stared out of the window, as if the answer was there all along, only we were too dim to notice.

Eventually he spoke. 'A good night's sleep and then we'll get up early, find Alice's boyfriend and nail him to the floor. We won't leave until we get answers. It will turn out fine, you'll see.'

'You honestly think so?' I loved Raff for being an eternal optimist and dearly wanted to believe him. I wanted his confidence to rub off on me.

'Alice has probably moved on to her next Get Rich Quick scheme.'

I so hoped he was right and I was wrong. My most immediate problem was how to get out of work tomorrow. Jerome would be furious if I bailed again. I didn't like the idea of lying to him, although I didn't feel I had much of a choice. I glanced at my watch: after nine, never a good time to make a call. At home, he answered after a couple of rings.

Bunching my fists, digging my nails into the palms, I pulled out the stops and went for it. 'Jerome, I'm so very sorry but there's been a family emergency.'

'Oh dear.' I could tell from the tone that he'd already worked out what was coming next.

'I really won't be able to make it to work tomorrow. I can only apologise for letting you down at such short notice.'

This could go one of two ways. A mercurial individual, Jerome would shrug his shoulders and mumble that it could not be helped, or fire me. He did neither.

'It is *très* inconvenient but these things cannot be helped. Take the rest of the week and we will rearrange.'

I didn't argue. 'Thank you,' I said earnestly. 'I'll make it up to you, I promise.'

'Yes,' he said, convincing me that the price might be quite high.

'Is there anything to eat?' Raff asked when I'd ended the call. Seeing as dinner was a write-off, I couldn't blame him. After a hard day's labour he was bound to be hungry. My appetite, on the other hand, had gone walkabout. 'Something quick and easy,' he said hopefully, picking up on my less than enthusiastic response.

'Sandwich?'

'Got any bacon?'

I confirmed we had and ferreted a pack out of the fridge. While I prepared our makeshift dinner and put the kettle on — you have to have a cup of tea with a bacon sarnie — Raff immersed himself in his Xbox. I tuned out to the sound of *Call of Duty*.

Sitting back down, plates on our laps, Raff's phone rang.

'Blast,' he said, looking at the screen. 'Dad,' he muttered, taking a massive bite out of his sandwich.

I watched warily. Was this about Craig or was this about Celeste and Orlando? I could tell Raff had the same thought. 'Yep . . .' he answered, chewing vigorously. 'Tomorrow . . . Not an issue . . . I know, I know . . .' He swallowed what he was eating. 'Calm down, Dad. Nobody is going to do anything stupid.'

No, I thought, *stupid had already been done a million times since I got here.*

'Yes, yes,' Raff said tersely, 'I'll let you know how it goes . . . What?' Raff said, rolling his eyes at me. 'Yes, she's doing fine. No, she doesn't think that . . . Goodnight, Dad.'

'Hell,' Raff said, taking another bite out of his sandwich.

'At least he cares what I think, I suppose.'

Raff grunted a reply.

'He's bound to be shaken up,' I said. 'We all are.'

Clearly cross, Raff finished his mouthful. 'Some more than others.'

We ate and drank in silence. I cleared away. Raff looked tired and pensive. I empathised.

'What do you think happened to Bonny?' I asked.

'God knows.'

'I know Craig said some terrible things but he seems genuinely concerned about his sister. I feel sorry for him.'

'Don't. Wren must be cracked to offer him a bed for the night. Hope she sleeps with one hand on her phone and the other with a knife.'

'That's a bit strong,' I said, shocked.

'He's a gold-digger, Rose, just like his sister and mother.'

'Thought you were sweet on Bonny,' I said, teasing.

Raff pulled a face. 'Who told you that?'

'Melissa.'

'Minx.' Raff grinned. The humour quickly faded. 'Hope she's okay.'

Not much I could add. I hoped Melissa was. I feared she wasn't. I'd heard that betrayed wives, in common with betrayed husbands, were slow on the uptake. Given the family's tradition of omertà, I thought it might be some time, if ever, before Melissa found out about her husband's affair with her mother.

I asked Raff whether he'd been in the dark about the letter sent from Bonny.

'The bloody cheek of it—' he chewed and swallowed. 'No, I did not know. Blasted woman was delusional. I mean fancy filling her kids' heads with malicious lies.

'If she'd been a decent mother, none of this mess with Alice would have happened.'

Part of that mess was mine. I'd made assumptions, misjudged and questioned my father-in-law's fidelity.

And then I remembered the picture of Shona Reid he carried close to his heart.

I remembered the rattle and roar of overheard conversation.

I remembered there was no word from Carmen.

Just when I'd glimpsed the seeming truth of a situation, a shift in gear and fast acceleration would take me hurtling straight into a brick wall.

CHAPTER SIXTY-SEVEN

ROSE

I listened to the birds tuning up for the day after a thin night's sleep.

'You awake?' Raff murmured.

'Yes.'

'Get any kip?'

'Not much. You?'

'Same.' I turned towards him. 'Goodness, you look like hell.' His face was bruised and he had a fat lip. I didn't like to think what the rest of him looked like.

'Well hard,' Raff joked. 'Should put the wind up Sean Stamp.'

'We're not going to put the wind up him. We're going to get answers.'

Raff grunted a reply and we got up and moved around like shadows. Eventually, fortified by tea and toast, we hit the road.

I had that bleary, irritable hangover feeling and was glad to let Raff drive my Mini. According to the satnav, it would take us over an hour to bomb up the M5 and into Worcestershire. We arrived around nine.

Stourport has a one-way circular system. It stands on a canal basin at the junction of the rivers Severn and Stour. The marina is impressive with cruisers and small boats bobbing in a blustery breeze. Red-brick Georgian houses give the appearance of a town punching above its weight, although this was historic. While once thriving, now its main attraction is an amusement arcade and funfair, set among fish and chip shops and fast-food venues near the bridge.

"Puffin" (we were reliably informed by Google) was in an industrial unit at one end of the car park I'd seen online. Two vans were parked directly outside, both similar to the one I'd seen outside Blackthorn. I hung back behind Raff to let him do the talking. An enquiry to discover where Sean Stamp hung out would come better from him.

The reception area was small and cramped, like you see in a backstreet garage. A youngster, with a choppy haircut, and a badge, stating her name was Samira, pecked at a computer keyboard. She was in conversation about a customer's machine with an older, capable-looking woman who I quickly intuited was the business end of the operation. Beyond, I glimpsed a workshop with washing machines in various states of repair.

'Hi,' Raff said warmly. 'Wonder if you can help.'

The older woman responded with a smile. 'We'll do our best.'

'Do you have an employee called Sean Stamp?'

Samira stopped tapping. The older woman's smile cleared off and out through the door. 'Who wants to know?'

Without missing a beat, Raff said, 'We're friends with his girlfriend, Alice.'

The woman crossed her arms and gave Raff a long, hard stare.

'And we're trying to locate her,' he ploughed on. 'Thought Sean could help.'

'Friends of Alice, you say?'

'Yes,' I piped up. 'To be honest, we're worried about her.'

The woman checked me out with a searching expression that left me sweaty and uncomfortable. 'And you want to find Sean to have a word?'

I ignored Raff's hands, which had automatically bunched into fists. 'Please,' I replied.

'Then you'd best get in the queue.'

'Popular guy then,' Raff said, darkly humorous.

The woman didn't see the joke. 'Not a man who makes friends and he no longer works for me. You'll find him at the funfair running one of the rides.'

Samira glanced at her watch. 'He won't be there now.'

'Do you know where he lives?' Raff appealed to both of them.

'We don't normally hand out addresses of employees past or present,' Samira's boss said, 'but I don't hold with men who hit women and, as Sean put a dent in the van he borrowed for private business, I'm willing to make an exception.'

Private business? I cast my mind back to the afternoon my path had crossed with Sean Stamp. Quiet road, violent man, lone woman — God, I'd got away lightly. But Alice had not and I worried it was my fault. I'd let on that the Percivals lived at Blackthorn and, by default, so did Alice. It was on me he'd tracked her down. I felt awful.

The older woman wrote down an address on a slip of paper and handed it to Raff. 'It's within walking distance.'

'Thank you so much.' He beamed.

'One other thing,' I said, curious. 'Why do you have a puffin as your logo?'

The woman cracked a smile. 'Because I like them.'

The only light moment in the day.

* * *

Sean Stamp lived above a Chinese chippy on an A road with a view of traffic lights. Cars and lorries thundered past shops with security grilles over the windows. Sandwiched between a nail salon and butcher's, the flat appeared to extend over two poky windows that were about to fall out of the masonry onto the street below. An alley led to a set of steel steps and the flat above. Raff was all for bounding up there and bashing down the door. I shot out a restraining arm.

'You heard what that lady said. The man's a thug. If you want answers, violence won't work.'

I could tell from his face that Raff strongly disagreed.

'What if Alice is locked in there?' I said. 'If she isn't, we need to find out where she is.'

'So what do you suggest?' Raff's voice rippled with frustration.

'Let me go first.' As far as I was concerned, Sean Stamp and me had unfinished business.

'That's not happening,' Raff said, adamantly. 'We know Stamp abuses women. He wouldn't think twice about taking a swing at you. The man could be a murderer.'

I really wished Raff hadn't pointed that out. 'I won't be alone. You'll be outside.'

'No, Rose . . .'

'I'll make it clear you're waiting. Then, if he cuts up rough, or whatever, you charge in.'

Raff was resistant. 'No way.'

'He won't talk if you're there. He sort of knows me.' Pushing it, he *might* recognise me.

Raff's hands shot to the top of his head in frustration. 'Bloody hell, Rose.'

'I'll be all right.' I wasn't convinced, if I were honest. All I knew was that people had a habit of telling me things. I was a collector of lies and secrets. My listening face was about to be put to the biggest test. *Please*, Raff. Trust me on this.'

He dropped his arms to his sides, muttering about it being a bullshit idea. He opened his mouth, changed his mind and then said, 'Three minutes and then I'm coming in.'

I tipped up on my toes. 'Thank you.'

'And I've got the cops on speed dial,' Raff warned.

I climbed the steps to a door that was battered and bashed and did not sit tight on its hinges, and rapped at the home of a man who could hit me.

CHAPTER SIXTY-EIGHT

MELISSA

In the light of her flagrant allegations, Melissa had expected a backlash. None had come. Yet.

Early morning, Orlando had walked down the lane for a solo swim in the bay and Melissa spent a happy hour pottering about with the children. Adept at blotting out problems and things that disturbed her, she'd erected a sturdy mental wall between her and the vengeful father of the former employee out for Orlando's blood. It was being taken care of, Orlando had told her. She had to trust her husband.

On his return, Orlando, toned and energetic, attended to his emails after which he suggested a family walk along the coastal path to Strawberry Hill. He sounded as if taking a break in his schedule for her and the kids was a heroic act. In return, because nothing came without conditions with Orlando, a very quid pro quo guy, he said he wanted to swim every morning for the rest of their stay.

'A little me time.' He grinned. Melissa was glad to agree because it meant part of the old Orlando, the knowable arrogant man to whom she was married, still lurked within.

Melissa packed snacks and drinks for the children and prepared the morning coffee. Orlando was very particular about brand and time. Elevenses meant elevenses. In the calm of the kitchen, Melissa gave her husband highlights of her conversation with Wren the night before that she'd been too wound up to divulge before bedtime. A bedtime that had seen Orlando act as an ardent and enthusiastic lover, and in a way she wasn't sure she quite enjoyed. His response to Wren's more lurid descriptions, of the fight and so on, was to sigh and grunt disapproval. 'Grown men fighting, it's risible,' he said, dismissive and reaching for a custard cream. 'As for Alice, seems I was right all along.'

Melissa bit back the retort threatening to choke her. Orlando had been entirely wrong in employing Alice in the first place.

'Anyway, the general consensus is that the boyfriend is involved in her disappearance,' Melissa said.

Orlando raised an eyebrow. 'Makes sense. Sounds like a lowlife. Where did you say he hails from?'

Melissa told him.

Orlando stroked his chin thoughtfully.

'Do you know the place?'

'Never heard of it. Now can we change the subject to something more uplifting?'

The weather was late September warm and the walk started off well enough. What had seemed like a good idea at the time '—It's only a mile,' Orlando had told her — took into account distance but not terrain. Unpredictably, and it wasn't on the forecast, the wind picked up. A choppy sea stared up from down below, jaws open. Autumn had a nasty habit of letting go of her hand and scampering on ahead. Edgar resented being bumped along in a backpack and let everyone loudly know about it.

Since Wren's revelations the night before, and despite Orlando's cool contempt, Melissa had found herself obsessively chewing things over to the point of giving herself mental indigestion. Dicing with death along a steep crumbly path, sharpened her thinking. What were the chances of so many random incidents occurring in the same time frame? People were coming and going at Blackthorn on a virtually revolving door basis, some never to be seen again. Melissa did not believe in coincidences. She didn't really believe in accidents. In the cold light of day, with a wind screaming in her face, she was no longer sure she believed her husband. A man like Orlando did not suffer fools (she should know). He didn't get driven out of his home and he didn't have things *taken care of*. A fixer, *he* took care of things. Efficiently. Ruthlessly. As Mummy had pointed out with passion: *he is the man with the sword.*

Melissa stumbled and came to an abrupt halt. Bile flooded her throat. Every hair on her arms and the back of her neck stood to attention. She couldn't move an inch. And it wasn't because she'd reached a fork in the path.

'It's this way, Lissie, left *left*,' Orlando bawled over his shoulder. Edgar, in his backpack, strained to look round. Autumn tugged at Melissa's hand.

'Come on, Mummy,' she whined.

Melissa thought of the numerous times her mother had spoken warmly of Orlando. Always coming to his defence, always sharing a joke with him, sometimes at Melissa's expense. Her mother liked to touch him too. A little nudge to his elbow. A sly pat on his thigh. An adoring and indulgent look. They were comfortable around each other. Too comfortable. And what was it Mummy had said when Melissa took Orlando home for the first time? He had potential. Because her mother sensed his virility? Because she fancied him? Melissa recalled how Mummy encouraged the relationship, gave it her blessing, gave it her all because everyone knew that if Celeste didn't agree to something, it didn't happen. *Christ.*

Dates popped up in Melissa's mind like symbols on a fruit machine. Orlando's weekends away, her mother's trips to London; the literary festival that never was because Mummy had fallen ill. But what if she hadn't been ill? What if Orlando had not been working his socks off? Now Melissa came to think of it, Belinda hadn't responded strongly to the suggestion that Orlando was overworked and under pressure. And why had Orlando embraced running in the woods so early in the morning when he'd never shown an interest before? Why had he suddenly turned into a generous and enthusiastic lover overnight?

'Mummee,' Autumn cried.

Jolted back to the present, Melissa nodded absently and planted one foot in front of the other, letting her small daughter lead the way.

'Good grief,' Orlando said. 'Get a shift on. It's not that bad.'

But it *was* that bad.

Her husband and her mother had been absent from Blackthorn on the night of Alice's disappearance. Her mother and her husband had keys and they knew Blackthorn intimately. Melissa recalled seeing Orlando humour Mummy when he'd first introduced the new nanny at the family gathering. At the time, Melissa had commented, *'I don't know how you pulled it off.'* Had some strange deviant scheme been plotted and planned from the beginning? Was this Orlando's idea of a sick joke? Silly naive Alice would not have seen the danger, no more than she had.

Melissa tried to shake some sense into her thinking. Why on earth would they do something like that? For kicks? Because they could? An argument from long ago carried on the wind and smacked Melissa in the face.

'You fucking killed her,' Violet raged.

'I will not have you swearing in our home,' Celeste thundered.

'You did. You did. You did. She was too nice and you were jealous.'

Was Mummy jealous of Alice, too?

A piercing sensation at the base of Melissa's skull fled to the top of her head. Her heart was racing. Inside, she was screaming.

And then she opened her mouth and let rip.

CHAPTER SIXTY-NINE

ROSE

I'd dragged Sean Stamp out of bed, bog-eyed and bare-chested. His jogging bottoms were grey with a white stripe down the side. He had black corduroy slippers with worn toes on his feet. A deep scratch cut a tramline down his face. I shuddered to think how he'd got it. Did Alice have sharp nails? I tried to remember and dropped my gaze to his hands. They were calloused and coarse, thick-fingered with dirty nails. Hands that would punch and pinch, hit and slap. Through red-rimmed, bloodshot eyes, he stared, trying to figure me out. Probably wondered if I were a cold caller, or someone from the council. I didn't think I could pass for a police officer, although, from the apprehension in his expression, it could have travelled through his mind.

'Remember me?' I said brightly. Before he did I took a bold step forward. Momentarily confused, he didn't argue and then a light appeared to switch on in his brain. He gave a startled noise, raised his hands, palms up in surrender. I was already in and had my back against his door.

'I want no trouble,' he said.

'Last thing on my mind,' I said cheerily.

A glance around the room confirmed that Sean Stamp took minimalism seriously. There was hardly any furniture: a chair with a suspicious looking stain on it, possibly curry, a small table and a TV on the wall with a 48-inch screen. A kitchenette suggested that Sean didn't do much cooking. The door to the bedroom was open. I didn't think he'd got Alice tucked up inside. Another door was closed. Bathroom, I thought, eager to take a peek.

Dragging my gaze away from his surroundings, I said, 'Alice.'

'Yeah, right,' Stamp said, clearing his throat in a way that suggested he had a pack a day habit. 'Thing is . . .'

'You tricked me.'

'No,' he said, with deliberation. 'I was trying to make sure she was safe, on the quiet like.'

'On the sly, you mean. And what do you care whether or not she's safe? You hurt her. I saw the burns on her arms.'

Colour fled across Stamp's pointy cheekbones. 'You wouldn't understand,' he muttered.

'Try me. You tracked her down deliberately.'

'I did not.'

'You were stalking her.'

He didn't deny it. He couldn't.

'How did you get that cut on your face?'

'Next-door neighbour's cat took a lump out of me.'

'Didn't know you had a next-door neighbour.'

'Flat above the loans shop. That away.' Stamp gestured to the right with his thumb.

'Must have been a tiger.'

'Yeah, well,' he said sullen.

Time to switch things up. 'Did you break into the grounds at Blackthorn while you were *delivering your washing machine*?' I asked with heavy sarcasm.

Stamp's response was to run a hand under his unshaven jaw.

I thought of the night I'd seen torchlight seeping through the trees, the lake, the cold water, the slime. 'You broke into the house, too, didn't you?'

Stamp dropped his gaze. 'I never.'

'Liar.'

Game up, he glanced up. 'Okay, okay, only once,' he insisted.

A hard ball of fear lodged itself inside my throat. People tell me things and it's not always very nice. What was Sean Stamp about to tell me? 'Go on,' I said, thinking any moment Raff will be through that door.

'I left a calling card.'

I frowned.

'There was a party at the house,' Stamp said, swallowing hard.

'You were there? You watched the family?' I was horrified.

'I didn't hurt anyone. I didn't steal anything. I was only looking and I waited until everyone had gone,' Stamp added ardently, as if this made sneaking around, breaking and entering all right.

Through gritted teeth, I reminded him that he said he'd left something.

Stamp's shoulders slumped. 'My brand of cigarettes.'

Pig. 'No wonder she was scared to death of you.'

He gave a start as if I'd hit him with a Taser. 'That's not true. She loves me. I love her. Always have, always will.'

I was taken aback by his passion. He didn't look away. He looked me straight in the eye. No ifs and no buts. In Sean Stamp's bashed-up mind he really did care. And then I realised what he'd said. He was talking in the present. *She loves me*, not *she loved me*.

'You don't know that Alice has gone, do you?' I said.

'What?' Stamp gave a terrible start, almost a shudder. His mouth dropped open, revealing a missing tooth. Fear quickly translated to anger. I'd been doing all right up until that point. He'd seemed biddable. Now he looked pissed off. He jutted out his chin and took an intimidating step towards me. Sweat and stale alcohol came off him in a sickening wave. In a flash, I sensed the smouldering violence beneath his skin. It wouldn't take much for it to ignite. Knees clanking, I stood my ground. Actually, I did more than that. I clutched my bag tighter and felt the outline of the scissors in the pouch inside.

'Where is she?'

'If I knew, I wouldn't be standing here having this conversation,' I snapped. 'She left, disappeared, vanished, where you and nobody else could find her.'

'No, she wouldn't do that. She always comes back. *Always*.' Distraught, he shoved his face in mine. 'You think I took her?'

'Why wouldn't I?'

'Bloody listen, will you? I never did nothing to her.'

I couldn't gauge how long I'd been there. Come on, Raff, rush in and save me.

Sean Stamp seemed to catch on. He sniffed the air like a terrier on the scent of a rat. 'Did you come alone?'

'My husband is outside. One wrong move from you and he'll call the police.'

Mention of cops had a subduing effect. The fight went straight out of him and I didn't think he was acting. I didn't know if it was fear of being found out for a crime, as yet unreported, or distrust of the law in general.

What kind of man was he? How had he come to this? What sort of upbringing had made him so crazy and angry? These questions came from the fact that I found it hard to believe that people are congenitally bad. You don't look at a child and think *they're evil*. Environment, poverty and parental neglect were the main drivers for crime. Prisons were full of headcases with horrible childhoods. I believed this when I looked into Sean Stamp's eyes. Yes, he'd done awful things, but he really didn't know what had happened to Alice, or where she was now. Sean Stamp was a run-of-the-mill bully. Confront him and he crumbled. I realised then he was no murderer.

Banging on the door alerted me to Raff's presence.

'You going to let him in?' Sean said quietly.

'No,' I said, 'I'm going to let me out.'

CHAPTER SEVENTY

MELISSA

Her head hurt. Her throat was sore, her chest felt as if barbed wire had bound itself around her heart and embedded itself deep. Betrayal was bitter and twisted and tasted of corked wine.

Melissa remembered little of the journey back from their cliff walk, apart from her children crying and Orlando wrapping his arms around her in a bid to keep the shattered pieces of her mind together. For some reason this had seemed terribly funny until a sharp slap across her face convinced her otherwise. Turning her sullen, shocked gaze on Orlando, she spotted fear behind his eyes. There was a tremor in his jaw. His nostrils flared like a racehorse about to keel over after winning the Cheltenham Gold Cup. His lips weren't pale. They were white. *Good*, she thought, his guilt was proof of her sanity. For a woman who had been unsure for so long, Melissa now had certainty. Her priority was to take the children, who were rightly scared of her outburst, and get away from Orlando as fast as possible. It would take patience and kindness to win back their trust. She would do all in her power to give them a settled upbringing. At least now that she knew

Orlando's disgruntled employee story was bogus, she didn't have to worry about an irate father threatening to pay a visit any time soon.

Past the post office and back in the car park, Autumn anxiously asked her father what was wrong with Mummy.

'She's had a funny little turn, that's all,' Orlando answered, swiftly recovering his composure. With deft efficiency, he put the children into their car seats. Melissa allowed him to assist her into the passenger side. He practically yanked the seat belt out of the buckle to strap her in, as if he could restrain her thoughts. Melissa entertained images of straightjackets and white sanatoriums. 'A rest and she'll be good as new,' Orlando told his daughter, chillingly casting Melissa a dubious glance.

It took minutes to drive to the rental.

Melissa fled to the bathroom and locked the door. Her reflection in the mirror revealed dark shadows and lines she'd never noticed before; the imprint of Orlando's slap, red and clearly visible. She was surprised he hadn't knocked out a tooth.

'Think I'll go for a lie down,' Melissa said weakly when she emerged.

'You do that,' Orlando said, clipped and in control. 'Do you need anything?'

'A cup of tea and aspirin would be good, thank you.' *Play nice. Play obedient.*

While he was gone she surreptitiously scrolled through the names of local long-distance cab firms on her phone. There was one, the only one, in fact, in Haverfordwest. She sent an email requesting a ride back to Gloucestershire with two small children, both requiring car seats, the following morning, around seven fifteen. Orlando would not pass on an opportunity to swim in the sea, however sick his wife. It would take split-second timing but Melissa was game and she was desperate. The thought of spending another night with her husband made her feel as if she had a false widow spider crawling slowly across her belly.

Orlando returned with tea, a glass of water and medication on a tray. She wriggled up on one elbow and thanked him. He went to leave and then, changed his mind, and sat on the bed. He reached over and touched her cheek where he'd slapped her. It hadn't hurt until now.

'I'm so sorry,' he said with false sincerity. 'I didn't know what to do.'

'I'll live.'

'But after what you told me about that man Alice was involved with.'

'Orlando, we've been married long enough for me to know you're not a wife beater.'

'We're good then?' he said hopefully.

'I think so.' She wasn't going to openly absolve him. Spotting a pressure point, Orlando made himself comfortable, crossing one leg over the other. 'What was all that about on the cliff then?' he asked.

Melissa took an avid interest in the duvet and tugged at the weave. 'I don't know. Panic attack, I think. Everything got to me. The fear of that awful man — the intern's disgruntled father you told me about, suddenly turning up, Alice's disappearing act, the move, you being away so much.' She chewed her lip, wondering if she'd over exaggerated. 'Obviously, I'll get used to it,' she added.

'Well, it's not forever,' Orlando said, ebullient.

'No,' she agreed, keen to avert her gaze.

'You're sure that's all? You scared us.'

'I know and I'm sorry.'

He tilted his head and viewed her as if he didn't know what to make of her. Her history of fragile mental health played for once in her favour. She saw his desperate need to believe that she really had suffered a mental health crisis. He wanted to probe yet feared where it might lead. Melissa felt empowered.

'So I really don't need to call a doctor?' Orlando let the question hang. Sedation would have suited him.

'No need, a few more days and nights of sea air and I'll be back on track.' Oh yes, Melissa thought. No doubt about getting back in the saddle.

'Good, good,' Orlando said, more to assure himself than her, she thought. She gave him instructions for preparation of the children's lunch and theirs. 'Consider it done,' he said patting the bed and standing up. 'I'll leave you to rest.'

Almost out of the door, he stopped, acutely embarrassed. 'Would you mind if I pop outside for ten minutes?'

'Oh?'

He screwed his face into a conspiratorial expression and dropped his voice to a whisper even though there were only the two of them in the room. 'Need to make a quick phone call. Work catch-up.'

Sure you do, Melissa thought. 'Not at all,' she replied. 'Take as long as you like.'

CHAPTER SEVENTY-ONE

ROSE

We argued all the way back to the car. Raff was infuriated I'd stopped him from "teaching the bastard a lesson", meaning Sean Stamp.

'Why the hell are you defending a man like that?'

'I'm not. I'm defending you,' I cried, exasperated. 'He's just the kind of guy who'd take pleasure in doing you for assault.'

'I'd like to see him try.' Raff balled his fists as if he were acting out his fury.

I stomped on ahead. Raff quickly caught me up. 'What exactly happened in there?'

I described the conversation.

'He could have killed you.'

'But he didn't.'

'No, he gave you a sob story and you fell for it.'

'That's absolute crap. He didn't ask for pity. Not once.'

Thwarted, Raff's grey-green eyes darkened to the colour of a stormy ocean. 'If I'd been there we'd have got to the truth.'

'I *did* get to the truth.'

'Only because he conned you.'

I stopped walking. 'I'm not a pushover, Raff.' I was so narked I stamped my foot.

Raff rarely sees me angry. Cars whizzed by. Pedestrians skirted around. We must have looked a right pair.

'I didn't mean it to come out like that,' he said, tugging at my sleeve.

Yes, you did. 'I know when I'm being lied to, Raff, and Sean Stamp didn't fake his surprise and dismay unless he's in line for a BAFTA.'

Raff slipped his hand through mine. 'I'm sorry. I wasn't there. I shouldn't judge.'

'No, you shouldn't,' I said huffily. 'You'll have to take my word for it. Sean Stamp is a nasty piece of work but he hasn't made off with Alice to do God knows what.' The most likely truth was more mundane: Alice saw the pack of cigarettes Sean had deliberately left and fled in panic. I told Raff what I should have seen all along. 'We're all running around like idiots while she is over the hills and faraway. You were right,' I said, feeling unaccountably hacked off.

'Although it doesn't explain the locked doors,' Raff said softly.

'Doesn't explain the security cameras not working,' I said. 'Think Alice disabled them?'

Raff laughed lightly. 'You really think she was that capable?'

I shook my head. No, I didn't.

'There's a way simpler solution. They were never on.'

I gave a start.

'Not what you're thinking,' Raff said with a grin. 'I spoke to Dad. He told me the contract with the security firm had lapsed.'

'Why would he let that happen?'

'He didn't think it good value for money now Blackthorn is no longer a wedding venue.'

'Do you believe him?'

The bridge of Raff's nose wrinkled. 'Why wouldn't I?'

Convenient timing, I thought, quickly scratching it. What was I saying: that Benedict had deliberately let the contract lapse?

We were back at the car. 'Now what?' Raff said.

'Home, I guess. I've got the rest of the week off.' And felt bad about it. Maybe I'd put some hours in for my course. About time, I took it seriously.

'I've got a better idea.' Raff grinned. 'Early lunch — my treat — and then I'll crack on and you can put your energy into finding us somewhere to live.'

Glorious, I thought.

We found a table in Côte in Cirencester's Black Jack Street. We ordered French lager and tartiflette for me and non-alcoholic beer and a steak for Raff. For the first time in ages I felt my body relax. I only needed my brain to catch up.

The restaurant hummed with couples dating, families with little kids and big kids, old married and young married, businessmen and tourists.

'Happy?' Raff asked.

'Happier,' I replied with a smile. Around me was real life. Living at Blackthorn was like being on a film set of a period drama with too much intrigue, dark relationships and mayhem. I was content to step away from my complicated world and sit back and observe.

I was draining my glass when my phone plinked. Immediately, my heart gave a great big leap. I showed Raff straightaway. He peered across and grinned. The image was of Carmen and Kai outside what looked like a castle with pointy towers. The message was simple: *Thank you xx*

I was so relieved I could have shouted my joy aloud.

'That's wonderful,' Raff said.

'The best news.'

He looked across at me, sharing my delight. 'All we need now is a similar message from Alice.'

That would be terrific. I tried not to think of Craig and his conviction that his sister had come to harm. I tried to eliminate my barking belief that she was dead.

Afterwards, Raff drove me home and picked up his truck to head out to price up a job in Ampney St Peter. I phoned a couple of letting agents about potential rentals and was told they'd been taken. Disappointed, I signed up and ignored the sharp intake of breath when I named how much we were prepared to pay. At this rate we'd be buying our own home at the same time as drawing our pensions.

I spent the next hour researching the psychological impact of hair loss for women. While it was accepted that not a lot could be done about genetics, busy, stressful lifestyles and air pollution were cited as potential reasons for a steep rise in cases. Dyed hair often shed more than natural, although it didn't interfere with the hair cycle and prevent hair growth. There were various products on the market to mitigate thin hair and balding scalps, a few more hardcore than others and requiring a doctor's prescription. I made notes about a more holistic approach to break the vicious cycle of stress leading to hair loss resulting in more stress, and so on. How I'd escaped alopecia in recent weeks was nothing short of a miracle.

Worded out and unable to concentrate, I grabbed a fleece and went outside onto our tiny patio. The woods were the other side of our picket fence, dark and intimidating. I suppressed a shiver at the thought of my last walk there. Unable to crush my fears, I turned my attention to Melissa instead.

Wrapped up in the *Sean is a murderer* saga I'd almost forgotten about my poor sister-in-law. Well, not forgotten exactly, rather pushed her to the back of my tired mind. Without breaking my promise to Raff, I'd have to do something about that when she returned.

CHAPTER SEVENTY-TWO

MELISSA

'Where the devil are my keys?' Orlando cursed.

Melissa watched impassively, standing in her dressing gown, as Orlando hurled about the living room, narrowly missing Edgar. 'Do you really need them? You could easily lose them on the beach and if you're only walking down the lane . . .'

'I don't like not having them,' Orlando snapped. 'It's like going out without your trousers on.'

Melissa resisted the salacious remark that was on the tip of her tongue. 'Have you looked down the sofa?'

'Naturally,' he said irritably.

Just go, for God's sake.

She'd spent a horrible night sleeping on the edge of the bed, as far away from Orlando as possible, trying not to involuntarily grind her teeth. She could do nothing about the stale stink of whisky on his breath. He must have done half a bottle.

Anxious that he might abandon his swim entirely, she adopted a soothing tone. 'I'll be here to let you in.' She kept her face relaxed and smiling. *Convincing.*

'I know that,' Orlando said peevishly.

'While you're gone I'll have a hunt around. They're bound to turn up somewhere.'

Entirely true, seeing as she'd disappeared them.

On a hot line between Little Haven and Blackthorn the previous evening (Melissa suspected) — Orlando had made a number of "work" phone calls. Whatever had transpired had put him in a foul mood and, consequently, he'd announced that he was going to extend his "me time" by walking down to the cove the following morning, bright and early, instead of driving there. Slipping into the bathroom, Melissa had texted the cab firm and cancelled the booking. While Orlando had glowered in a corner with a tumbler of scotch, getting pissed in every sense of the word, she'd stolen his keys and disappeared them in the bottom of her holdall. She reasoned he would not need them again. Not ever.

Orlando emitted a gale of a sigh, gave in, pecked Melissa on the cheek and, hurling goodbyes to his children, left for the beach. The door shut with finality. Melissa thought it the sweetest sound.

Mentally, she put on her running shoes. First, she put the TV on for the children.

'Daddy doesn't let us watch telly before breakfast,' Autumn announced, her little face serious.

'Daddy isn't here, buttons,' Melissa assured her with a smile.

'He'll be *so* cross.'

Melissa crouched down to the same level as her daughter. 'I won't tell if you don't,' she whispered.

Autumn's eyes widened with glee. 'Okay,' she whispered back.

'Good girl,' Melissa said. 'We're going to have fun today.' To emphasise the point, she handed each child extortionately expensive fruit bars bought from a local farm shop in the Cotswolds. Children occupied, she hurried off to dress, throwing on sweats and hoodie and sneakers.

Next, she packed drinks and treats and put these into the car, alongside the holdall from which she'd first retrieved

Orlando's keys. Toys that travelled everywhere with her children were packed next. She didn't bother with clothing. Outside, Melissa couldn't help but tip up on her toes and scan the lane anxiously to make sure that Orlando had really walked down the hill and wasn't lurking in the bushes making another of his ghastly phone calls. With every passing second she had a genuine horror of Orlando returning unexpectedly. Flying back inside, her fingers trembled as she changed Edgar's nappy.

'Right, buttons, let's go,' Melissa said. 'Time for an adventure.'

'But I'm still in my PJs, Mummy.'

'That doesn't matter.'

Autumn's nose wrinkled into a frown. 'You said we were going on an adventure.'

'And we are.'

'Then I want my ballerina dress. And my silver shoes.' Autumn twirled around on her toes.

Frustration nipping at her ankles, Melissa said, 'We'll take them with us.'

'No, Mummy.' Autumn's small hands reached for her hips. 'You *said* we were going to have fun.'

Normally Melissa would have reasoned and argued. She didn't have time. In an agony of anxiety she wrangled Autumn into her chosen clothing, pulling her little girl's hair accidentally in the process and making her cry.

'I'm so sorry, sweetie,' Melissa said. 'Here, cuddle.' Cuddle duly administered and with time ticking, she bundled both children into the car with tablets set up for their favourite programmes.

Beads of perspiration popped up on Melissa's brow as she climbed into the car. Heart hammering in her chest, Melissa started the engine, set the satnav and took off. The whole operation had taken forty-five minutes. Orlando would be back in less than an hour. *Screw him*, she thought.

Melissa didn't slow down, or calm down, until she was the other side of Haverfordwest. Forty minutes later, she received a call on the hands-free from Orlando.

'Where the hell are you?' he boomed down the line.

'Approaching Carmarthen,' Melissa replied.

Stunned, it took Orlando longer than she'd expected to process the news. When he finally got his head into gear he sounded as if he'd eaten sand for breakfast.

'What the fuck are you doing there?'

'Orlando, language. The children are with me in the car.'

'Then I'll ask again,' Orlando said through gritted teeth, no doubt about that. 'Why are you going to Carmarthen?'

'I'm not. I'm going home.'

'What do you mean you're going home?'

He sounded like an adolescent boy with a voice on the verge of breaking.

'I'm not repeating myself,' Melissa said, imperious.

'You can't leave me here,' Orlando screeched. 'I'm bloody locked out.'

'Then you'll understand how I've felt for most of our marriage.'

'Don't be ridiculous.'

'I don't appreciate your lies, Orlando.' Melissa glanced in the rear-view and caught Autumn's eye. *Fibs,* she mouthed. Autumn nodded and went back to Peppa Pig and George.

'I have no idea what you're on about.'

'I think you do.'

The silence at the other end of the line extended. Melissa pictured Orlando stalking up and down, phone aloft, the edge of his tongue grazing the side of his mouth, something he did when under pressure.

'Look, I need a shower and warm clothing.'

Melissa indicated to turn left onto a roundabout.

'Come back and we'll talk,' Orlando said.

Did she detect a plea in his voice? She smiled. Orlando the great man with the bloody big sword was worried. 'We are done with talking.'

'Jesus Christ, when will . . .'

'Tell you what, why don't you give Mummy a ring? I'm sure she'll drop everything to come and pick you up.'

'Now, look here . . .'

'Don't you dare deny it, you conniving treacherous adulterous bastard.' Another quick glance in the rear-view and Melissa was relieved to see that Autumn had fallen asleep. 'And, trust me, I *will* be talking to my mother.'

Melissa listened and heard Orlando inhaling strongly through his nose. Anyone innocent would have hotly denied such a flagrant accusation. Orlando could huff and puff all he liked, he and her mother were guilty as charged and she was going to tear their bloody house down. What else was on his conscience, Melissa wanted to know.

'What did you do with Alice?'

Orlando's roar was loud enough to wake their sleeping child.

Melissa killed the call and phoned Ava.

Having bored her old friend to death for years about the state of her marriage, Ava was not surprised to hear that Melissa had left Orlando.

'Well done, you.'

Revealing the tipping point could keep until they were alone, Melissa thought, thinking that Ava the unshockable would be astounded. 'Thing is I don't want him having access to our rental in Sapperton,' Melissa said.

'I'll send a locksmith around this afternoon.'

'Perfect.'

'Anything else you need?'

'Apart from a new life?'

Ava laughed. 'You'll find yourself *and* a new life, promise.'

Melissa hoped Ava was right.

'Actually, there is something,' Melissa said, thinking on her feet, not something she'd done in a while. 'Could my kids crash in with yours for a few hours? I know it's a huge imposition but . . .'

'It's fine. My mother is down from Surrey for the week.'

'She won't mind?'

'Not a bit. Adores little ones. Big ones not so much,' Ava said ruefully, referring to her teenage daughters from a previous marriage, Melissa surmised. 'I'll let her know to expect Autumn and Edgar.'

At the mention of her name, Autumn's ears pricked. 'We're going to Auntie Ava's?'

'We are,' Melissa said cheerily and then to Ava, 'As long as I'm not putting your mother out.'

'Stop worrying, Melissa. We all want to help. This is your chance to strike a blow for freedom.'

Glowing inside, Melissa ended the call. Home first, feed the children, drop them off and then on to Blackthorn to have it out with her mother and shatter her father's life.

CHAPTER SEVENTY-THREE

ROSE

I returned to my studies. Sort of. Perched on the window seat, and in pole position, I saw Benedict fly out and, a little later, Melissa in the Range Rover fly in.

I stood up with a jolt. I couldn't see Melissa's face. The vehicle, going too fast and pebble-dashing the lawn with gravel, told me everything I needed to know. Melissa had found out about the affair and was back for retribution. Where Orlando was or how he was, I'd no idea. I phoned Raff to warn him of impending aggro — as if we hadn't had enough of it.

'You're kidding. How the hell did she find out?'

'It wasn't me. It has to be Orlando.'

'Doubt it.'

'I'm staying out for as along as possible,' he said. 'I suggest you keep your head down.'

Great, I thought. My life was getting better and better. Unable to settle, I admit I briefly entertained *accidentally on purpose* dropping in to the big house to see if I could calm things down. Once upon a time I'd have been curious to know how Celeste would defend herself. That time was over. Curiosity killed the cat and it had certainly done for me. I'd learnt my lesson. I could lie low, carry on with my studies — fat chance — or sort out the unappealing mound of washing that had accumulated because I'd been too proud to accept an offer of free laundry. About to tackle the load, Wren burst in.

I looked at her sharply. 'Don't you knock before you come into someone's home?'

'This *is* my home.'

I couldn't be bothered to argue. 'What do you want, Wren?'

'Have you seen Craig?'

'No.'

'Fuck it.' Wren plumped down on the sofa, pulled out her phone and stabbed at it as if she were piercing film for a microwave dinner. 'The tosser's cleared off with my wallet and stolen a grand from my account.' The way she viewed me you'd think it was my fault. 'Yes,' she snapped to whichever poor soul was at the other end. 'My debit cards have been stolen. I need to cancel them.' Gales of tutting and complaint erupted from the depth of the cushions — standard Wren operating behaviour. I waited patiently and wondered how it was going at the big house and who had eviscerated whom. If I had to bet, I'd put my money on Melissa.

'God, you need me to write to confirm?' Wren blustered. 'Can't you take my word for it?'

I wouldn't if I were you, I thought sourly. After a lot more huffing, Wren finished. Her cross little face looked into mine. 'Raff was right. They're all bloody rip-off merchants. And after all I did for the ungrateful little scrote. I fed him alcohol, listened to him droning on half the night about his rotten childhood, virtually had to put him to bed, *and* I gave him a hearty organic breakfast. He must have scarpered as soon as I went to take my yoga class.'

Alarmingly, now that Wren was here she seemed quite happy to stay. Tucking her legs up underneath her, she invited me to scooch down beside her on the sofa. Reluctantly, I did.

'Did you track down Alice's bloke?'

'Uh-huh.'

'And?'

'He's a thug but I don't believe he made off with her.'

'So she went of her own accord?'

'I suppose she did.'

'It's all Melissa's fault.'

I couldn't have disagreed more and tried to change the subject. 'Have you heard from her?' I asked.

'Spoke to her a couple of nights ago to give her the highlights. She didn't say much,' Wren said, evidently disappointed. 'How did you read the room?'

What a question. 'I didn't.'

My answer as unsatisfactory to Wren's ears as her sister's, she continued to gripe. 'If only Melissa hadn't meddled with arrangements. Alice was perfectly happy here until she was told the family were moving out.'

'It's not Melissa's fault,' I pointed out frostily. 'The only reason Alice was here was to extort money.'

'Hmm,' Wren said. 'Do you think Alice really believed Bonny's lies?'

'That she was Benedict's daughter?'

Wren's teeth rested on her bottom lip, anguished at the thought. She was probably thinking about inheritance and how it might affect her.

'I don't know. Probably not,' I said, for Wren's benefit.

Wren sniffed. 'I think Mummy was right about Bonny getting pregnant *after* she left Blackthorn.'

I wondered who the father was. I also wondered what the "dragon nanny" made of her daughter's pregnancy. From the sound of Beatrice Cole she'd have gone apeshit and filed a lawsuit if she thought for one second Benedict was responsible.

'Horrible of Bonny to blame Daddy,' Wren said conclusively, 'although . . .' The tip of Wren's tongue rested in the corner of her mouth. She was building up to something, I thought. 'You don't know Daddy like I do,' Wren said tentatively. 'He's laid-back. Never loses his temper. A really cool dad.' Wren fastened on to me with a frightened gaze. 'In all my life I've never *ever* seen him behave like he did last night.'

CHAPTER SEVENTY-FOUR

MELISSA

Melissa viewed Blackthorn, the seat of all her problems, with quiet hatred. She'd believed that by moving on and creating her own world and family, she could leave the past behind. But her mother had conspired to deny her. Entering through the great door instead of the usual entrance, round the side and used by family members, Melissa felt murderous.

Her mother was in the kitchen, seated at the table. A pot of tea and two china cups, with milk, no sugar sat on a tray, as if in readiness. It would take more than tea and sympathy to bridge the chasm between them. For an adulterous woman Celeste sat calm and composed, her hands folded in her lap. Maybe if she stood up, Melissa would notice them tremble. She hoped so.

'I assume Orlando warned you I'd be coming?'

'He did.' Celeste poured milk into two cups and topped them up with tea. 'Might I know how you found out? Did Raff tell you?'

Melissa pinched inside. 'Raff knew?'

Celeste nodded.

'Christ, then he will have told Rose.'

'He assured me he hasn't.'

'So who *does* know?'

'Only the four of us.'

Melissa clicked her tongue. 'That's all right then. Now that we've got the *housekeeping* squared away, where's Daddy?'

'I sent him out.'

'To fetch your lover?'

A pulse ticked above Celeste's top lip. 'To protect your father.'

'Too late for that. When will you confess to your sordid affair?'

Celeste's top lip twitched. 'Sit down, Melissa. Please.'

'I'd prefer to stand. I won't have tea, incidentally. This won't take long.'

'Will you let me speak first?'

Her mother sounded solemn, if not especially contrite. Melissa crossed her arms. This had better be good, she thought. 'If you must.'

Like a solo trumpeter, Celeste took a breath. 'I know you're hurt and I understand your sense of betrayal. I'd like to put all the blame on Orlando but I can't. It was entirely consensual and . . .'

Melissa cupped a hand to her ear. 'Did I hear the word *sorry*?'

'Of course I'm sorry. I wished it hadn't happened but we are where we are.'

'Spare me the homily. How long has it been going on?'

Celeste lowered her gaze.

'Months? Years? When I was pregnant?' Melissa was breathing hard, struggling to find the right tempo.

Recognising Melissa's struggle to contain her emotions, Celeste glanced up, the suggestion of a smile on her lips. 'Melissa, darling, as you're very aware, marriage is tough. Especially so when you're running a business together. It takes energy and commitment and a certain amount of give and take . . .' Celeste broke off, cleared her voice. Melissa didn't interrupt. She shot her mother a look that, had it been fired from a gun, would have killed her. Celeste blanched. She didn't so much as pick up the thread; she snipped it in two. 'My life with your father has not always been easy.'

'You expect *me* to feel sorry for *you*?' Melissa let out a peal of laughter. It sounded like shattering glass.

'I'm trying to explain.' Strain tugged at Celeste's mouth and distorted her voice.

'I'm not interested in your explanations.'

'Then why are you here?'

'To tell you that you can have Orlando. He's all yours. You're welcome to him.'

The lines underneath Celeste's eyes deepened. Her lips, so pale, tugged down at the edges. For the first and only time in her life, Melissa thought her mother looked scared. So she bloody should.

Melissa craned forward. 'You think you can pick up the reins of your marriage and carry on as if nothing happened? You *think* I'll bring my children here to play with their grandmother, the same woman who screwed their daddy?'

Celeste paled. She emitted a sound. Possibly a whimper.

'I'm sorry. I'm sorry. I'm sorry.'

'It's too bloody late.'

'I'm begging you, darling. Edgar and Autumn have nothing to do with this.'

'And neither does Daddy but he'll soon know what an evil duplicitous bitch you really are.'

Celeste started as if she'd had scalding water chucked over her.

But Melissa was not finished. Melissa didn't care. She was on a cathartic roll.

'You disgust me. For years you've told me that I'm fragile, that I have *issues*,' Melissa spat, with contempt. 'When it's you with your vile thoughts, petty jealousies and obsessions who's the crazy one.'

Her chair scraping back on the tiled kitchen floor, Celeste staggered to her feet. 'Please don't ruin your father's life.'

'There it is. Twist it around to make it my fault. Just like you did with Violet. *Me* ruin my father's life? What about *you*? What about what *you've* done to ruin mine and my big sister's lives?'

Celeste let out a startled cry. A hand flew to her mouth and it was shaking.

'You honestly expect me to keep my mouth shut about that too?'

Celeste's lips parted, pleading.

'Not this time,' Melissa said.

CHAPTER SEVENTY-FIVE

ROSE

I saw the car speeding down the drive. For a terrible moment I thought Melissa wasn't going to brake in time and the Range Rover would wind up crashing through our front window. Tyres spitting dirt and gravel, it skidded and came to an untidy halt. The driver door swung open and Melissa, hatchet-faced, climbed out, strode to the door and rapped on it so hard the frame rattled.

Wren leapt to her feet first. 'What's got into her?'

I had a rough idea and pushed past Wren to the door. Under Melissa's accusing gaze the rough thought assumed shape and form. 'You knew, didn't you, and you never breathed a damn word?'

'Knew what?' Wren said, crowding in behind me.

'It wasn't like that, Melissa.' Although it really was like that. 'Please, come inside,' I said gently. Seeing the pain in Melissa's face I wished I'd confessed what I'd seen to her first. The result couldn't be any worse than this.

Tossing her chin, defiant, Melissa brushed past, almost knocking me over, and planted herself in front of the log burner.

'Would somebody please tell me what's going on?' Wren whined. The room was so small she had to stand on the threshold of the kitchen.

'Our mother is shagging my husband.' The rest came out in a torrent of cold rage, hot rage and incandescent rage. After the initial *Holy crap* response, Wren let out a little gasp with every revelation.

'So,' Melissa finished, breathless and triumphant, 'I bloody dumped him in Wales, and see how they like him, *and* I'm having all the locks changed on our property so he can't come back. Ever.'

Wren assumed a condescending tone. 'Melissa, don't you think you should calm . . .'

'I do not need to calm the fuck down.'

'It's horrible but it might be helpful to think of it as a one-off.'

Melissa viewed her sister as if she'd announced she was joining a nunnery and taking a vow of silence. If only. 'Their sordid affair has been going on for years,' she snapped back.

'Are you sure there isn't some mistake. Did Mummy really admit to it?'

Giving a passable impression of her mother, Melissa said, 'It's complicated because of the dog's life your daddy led me.'

Wren's face pinched. 'She actually said that?'

'In so many words.' Melissa turned accusingly to me. 'When did Raff tell you?'

'Raff?' Wren interrupted, aggrieved. 'Am I the only one who doesn't know?'

'You *and* Daddy,' Melissa fired back. Again, to me, uncompromisingly, 'Rose?'

'Raff didn't tell me. I told him.'

Melissa's mouth dropped open. Her eyes swam with tears. Before her legs gave way she sat down with a thump. I sank down beside her and put an arm around her. She felt thin and bony. There was nothing to her.

'Budge up,' Wren said, sneaking in, the three of us sitting there: me ashamed, Melissa distraught and Wren in shock.

Eventually, Melissa got it together and I told her as calmly as I could how I'd stumbled across the adulterers in the woods.

'I wanted to tell you, Melissa, but Raff thought it best to hush it up — at least in the short term. He was trying to protect you,' I added, aware that a decision made for the right reason can sometimes create the wrong result.

'Law of unintended consequences.' Melissa sounded horribly like her husband.

'I can't frigging believe it,' Wren said. 'It's so *gross*. And what with Alice's brother showing up and robbing me blind, I wish I'd never come back.'

'Alice's brother stole from you?' Melissa said, surprised.

I let Wren bring Melissa up to speed on the latest development. Wren would exaggerate a trip to the village shop. She had no need to embroider events of Craig's rip and run.

Melissa took a breath, thinking and taking it all in. 'Did you find Alice's boyfriend?' she asked me. 'Wren said you and Raff had gone looking for him.'

I told her we had and shared the detail of my conversation. 'I believed Sean Stamp's account,' I added.

'I wouldn't be so certain,' Wren said.

'He definitely followed her to Blackthorn,' I confirmed. 'I think he put the fear of God up her, but he's as much in the dark about Alice's disappearance as we are.'

Melissa listened, thoughtful. I don't know whether she doubted Stamp's word, was reliving the bust-up with her mother, thinking how once she had loved Orlando, or plotting how she could turn the screw on her unfaithful husband. I had little doubt that Florence's expertise would be required sooner or later.

'What now?' Wren put her hands above her head and stretched.

I turned to Melissa who, seemingly tuned to a different wavelength, didn't answer immediately.

'Liss?' Wren prodded.

Melissa appeared to come to a mighty decision. 'What are you doing for the next couple of hours?' she asked her sister.

Wren's eyes thinned with suspicion. 'I was going back to the Granary to meditate. Why?'

'Could you do me an enormous favour?'

'Well, I . . .'

'Pick up the kids from Ava's and take them back to Sapperton.'

Me?'

'You can practice your auntie skills.'

What auntie skills? I wondered.

'But they barely know me.'

'Then here's your chance.' Ignoring Wren's panicky protestations, Melissa asked if I had plans.

Intrigued if perplexed, I confirmed I hadn't.

'Excellent. Can we take your car?'

'Now hold on a moment . . .' Wren began.

'I'm not taking no for an answer,' Melissa warned, firmly pushing the Range Rover keys into Wren's hand.

'But where are you going?' Wren wailed.

'To visit Violet.'

I stifled a reaction. Violet, the pariah of the family; Violet, the drug taker and woman who'd fried her brains; Violet, the eldest child who'd known Shona Reid as well as anyone.

Wren pushed her head forward, doing a fair impression of a chicken. 'What for?'

'Because I have things I need to tell her and things I need to say.'

And things you need to hear, I thought.

'Now?' Wren said. 'Can't it wait?'

'No.'

'But . . .'

'And I swear to God, Wren, one word to the parents, and I'll swing for you.'

Melissa stood up and belted out the room. Grabbing my bag, I pulled what I hoped was a convincing *search me* face at Wren and followed Melissa to where my car was parked.

Rain was in the air. Mist, like smoke, drifted through the trees, muting the colours of autumn. Unexpectedly, my positive mood deserted me.

We climbed into my Mini. Melissa put her seat belt on. I did the same. Before I pushed the starter button, I took a breath.

'Why are we really going to see Violet?'

Melissa turned to me. 'Metaphorically, she knows where the bodies are buried.'

I supposed I should have felt honoured, favoured, and chosen. I felt none of those things. 'Why me? This is Percival business, isn't it?'

Melissa returned my straight-talking with a straight look. 'You're as much a Percival as I am and you don't believe the lies we've been spun any more than I do.'

CHAPTER SEVENTY-SIX

ROSE

My head swam.

'I ought to let Raff know where I'm going.'

'I can drop him a text, if you like,' Melissa said.

'Thank you.'

Melissa located his number and tapped out a message while I drove. We'd barely travelled a mile when Melissa's phone bleeped with an irate text from Wren. Greatly amused, Melissa read it aloud.

Your car is disgusting. It stinks of vomit.

Thanks for letting me know, Melissa tapped back. *I'll book it in for a valet.*

My sister-in-law was jaunty and upbeat — alarmingly so. 'Autumn was sick on the way down,' Melissa explained, as if it were a hoot.

I glanced across. 'Are you feeling okay?'

'Never better.'

'I'm so sorry about everything.'

'Rose, stop apologising for things that have nothing to do with you.'

It sounded like a command. Even Melissa displayed the Percival trait of imperiousness on occasion.

'Will you speak to your dad?' I asked her.

'About *it*?'

I nodded. I couldn't picture that conversation. I didn't want to.

'In time.'

'But you definitely will?'

She evaded my question and asked one of her own. 'You were there when Daddy got into a fight with Alice's brother, weren't you?'

'I was.' I paused. 'Wren obviously told you what sparked it.'

'A risible lie.'

I didn't comment. 'Speed camera,' I murmured, slowing down.

'My father would not be that stupid.' Melissa said more to herself than to me.

I saw that the trip to see Violet was important because it was connected. Melissa needed answers before she spoke to Benedict. I grimaced at the thought of the photograph of Shona Reid I'd found in his jacket. Keen to offer some good news I told her that I'd heard from Carmen.

'She sent a lovely photo of her with Kai.'

Whatever Melissa was going to say she didn't say it.

'You're not convinced?'

'If you say Carmen is fine then I believe you.' Melissa glanced out of the window.

'I saw the photo, Melissa.'

'Then I'm sure you're absolutely right.'

'And I was wrong to be alarmist,' I insisted. 'I thought we had two missing women.'

'Maybe we still do.'

She meant Alice and Bonny. Mother and daughter, what were the chances of that? Then I had another idea: perhaps Alice had panicked and somehow found Bonny. Maybe they were together. Except it didn't compute with Craig's account of Alice staying in touch. Why would she leave him out in the cold if she were safe?

Melissa's phone bleeped. She viewed the screen and smiled. 'Raff says *received and understood*.'

'Did you tell him where we were going?'

'Should I have done?'

'I suppose it doesn't matter,' I said apprehensively.

'Says he's going to drop in to see Tom on his way home and might cab it back.'

Pints of beer followed by vindaloo at the Rajdoot. I stifled a groan, although, hand on heart, I couldn't blame him for wanting to get wasted.

* * *

The Forest of Dean covers the western part of Gloucestershire and is home to twenty million trees. Parts of it have a funny old atmosphere, as if ritual sacrifices took place there long ago. (Or maybe Blackthorn had rubbed off on me. I'm sure the people who live there don't feel quite the same). Travelling along A roads, it took us around forty-five minutes and then the fun started. Melissa thought it was one way and then, changing her mind, another.

'It's been a long time since I visited,' Melissa said.

We doubled back on ourselves once and then, as if she'd suddenly got with the programme, Melissa cried, 'Right, that way.'

I went *that way*, up a steep incline that took us deeper into now dripping woodland and places that looked as if they'd been banged together with items from a skip. More than that, they looked like versions of the house that Jack built when Jack had dropped acid. In Violet's case that would have been appropriate. We passed a sign that said Lydbrook.

Melissa became more alert and excitable, an indicator that we were on the right track. Finally, we found Violet's home tucked away, remote, up a private drive. It didn't say Keep Out. It bellowed it. I would have never found it without Melissa's help. Toy town in appearance, it was a patchwork quilt of a house.

We drove onto an area of hard core. There was no other vehicle there. Entrance to the property was up three steps onto decking. It was made up of three sections, possibly shipping containers, with glass fronts. I could see a bed in one area and a dining table in another. The kitchen was directly ahead. Mechanisms were inset into the window frames to allow metal grills to drop down for privacy and security. The roof was covered in solar panels. Sprouting out of the top, a steel funnel suggesting a log burner. I wondered if Violet was off-grid and, as lonely as the place was, it looked idyllic to my eyes.

Our shoes clattered across the decking. 'Is Violet expecting us?' I whispered to Melissa.

'No, but she's in. She never leaves.'

Melissa tugged on a bell pull. 'There's a small garden out the back where Vi grows vegetables. She's probably out there.'

Unaccountably nervous, I waited, shifting my weight from one foot to the other. Violet appeared and opened the door. Short and wiry, similar to Wren in build, she wiped her hands on her trousers and, next, her brow with the back of a hand. Thick-framed spectacles dominated a face that was deeply tanned from working outside. I tried not to look at her head, the same colour as the skin on her cheeks and was completely bald. Lines radiated from the corners of her eyes but they weren't from laughter. These were sad lines, *hard work* lines, *telling a story* lines and I wondered what kind of tale Violet would speak. As much as I longed to know, I dreaded it, too.

'Hello, Violet,' Melissa said softly.

Violet stood for a moment, viewing her sister. I saw warmth and shared affection. A fragile smile broke out on Violet's face and for a second she lit up. Fading as quickly as it appeared, Violet scratched distractedly at her scalp, and without glancing at me, motioned for us to come inside.

It was a home of primary colours, how I imagined a playschool to look inside. Jolly cushions in rich shades of red and gold, orange and blue, and covers and throws in various textures and hues. Art on the walls was bright and primitive. I wondered if Violet had painted them herself. There were pots and china and assorted stuff, like I'd seen in the Corn Hall when the antique market was in full swing. The interior was a dazzling array that grabbed hold of your visual senses, giving every impression of a life that was riotous and fun and uncomplicated. As much as I admired it, it felt as convincing as the smile on a man intent on committing suicide. What lay beneath?

We were in the living area, a cosy space with built-in seating and a log burner that was alight. A fluffy grey cat with the most extraordinary topaz-coloured eyes jumped off a chair with an indignant stare. Coiling its tail around Violet's legs, it scurried into the kitchen; evidently an animal as antisocial as its mistress.

Melissa sat on one side of the hearth, Violet the other. I hived myself off in the corner, out of sight, out of mind. So far, Violet had not uttered a word. Was she mute?

'Vi, you remember Rose, don't you? Raff's wife,' Melissa said conversationally.

Violet nodded, without acknowledging me.

'How are you keeping?' Melissa asked her sister.

Violet took her time, as if checking her vital signs. Eventually, she said, 'I'm quite well . . . thank you.'

Her voice sounded shrivelled, as if she hadn't spoken to another soul for years.

'That's good,' Melissa said cheerily. 'Vi, do you know why I'm here?'

Again a long pause. 'Perhaps.'

'Remember what we spoke about on the phone?'

Violet inclined her head, scratched at her scalp again. *Her tell*, I thought. Yes, Violet remembered.

'You asked me to consider why Shona had gone to live in Bath after her brother died.'

Violet nodded slowly.

'Daddy set her up there, didn't he?'

When Violet answered she didn't look at me. Her gaze was fixed on Melissa. It was as if I wasn't there. 'Because he loved her.'

'As much as us?' Melissa asked.

'More.'

My throat felt dry.

Violet tipped forward, for Melissa's ears only. 'I was there.'

'That day?'

On the edge of my seat, it took everything I had, not to move a muscle.

Violet nodded furiously.

'Tell me.' Melissa's voice was honey and silk.

Violet recoiled, instantly ripping out the communication line. 'I must see where Puddles is.' Her gaze twisted towards the kitchen. She made a move to get up. Melissa's hand shot out, staying Violet's arm. She'd come this far and, though she wasn't going to blunder in, she wasn't giving up.

'You think I won't believe you,' Melissa said.

'Nobody did.' Violet's voice throbbed with pain.

'It was wrong what happened, Vi, but I believe you. I *trust* you.'

Violet's fingers fled to the top of her head. The light caught her scalp. I was sure I could see fine hairs growing there. 'They made me promise not to tell.'

'Who made you promise?'

'I think . . .' Violet drifted off, looking out of the glass, staring into the distance.

Melissa leaned forward and took both Violet's hands in hers. 'You said you were there. Do you remember if the sun was shining?'

'It was raining,' Violet said. 'Pouring and cold.'

'And where were we?'

'At school.'

'Why weren't you there?'

'Poorly . . . mumps.'

'Oh my God, I remember,' Melissa said, chuckling lightly. 'It went through the lot of us like a bush fire.'

Happy to share common ground, Violet's face lit up. 'Yes . . . yes . . .'

'What about baby Wren? Was she home with Daddy?'

'No, I had to look after her, see she didn't make a fuss.'

This sounded odd to my ears. Melissa's frown mimicked my thoughts.

'Where were you when you with Wren?'

'We were all in the car . . . Mummy's,' Violet said.

'And where did you go?'

'To Bath.'

'To visit Shona?'

'Yes.'

'At her flat?'

'House. It was a house.' Violet's voice rasped, breathy and distressed.

'You went inside?'

'No, no. We weren't allowed.'

'You sat in the car on the road in the rain?'

'Yes.'

'On your own?'

Violet nodded.

'And Mummy went inside, right?'

Violet violently pulled away and reached for the top of her head with both hands.

'Hush, Violet, take your time.'

I watched Violet's eyes dart around the room, searching for an escape route. Melissa was patient, talking softly, coaxing Violet to speak of the past and the things that terrified her the most.

'We waited and waited,' Violet said, dismayed. 'Wren started crying. I think she was hungry. I tried to comfort her but I couldn't make her stop. She got louder and louder. I thought she was going to choke.'

'That must have been very frightening,' Melissa said soothingly. 'You were only a little girl.'

'I was and I was so scared,' Violet said, in a bleak whisper. 'I needed Mummy to come back. I didn't want the *noise*.'

'Of course you didn't.'

'It was . . .' Violet heaved a big breath. 'Horrible.'

'I understand.' And Melissa genuinely looked as if she did, I thought.

Violet nodded and muttered something under her breath. Her expression told me she was right back there in the moment and it was traumatic.

'What did you do?' Melissa asked tenderly.

Violet glanced over her shoulder. She saw me, I think, yet her brain didn't connect. 'I climbed out,' Violet said, pale-faced. 'A man in a big car beeped his horn at me. I nearly got run over.'

Melissa's hand shot to her chest. She was imagining Autumn doing something similar. Violet had had a narrow escape.

'Rain and wind in my face,' Violet continued haltingly, 'I ran along the street to the front door. It was ajar and . . .'

I think Melissa squeezed out a 'Yes?' I couldn't be sure.

Violet's trembling hands flew to the top of her head again. 'I peeped inside. I saw legs and a foot with one shoe on, a lady's shoe. It looked funny. I didn't know who it was. Not then,' she gasped.

'What did you do next?' Melissa asked. I noticed her knuckles were white.

'I pushed inside. And there she was.' Violet dropped her hands to her lap, smiling briefly at some long-forgotten memory. 'I was so happy and pleased because I'd found Shona. She was lying down and I thought she was sleeping.'

'Oh, Vi.'

'But she didn't look comfy and I wanted to wake her up but . . .'

Violet pressed her fists into her face. Her shoulders heaved. She gulped air. Melissa reached out and prised Violet's hands away and held them in hers again. 'Breathe,' she said. 'Nice and slow, just breathe.' Melissa motioned for me to fetch a glass of water.

Stiff-limbed, I'd almost forgotten how to move. I hurried to the kitchen, found a dirty glass on a worktop, rinsed and filled it from the tap. Returning to the living room, I handed it to Melissa who gave it to Violet. I returned to my seat on shaky legs.

'Small sips,' Melissa advised her sister.

Minutes ticked by like hours. Eventually Violet settled down, yet I very much feared that she'd gone as far back as her wounded mind would allow. And then she suddenly spoke.

'I'd wanted her to be alive so much I couldn't see what I was looking at.' Violet let out a dry sob. 'She was on her back . . . bottom of the stairs. Her face . . . her face was horribly twisted to one side. Oh God, oh God,' Violet cried, clawing at her sister. 'I can't forget her eyes. They were open, Melissa. Wide when they should have been shut. That's when I knew she was dead.'

'And where was Mummy?' Melissa asked, anguished.

I held my breath.

Violet froze. Her lips moved, but no words came out.

'Vi?'

With a fierce look, Violet said, 'She was coming down the stairs and she was furious.'

CHAPTER SEVENTY-SEVEN

MELISSA

You could have heard a feather drop.

Melissa prised her fists from her mouth. She didn't remember placing them there or registering pain at biting down hard on her own knuckles. Good God, Violet, all these years and you never said you'd seen Shona lying there at the bottom of the stairs. You didn't speak a single word to the police when you could have done. You never told another soul that you were a witness. What sort of sick woman lays such a dark secret on a grieving child? The same woman who'd sleep with her son-in-law. *My mother*, Melissa thought, seized with a hot surge of anger.

Spent, Violet shrank down into the chair. She seemed so much smaller than she was less than an hour ago, as if the weight of the burden she'd carried for most of her life had lifted. Melissa reached out to her sister, pulled her in tight, like she did with Autumn when she'd fallen and hurt herself. And Violet let her. 'Sorry,' Violet stammered. 'Should have said.'

'You have nothing to be sorry for. *I'm* sorry it's taken so long.' Melissa caught Rose's eye, taking in that she was hunched and deathly pale.

'Think I'll pop outside for some air,' Rose said, eager to escape.

'I won't be much longer,' Melissa assured her.

Waiting for Rose to go, Violet became suddenly anxious. 'Will I get into trouble?'

'No,' Melissa answered, firmly patting her sister's knee.

'If I am, Granny Maud . . . she will look after me.'

'*I* will look after you.' Adopted sister or not, this wasn't the time to ask.

Melissa felt Violet's arms snake around her in a clumsy hug. In Violet's world it was the greatest gift she could bestow.

'You will visit soon?' Violet asked.

'I will. I promise. I'll bring the children and you can read them your story.'

'And they can meet Puddles.'

They embraced awkwardly again and Melissa stood up and walked with Violet to the door. Waving goodbye, she found Rose already in her car.

'The utter, utter bitch,' Melissa cursed.

'You weren't listening,' Rose said quietly.

'Come again? You heard what I heard.'

'Violet only mentioned your mother.'

'Precisely. Daddy didn't get a look-in.'

'That's because you didn't ask.'

'What are you talking about, Rose?'

'You asked if Wren was home with your father and Violet said he wasn't.'

'Which explains why she had to look after Wren.'

'Where was your father and why wasn't *he* caring for his baby?'

Melissa didn't like where she thought Rose was taking her. 'How should I know? Is it essential we know?'

'Extremely. Violet said that they were *all* in your mother's car. How do you know your father wasn't there, too?'

Melissa gaped at her sister-in-law. 'Because Violet would have said so.'

'Because you didn't ask.'

Melissa clicked her tongue. Why was Rose being so deliberately difficult? Unfortunately, she continued to be so. 'You asked Violet if your mother had gone inside Shona's house.'

'And Violet confirmed that she had. Violet also said our mother was *furious*. Why would she be angry? Why wouldn't she be upset, traumatised, devastated, reaching for a phone to call an ambulance?'

Melissa could see that Rose had no answer. What would she spout next?

'I don't know much about your sister,' Rose conceded.

'We can agree on that.'

'Melissa, I'm really not trying to be awkward.'

'Accepted,' Melissa said stiffly.

'I care about you, believe it or not.'

Melissa softened. 'Thank you.'

'Violet only answers direct questions with direct answers.'

'That's because of the drugs.'

Rose appeared to concede this point too. 'It could also be because you didn't ask the right questions.'

'You think my disgust of my mother has blinded me to other scenarios?'

Melissa followed Rose's gaze to a squirrel scampering up a tree. She refused to answer.

'This is ridiculous,' Melissa said hotly. 'You still maintain my father was there?'

'I'm saying you can't rule it out.'

'But that's grotesque. I don't believe it. Violet would have told me. I know she would.'

'Perhaps she wants to protect him. Look, you and Violet loved Shona. I think Violet was right about your father's love for her too.'

'See, that confirms he wasn't there.'

'It confirms he didn't harm her,' I countered.

Melissa shook her head. 'My mother was at that house when Shona died.' God, they were going around and around in circles.

'It doesn't mean she was responsible for Shona's death.'

Melissa felt her face flush with indignation. 'Of course she was. just like she was responsible for the affair with my husband. And at the risk of repeating myself, you heard Violet. She said my mother was furious.'

'At Violet for getting out the car. At Violet for stumbling across a horrific situation.'

'Would you be furious with a child given similar circumstances?'

'I don't know. I'm not a mother. I'd like to think I'd be kind, but this is Celeste. Everyone behaves differently. Hate is the other side of love. Anger is the other side of fear.'

'This is horseshit.'

'I understand where you're . . .'

'Spare me the clichés,' Melissa snapped, strapping on her seatbelt. 'There's a very good way to find out.'

'I'm not taking you to Blackthorn this evening,' Rose said.

'Wren can hold the fort.'

'That I doubt. And what happens if Orlando shows up? Wren would probably invite him in for a drink.'

Frustration billowed inside Melissa. Rose was right when she wanted her to be wrong. 'Please, Rose, I need to nail this down once and for all.'

'I know you do and you will, but not tonight. You're upset. Understandably so. The children will be wondering where you are. They're not stupid. They'll sense something is up.'

Melissa ran her tongue over her bottom lip. It felt cracked and sore. As much as she hated to hear it, Rose had made her think. She hated herself for feeling hot and resistant to what her sister-in-law was saying. She hated even more taking it out on Rose who was nothing but kindness.

Rose's phone signalled an incoming text. Melissa watched as Rose read it. 'It's from Celeste.'

The mere mention of her mother was like a gust of air on smouldering embers. Melissa felt an immediate danger of her temper catching light again and knew it. 'What the hell did she want?'

'To know whether I'd been in contact with your father.'

'She told me she'd sent him away.'

'To where?'

'She didn't say.'

'Well, he's not answering his phone.'

'Does she sound worried?'

'Must be to contact me.'

'Maybe she told him about Orlando.'

'She never said.'

'I'll try to get hold of Daddy . . . to establish his whereabouts,' Melissa said in answer to Rose's nervous expression. 'Nothing more.'

Melissa found her father's number and held up the phone as if it were a trophy. 'Damn, he's not answering. I'll leave a message. Maybe he's drowning his sorrows with Raff.'

'I bloody hope not,' Rose said, starting the engine.

Hello. My mother is looking for you. Could you contact her, please? Thank you. She read it out to Rose.

'That sounds stern.'

'How do you expect me to sound?'

Rose shrugged and changed up a gear. 'Try him again, maybe, once we're back in civilisation.'

'Is that what they call it?' Melissa said with heavy sarcasm.

CHAPTER SEVENTY-EIGHT

ROSE

I felt mangled, the thoughts in my head jumbled and tossed all over the place.

What if Celeste and Benedict were involved in Shona Reid's death, together?

I'd wanted to butt in when Violet was speaking, but feared breaking her flow.

Lost in thought, the journey back was more silent than the journey out. I would have heard Melissa's brain whirring if my own hadn't been quite so noisy. Attempting to stay rational and apply logic to an argument with a woman consumed by passion and betrayal defeated me. Violet's childhood trauma massively complicated things. Whatever the truth of Shona Reid's death, it was not necessarily connected to Alice and Bonny's disappearance, I doggedly told myself. It was likely to be quite separate. Not keen to sit at home to analyse and obsess with my best mate, Pinot Grigio, I decided I'd call in on Florence. I hadn't seen her since promising to be good i.e. stop interfering. Promises were made to be broken; they weren't meant to be shattered and trampled underfoot. My best friend would be disappointed.

Melissa sat up and craned her head as we entered the village. I think she feared sighting Orlando after his escape from the seaside. No sign of him. *Thank you, God.*

I pulled up in the drive. Melissa turned to me. The anger had gone from her face. She looked like Melissa again. 'Thanks for this afternoon,' she said awkwardly. 'I recognise it was a big ask and it wasn't very nice.'

Not nice was an understatement.

'Which is why it's hard for me to ask another favour.'

I braced and tried to look dumb.

'Come with me tomorrow.'

I blew out between my lips. I felt wedded to Alice and Bonny. I didn't feel invested in Benedict and Celeste. But what if they were not only connected, what if one led to the other?

'Please. I'm not good on my own,' Melissa implored me.

'You seem to be doing a pretty fine job to me.'

'I'd rather have backup with the parents.'

I drummed my fingers on the steering wheel, making a play of weighing up pros and cons. 'What will you do with the children?'

'I'll bribe Wren to stay.'

'Good luck with that.'

'Are we agreed?'

I nodded slowly. 'Let's get it over and done with early.'

'I can be at yours for nine tomorrow.'

With that sorted, I watched Melissa climb out and cross the drive. The door was already open by the time she reached it, Autumn flying out to greet her, Wren standing with Edgar in her arms. I drove out of the village and pulled over. First, I called Florence to make sure she was in. She was. And then I called Raff.

'Hello, gorgeous,' he said. 'Have you survived the fallout?'

Compressing an afternoon's dramatic revelations into a phone call wasn't possible. Not keen to lie, I stuck to more palatable truths. I let Raff know that Craig had ripped off Wren and that I'd spent the afternoon with Melissa.

'How is she?'

'How you'd expect.'

'Get you, the agony aunt.'

I screwed my eyes tight. There was no way of getting around it.

'We visited Violet.'

'Christ,' he spluttered. 'What were you doing there?'

'Melissa needed a sisterly chat.'

Raff went so quiet I thought he'd dropped his phone. 'Rose, I'm not thick. Is Melissa gathering evidence against my mother?'

'Why do you say that?'

'My big sister is looking to stick the knife in.'

'Are you saying you blame her?'

'I'm saying Melissa has a soft spot for Violet . . .'

'Because she's a nice person.'

'I'm not saying she isn't.'

'Who? Violet or Melissa.'

'Both,' Raff said, audibly rippling with frustration. 'But Violet has a bloody big axe to grind with my mother. It's called closing ranks.'

It was called a lot more than that. What would Raff say if he knew I was accompanying Melissa for the showdown, tomorrow? Perhaps Raff should be there too. Toying with asking him, he said, 'Look, can it all keep? We've had a hell of a few days.'

Sounded like a plan. 'Melissa said you were going out with Tom the Tree.'

'Yep. If I can't get a cab, I might stay over.'

'Rather you than me.' Tom and Amber lived in a hovel. 'I'm popping over to see Florence.'

'Give her my love.'

'One other thing, Raff. Your dad's gone walkabout and nobody can get hold of him. Has he been in touch with you?'

'Bloody hell, has he found out?'

'Don't think so.'

'Mum hasn't told him?'

'Not that I'm aware.'

'What about Melissa?'
'Nope.'
'Orlando?'
'Hardly.'

'No, you're right there.' Raff thought for a moment. 'You don't think he's hurt, do you? He took some pretty big knocks from that little turd, Craig.'

I hadn't considered the possibility. 'I could drop Melissa a text and suggest phoning the hospitals.'

'I'll do it,' Raff said. 'And I'll ring around his pals too.'

'That would be grand.' It was lovely to have him step up and share the load. 'Your mother is genuinely worried.'

The noise Raff made from the other end of the line was a combination of dry bark and snort. I pictured him making the biggest eye-roll ever.

CHAPTER SEVENTY-NINE

ROSE

Florence went to loads of trouble. There was a tapas selection from a deli that included all my favourite bits and pieces: olives with feta cheese, marinated aubergines, pickled anchovies, fat red peppers in olive oil and flakes of honey-cured salmon. There were salads and dips, tortilla chips and flatbreads. We polished off the lot with most of a bottle of Albarino, Florence's favourite. She implored me to stay over so 'we can get drunk together'. I declined and stuck to one small glass of wine. I hadn't realised how hungry I was and, preferring not to give either of us indigestion, stuck to mundane stuff about Mum and Dad's holiday and my coursework. I also told Florence about Carmen dropping me a message and picture.

'Told you so,' Florence said, with a playful grin — a grin that I have to say disappeared fairly smartly when I spilled the beans about Melissa, Orlando and Celeste.

Florence's baby-blue eyes positively popped. 'Jesus wept, a love triangle?'

'Not sure love has much to do with it.'

'I'll say,' Florence said, visibly taken aback. 'Not unheard of, unfortunately.'

'As you might imagine, it's caused a hell of a stink.'

Suddenly, Florence brightened. She didn't quite rub her hands together in glee but I got the picture. 'Imagine the size of the pot. Will you put in a word for me? It would be so cool if our firm got the case and it would do masses for my street cred.'

'I'm starting to understand why the general population has such a poor opinion of divorce lawyers.'

'Don't believe a word of it.' Florence grinned. 'I'll make damn sure Melissa gets every cent she's entitled to and more.'

'I don't doubt it. You've been gunning for Orlando Rhodes for years.'

'Prick,' Florence said, her final word on the subject.

It wasn't until I had a decaff coffee in my hand that I moved on to Craig's visit to the seat of power.

'Back up,' Florence cut in. 'Alice is officially missing?'

'Unofficially.' I filled Florence in on Craig, Alice's brother and the plot to extort money from Benedict, including Craig's allegations about Bonny and Alice.

Florence scratched the end of her nose. 'That's one hell of a mess. You think the brother was telling the truth or was it all part of the dastardly plot to rinse the Percivals?'

'I'm not sure I can tell anymore.'

Florence gave me a funny look and took a moment to consider. 'It's not the first time we've discussed whether or not Benedict is sketchy.'

'And we've always agreed that he finds women attractive but . . .' I ran out of road.

Florence pounced with the tenacity of a cat trapping a vole. 'You don't get off that easily.'

I took a breath and began. As much as I wanted to be clear and concise for Florence's benefit, Shona Reid, Alice and Bonny all came out in an untidy, disorganised mess. I even detoured into the #MeToo movement and blithered on about values today being different to yesterday and thank goodness for that.

Florence being Florence cut the crap and went straight to the chase. 'Fact is the police didn't pursue an enquiry into

Shona's death and they would have done if they thought it suspicious. In their eyes, no crime was committed and it was simply an unfortunate accident.'

'But after hearing Violet's story, it looks less likely.'

'She was a child.'

'So what? Children are more likely to tell the truth than an adult.'

'I'm not unsympathetic,' Florence said. 'However unless Celeste and Benedict put the record straight with their version, it's a dead end — pardon the pun.'

'Not according to Melissa.' I told Florence about her intentions for the following morning.

'Bad idea. Melissa is already gunning for her husband's lover who also happens to be her mother. Guaranteed to descend into an ugly scene.'

'That's what I'm afraid of. Melissa asked me to go with her.'

Florence gave me a hard look. 'What were you planning to do — referee?'

'I promised,' I said weakly.

'Pushover.'

'I'm not.'

'No, you're bloody nosy.'

I didn't argue the point.

Florence poured herself another glass of wine. 'Helps me think,' she said, as if I'd criticise. 'You said Bonny Cole is Alice's mother.'

'Correct.'

'Pity you can't talk to her.'

I explained that she'd also gone missing. 'She hasn't been seen or heard of in the past four or five years.'

'Didn't you say that the son, Craig, alleged Bonny had a habit of moving around the country with different men?'

'He did.'

'Mystery solved.'

I went to open my mouth to protest. Florence got there first.

'It's hard to disappear deliberately without leaving a trace.'

'Who said anything about deliberate?'

Florence waggled a disapproving finger at me. 'The likelihood is she decided to strike out on her own. Maybe change her name.'

'Why would she do that?'

'To conceal her identity.'

I repeated my question.

'There are loads of reasons,' Florence replied airily. 'Debt, bother with a boyfriend, crime — committed by the name-changer, crime — committed by someone else but witnessed by the name-changer, the need to disassociate from a particular event, which amounts to the same thing, I guess.'

'Aren't there innocent reasons?' I managed to cut in. Not easy with Florence in full spate.

'Some women revert back to their maiden names after divorce. Obviously, if Bonny becomes Barry, she might want to align her gender with a new name. When kids are brought up by their grandparents they sometimes want to honour them by taking their surname rather than the adopted one.'

This all sounded tame to me. And tame didn't fit the context.

I nodded, giving the impression that I bought into Florence's version. 'I still don't get why someone like Bonny would change her name . . .'

'*If* she changed her name,' Florence butted in.

I sighed in frustration. Thanks to Florence, we'd bumped down a name-changing bunny hole together. 'Whatever,' I said, dismissive, 'Bonny hasn't been in contact with her children after she made a point of staying in touch for a number of years.'

'Oh come on,' Florence said in a *wake up and smell the coffee* tone. 'From what you describe, she wasn't exactly close. She most definitely wouldn't win any Mummy of the Year awards.'

'Do I detect a note of criticism?'

'I'm stating facts and, according to you, Bonny Whoever had a tendency to embroider situations.'

'Allegedly,' I said, keen to score a point and use a word Florence used far too often. Annoyingly, she didn't take the bait.

'Fantasists make shit up. A disappearing act could be part of Bonny Cole's routine.'

'And Alice?' I asked.

'Different person. Different context.'

'Don't you think it's a weird coincidence that mother and daughter go walkabout within a few years of each other?'

Florence waited a beat. She was giving it serious consideration.

'Are you really certain about the boyfriend?' she asked. 'Statistically speaking, an abusive partner is a more likely bet.'

'It wasn't Sean Stamp,' I said, finishing my drink.

CHAPTER EIGHTY

SEAN

Sean Stamp didn't often tell the truth. On the rare occasions he did, he couldn't help but slip in a lie. Second nature.

This was not uppermost in his mind. He'd been thrown out of the pub again and this time barred for mouthing off. *Fuck 'em*, Sean glowered. *They can't do me for standing on the bridge with my can of cider.* He leaned over the side. After the rain the river was high. Dark, inky water swirled past. Sean thought how cold it would be.

Crushing the can in his hand, the crackle of aluminium like the sound of a bone breaking, he threw it through the darkness and into the water with a satisfying splash. Got to get your kicks somewhere. In next, an abandoned shopping trolley, parked at the top of the cast iron staircase leading to the towpath on the eastern flank of the river. That made an even bigger splash. He fancied it was like the sound of a body being disposed of. The sick grin on his face quickly faded. Everything bad that had happened to him lately was Alice Trinick's fault. *Bitch*. Should have got rid of her sooner.

Sean turned on his heel and, with a rolling gait, zig-zagged his drunken way to Engine Lane. A man who hoarded grievances like shopping coupons, Sean recalled the other nosy bitch who'd disturbed his sleep that morning. Cat scratched his face, my arse. If the silly cow believed that she was thicker than she looked. Not like those bastard cops who'd come for him in the early hours. Sean hawked phlegm from the back of his throat and spat it out onto the pavement where it sat glistening under the streetlight.

Be nice to a woman and what do you get? Fucking trouble. Touch her arse, and you're a rapist. All he wanted was a little bit of comfort, a little bit of love. Where's the harm in that? But this kid he'd met — she'd loved his chat-up lines — had been up for it, right enough. What was her name? Marnie, or maybe it was Maddie. He scratched at the waistband of his sweat pants. Fucked if he remembered. Bought her loads of drinks from money put on a tab and which he stood no chance of paying. Wasn't his fault, she cut up rough when he tried it on. Gave her a little tap — that was all. Got to silence the screamers. Alice never fucking complained. She liked it. Showed he was a proper bloke not some pathetic weed. This girl, Marnie, or whatever, nearly took his eye out. And *she's* the one that goes to the cops and cries rape. *Fucking hell, darling, if I'd raped you, you'd know about it.* Sean let out a wheezy laugh almost doubled up it was that funny. Couldn't stop.

A crowd of lads on the other side of the street pointed at him. 'What you looking at?' he roared, colliding with some tosser walking past with a comma in his ear. 'I'm talking to myself, aren't I?' Sean yelled. 'No law against it.' The man hurried on. Got nobody else to chat to now that Alice was well and truly gone.

If Alice hadn't been so stupid with her fucking fairy stories he wouldn't be drinking all hours. He wouldn't be chasing other girls. He wouldn't be in trouble with the law. They'd nearly broken his door down when they'd come for him. Dragged him out of his pit and bundled him into a cop car. Fucking arrested him and took a swab of his privates, the bastards. 'Didn't do nothing,' he protested, fronting it out.

Released pending further enquiries, he was told. *Cunts.* When he turned up for work as usual he was told he wasn't welcome.

Fucking bitch, Alice. I was good to you. I still love you and look what you did to me. Look how you repaid me. Look at the trouble I'm in.

Lost in recrimination, Sean stepped off the pavement to cross the road. He didn't register the SUV that had been tracking him. Didn't hear the purr of the electric motor. Didn't notice it speed up and didn't see it until it was on him. Too slow to react, Sean sucked in one last hot breath before the crash and bang. Catapulted into the air, legs and arms splayed out, he was dead before his head cracked open and blood and brain splattered over the tarmac.

CHAPTER EIGHTY-ONE

ROSE

I stayed awake late into the night and listened to the rain and thought about Alice.

Eventually, I fell asleep and woke around six. After a cuppa, I showered, washed my hair and applied a mask, leaving it on for twenty minutes before washing off and conditioning. Out of my normal routine since I'd arrived at Blackthorn, I'd got out of the habit.

I dressed warmly in a soft green sweater and jeans. A quick search produced a pair of brown leather ankle boots that I hadn't worn since the winter. I did a quick tidy round and put a load in the washing machine from the never-ending pile. I'd kept on top of Raff's work clobber — always filthy — and the clothes I wore for work, yet there was still a suspiciously large amount of coloured stuff that lurked in the bottom of the laundry basket. Maybe I'd pop to Mum's later. In a good mood after the holiday, she might even iron it for me. Happiness at seeing my parents again disintegrated at the thought of how they'd react to the goings-on, as Dad would put it, at Blackthorn. He'd be crowing about it for months.

Looking through the window, I noticed that Benedict's car was back. Perhaps it would have been better if he'd stayed away.

My phone rang. Raff.

'Hiya,' I said. 'Good night?'

'Boozy night. How was yours?'

'Restrained. Your dad's come home.'

'Thought he would. I tried him several times and gave up. So what's the craic with Violet?'

I deliberately swerved the question. 'How long have you got?'

'Sounds juicy.'

'Not quite how I'd put it.'

'Now you've got me interested. How about edited highlights?'

I bit down on my jaw to stop from blurting everything out. 'Best saved until later.'

Hearing a car pull up outside, I stole a glance, anxious that Raff would somehow read my mind, and was mortified to see that Melissa had Wren and the kids with her.

'Okey-doke, enjoy your day,' Raff said.

'Will do.'

'Before you go, I might have a lead on a rental.'

'Great.' Any minute now, Melissa and the children would burst through the door.

'You okay, Rose? I don't know but you seem . . .'

'Absolutely fine. Love you,' I trilled.

'Love you more.'

I ended the call and set my shoulders back.

The children piled in first with Melissa in pursuit. Wren, with a face like someone had slapped it with a wet piece of haddock, followed.

'She insisted,' Melissa hissed under her breath, meaning Wren.

'I'm not going to see your parents if she's coming,' I hissed back.

'I'm staying here with the kids,' Wren announced loftily. 'They can wreck your home instead of mine.'

Melissa arched a questioning eyebrow. *Are we still on?*

'I guess that's all right then,' I said in a loud voice. 'It's not that I have anything of value.'

Wren gave a dry smile of agreement. *Cow*, I thought.

Like a magician, Melissa produced a plastic tablecloth that she spread on the carpet; pads and pens, packets of crisps and biscuits appeared.

'I'm not feeding them that crap,' Wren said.

'Up to you.' Melissa shrugged. 'Shall we?' She motioned me towards the door.

'Don't be long,' Wren bawled after us.

Outside, padding up the drive, I asked Melissa how her evening had been.

'Fairly bloody,' Melissa replied. 'I had Orlando in one ear and Wren in the other.'

'Orlando turned up?'

'Good God, no. He's back at the flat in London.' *All right for some*, I thought. *I only want one home. He's got two.* 'He spoke to my father, apparently.'

Brave move, I thought. 'Face to face?'

Melissa nodded. 'Explains why we couldn't get hold of Daddy afterwards.'

Made sense. Probably drowning his sorrows. 'Did Orlando say how your father took the news?'

Melissa frowned. 'Hard to gauge, quite honestly.'

I didn't know whether Melissa found it hard, or her husband.

I stopped walking. 'There was no big bust-up?'

'I wouldn't put it like that. There were extremely strong words.'

'I'm surprised there weren't extremely strong fists.' What planet were these people on?

Melissa gave me a long slow look as if to say that this wasn't how the men in the family did things.

'In the interests of equality, I take it you won't be ripping off your mother's head any time soon then.'

Melissa's answering expression was withering.

'I was with Florence last night,' I said, taking a detour.

'I suppose you told her about me and Orlando.'

'Did I do the wrong thing?'

'Everyone will get to know sooner or later.'

'If you need a good divorce lawyer, Florence's firm would be happy to help.'

Melissa stopped, turned to me and smiled.

'What?'

'Thank you.'

'For what?'

'Looking out for me.'

We were at the front door, the entrance used, not by the family, but by tradesmen and acquaintances. It felt symbolic, as if Melissa was distancing herself, and no longer one of them. I could have turned back. I should have done. *Guaranteed to descend into an ugly scene*, Florence had said. More profoundly, *unless Celeste and Benedict put the record straight with their version, it's a dead end . . .*

But what if it unlocked the mystery of the missing mother and daughter? Wasn't a slim chance better than none?

'Come on,' Melissa said, 'let's get this over with.'

So I followed.

CHAPTER EIGHTY-TWO

ROSE

Benedict came to the door. The transformation in his features startled me. His face, a mixture of dark shadows and lines, was gaunt, the skin beneath his eyes pouched and puffy. Wrinkles, like weeds after overnight rain, had sprung up everywhere. Defeat sat heavy on his shoulders.

He hugged Melissa close, mouthed hello to me and thanked me for coming. I nodded a non-committal reply.

Melissa drew away, but clung on to his hand. I had a flashback to one of the photographs in the study: Melissa, the little girl lost. 'How are you doing, Daddy?'

He shook his head sadly. 'It's you I'm worried about.'

For a man blatantly cheated upon, Benedict seemed peculiarly composed. Perhaps he'd always known about Celeste's extra-marital activities and turned a blind eye. Or he'd done all his raging and roaring the night before when nobody could see or find him. Missing people was a recurrent theme with the Percivals, temporary or otherwise. It didn't make me feel any less apprehensive.

'Celeste's in the drawing room.' Then, dropping a hand on my shoulder, Benedict asked, 'Mind if I have a quiet word with my daughter?'

The thought of spending minutes alone with Celeste was as appealing as swallowing fire. I made an excuse to visit the cloakroom. Inside, I did a slow count to twenty, flushed the loo and washed my hands with soap that cost more than my body lotion. My tired reflection in the Victorian-style mirror confirmed that the past weeks had taken a toll. I'd lost my natural smile. I'd lost my sense of humour. I'd lost my optimism and youthfulness. I was in my early thirties, for God's sake, and I felt like an elderly aunt. Worst of all, I'd mislaid my moral anchor, if that didn't sound too lofty. The values my parents had instilled in me, of courage and tenacity, of doing the right thing when the wrong thing is easier, of protecting those you can — felt like strangers. When I thought of the sacrifices my parents had made through Poppy's illness, their stoicism and their love, it made me want to weep, not with sorrow but with pride. In a dysfunctional family I was becoming dysfunctional: my thoughts, my actions, everything. How Raff survived in it I'd never know. I cracked a grin. My face belonged to a clown. If we didn't flee soon we'd be trapped here and I'd be lost forever. I didn't care where or in what Raff had found for us to live. I'd settle for a kennel.

I let myself out, crossed the hall, believing it would be for the very last time, and entered the drawing room. A fire crackled in the grate. Portraits of ancestors stared down at me. Had they heard it all before? What secrets could they tell?

Benedict and Celeste sat close, near a table holding a jug of water and four glasses. Perched at the edge of a sofa, legs and shoes together, Celeste sat stiff and tense. She could have been a waxwork. I'd never seen her without make-up. She looked wan, her eyes, once sparkling, were dull. No amount of foundation and blusher would change a thing, I surmised, the way she looked a reflection of how she felt: washed out, washed up.

Melissa, already seated, indicated that I sit down. I pulled up a straight-backed chair some distance away. Whenever I'd been summoned to a family gathering or meeting, either Benedict or Celeste kicked off the proceedings. They didn't stand a chance. Flat out, Melissa said, 'Which one of you killed Shona?'

Celeste's hand braced. Benedict's jaw dropped, as did mine. He began to speak. Melissa raised a hand to cut him off.

'I know you were there,' Melissa said, coldly staring at her mother. In Melissa's heart, I still didn't think she believed Benedict had been present.

'It was an accident,' Celeste bleated.

'I don't believe you.'

'Melissa, darling . . .' Benedict began.

'Violet saw Shona and she saw *you*.' Melissa's gaze fastened on Celeste. 'Why were you furious?'

'Furious . . . Was I?' Celeste stammered. 'I don't remember.'

'That's a lie. You've never forgotten.'

And neither had Violet, I thought. It wasn't drugs that had broken her mind. It was shattered long before.

'You murdered her, didn't you?' Melissa never dropped her gaze. It was like watching someone expertly pressing a pressure point, creating extreme pain.

'That's not true.'

'Gave her a push, a shove.'

'No, no, no.' Celeste pitched forward, anguished.

'Sent her flying down the stairs.'

Benedict's voice was a roar. 'She didn't do it.'

'How do you know?' Melissa roared back.

'Because I was there.'

I caught my breath. Astonished that I was right, any satisfaction squashed under a ton of questions that remained.

'There is a lot you don't understand,' Benedict murmured.

'Then help me,' Melissa said, shaken.

Benedict looked at Celeste. I couldn't decipher what passed between them. Were they complicit or was it confession time? After a pause, she nodded for him to speak.

'I was young. I was arrogant and I fell in love with Shona,' Benedict began. 'It was wrong.' He lightly touched Celeste's knee, making her flinch. 'You might not remember but Shona's brother died.'

'Hamish,' Melissa said.

Benedict nodded. 'Shona was deeply upset and I was her shoulder to cry on. Too often,' he admitted, 'and we became careless. Your mother saw what others didn't. When she discovered our affair, Shona was fired.'

'But it wasn't the end of it?' Melissa said.

'It wasn't. I lied to your mother and set Shona up in a property in Bath.'

'So that you could visit and continue?'

'Yes.'

'And you held the lease?'

'I did.'

'That's why the police came to Blackthorn when she died,' Melissa said, fitting the pieces together.

'You remember that?'

'And more,' Melissa said, threat in her voice. 'What was the cause of death?'

Celeste answered. 'Trauma to the spinal cord.' Benedict crossed and uncrossed his legs. A tiny gesture but I thought he seemed uncomfortable. Melissa indicated for him to continue.

Clearing his throat, Benedict began again. It was like listening to a car with a cold battery starting up. Eventually, he got rolling. 'Your mother rightly became suspicious and followed me. When I returned home she gave me an ultimatum.'

'Either you finish it with Shona or clear out,' Melissa suggested.

'If your father left it would have been catastrophic for the family,' Celeste said earnestly. I winced inside at how crass that seemed now. Melissa's response was similar to mine; she stared straight through her mother as if she were sheet glass.

'She's right, Melissa,' Benedict said, pouring himself a glass of water.

'I think we can agree to disagree on that,' Melissa said, stony. 'Go on . . .'

Benedict drank deep as if he were necking a shot. 'I knew the game was up for good. Men of my age never dumped women by text or email, as happens nowadays.' He tried to smile and gave up when he had no takers. 'I insisted on seeing Shona one last time to talk to her, face to face. Your mother agreed with one condition. She insisted on coming with me.'

I leaned forward so that I didn't miss a thing. Truth or another lie, we were getting to the heart of the story they wanted us to believe.

'In retrospect, it was a mistake to take the children,' Celeste said with a nervous smile, appealing to her daughter. The way Melissa sat, grim and immobile, it cut no slack.

Benedict picked up the story again. 'Shona answered the door. We entered her home and, in one of the most painful episodes of my life, I explained I couldn't continue seeing her. As you'd imagine, Shona was confused and deeply upset. We all were,' he said, squeezing Celeste's knee, as if to say *how am I doing?* 'Shona became hysterical and your mother went into the kitchen to fetch a glass of water for her.'

I could not picture this scenario. Celeste didn't fetch anything for anyone, least of all her husband's lover.

'I tried to calm Shona down. She was screaming at me, punching and slapping and scratching, out of control.' Benedict paled at the memory. 'Enraged, she flew upstairs, all three storeys, to pack her things. At the top, she missed her footing.' He swallowed hard. 'I watched her fall.'

'It was very quick,' Celeste said, clipped, as if it were a blessing.

'How would you know?' I asked. 'You were in the kitchen.'

Everyone turned to me. My ears sizzled and my cheeks burned.

'It's what I understood happened,' Celeste answered self-consciously. 'There was tremendous noise.'

'Tumbling down three flights, there would be.' I didn't need to spell out that it would not be a fast descent unless she'd been pushed hard. The velocity required for Shona to fall from the very top down to the very bottom must have been profound.

Celeste raised her eyebrows and gave a brittle sigh. 'It was how your father described it to me.' She aimed her last remark at Melissa. I was dismissed: toast.

'So you see, Melissa,' Benedict said, 'quite rightly, your mother was furious with *me*, not Shona, and certainly not little Violet.'

'And taking my husband as her lover all those years later is her perverted form of revenge, right?'

'Please, Melissa, forgive me,' Celeste implored. Tears sprang from her eyes and dribbled down her cheeks.

'Forgive *us*,' Benedict said. 'The present has nothing to do with the past. We handled the situation badly, darling, but it really was a terrible and very unfortunate accident.'

My sister-in-law could believe what she liked. I didn't believe a word of it.

CHAPTER EIGHTY-THREE

ROSE

'Can I say something?' I could have ripped into them. I could have torn their story apart. I could have argued that it was Benedict in the kitchen getting that glass of water when Celeste raced to the top of the stairs, Shona after her, before she was pushed. I had more urgent concerns.

'Bonny Cole,' I said.

If they were delighted I'd changed the subject, neither Benedict nor Celeste let on. Perplexed, Melissa mouthed, *What?*

'The letter she allegedly sent.'

'She *did* send a letter,' Celeste insisted.

'Where is it?'

'We don't have it.'

'You destroyed it?'

'Yes, it was a horrible . . .'

'How did she sign it?'

Celeste looked to Benedict.

'Bonny Cole,' he answered.

'Not Bonny Trinick?'

'No.'

'And Bonny never mentioned her daughter, *your* daughter?'

'For goodness' sake, Rose,' Celeste burst out.

'She mentioned dependents,' Benedict blustered, equally irritated.

Out of the corner of my eye, I noticed Melissa sitting, rapt.

'When did you receive the letter?' I asked.

'God knows.'

'Surely, you have some idea?'

'As we already told Alice's brother when you were here,' Celeste answered, enunciating each word, as if I were deaf, '*several* years ago.'

'Define several.'

Benedict sighed with frustration. 'Four, five, I don't remember . . .'

'And how did Bonny want the money — cheque, cash, or what?'

'Cash,' Celeste said, comfortable with telling the truth.

'Ten thousand pounds,' Benedict chipped in.

'Where did she ask to meet?'

'What?'

'To hand over the money?'

Celeste and Benedict exchanged glances. Celeste shook her head, either because she couldn't recall or didn't want Benedict to tell me. 'We don't remember exactly.'

'In the UK, presumably?'

'Oh, yes.'

'No postmark on the envelope?'

Celeste's mouth creased into an apologetic smile, one I didn't return.

'Come to think of it,' Benedict said, scratching his leg. 'Might have been Wales.'

'You're right,' Celeste said, eyes brightening.

'A friend was mentioned as a sort of go-between,' Benedict said, warming to the lie.

'A male friend?' I asked. Bonny had plenty of those.
'Girlfriend.'
'What was her name?'
'Totally escapes me.' Celeste's final word on the subject, her mouth snapped shut like a trap.

Satisfied that I had nothing to go on, I was practically dismissed. I left Melissa to draw her own conclusions and make her own way back.

Necessity is a wonderful thing. I'd learnt from Mum and Dad that if you can't tackle a problem one way you go at it another.

Wren was outside the lodge, guiltily puffing a vape. The cloud of whatever it was she was inhaling was sweet and noxious. At my approach she jumped in defensively before I could accuse her of child neglect. 'No need to get antsy,' she said, tilting her lips into the semblance of a smile. 'Kids are fine. Edgar's dropped off.'

'Dropped off where?' It wasn't as if we had facilities for small people.

'On the floor,' Wren said, as if my intelligence was compromised. 'Autumn is playing with her dolls,' she added. 'How did it go with the parents? Frankly, I thought Melissa was tapped for tearing dirty plasters off old wounds.'

'How much did Melissa tell you?'

'Nobody tells me anything around here,' Wren huffed. 'I'm always the last to know.'

'That's not quite true,' I said. 'You've got the drop on the lot of us.'

'I have?' From the shine in her eyes I could see the idea held enormous appeal.

'Craig talked to you, right?'

'Bored the tits off me.'

'Told you his life story.'

'His *miserable* life story.'

'And you fed him with booze.'

'I did. Bum move.'

'Told you all about his mum, Bonny.'
'Yada yada yada.'
'Told you about the men in her life.'
'Endlessly.'
'Told you about his mum's bestie.'
'Alice's godmother, such a yawn.'
'Do you remember her name?'
'Kelly, lived out in the sticks, place I've never heard of.'
'Any idea where?' My pulse quickened.
'Sounds like a revolver.'

No, no, no, it has to be less cryptic than this. I wouldn't know one gun from another.

Wren's tongue poked out between her teeth. Her brow furrowed. Quite animated, she strained to remember.

'Give it your best shot,' I said, ignoring my own pun.

'Webley,' she said, with a ta-da.

I looked it up on my phone and shook my head. Screeds of stuff on the actual gun; nothing about a place.

'Here, let me take a peek,' Wren said, snatching my phone.

Her thumbs tapped at the screen as if they had independent existences. Maybe she was warming to the fact that helping people can actually feel nice. After a lot of head shaking, Wren let out a triumphant shriek. 'Weobley,' she shouted. 'See,' she said, handing me back my phone, 'different spelling.'

I hate embracing Wren. Forced to on social occasions for the sake of keeping up appearances with the family, I found the process dispiriting, but I could have hugged the life out of her.

'You're a star,' I said, meaning it.

She beamed for all of two seconds. Tightening my grip on my bag, I headed for my car. 'Rose, Rose,' Wren hollered, 'where are you going?'

'Where do you think?' I called back with a laugh.

CHAPTER EIGHTY-FOUR

ROSE

Weobley is a small town in Herefordshire. According to the satnav, it was fifty-four miles away and would take me an hour and a half.

Riding high on what felt like a breakthrough, gremlin doubts set in on the approach to Gloucester. I didn't know Kelly's surname. I didn't know if she still lived in Weobley. I didn't have an address. I considered driving straight home to my parents except they'd be at work. What would they advise if they knew the half of it?

Of the "leave no stone unturned" philosophy, they would encourage me to listen to my heart and follow. It's what they'd done with Poppy, my little sister, at every stage of her short and unpredictably awful life.

Fact was, Kelly was Bonny's friend and Alice's godmother, so that amounted to something.

Arriving on the outskirts of Hereford, I followed the Roman Road and continued to a *Game of Thrones* sounding place called Raven's Causeway. From there it was another ten miles or so to my destination.

I'd never seen so many black-and-white half-timbered houses. It was like stepping back in time. The High Street was like no other. Shaped into a triangle, the road went up one side and down the other. In the middle: a patch of grass flanked by a grey dry-stone wall; a rural market town without a discernible market.

Set back from a wide pavement, medieval buildings and, later additions, shops, some more ancient than others. On my way in I'd spotted two old-fashioned petrol pumps for diesel. I'd no idea if they were still in use. An easy place to park, I slotted the Mini outside a café that also sold organic produce. I wasn't looking to sightsee although I couldn't help but clock a couple of hair salons. If Kelly lived in Weobley I guessed she did her main shop in Hereford. For everyday items, milk and so on, she would probably use the local supermarket and grocery store. This was where I headed.

I waited my turn in the queue. It took a while for a friendly-faced blonde with a ready smile, wide features and a dimple on her chin to get around to me. Every customer wanted a chat and she was happy to oblige. I was staggered by how much could be pushed into a single shopping trolley. Cash, a novelty, was often exchanged instead of card transaction. Nobody appeared to be familiar with using phones to pay.

When it came to my turn I was treated with the same courtesy extended to other customers. There was none of that *you're a foreigner in these parts* here.

I bought a chocolate bar and paid for a coffee to go. 'I need your help,' I began, tapping my phone on the payment reader. 'I'm trying to trace a woman who I believe lives here. Her name is Kelly.'

'Kelly Devon?'

I smiled weakly. I'd no idea.

'Pulling your leg. That's what we call her,' the woman said with a wink. 'You mean Kelly Tucker. Lives opposite the church.'

'Is it far?'

'Where are you parked?'

I told her. She walked with me to the door and pointed across the street.

'Walk to the end, bear left. You'll see a car park. Bell Square,' she added helpfully. 'Take a right before it, mind, else you'll find yourself walking out of town. It's about seventy-five yards down the road. Red brick. Yew in the front garden. Tell her Mags sends her love.'

Mags gave me the number of the house. I thanked her and set off. The rain had eased, as had the bitterly cold wind. From what Mags had told me, I guessed that Kelly's nickname was due to her West Country connection. It's how she'd met Bonny, I realised. Godmother to Alice, she must have known Bonny for well over twenty years.

Kelly Tucker lived in a 1950s style red-brick bungalow behind a thick yew hedge. Double-fronted, compact, slightly raised above the lawn on which it stood, it had a commanding position. It was one of those properties that I bet was modest on the outside, inside a palace.

I won't lie. I was nervous. Why would Kelly Tucker give the time of day to a stranger about a friend she might not have seen in years? Alternatively, Kelly could have been sworn to secrecy about Bonny's whereabouts. There was another option: Bonny Cole was living right here, under everyone's nose. Could I be that lucky?

I pressed the doorbell. A slim woman in a soft grey onesie, that matched her hair colour, answered. Her eyes were brown and her expression wary. She had nothing on her feet and her toenails were a deep shade of pink. I pegged her to be mid-forties, but she might have been older.

'Are you Kelly Tucker?' Not my best opening line.

'Who wants to know?'

I tried a smile that was not returned. 'My name is Rose Percival.'

The door began to close. I stuck my foot out. 'I'm searching for Bonny Cole.'

The pressure on my foot increased considerably. 'And I'm looking for your goddaughter, Alice Trinick,' I squeaked. 'She's gone missing.'

The door opened a crack. I kept my foot right where it was despite the throbbing sensation in the joint in my big toe. I'd not come this far to have a door slammed on me.

'Alice?'

'Yes.'

'Is she all right?'

'I'm hoping you can help me with that.'

The door flew wide. Kelly turned and crossed a big hall with thick carpet that smelt freshly laid. 'You'd best come in then. Make sure you take off your shoes.'

I did as asked and followed Kelly into a kitchen that was clean and comfortable with bright under-cupboard lights and quartz worktops. The cooker looked brand new. I scraped back a chair at the round pine table while, silently, Kelly put water in the kettle, switched it on, took instant coffee from a cupboard, and milk from a tall fridge that ticked quietly in the corner when she opened the door. She didn't ask me if I wanted a drink. She made me one anyway. No sugar was offered and I didn't ask. I think she used the time to recalibrate and consider what she would say and, more importantly, what she wouldn't. Finally she sat across from me, eyeing me as if I were a venomous spider that had hitched a ride on a flight from Australia.

'How old are you?' she asked.

An odd question, I answered truthfully.

Kelly inclined her head and blew across the surface of her mug. Tiny lines appeared around her mouth.

'So where do you fit?'

'Fit?' I said.

'Yeah.'

I saw where this was going. 'I'm an outsider, an in-law. I'm a Percival by marriage. I'm not one of the sisters.'

I thought this might change the dynamic. Kelly didn't miss a beat. 'What do you want with Bonny?'

'If I find Bonny, I'll find Alice.' I didn't know this to be true. It was a hazardous guess.

'And what do you want with Alice?'

'To know whether she's alive, or not.'

Kelly gave a start. That *did* change the dynamic.

'You think something happened to her?'

'That's what I'm trying to establish. So why don't you tell me how *you* fit?'

CHAPTER EIGHTY-FIVE

ROSE

'I haven't seen Bonny for years,' Kelly began, wary. 'She was always moving around, going under different names, ducking and diving, usually with a man in tow. Like sticking jelly to a wall trying to stay in touch with her, but she always showed up. Eventually. To me, she was always Bonny Cole from Ivybridge.'

'You're from that part of the world too?'

Kelly nodded fondly. 'We met over a cup of tea at a baby group.'

'You were pregnant?'

'That's what a baby group means,' she said, with a flat stare.

'Sorry, yes,' I said, flustered.

'Soon to be single teenage mums, we were the odd ones out. Weren't made to feel that welcome by the respectable mothers and we instantly bonded.'

'And why you became godmother to Alice.'

'That's right.'

'When was the last time you saw Alice?'

Kelly narrowed her eyes. 'When she was little, her and Craig, not so much now.' Her eyes darted to the clock on the wall.

'Have you seen her in the last twelve months?'

Kelly bowed her head. Yes, she had. I let it go. 'Who was Alice's father?'

'I don't know.' Kelly blew out a soft breath.

'Bonny never told you?' I leaned forward.

'Sure, she did, Benedict Percival, but I'm not sure I believed her. She never told her mother who the father was at any rate.'

I thought about that. 'Do you have a photo of Bonny?'

'Somewhere.' Kelly reached for her bag and fumbled out her phone. Tapping in the password, she located the app, scrolled through photos and, with a nervous smile, showed me.

Bonny Cole was simply stunning and made Alice seem plain by comparison. Tall, statuesque, dark-eyed, with a glossy mane of chestnut hair, she oozed old movie star glamour. Rocking a classic black dress with a plunging neckline, she beamed at me as if she'd cracked the secret of a happy life, yet beneath the teeth and smiles I caught something fragile in her expression, the same fragility I'd picked up on in her daughter, Alice. Unnerved, I handed back the phone to Kelly.

'Lovely, isn't she?' Kelly said, smiling fondly before clicking off the picture.

'What was she like?'

The smile on Kelly's face faded a little at the edges. She didn't answer straightaway. 'Bonny was the best fun, a proper good-time girl, always up for a laugh, but she had issues.'

'Like?'

'Men. And she was a hell of a dreamer. Wanted nice things, expensive things, would never settle for second best. Basically Bonny wanted what she couldn't afford. She had it in her head that she was owed a better life, without putting the work in to get it. I don't like speaking about her like this,' Kelly said, breaking off, suddenly earnest, 'but it's the truth. She was sometimes a difficult friend. And she lived in the past. She had this grand idea that she came from aristocracy. I think because she couldn't cope with the fact that her dad had abandoned her.'

'And that's how Benedict Percival became the centre of her universe.'

'Could be right.'

'But did he get her pregnant?' I pressed again.

Kelly took her time to consider. 'Do you know what? I don't think even Bonny knew for sure.'

'Yet she'd passed this so-called folklore on to Alice. And you didn't enlighten your goddaughter. You encouraged it.'

Kelly sat still for a second, uncomfortable.

'What was the deal?' I asked. 'Did she promise you a cut?'

'I . . .'

'You let her believe that her mother was right. You allowed her, *helped* her, put together a plan to rinse Benedict Percival for his so-called crime, without the slightest evidence that it was true.'

Kelly flashed with anger. 'She was desperate. She'd got this horrible boyfriend who knocked the shit out of her. What was I supposed to do?'

'Put a roof over her head, feed her, help her find the work you believe is so important for a better life. Alice needed you. Have you any idea what you've started, what you've done? And for what — a couple of grand?' I'm not a shouter but I was shouting now.

Kelly's shoulders slumped. Shame glanced across her cheeks.

'Has she visited you in the past two months?' I felt weary and sounded it.

Kelly met my eye and shook her head. I believed her.

'Going back to Bonny, you said you saw her four years ago.'

'After Beatrice died.'

The *dragon nanny*, I reminded myself.

'Bonny came for a couple of weeks after her mother's funeral,' Kelly said.

'When was that?'

'Four years ago. Between men, Bonny promised to stay for Christmas.'

'But she didn't?'

'Cleared off and left me high and dry.'

'Cleared off and cleared out?'

Kelly raised an eyebrow, not understanding.

'Did she take all her stuff?'

'Not all, but that wasn't so unusual.'

'Did you keep any of it?'

Kelly gave a nervy laugh. 'It's a small place. I gave it a couple of years and then I got rid of it. I thought she'd taken up with one of her blokes,' she said, defensive. 'On my Jack Jones, I never heard from her again.'

I gripped the table with both hands. Blood pounded through my head. I recalled Benedict's remark about when he'd received the letter: *four, five. I don't remember.* I bet he did. I had one final question: 'Would anyone miss Bonny if she disappeared?'

'Me,' Kelly replied.

'And Alice?'

She gave it to me straight. 'Me, Craig, and now you.'

CHAPTER EIGHTY-SIX

ROSE

My chest was tight and a headache hammered furiously against my skull. I didn't notice the road, other cars, motorists, or pedestrians. I drove by rote.

I had the chilling scenario all mapped out and ran it through my tortured mind.

True to form, Benedict had an illicit affair with Bonny Cole. Years later, Bonny asks for money in exchange for silence about their daughter, Alice. Benedict and Celeste hatch a plan to silence Bonny forever.

Some might ask what's the big deal? People don't kill for an indiscretion. Social media and agony columns in tabloids are plastered with illicit affairs. People get up to all sorts of crap in their downtime, peculiar relationships so commonplace they are practically boring. *But this is the Percivals*, I thought, and they'd already drawn a spectacular amount of heat with a woman's death months before Beatrice and Bonny's arrival. If it snuck out that Benedict was the father of child by a sixteen-year-old, friends, neighbours and the wider community would gossip. What other awkward questions might be asked?

And what in hell was I going to do about it?

Florence would say I was speculating. She would tell me that the information I'd stumbled across was purely circumstantial and open to interpretation. No proof, no hard evidence. No confession.

Yet still two women, mother and daughter, were missing.

When someone takes a life it crosses an unimaginable line. In robbing the victim, the perpetrator forfeits a part of him or herself. Moral codes are broken, values distorted. I'd observed the Percivals at close quarters in past weeks. I'd heard their brand of ethics. I'd watched them group together, fight each other yet unite in a common aim to dissemble, confuse and shut down the truth.

I pictured Benedict and Celeste agreeing to meet Bonny with the sole intention of picking her off. I could imagine them luring her with more money than she'd demanded to make the deal sweeter, but on the strict condition that she told absolutely nobody and came alone. They would have found somewhere quiet and isolated. One or both of them had killed before, I reasoned, so another would make no difference. That way, all their problems would go away. They simply hadn't bargained on Alice showing up later and raking up the past.

And that meant she had to go too.

I desperately wanted to be wrong, like I wanted my parents and the doctors to be wrong when they told me that my little sister was dying from a rare form of liver cancer. Our family was never quite complete without her. It felt as if there was always one missing. Perhaps this explained my obsession with two missing women, one I vaguely knew and the other I'd never met.

I was almost back at the lodge. Clear-sighted, I'd decided to phone Raff and ask him to come home. I'd book rooms in a hotel in Cheltenham, pack overnight bags for both of us, tidy up and silently wait. With his arms around me, I would talk and confide my deepest fears and he would listen, like he always did, and we would leave. He would know what to do and we'd get through it all.

Reaching Blackthorn, I drove past the Granary and, to facilitate a speedy getaway, parked outside the lodge. I called Raff from the car.

'Can you come home?' I asked.

'What? Now?'

'Yes.'

'Has something happened?'

'Yes.'

'What?'

'Raff, come home.' My voice caught and I was close to tears. 'I can't do this on the phone.'

'Jesus, you're not going to leave me, are you?'

'Silly, whatever gave you that idea?'

'You seem . . . duh, I don't know . . . strung out.'

Because I was. 'Please, Raff.'

'Okay. Let me finish up here at the unit. I'll be as quick as I can.'

'Drive carefully,' I said, finishing the call.

Melissa had made an effort to clear up the human debris left by her children. The stain from a spilled drink on the carpet was someone else's problem now. Coat still on, I went upstairs to our bedroom and lifted down our bags from the cupboards on top of the wardrobe. I selected sweaters and shirts, underwear and toiletries, including my contraceptive pills, and laid them on our bed. Raff's best jeans were hanging up. I slipped these off the hanger and retrieved a couple of shirts for him and a smart pair of trousers for me. Once I'd got everything covered, I packed my bag first and then unzipped Raff's. Inside: his favourite navy shirt. I'd no idea what it was doing there and pulled it out. Thinking it might need a wash I lifted it to my nose and reeled at the fragrance. It wasn't mine and it wasn't Raff's aftershave. I'd inhaled that cheap perfume before. The horror of the discovery suddenly dawned on me.

I sat down on the bed with a thud. This was stupid. This was ridiculous. With shaking fingers, I held his shirt up to the light. No blood. That was good. It had a single pocket on the left hand side. There was no bulge and it appeared empty. To be certain, I plunged my fingers inside, feverishly exploring, willing the chilling thoughts rampaging through my mind to vanish. I withdrew my hand relieved to see it was empty. Then I looked again and felt as if a stranger had come up to me in the street and punched me in the throat.

I stared at the single hair caught underneath the nail on my index finger. It was long, coloured red and dark at the root.

CHAPTER EIGHTY-SEVEN

ROSE

I didn't wait. I grabbed my bag and drove.

My beautiful man.

My life.

My everything.

Keen to pin the blame on Sean, Raff had been eager to listen, to offer his help in my doomed quest to find out what happened to Alice. As I'd dismissed Sean's involvement in her disappearance, Raff had agreed and walked away too.

So plausible.

So credible.

Such a liar.

I'd always thought Raff a many-faceted man: husband, dutiful son, best mate, lover, provider and skilled at his job. I didn't know he was an abductor and murderer too. I'd thought he'd survived his dysfunctional family; that he really hadn't been sucked in like the rest of them. I hadn't realised that he was more expert at concealing it. I didn't know when the rot set in. I guessed it was when his sensitive thirteen-year-old self, hormones raging, had a crush on a young girl called Bonny Cole; the same girl who had rejected him, to his mind, and fallen for his father's charm, the same father who'd had an affair with Shona Reid, who might, or might not have covered for his wife's crime. Might, or might not have been involved himself.

I pulled up alongside Raff's dirty old truck, climbed out on numb legs and let myself into the unit.

My husband was a tidy man. Ladders, chainsaws, hedge cutters and axes, each had their own compartmentalised spaces, any one of which he could use to kill me. With a trembling hand, I slipped out my hairdressing scissors from my bag, pushing them into the back pocket of my jeans.

A ride-on mower sat alongside a couple of lesser beasts for smaller jobs. Cans of petrol carefully set aside, there was personal equipment: helmet, climbing spurs and harnesses attached to a rack on the wall, symbolic of who he was, or what I thought he was. Beneath, six fifty-five gallon oil drums stowed for Amber, Tom the Tree's girlfriend, as part of her pizza project.

Raff was sorting through paperwork in the part he'd hived off as an office. He looked up and gave a start when he saw me.

'What are you doing here? Thought we were meeting at home.'

'When did you find the letter, Raff?'

'What letter?'

'The one that led you to Bonny Cole.'

He flicked a nervous smile. Innocence shone out of his eyes. I think he truly believed he'd done nothing wrong, that in his head he'd restored family honour, in defence of his mother, or some such crap, or maybe, with Bonny, it was plain payback for her preferring his dad to him. Whatever the motive, he'd met her and hurt her and entombed my heart in ice.

'Rose, Rose? You really think I'm capable of murder?'

I spoke softly, no sudden movements, and tightened my hold on my bag. 'I never mentioned anything about murder.' I had him yet still he swerved it.

'Rose, hun, you've been under a lot of pressure.' He cracked an unsteady smile.

'Why the sudden trip abroad the Christmas we were supposed to spend together?'

He crossed his arms and laughed. 'You're not still banging on about that? Jesus, I made the wrong call but it wasn't my fault my uncle couldn't come to our wedding.'

'The wrong call,' I said, making air quotes with my fingers, 'was murdering an innocent woman. You left to go to New Zealand, as far away as possible from the scene of the crime, to escape.'

His face creased with anger. 'That's utter bullshit.'

'I found your favourite shirt, Raff, the one you wore when you lured Alice to her death. Did you wear it for Bonny too?'

'I don't know what the hell has got into . . .'

'Stop lying!' I shouted. Spit flew from my mouth. I was so loud, Raff physically jumped. He sat down before he fell down. Strain tugged at the corners of his mouth. He lowered his eyes; he couldn't bear to look at me.

With a weary sigh, I took a step towards him and softened my tone. 'We've never lied to each other, have we? Did you know that Poppy would have been the same age as Alice if she'd survived?'

He found my eyes and held my gaze. 'I didn't know that,' Raff said. 'I'm sorry.'

'Talk to me,' I said.

His face fell and his shoulders sagged. He picked up a paperweight and put it back down. 'I've known for years about my father's affairs. The man's a dog.' He raised a hand to prevent me from interjecting. 'It badly affected my mother, the humiliation and hurt unimaginable. I couldn't bear it.'

'You wanted to protect her?'

He nodded slowly. 'You have no idea what it was like growing up in that environment, with all those fragile women.'

I saw then why Raff had chosen me. He saw me as level-headed and straightforward.

'Violet was . . .' He struggled to find the right description and stared at the table as if the answer were written in one of the carvings. '. . . off her head, first at Mum and then with drugs. She would bang around the house calling Mum a murderer.'

'Did it ever occur to you that she was right?'

His head snapped up.

'Your parents were at Shona Reid's the day she died.'

'No,' he said, 'that can't be right.'

'Ask them, Raff.'

His lips parted. The colour drained from his cheeks. I'd seen the same expression on his face when I'd revealed his mother's affair with Orlando. It had made him question who the real guilty party was in his family. Up until then, it was always his father who'd received a bad rep.

Raff dropped his gaze. I got it. He couldn't face the prospect of being wrong because that meant everything he'd done to *right* things, in his messed-up head, and protect the family unit, was flawed from the outset.

'Why did you bring me here if you believed your father was so predatory?'

'I always knew you were safe. You're not his type.'

I bridled. 'Not because you knew you could trust me? Not because I loved you? What was it your mother said? She compared me to a Land Rover Defender: dull but reliable.'

'Rose, Rose, that's not the case.' He stood up so fast the chair toppled.

'Stay back,' I barked.

Raff spread his hands, patted the air in a gesture reminiscent of his father. 'It's true I found the letter,' he began.

'You contacted Bonny?'

'We agreed to meet.'

'Somewhere quiet,' I sneered.

He blanched. 'I never intended to hurt her. I simply wanted her to leave the folks alone. She got nasty.'

I crossed my arms. 'How?'

'She became violent.'

'I don't believe you.'

A pulse twitched above his top lip. 'It wasn't meant to happen.'

'Was she your first love?' I asked softly.

His bottom lip trembled at the memory. 'I thought I meant something to her.'

'She strung you along?'

He looked at me with haunted eyes. 'It was always my father the girls fancied.'

'How did you do it?'

Ashen, his gaze hit the concrete floor with a resounding thud. 'I strangled her.'

My hand flew to my mouth.

'And Alice?' I stuttered.

'Same.'

'Jesus Christ, Raff,' I cried. 'Where is she?' *The woods*, I thought, answering my own question. All the time I thought, in my delirium, Raff was in bed next to me, he was disposing of Alice's body, clearing her room. 'Where did you bury her?' I persisted.

'I didn't.'

He tilted his chin towards the open door. Couldn't think what he meant and then I remembered the oil drums I'd seen on my way in. I felt as if I were walking thigh-deep through a sea of molten lava.

'I took her to the woods, moved her the next day.'

The day he'd overslept, I recalled. He'd shot out of bed late. When I'd asked if it were possible to access the woods by the road, he'd been evasive.

The light in Raff's eyes changed. They were hard and dark and murderous. My gaze fell on his hands, hands that had stroked my cheek with tenderness, hands that had held and explored me, strong hands, a strangler's hands.

Speechless and terrified, I stumbled back and hit the side of a metal filing cabinet. The outline of the scissors jarred against my rear. When Raff advanced I twisted and jerked them out of my pocket. Razor sharp blades glinted under the fluorescent lighting. With one stab I could fatally wound him and he knew it. Shock invaded his features. I was no longer plain old dependable and bloody gullible Rose.

'Get back,' I cried, scything at his chest.

Still he came and, in one swift movement, his hand caught and clamped on my wrist. With his other hand, he disarmed me. I let out a scream that he smothered with a kiss. Out of the corner of my eye I saw the point of the blades flash as he raised it then brought the scissors down towards me. In blind terror, I thought of Poppy. I thought of my mum and dad and their complete and utter devastation.

I feared pain.

I feared death.

And this was mine.

No time for regret; only one last breath.

I knew exactly how this was going to end.

CHAPTER EIGHTY-EIGHT

ROSE

And I was wrong.

With terrifying force, Raff plunged the tip of the blades into his neck and twisted. His eyes shot wide in agony as blood, warm and rich, fountained from the wound. I grabbed hold to try and staunch the flow. Like holding back a river in full spate, it was hopeless. Blood shot between my fingers, over my sweater, down my jeans, over my boots and onto the floor.

Raff's eyes rolled and his knees buckled. I went down with him, breaking his fall.

'Christ, Raff, why did you do it?'

'Better this way.'

He looked into my eyes. 'I could never hurt you,' he said, dreamy.

'I know.' Tears trickled down my cheeks.

'I'm cold.'

I fumbled off my jacket and covered him. There was blood everywhere, up the walls, on the floor, every surface, over me. I'd never seen so much and it was still coming.

I held him tight, told him to close his eyes, rocked him. I didn't speak. There was nothing left to say.

In minutes it was all over. 'You'll make a great mother,' were his last words.

CHAPTER EIGHTY-NINE

ROSE

I lost the plot, lost weight and lost my hair. How's that for karma?

I moved back into my old room at Mum and Dad's and for a whole month I barely got out of bed, except to talk to police officers, totter about, watch a bit of telly (not the news), nibble at what Mum tried to persuade me to eat, before returning to bed to sleep and sleep. Blindsided by the *whole bloody perverted nonsense* (Dad's words, not mine), he popped his head around the door from time to time but generally kept his distance. There was talk about medication, which I rejected, and talk about psychological intervention, which I said I'd think about.

With Raff dead in my arms I'd phoned the emergency services. Teeth chattering with shock, I remember little of the call. Police and two ambulances arrived in tandem. Bursting in as if they were busting a terrorist cell, I feared violent arrest. Covered in blood, the medics initially thought I'd been injured in a domestic. It took a while to straighten things out and a whole lot longer for the truth to emerge. The decomposing body of Alice Trinick found in one of the oil drums went some way to corroborating my story. A lead detective, called Dench, headed up the murder investigation although the police said they weren't looking for anyone else in connection with the enquiry. Another enquiry was opened into Bonny Cole's mysterious disappearance. Some weeks after that, human remains were discovered in a shallow grave near Ross-on Wye. A week after that it was confirmed through DNA that they belonged to Bonny. The media, according to Mum, were all over the mother-daughter murders. I took Mum's word for it.

I emailed my notice to Crowning Glory and felt bad for Jerome. I bailed from my degree. I heard through Florence, whose firm was indeed handling Melissa's divorce, a steady stream of police continued back and forth to question the Percivals. Benedict and Celeste had gone full Fortress Blackthorn, dropped out of every social fixture and disappeared from view. Wren moved in with Melissa — a bold move on Melissa's part, I thought — and the sisters visited Violet often. In my more visionary moments, and there were a lot of them, I quite fancied going off-grid myself and hiding away, an idea put a determined stop to by my parents.

Sean Stamp, I discovered, had been killed in a hit-and-run. My suspicious mind reeled back to the night Benedict went missing. Raff, also, flew to the top of my personal suspect list. The truth was more mundane. The brother of a woman Stamp had assaulted confessed to the crime and was charged.

I saw danger when there was none. I heard threat in every well-intentioned word. My parents deserved a New Year's Honour for putting up with my mercurial moods. I didn't feel like Rose anymore. I was a pale shadow of the woman I used to be.

Until, one day, Dad came home, looked at my mum and said, 'It's all sorted, Lindsey. We're on the move.'

CHAPTER NINETY

ROSE
Five years on

'That will be seventy-four pounds, Deandra.'

Deandra, one of my regulars, paid and requested a cut and colour for her next appointment.

'Seven weeks suit you?' I asked.

'Perfect, Rose.'

I scrolled through the calendar on the salon computer, booked a two-hour appointment, printed off a reminder and handed it to Deandra.

'Did you have a jacket?' I asked.

'Barbour,' she said.

I found it hanging up among several other coats, helped her on with it and wished her well. Looking at the time, I told Mel, our receptionist, that I was shooting off. My last client had cancelled due to sickness and I'd promised Mum I wouldn't be late because it was her book club night. Hoofing out to the back to grab my bag, I found Mike taking a sneaky bite out of a jam doughnut.

'Caught red-handed,' he said with a grin. Tall, wiry, with an angular face and curly dark hair, Mike had the constitution of a teenager with the metabolism to match.

'How did you snaffle that?' I asked.

'A loyal customer.'

'Don't tell me, Mrs Dinsdale.'

'Who else? Perk of the job.'

'None of *my* clients bring me pastries.'

'You're just jealous.' Leaning over, he dropped a big sugary kiss on my lips.

'Get off,' I said, laughing, pushing him away. 'And wash your hands, for God's sake.'

Licking his fingers, Mike gave them a rinse under the tap in our tiny kitchen area. I stayed still, watching him, not quite believing that this uncomplicated big guy with an even bigger smile loved *me*.

A couple of years after I'd moved with Mum and Dad to a three-bedroom flat, I finally got my degree and met Mike at a hairdressing convention where we immediately hit it off in a way I'd never dreamed possible. Mike Coverdale didn't patronise, take the piss out of my accent, or me. His sense of humour and down-to-earth approach to life won me completely over. Bar Jerome, Mike was the most impressive hairdresser I'd ever met. My parents liked him, particularly my dad, who had someone equally as sports mad to discuss the footie with when he wasn't with his new best friend, Ronnie, a carpet-fitter. Mike also got the Florence seal of approval. Through it all she and I had remained in touch. My oldest friend had visited solo and a couple of times with Jamie. Me? I never went back.

'Better get cracking,' I said, making a move.

'See you back at the ranch.'

Outside, I put up my umbrella and set off for the twenty-minute walk home through the drizzle. A tourist hotspot, steeped in history, with a prestigious university, I loved York with its narrow streets and alleys. From Bishopgate Street I headed to Skeldergate, a smart residential area where old warehouses had been converted to trendy apartments. Beyond, my home, in a road of terraced Victorian houses with bay front windows and lovely views over Knavesmire and the racecourse.

I let myself in and found Mum on her hands and knees playing with Mara. There were toy bricks and teddies everywhere. My daughter immediately looked up and beamed, scuttling towards me like a wind-up toy. I scooped her up into my arms and dropped a soft kiss on her cheek. She smelled of wheat and joy.

'She's been an absolute poppet,' Mum said, getting to her feet, knees cracking. Then, looking at her watch, 'I'd better get moving. Same time tomorrow?'

'A few hours in the morning would be grand.' I said.

'Looking forward to it already.' Mum chucked Mara under her little chin. 'Ooh, and I've left a pie in the fridge for you and Mike,' she said, giving me strict instructions about how to heat it up.

Since the move, my mother was having the time of her life. She'd found part-time work at a florist and, on her days off, helped me out by looking after, Mara Poppy, my daughter's second name in honour of my little sister.

I thanked Mum and saw her to the door.

'Bye, pet,' she said.

I stood in the doorway, breathing in the damp evening air. Mara twiddled a lock of my hair in her fingers. After I'd given Mara her tea and bathed her, Mike would be home soon to kiss his daughter goodnight. I didn't think of all that I'd lost, but all that I'd found.

THE END

ACKNOWLEDGEMENTS

A big heartfelt thank you to my co-partners in literary crime: my agent Broo Doherty at DHH Literary Agency, who has kept me going all these years (apologies for sounding like an old car!), Kate Lyall Grant, editor and publishing director at Joffe for her commitment and astute editorial input, and Jasper Joffe who *is* Joffe Publishing. Copyeditors Sam Matthews and Sarah Tranter deserve special mention for individually and collectively saving my blushes. Once more, thanks to Becky Wyde for giving the story a final once-over and similarly saving my blushes.

I must also thank the unsung heroes: my hairdressers past and present. It was you lot that gave me the idea to make my main protagonist, Rose, a hairdresser and you have generously furnished me with enough knowledge to make her authentic.

Final thanks to Ian for putting up with me scribbling away during a house move. It has not been easy but we did it and in style.

THE JOFFE BOOKS STORY

We began in 2014 when Jasper agreed to publish his mum's much-rejected romance novel and it became a bestseller.

Since then we've grown into the largest independent publisher in the UK. We're extremely proud to publish some of the very best writers in the world, including Joy Ellis, Faith Martin, Caro Ramsay, Helen Forrester, Simon Brett and Robert Goddard. Everyone at Joffe Books loves reading and we never forget that it all begins with the magic of an author telling a story.

We are proud to publish talented first-time authors, as well as established writers whose books we love introducing to a new generation of readers.

We won Trade Publisher of the Year at the Independent Publishing Awards in 2023. We have been shortlisted for Independent Publisher of the Year at the British Book Awards for the last four years, and were shortlisted for the Diversity and Inclusivity Award at the 2022 Independent Publishing Awards. In 2023 we were shortlisted for Publisher of the Year at the RNA Industry Awards.

We built this company with your help, and we love to hear from you, so please email us about absolutely anything bookish at feedback@joffebooks.com

If you want to receive free books every Friday and hear about all our new releases, join our mailing list: www.joffebooks.com/contact

And when you tell your friends about us, just remember: it's pronounced Joffe as in coffee or toffee!